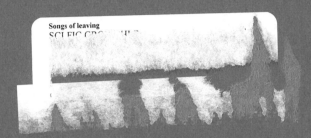

Songs of leaving

Pete Crowther

Songs

of

Leaving

Songs

PETER

of

Leaving

CROWTHER

SUBTERRANEAN PRESS · 2004

FIRST EDITION

ISBN
1-931081-85-9

Subterranean Press
P.O. Box 190106
Burton, MI 48519

email:
subpress@earthlink.net

website:
www.subterraneanpress.com

Contents

Peter Crowther: Tales of Wonder

Adam Roberts

What, you may wonder, is the nature of the book are you holding in your hand, right now?

We might call it "SF," but that only begs the question. One way of approaching the much-debated matter of a definition for the sort of writing — science fictional, fantastical, horrific, imaginative — that is categorized as "SF" by marketers and booksellers would be to look at the titles of the various magazines that have serviced the public appetite for it over the years, the so-called Pulps. Nowadays, it is true, the taste in magazine titles runs rather to the oblique: *Interzone*, *The Third Alternative*, *Spectrum*, *Analog* — suggesting a sideways, allusive avoidance of the whole question of definition. But once upon a time, in the Old Days, SF magazine titles were much more what-you-see-is-what-you-get. If a 1930s punter spent money on an issue of *Astounding Stories of Super-Science* he or she might legitimately have expected to be astounded; *Amazing Stories*, likewise, strove to amaze its readership.

Now, as then, there is a type of contemporary SF whose aim is to astound and amaze, to batter the reader's perceptions with gigantic spacecraft, cosmic locations, catastrophic happenings, aeon-long timescales. Other writers today are more level-headed, extrapolating particular scientific circumstances and social trends into possible scenarios of the future: writing *Tales of Tomorrow*, or *Futuristic Science Stories*, to borrow the titles of two short-lived British SF mags from the 1950s. A third approach common today is to unsettle the reader, to concentrate on the bizarre, the revolting or the outright strange — to write *Weird Tales*, as the title of one long-lived US-Pulp had it.

But although he sometimes writes astounding tales, sometimes deals with futuristic science, sometimes writes about the weird, Pete Crowther's stories aren't really described by any of these titles. His writing is at once difficult to pin down and enormously distinctive, his voice uniquely his own. If I had to pick one magazine title to describe the sort of writing he does, it would be the first British SF pulp aimed at an adult market, a publication that ran from the late 1930s to the early 1940s. Pete Crowther writes *Tales of Wonder*.

"Wonder" in this sense is the core of his art; not a saccharine Hollywood shortlived emotional uplift, those imitation smiles and tears, but a deeper, more considered, deeply humane sense of the wonder of everyday life. Crowther's "sense of wonder" is predicated not upon sheer scale, not upon giant technology or millennial spans of time, but upon heart, on life. His is not the science fiction of E. E. "Doc" Smith, or Isaac Asimov; it is the fiction of Ray Bradbury and Ursula Le Guin.

Perhaps it is misleading to bracket him with SF at all. In many ways he is simply not a genre writer: he treads his own path, he avoids conventional touches and cliché. Of course he is aware of, and utilizes, the techniques of those sorts of Pulps, the importance of plot and incident, writing in a way that your reader can follow, of "imagination" and so on: as his character Adam says of those kinds of magazines in "The Invasion," "they're kinda schlocky...but there's some good stuff, too." But nobody could call Pete a "Pulp" writer. His prose is too clean and well-crafted; his imagination is too eloquent, his stories too thought-provoking. If it didn't smack of elitism (and he is the least elitist writer in the world) I might be tempted to call him a "literary" writer.

His narratives lead us towards understanding certain truths so deep that, simply cited in aphoristic form, they can seem banal, but which when "earned" by seeing them worked through in real people, real lives (which is what Pete always writes about) start to assume their true significance. To take one example: in "The Invasion" it is the multiple portraits of ordinary people, with their ordinary frustrations and delights, that gives depth to the unusual alien "invaders." The story ends — I'm not giving anything away by saying this — by observing of the invaders that "filled with newfound understanding and a wealth of information, they went accepting their fate. It's all any of us can hope for." The line by itself sounds as flip as a slogan from the *Little Book of Calm*; but the same line encountered in its proper place in the story, after we have become absorbed in the lives of the protagonists, after we have worried and then wondered at the alien lives that intersect theirs, achieves much more than this.

All the stories in this collection articulate actual wisdom, all of them express a basic humanity, all concentrate on the little people, on small-town life or ordinary folks isolated in strange environments. SF is seen by some of its critics as nothing more than escapist fantasies; and if that's true (which I don't believe) then Pete is actually an *anti*-SF writer, a writer absolutely committed to the Real, to getting back to what really matters. "Setting Free the Daughters of Earth" reminds me of Bradbury's masterful *Fahrenheit 451* not only in its premise of a State-controlled Authority hostile to the written word, but in its awareness of the strength of the Real when compared to the hollow escapist addictions of TV and cinema. The story is set in a world where TAPpers pump escapism directly into their brains via

Frankenstein-monster-like bolts in their temples; a cyberpunkish Hell which people can only deal with by various addictions, "everyone had his or her way of dealing with life in the domes...." But the protagonist of the tale, known only by the ironic title 'the addict' is different; his addiction is not for escape but for return. His delight at the sheer smell of books will be familiar to any bibliophile, as will his excitement at being in the presence of "Dickens, Homer, Tolstoy, Shakespeare...Melville, Bradbury, Updike, King." This addict is more than addicted to books, in an important sense, addicted to Reality. The story ends with a beautiful image, of fertility, of hope for growth and for the future.

"Surface Tension" shows that Pete can use the good-old Pulp tricks when he wants to. Right through, from its slap-bang opening ("when the rock-thing upped and ate Davenport...") I found this short sharp tale absolutely hilarious—but also absolutely gripping, and insidiously scary. Crowther's man-crunching rock aliens are splendid creations, thrilling and amusing in equal measure, but by the story's end the laughter has switched around from reader to story in a lovely, unexpected way. "Elmer" is another story that inhabits a Pulp premise—the asteroid that crashes into the Earth—only, once again, to turn it wholly around. This asteroid turns out to be something stranger and more wonderful than we could imagine; not only does it bounce harmlessly off the world and back into space, it leaves behind something extraordinary. It is typical of the humanity of Pete's imagination that he is able to paint the consequences of this wonderful, wonderfull encounter in colors that are uplifting without ever quite losing their melancholy.

"A Worse Place Than Hell" is a story that does something that Pete is expert at; deftly weaving together several seemingly unrelated narrative lines, the point-of-view switching between the 'present' and a variety of pasts as the reader begins to understand—at the pace that Pete already determined—the secret at the heart of the tale. As in several other stories here there is a wicked comedy at work here: is this really President Lincoln standing in a seedy modern sidestreet watching a drunk peeing against a wall? I particularly liked the moment when a child, scolded by his teacher, is told to show the whole class what he's playing with, only for it to turn out to be a part of the President's head. But there is a more serious point behind the dark humor. This story embodies a concern that runs throughout Pete's writing: the way the past relates to the present. This, of course, is one of the Great Themes of literature, encompassing memory, history, life and death; and the fact that Pete always deals with it in a thoroughly entertaining manner shouldn't distract us from the sophistication and depth of his insights. "A Worse Place Than Hell" presents us with a range of apparently dissociated episodes that in fact form a continuous chain between death and life—between death and rebirth. The way that memory and love can bring a person back from death (actual or metaphorical) is Pete's greatest subject. I think the best stories in this collection are the ones that tackle this idea straight on.

"Songs of Leaving" is one of the Greats, and it contains all the elements that make Pete's writing so wonderful. The premise starts as "SF disaster blockbuster," *Armageddon*-style, with an impending comet threatening the destruction of the whole world. But then Pete takes us in a wholly unexpected, wholly Crowtheresque direction. The world is *not* saved at the last minute by a muscled hero; death can not be dodged — Pete is wise enough (wiser than many) to appreciate just how true this is for each and every one of us. His stories confront this fact not as tragedy but as a bittersweet and beautiful necessity. What I admire most about "Songs of Leaving" is the extraordinary technical skill with which it is written. Pete's prose is never flashy or pretentious, but he is always in complete control of its effects. The earlier portion of "Songs of Leaving" achieves an almost goofy mood, the coming catastrophe related in a jokey prose bristling with references to popular culture. But halfway through the story undergoes the most extraordinary shift, as the runaways leave the doomed earth and the remainder of humanity faces up to the inevitability of the end. The prose changes, organically, to a lyrical, elegiac timbre to tell how the dead return to life for a little time before the end of everything. The reunions and reconnections this makes possible are rendered plainly, vividly, and most movingly. The reader who can finish "Songs of Leaving" without being genuinely touched is a colder fish than I.

Two other exceptional stories from this collection are similarly fascinated by the inter-relation of past and present, and the place of death in the nature of things. "The Killing of Davis-Davis" starts out like New-Wave-on-speed, Churchill wading through a sea of entrails and Kennedy being assassinated on a drive to Dachau — Barry Malzberg or Ted White come to mind. But this is a story that wants to do very much more than disorient and shock the reader. Or to be more precise, its dislocations all serve precise purposes in the story's elegant construction. As we read on, piecing the achronologic pieces together, we understand that Pete has found a way of dramatizing a temporal feedback-shortcircuit. A time-assassin is sent back to the past to kill a commercial rival before he became so powerful as to be untouchable: but one man's death is, in a sense, everybody's death, and Fate — or God — or whatever Entity is in control — is compelled to try and undo the damage done by endlessly shuffling and re-dealing the millions of cards that make up the events in our lives. As ever in Pete's writing, the past and the present are intimately interpenetrated. As the assassin gets closer and closer to his target, and as we begin to understand the consequences of his victim's murder, the inevitability of it all actually enhances the excitement of our reading. We hurry through the story eager to find out what will happen next; only when it is over do we have time to think how cleverly Pete has constellated meditations on chance and life, on the way little things and big things interact, on the past and the present, on randomness and power.

"Some Burial Place, Vast and Dry" is also about memory, about the tight relationship between past and present, about death and life. In this story above all we can see the influence of Ray Bradbury (the story is dedicated to him) — one of the greatest writers of that indefinable sort-of-SF sort-of-not-SF mode of writing, that unique and brilliant genre in which Pete also works. Taken as a whole Bradbury's short fiction (and for my money, his greatest achievements are to be found in his short stories) constitutes a stunning assemblage of "tales of wonder." "Some Burial Place, Vast and Dry" is worthy of him, and that's amongst the highest praise I can think of. The distant planet of "Orgundy" is rendered as vividly as a 1950s *Galaxy* cover illustration, its rust-colored lawns and purple sands, the view across its deserted landscape towards "the egg-shaped bulk of distant Quextal which lay as though partially submerged in Orgundy's horizon, its twinkling rings sparkling in the encroaching shadow." The sole character in the story, Will Gainsborough, is an old man stranded on this world for decades who enjoys one special Day every year. On this day phantasmagoric buildings from every portion of his Earthly life float through the sky, insubstantial as smoke, trailing "the smells of the past, hamburgers and hot dogs, popcorn and lemonade" in their wake, to settle together in one gigantic city at a certain place on the planet, topped by the Empire State Building — the whole architectural carnival a brilliant imaginative device. We never quite know whether this shadowy city is the hallucination of a man driven mad by solitude, or whether it has been conjured, as in Lem's *Solaris*, by the planet itself as some sort of alien compensation for his lot. Yet the story's end, though tinged with sadness, achieves an almost triumphant consummation, neither forlorn nor tragic. Achieving this exquisite tone in so short a story is a fantastic writerly achievement.

"Songs of Leaving," "The Killing of Davis-Davis" and "Some Burial Place, Vast and Dry" are, I think, the jewels of this collection; but there's not a story here that isn't wonderful. In the haunting (in several senses) tale "Halfway House" a dying astronaut is represented as the sum of his memories, and the power of that lived mental past is seen as simply greater than the trials of the present. The "halfway house" of the story's title is the half-alive, half-dead condition the protagonist Glogauer finds himself in, floating helplessly in space; but it also refers, I think, to the way human beings live half-lives, caught up in the stresses and minutiae of our jobs and our struggles, and forgetting the things that are actually important. Glogauer is frightened of dying, "but Monica smiled again. He had forgotten how beautiful she was when she smiled. He had forgotten so many things." Pete finds a way of suggesting that dying, if it means a coming to terms with life, can be a remembering rather than a forgetting.

Then there is "Late Night Pick-up" one of the strangest and funniest stories ever written about alien abduction. As Ben plays and replays his bizarre interrogation, diminishing each time, it's like reading Whitley Streiber rewritten by Samuel Beckett collaborating with Groucho Marx. "Palindromic," one of Pete's cleverest plotlines, is another space-alien story; but as we might expect, past and present, memory and hope get tangled up in important ways. And "Heroes and Villains" revisits the territory of Alan Moore's excellent graphic-novel *Watchmen*; what if comic superheroes and supervillains were real? How would they operate in the world. Pete's twist is to humanise his villain, to follow him on a moving visit to his dying mother, and to suggest that both yin and yang are necessary to make the whole.

All these stories, then, champion the human rather than the technological, champion the Real rather than the escapist — and more than that, manage to convince us that the Real *is* more imaginative, more fantastic and wonderful than the tacky shifts of escapist schlock. All of them reveal Pete Crowther to be the heir of that profound humanist and extraordinary writer Ray Bradbury. In the genre of imaginative writing today, however you want to describe it — science fictional, fantastical, horrific, imaginative — there are too few writers who could wear that accolade as convincingly as Pete.

Some Burial Place, Vast and Dry

What weeping face is that looking from the window?
Why does it stream those sorrowful tears?
Is it for some burial place, vast and dry?
Is it to wet the soil of graves?

Walt Whitman, from "Debris" (1860)

T he first parts of the colossal architectural complex drifted into the town in fragrant traces, myriad vapors floating on the winds of Orgundy like the memory of a cigarette or the promise of a delicate perfume.

The hint of its crenellated towers brought with it all the smells of the past…hamburgers and hot dogs, popcorn and lemonade, toffee apples and candy floss, all long-ago faded into a billion sunsets but here again, *now* wafting across the barren landscape. The scent of its storm-worn front porches and tall, fluted columns filtered into thousands upon thousands of forgotten wispy rocket exhaust residues and settled like fairy dust onto the softly-sighing stamens of the peach flowers.

The old man looked up from tending his crops beside the glimmering Plexiglas of Dome 12 and stared, responding to the faintest tingling in his bones, a song of sorts which whispered regularly of youth and mystery, and most of all, of Earth.

Home.

He stood there, amid a patchwork quilt of rectangular crop partitions, most of which, long untended, had grown over with the ever-present, orange weed of Orgundy, and mouthed the word silently as, above him, the strange yet familiar constructs of the past swooped and glided like summer kites or playful birds.

Home!

It was a mantra of sorts — *aum* — a single word comprising all that was dear and all that was distant. Maybe the two went together, *always* went together.

*The grass is always greener…*he thought, as a thin, gossamer line of picket fencing unraveled like railroad tracks above the domes and drifted off toward the usual site, breaking apart and then reforming en route. But the grass on Orgundy was not green at all, he suddenly remembered, looking down at the rust-colored sward and the fine, mauve sand he so lovingly — so absently — tilled every day.

He hadn't realized The Day had been so close. The old 2069 calendar thumbtacked on his cot-room wall still showed April…a different year, a different month. What year *was* it? he wondered. But that was so unimportant now: The main thing was that today was The Day, come again to entertain him and fill him with wonder and memories.

He laid the crude tilling device on the loamy soil and walked slowly to the dome's hatch, hardly daring to breathe lest his discarded energy should disturb the ghostly constructs that swooped and swirled outside. He keyed in the password, a solemn configuration of uncaring numbers, and stepped back to allow the hatch-guard by his feet to disengage. When it was fully open, he slipped inside and keyed the hatch-door closed again.

The air inside the dome was thin and tainted, redolent with inaction and age. The old man moved through the doorless rooms, suddenly noting the fine covering of years-old dust which lay on the furniture and the piles of books that towered and tottered in every corner and littered every corridor with a literary loam.

He lifted the old Timberline jacket, corduroy and fleecy-lined, from the foot of his cot and shrugged his way into it. It had been a long time since he had worn the jacket. Too long, he realized sadly. The Orgundy climate was constantly early autumn and he needed only his regular workshirt and vest while working in his garden. That was all he did these days, work in his garden.

The old man shook his head, scattering the first settlings of self-pity, and then straightened himself up. He savored the stillness and the familiarity of his dome while he tried to gain his bearings…not in a geographical sense but a temporal one. How long was it? Fifty years? It must be at least fifty years." The face that stared back from his silver-cracked mirror was now that of a grandfather.

There was a time, once upon a time, when he would walk away from the domes to the distant foothills and visit with everybody. At first, he went with Margaret. But then Margaret left him, too. The old man shook his head again, dislodging the memory and bouncing it around in his mind to stop it from settling and taking foot. He zippered up the Timberline and shuffled back into the memory of the coat.

That was the last time he had worn it, he realized. When, on a particularly bad day, when the lonesomeness had tugged at every nerve ending and pounded in his temples like a migraine, he had gone to talk to Margaret. That was the last time he had needed to wear the jacket. That was…how long ago was it? *Too* long.

He turned sharply and walked back to the hatch, ignoring the silence and the loneliness that surrounded him.

Back at the hatch, he keyed in the password. Then, as always, he closed his eyes and breathed in deeply.

The smells of Orgundy filled him, sank into his soul through mouth and nose, swirled amidst his creaking ribs before spiraling outward to the very tips of his outstretched arms. Then, pulling the old Timberline collar up to his chin, he opened his eyes and stepped outside.

Like a child's breath across a set of pipes, the Orgundy wind whined and hummed, a calliope melody of false starts and delicate refrains.

He slackened the dirty bandanna around his neck and pulled it over his mouth, preventing the lavender-hued dust from turning his saliva into purple goo. He raised his left hand to shield his eyes and watched.

Up ahead, near the foothills and the Resting Place, the first parts of the complex were settling, miragelike, a curious but heady amalgam of French chateaux, Italian palazzi and Elizabethan manor houses. He threw his head back and laughed out loud, laughed in spite of himself and his loneliness, laughed both against and with the tears he felt welling deep inside…stretching his arms out like a man in a desert feeling the first fulfilling drops of cool rain on his parched body.

"Here it comes," he shouted.

And it did, filling the air with glints and reflections, casting creeping shadows across the mauve sand…

It was the ultimate airborne craft, sky-wide and horizon-deep, a veritable city of lines and curves, the last word in what they used to call unidentified flying objects. But the old man knew every corner and every tile, recognized every piece of stone and every gable-end, every sun-blasted shard of brick and every weatherworn section of polished beech and oak and cedar.

Stuccoed walls, tiled roofs, loggias, open courtyards circled by elegant ironwork; wooden sash windows decorated with thin strips of white marble trim along their sills; dolman windows enriched with crockets and finials…square towers, tall chimney stacks, ornately carved balustrades and a million-and-one gargoyles resting, sitting, flying, hiding.

And it didn't stop there.

Gliding above him, shimmering as still it pulled together its composite parts, a colossal potpourri spaceship of construction and style and architectural fashion rode the alien winds…fifty — no, one hundred! — times bigger than the tiny, cold and futuristic silver needles that had brought the old man and his wife, Margaret, and all of their friends, here all those many years ago.

A vaulted banqueting hall pirouetted to his left, its tapestries and enormous hooded stone fireplaces catching the wind and the light while the whole affair steadied itself as it prepared to join the others.

Alongside, like suckling calves, other rooms and smaller buildings nestled in the shadows of the great hall. Colossal pilasters, arched windows and doors and rusticated bases leveled off amidst a cornucopia of scrollwork, console brackets, fascias, garlands and cartouches as they all approached the foothills up ahead.

The old man spun around, laughing, spittle flecking his lips as waved to one and all and bade them *Welcome!*

To his right, a shingle-style homestead bumped on the air currents, a single-prop dwelling beside the ostentatiously sleek great-hall airliner. At its back hung a coal chute and from its oak-paneled doorway a flagstone path passed…though, miraculously, disturbing not a single spicule of the mauve sand. As he watched, the building leaned to negotiate the wind and this side fell slowly open like a doll's house, exposing bedrooms and servants' quarters, an oak-beamed kitchen area, and a circular wooden staircase whose ornate carvings the old man could make out even from this distance.

Pausing for breath, he steadied himself and watched the latest arrivals settle down into the usual place amidst the gentle rises and slopes of the foothills. He was near enough now that he could make out the weathered markers of his friends and, just for a moment, he felt a wave of sadness wash against his insides. But, like any wave, it passed almost as soon as it had appeared, retreating, perhaps, to consolidate and return, strengthened and more determined.

No matter, he thought. It would not spoil The Day. And just for a second, his mind drifted back to his grandfather telling him about how he would jump up on Fourth of July morning, trampling dogs and siblings underfoot. To race into the Illinois dawn in a frantic effort be the first kid on the block to let off a firecracker. Orgundy might be a long way from Illinois, Earth, but he reckoned he felt the same way as his grandfather had felt all those years ago. Just the same.

Taking a deep breath, he leaned forward into the thickening breeze and took the first of many steps that would take him Home.

Up ahead, the first parts of the "ship" had landed, its building-sections settling into place, becoming one huge composite of line and curve, stone and wood, plaster and brick.

And now, as ever at the start of The Day, he wondered — marveled — at how this could be. That a planet somehow could transpose memory and feeling, hopes and dreams, wishes and regrets into one mountainous construct of all that once was — and forever would be — Earth.

For this was a strange sentience indeed, a bizarre ability. Perhaps it was even a need. Perhaps the planet sensed his loneliness. Perhaps it sent these corporeal translations of his mind as some kind of reward…a payment for attention and affection, for friendship. Whatever.

The Day was his and his alone. It had never come when they were all together, not even when he and Margaret were alone. But then, in July of — of when? 2068? '67? He couldn't remember. There was so much he couldn't remember, which was, of course, what made The Day so special — the buildings had come. It was the fourth day, the Fourth of July, some year. Independence Day. Which was why he had christened his own personal Eldorado as Independence.

He quickened his step. And as he walked, he thought.

On that first Day, that first and dimly remembered Fourth of July, two thousand something or other, he had thought the buildings were indeed spacecraft. That they were some huge, intergalactic flotilla, lost in the vastness of space and happening upon his lonely personal world by pure chance.

They had come — as they always had come since that first Day — silently and without warning, darkening the skies above the domes as though a swarm of insects blotted out the light of Orgundy's twin suns. He had rushed outside, responding to the gathering darkness inside the dome, and looked up, covering his eyes. Many of them he had recognized immediately; others he recognized only after time.

And each year, there were more.

He spent the long months between Days structuring his thoughts the same way that the planet seemed to structure his Independence for him. He fought to remember. And with each memory of buildings and homes, so came memories of the times around them…memories of the people he had been with. But, for a while at least, the planet had seemed only able to replicate inanimate matter.

Then that, too, had changed.

He shuddered involuntarily. The best was still to come, he thought, and the sudden realizations…the heart-speeding certainty of what was to follow roiled inside him like a warm storm.

As he neared the foothills, he rested again, turning back the way he had come.

He was already quite high. The domes lay beneath him, scattered on the mauve carpet of Orgundy like droplets of mercury. He looked up into the air, watching the last shacks and bandstands and outhouses shudder across the sky and disappear over his head to take their places behind him. As always, the biggest would come last.

The old man sat down to wait.

The spire showed first, far away, where sky and sand met in a shimmering, fluctuating line, far beyond the broken remains of the smashed rocketships that had brought him and his friends here, sunlight glinting from their still-polished hulls…far, far away, framed against the egg-shaped bulk of distant Quextal which lay as though partially submerged in Orgundy's horizon, its twinkling rings sparkling in the encroaching shadow.

Am I the first, old man? said a voice by his side.

The old man turned in the direction of the voice and stared into the eyes of himself — but this was him as he was years ago…maybe thirty, forty years ago.

"Yes, you're the first," the old man said with a smile. "I'll call you 'Thirty.'"

The younger man tilted his head to one side as he considered the name, and then he frowned. *But I'm still you,* he said, *Will Gainsborough.*

The Old Man — who was, indeed, William Gainsborough — nodded and turned to face the swelling shape that now seemed to fill the horizon. "Yes, well, it'll make it easier when we're all here," he said. He sensed the other man chew on that and then turn his head, apparently appeased if not entirely satisfied, and together they watched the end of the first act.

The first half of its 1,454 feet could now be seen: some fifty or more of its 102 stories, one thousand or so of its 1,860 stairs and maybe 200,000 of its reputed 365,000 tons of building materials. It seemed to hover, but the old man knew it was actually moving, drifting silently toward them, filling both the sky and his own mind with all of its majesty.

"You know," the old Will Gainsborough said to his younger self, "she took nineteen months to build and was so strong that, in 1945, a B-52 bomber crashed into the seventy-ninth floor and it didn't even shake her."

Mmmm, said the other Will Gainsborough. *And an elevator operator — her name was Betty Lou Oliver — managed to survive her elevator car plummeting seventy-six floors as a result.*

"You remembered," the old man said.

So did you, came the reply.

"And by the time we left Earth in late '66, thirty-eight people had jumped from her to their deaths," said the elder Gainsborough. "Would have been thirty-nine except that, in 1979, Elvita Adams threw herself from the eighty-sixth floor and a gust of wind blew her back onto a lower ledge."

Thirty-eight, said Thirty thoughtfully. *That's a lot of unhappy people,* he added.

The old man shook his head. "I sure do miss her," he said.

Margaret? Or the Empire State?

"Both. But mainly Margaret. How is she?" As he turned to face Thirty, the shadow of the magnificent Empire State Building fell across them and for a moment, the air seemed slightly cooler. "How is she right now?"

You remember, Will Gainsborough. She's wonderful and healthy and she fills my every waking and sleeping moment. We've just had our second child — a boy, Timothy.

"Then it's 2064."

Right.

William Gainsborough lifted his head as the end of the building drifted soundlessly above him. "I was twenty-eight," he said.

That mean you're going to change my name?

He laughed. "No, I'll keep calling you Thirty."

How about me? said a younger voice.

The old man lowered his head and smiled at the boy standing before him. The boy had a thick, unruly thatch of brown-blonde hair that stood proudly off his head. He wore short pants that stopped inches above scuffed knees, below which two sock tops hovered at different heights on scrawny legs.

"You," he said, "you I'll call Twelve. Is that what you are?"

The boy nodded.

"Good guess," said Will Gainsborough.

You gonna play? Play ball, maybe?

"Maybe, Twelve. Maybe I'll pitch a couple to you later. But first…first we have to watch the rest of the show.

The old man got to his feet and turned around in time to see the Empire State Building settle silently into place between an old brownstone that he had lived in when he was a small child and the bandstand that his mother and father used to take him to on a Sunday afternoon, its clapboard sides magically twisting into the exhaust-darkened brickwork of 289 Third Avenue in midtown Manhattan.

It looked just the way it used to look, before his old home became the only brownstone left on the block, cowering in the shadows of the skyscrapers and clashing with, to its left, the blue-glass and stainless-steel of the adjoining French restaurant, with its garish red awning, and to its right, a concrete block containing a branch of First National.

He remembered its brickwork and its sad window-eyes, each sided by blue, latticework shutters and topped with bracketed moldings, the latter providing the eyebrow curves essential to the Italiate style.

These were the things that had led him to architecture and design all those many years ago. These were his loves — the old buildings, the homesteads, the mansions. They were his children, his friends. Each brick and each board, known to him personally. It was they who had whispered to him, sung to him of their constructive and beautiful magic, first in school, then at college and then at various design agencies until the space program asked him on board to work on the life-support units for the first planned outpost beyond the Milky Way.

He felt a trickle on his cheek and tasted the unmistakable bitterness of salt.

Who's that? Thirty asked, pointing to a figure sitting cross-legged in the sand between them and the collection of buildings, his back to them.

Will Gainsborough squinted his eyes at the figure and immediately recognized the lowered shoulders. "That's Forty-four," he said, and he started toward the figure, his heart heavy with sadness.

He crouched down by the side of himself so many years younger and felt a strange mixture of emotions. First, he felt jealousy: After all, the person by his side had such fresh memories of the woman he had loved. *Still loved!* But he felt a profound sympathy, too, for the younger Will Gainsborough had just lost that woman while he himself had long since come to terms with her absence. For this reason, he felt pleased that those were not his present feelings, not his present suffering. Will Gainsborough Senior (as he liked to think of himself on The Day) remembered those feelings all too well, even though some thirty years or more had passed since he first experienced them.

"Take it easy," he said. "It gets easier."

Easier? the other said, his words echoing in the old man's ears. *Will it really?*

"Yes. You won't miss her any less, but the pain will become more bearable."

The younger man lowered his head into his hands and sobbed.

William Gainsborough forgot for a moment and tried to place an arm about his younger self's shoulder, suddenly starting as the sleeve of the old Timberline seemed to shudder in mist.

You many not touch us, old man, the figure said into its hands.

He withdrew his arm and clasped his hands tightly, "I forgot," he said.

You must not forget.

"I know."

He got to his feet, rubbing his knees — the first signs of arthritis, he reckoned — and turned round. There were more of them now, many of their ages making it difficult for him to distinguish one from another. He could only recall the occasions, the landmarks in his life.

There, at the back, running around the dunes amidst the other figures, was Eight, fresh from asking his father on Christmas morning if Santa Claus had really brought the bulging pillowcase of gaudily wrapped presents that stood beside his bed. And there was Eighteen, the round face of adolescence now surrendered to the finer features of approaching adulthood, wearing the stern, proud gaze that came from graduation and the keys to his first automobile.

They were all there: first kisses, winning football games, exam passes, first building design, successful interviews…and all the Margaret memories.

They came in a swarm, flooding his mind with pictures of the past. He shook his head, fighting the tears, and turned around, away from them all, to see the finished construction.

It was the greatest building that had ever existed, a castle of such magnitude and invention that it dwarfed all other contenders in both size and concept. Never…not in all the years that it had come…had it ever reached such magnificent proportions.

Shack stood upon brownstone upon tenement.

There was the Whaler's Church he had marveled at on a long-ago visit to Sag Harbor, butting its Egyptianate boundaries with the stark symmetry of Louis XIV's orangery at Versailles.

There was…

There was…

Mansard roofs, columns, pediment and entablature, fish-scale shingling, Adamesque fanlights, Italianate porches, Greek transoms, robustly paneled shutters, conically roofed gazebos aside scissors-trusses and pierced-wood paneling, all leading onto old brick sidewalks swept with fine sand and protected by white picket gates which, suspended magically in the air, circumnavigated high stories of the many magnificent and wonderful adjuncts and extensions. Bargeboard frames with elongated quatrefoils, paired dormers opening onto Mosque rooftops which themselves led onto buttressed dormer windows of striking Pre-Raphaelite beauty…

William Gainsborough was breathless just looking at it.

It was every building he had ever known, every style he had ever studied and every color he had ever seen.

It was Gormenghast and Tintagel, magnified a thousandfold.

It gleamed and glimmered, catching light and diffusing its rays, sending them spinning and pirouetting across roof and window, gargoyle and gable, dulling brick and shining shingle.

Its highest points scraped the sky, tore its blueness in thin gashes so that its steeples disappeared from view into the strangeness of space. And of all the high points, of all the distant, towering curves and lines of this castle of castles, the Empire State reigned supreme.

It was finished. Now was the time.

Now it would start to shimmer, its bonds and joinings begin to fade, to grow dissolute and drift with the wind. Now it would fall apart, its beams and its masonry stretch and fold in upon itself like smoke dreams cast by the most ancient of tribal pipes.

He waited, watching, staring, drinking in with his eyes and his mind, recharging memory and dreams alike.

But still the Castle Independence remained.

He waited some more.

And still it remained.

William Gainsborough Senior turned around and was startled to see that he stood alone on the sand. He looked again, first one way and then the other, wondering if, perhaps, the many other versions of himself over the years of his life had huddled together to surprise him. But there was nothing, only the distant dome-droplets on the plains below, and the far-off egg of Quextal sitting astride the horizon and, nearby, the marker-clad carpet of the Resting Place. And all about him, the wind sang softly.

Then he heard the rusting grind of metal on metal and the throaty churn of creaking wood.

The old man tensed, hardly daring to turn. There had never been a noise before, never a sound from the collective monolith that had visited his space-born island, never a whisper from the fluttering drapes or a squeak from the gently wafting picket gates. The sound continued, growing heavier and deeper, until there came a distant thud and the ground beneath him trembled.

Silence returned.

Twisting himself around, inch by inch, he turned his head to see what had happened.

The Castle still stood there, its every gable and turret, its every rooftop and minaret, its every column and bracket...all strikingly complete and sturdy. But, in the middle of it all, a tiny square on the front of its seem-ingly endless facade had opened by virtue of an old portcullis drawbridge which now rested flat upon the sand. And, as he looked, the old man could see the faintest traces of wafting sand released into the air by the sheer force of the gate, and, within the gaping maw of the entrance, the vaguest hint of shimmering light, eating the blackness around it as it grew in inten-sity. Something was coming toward him.

Suddenly he felt afraid. The mirage had become real.

Now the castle seemed to take upon itself an altogether more Gothic appearance. Now, it seemed murky and melodramatic, dreary and dolorous...brooding, lugubrious, and woeful.

Now, the building before him seemed a place more in keeping with surroundings of weeping willows, howling storms, and subterranean, ni-ter-encrusted crypts...a monolithic maze of secret passages, hidden recesses, and tattered tapestries.

Now it felt less like the Fourth of July and more like November, the thirteenth of November, perhaps, with summer lying long-dead with the bluebonnets in the fields, and the final stroke of midnight still echoing in the darkening air.

The old man looked up and saw that it was, indeed, getting darker. He turned and saw that the twin suns of Orgundy still seemed to burn as brightly as ever but now they seemed to burn behind cloth — thick, dark cloth, that stole clarity and precision.

He turned back and saw that the light now filled the entrance to Independence. And he saw that, encased in the light, a lone figure stood, motionless. Waiting.

Waiting for *him*.

William Gainsborough Senior took a step back, away from the towers and the wood and the stone. Then, as he was about to take another step, the figure raised an arm and beckoned to him. He stopped and squinted his eyes. There was something familiar about that wave. Something he recognized.

He withdrew that step. And then took one more.

Then another.

His heart pounded and his eyes widened. The figure moved again…and he started to run.

Surely it was his imagination. Surely it was a trick…a trick of the twin suns, of the desert breeze, a construction of his active mind or a reflection of his inner thoughts or of some distant star whose light had traveled many millions of years to create such an effect purely for him. He felt his teeth jangling together as he ran, his jaw flopping with the effort. And then, suddenly, he had the strength.

It came in a flood into every pore of his body, a rush of energy and determination.

As he ran, the figure stepped back, her arms still outstretched the way she always stretched them to him. And he saw her hair now, blowing around her face and her shoulders.

He ran through the sand, kicking it around his feet in purple gusts until he reached the drawbridge in the shadow of every building he had ever known, all of which now gathered around the skirt-tails of the Empire State Building where, so many years ago, he had first met Margaret.

His feet clattered on the wood and he laughed at the sound they made. He shouted her name, over and over again, and he heard her shout back, his own name spoken again by another voice after all these long years. *Her* voice.

And now he understood this monolithic construct…this unidentified flying castle.

He knew that, inside, he would find King Arthur and Gandalf and Steerpike…and Herman Melville and Edgar Allen Poe and Edgar Rice Burroughs. He knew instinctively all its rooms and its corridors, recognized all of its thick-pile carpets, stone floors, and polished bare-board rafter walkways.

Margaret had stepped back now, well back into the first of those corridors. But now he could see her face and her smile.

And as she bade him welcome, he could hear, above the sound of the drawbridge closing behind him, every single syllable of her words, and every tiny consonant. And each was as important to the message as each slate of Independence's roof and each brick in its sides and each board in its floors was essential to the final construction.

And then he fell once more into her arms, to build again.

✧◉✧

Over time, the patchwork quilt of rectangular gardens was covered by the sands though the domes remained, still looking like tiny droplets of mercury on the otherwise arid plains.

Over still more time, the sand covered the distant polished-steel skeletons of the broken rocketships in their silent tombs and, finally, even drifted up to the Resting Place, where the winds had blown down the crude markings whose words had long since faded.

Each year, the airborne domain of memory and hope returned, its ghostly gables drifting again on the strange breezes. And each year, it seemed a little different…though there was no one there to appreciate the modifications.

Finally even the faded corduroy of the Timberline jacket had faded from sight.

> I raise high the perpendicular hand, I make the signal,
> To remain after me in sight forever,
> For all the haunts and homes of me.
>
> Walt Whitman, from *Salut Au Monde* (1856)

For Ray Bradbury

The Killing of Davis-Davis

All my wishes end where I hope my days will end, at Monticello.

Thomas Jefferson

The sound was that of a gigantic pack of playing cards being fanned across the sky, echoing around the clouds in time to the distant flares of color that split the horizon into thick, weeping gashes. It reverberated and filled the entire cosmos and bounced off the weakening walls of time, dark winds whipping up great fragments of the continuum like street blocks of sidewalk and pavement, bombarding the billowing fabrics of the universe and sending them spinning and pirouetting like enormous gossamer curtains.

Amidst the carnage and confusion, the voice screamed again, hoarse now, crying into the deathless winds. And deep within the maelstrom of movement and noise, a frail body writhed as if possessed.

Billion-mile rips, like gangrenous tears, breached the boundless heavens and pieces of history tumbled from the wounds onto the battlefield. Cries of the newborn mingled with the tearful oaths of the dying while, across the ground, the blood of the centuries ran, and formed pools, and then scabbed, and then disappeared.

The air was filled with a multitide of odors.

Here a shape fell and decayed in seconds...only to reform its flesh and rise again screaming. Lying among the tortured souls, a fat man with a cigar gave a two-fingered sign as his legs crumbled into the river of entrails that washed around him. High above in the mists, red clouds scurried with crashes of thunder, and lightning raked the ground leaving craters and fires that later had never been but soon would be.

A young man slumped froward in a car as a bullet scattered pieces of brain across his driver, and the whole entourage plowed into the gates of a camp that made lamp shades out of the skins of babies. Aove the scene, appropriately placed in a presidential box, a man raised high his weapon and screamed his assassin scream yet again…as peace was declared and war broke out.

And this was as it would always be.

Thus had it ever been.

The countdown for the final performance approached…and it was about time.

⚜

"Then it's the only way?"

"It's the only way. Will you do it?"

He turned a card, a red seven, and placed it on the eight of spades. "I'll do it," he said, fingering the pack.

⚜

The door slammed open and Mandrain burst in waving a piece of paper, his face pale and drawn.

"What is it?" asked DeFatz, his hand resting on the roulette wheel.

"The computer…it came up with this: We didn't know."

DeFatz spun the wheel, took the printout, and read.

"We didn't know!" screamed Mandrain, and he watched the little white ball bounce among the slots, waiting for the motion to stop.

⚜

"When will you leave?" she asked, stroking his head.

He stared at the spread of playing cards and gently rubbed those still to be turned. "Tomorrow, but you'll hardly know I've gone."

She sighed.

He turned a card.

The fire crackled.

⚜

"It's as simple as this," said Smutbath, waving his baton at the blackboard. "East Side Spare Parts now covers the world; from London to Adelaide, New York to Moscow." He paused and gesticulated wildly, unable to think of any other cities offhand. "In fact," he continued, "just about every damn place you can think of except—" And he turned again to the blackboard. "Except here." He prodded Jersey with his baton and stepped away from the blackboard.

"See," he started, "the past eighty, ninety years have seen massive progress in cooperation between the Federation and the..." He paused, seemingly trying to think of a word.

"The Jeffies, sir?" a voice shouted.

"The Spacers?" another voice enquired querulously.

Smutbath searched the room myopically, nodding. "Yes, quite," he said, "the Jeffies and the Spacers...indeed, such quaint pieces of terminology. Rather," he tapped the side of his leg with his baton, "let's call them free thinkers and free movers, shall we?"

There was no response.

"Anyway," Smutbath continued, "there has been, as I said, considerable progress between the Federation and the free-thinking and free-moving elements of our society in terms of business development and open communications...progress that has enabled East Side Spare Parts to expand beyond our one-time wildest dreams. Now" — he strode determinedly back to the blackboard and brandished his baton — "the Earth is effectively ours, at least in terms of strict commercialism, and similarly — thanks to last century's black hole discovery plus advancements...albeit of a limited success...in robotics and nanotechnology — delivery and production levels are off the scale."

Smutbath paused. "Everything in the garden is exceptionally rosy indeed...apart from one small slug wandering the flowerbeds." He pulled down the flip-chart and displayed Jersey Replacements' well-known emblem.

"Why don't we just bomb them?" asked Filbean, in a shrill voice that sounded like Smutbath's chalk on the blackboard.

Everyone nodded and muttered mutual agreement.

"Because Jersey Replacements is too good a concern to just wipe off the map. Its reputation goes back decades...back to the early two-thousands I should think. Their ground-breaking work in spread-spectrum radio, steganography, and encryption, for example — and those are but a few of many such examples — has made them a highly respected element in the electronics and surveillance society of 2271."

Smutbath left the rostrum and all eyes followed him. "So, no," he continued, "we don't just bomb them. And Davis-Davis will not sell out — my God but we've tried."

"Then we kill Davis-Davis," said a voice.

Pilking, a small, sharp-faced man, rose to his feet and turned to face the speaker. "We have tried every way to blot him out. For years. The entire assassinations sections has been geared to that very goal for the past eighteen months, even to the point of evaluating usage of the recently discovered black-hole singularity...but beams and devices used in that way cannot be effectively controlled.

"So…" his voice trailed as he turned to face Smutbath at the front of the room. "We cannot get near him. The island of Jersey is impregnable, his bodyguards number in the thousands, and his clones exist in every corner…offworld as well as onworld, hidden, waiting to be called to duty should the Davis-Davis on the island be killed." He shrugged. "It would solve nothing even if we *could* kill him now…." He paused and faced the room. "But if we had killed him as he moved up the company…that would have been different. We had opportunities then. We should have foreseen this situation when we killed his father." He nodded to nobody in particular and, turning, smiled up at Smutbath. "We blew it," he said. Then he sat down.

Smutbath returned the smile and walked quietly down the aisle between the desks until he reached the second desk from the back of the fourth row.

There, a dark-haired man sat playing Patience.

The murmuring that had resulted from Pilking's words faded into absolute silence. The man looked up at Smutbath and then turned his eyes to Pilking, who had turned around in his seat and now sat staring at him through the sea of faces and backs of heads. The man held his cards tightly and said, "Then it's the only way?"

"It's the only way. Will you do it?"

He turned a card, a red seven, and placed it on the eight of spades. "I'll do it," he said, fingering the pack.

⚜

DeFatz ran from the data-control block to the management sector, horror in his heart.

Smutbath looked up from the four neat piles of playing cards on his desk as DeFatz burst into his office. "What the —"

DeFatz leaned on the dask, panting, and stretched out an empty right hand. "Read this," he gasped.

Smutbath frowned. "Read what?"

"This print —" DeFatz stopped and looked around the office. "Did you want me?" he asked.

"No." Smutbath lifted one of the piles and fanned it out, counting the points.

"Then why am I here?" muttered DeFatz, scratching his head.

⚜

"I've been expecting you," the man behind the desk said.

He kept the laser trained on the man and searched the smoldering office for opposition.

"This is the end, then," said Davis-Davis.

He nodded and pulled back the trigger.

❦

He turned an ace and moved it to the side.

"I have a feeling about this one," she said.

He said nothing and turned three cards, the three of clubs on the top. There was no red four and the ace of clubs had yet to be played.

"He's too clever for you," she said, reaching for her drink. "And Smutbath, and Pilking."

He turned more cards. Queen of hearts.

She held his head inches from her own and the tears trickled sown her cheeks. "They've been trying for years to nail him and…"

But he wasn't listening.

She sighed and sipped her drink, feeling the soft coldness travel down her throat. "When will you leave?" she asked, stroking his head.

❦

"It will be normal," said Meatle, walking around his machine. "Just the initial dizziness, muscle recoordination—that's the tightness in the arms and legs," he interrupted himself, "and a sick feeling; then you're home and dry."

Smutbath stepped forward nearer to the console and thrust his hands deep into his pants pockets. "Any questions?"

The man continued to toss a coin, watching it twirl in the air and then land again on his outstretched palm. He checked the face of the coin and, tossing it again, said, "No."

"Even at that time, Davis-Davis had bodyguards, and the channel was constantly patrolled by Jersey Replacements vessels—although ships from France docked there daily, so that'll be your means of crossing. How you actually get onto the island will, I'm afraid, be your own problem."

He twisted the coin in his fingers and nodded.

"At the time," said Smutbath, "Davis-Davis was deputy managing director. It was three years before we assassinated his father, thereby allowing him to gain full control of the company. Perhaps he was even contemplating it then. We have no way of knowing, of course, but at least in retrospect, it would seem as though we did Davis-Davis a big favor.

"Eighteen months from the time you will arrive, key men in the cabinet were replaced by militants from the Davis-Davis camp. At that time, his father ceased to have any real control and thus merely became a figurehead, kept alive only, I'm sure, until new relationships with the rest of the world could be effected." Smutbath paused and shook his head. "If only we had thought, and paid more attention to the signs, then all of this might not have been necessary."

"But there is no real danger," Meatle said, rubbing his hand across the bulkhead of his machine. "And he has used it before," he added, turning to smile at the somber gathering.

"But this time we will be altering the entire time flow," Smutbath pointed out in a voice that bore traces of tiredness and something else. "This time, we will be removing a complete piece of history."

⚜

All in sight was fading and returning, and still the body lurched and cried deep, sobbing moans.

⚜

"Then it's the only way?"

"It's the only way. Will you do it?"

He turned a card, a black four, and started to place it on the eight of spades. He frowned and pulled back, puzzled. "I'll...do it," he said, fingering the pack.

⚜

DeFatz spun the wheel, took the printout, and read.

"We didn't know!" screamed Mandrain, and he watched the little white ball bounce among the slots, waiting for the motion to stop.

The paper carried the legend FILE AMENDMENTS. Under the sub-heading DELETIONS was the name Davis-Davis, complete with relevant date, time of birth, personal appraisals, and an estimated MAIN FILE CORRECTION run of 716,421,763 pages containing 8,162,946,344,446 entries. Beneath that was another name. **Finnegan.** It was double-printed, making the word stand out from the rest.

DeFatz looked up as the wheel came to a stop and the little white ball slowed. "Finnegan?" he asked.

Mandrain leaned across the desk, his wet face inches from that of DeFatz. "Look at the date of his death," he sobbed, grabbing the paper and pushing it toward the other man's face. "Look at the date!"

❧❀❧

"That depends," said Captain Ferrarro, a grizzled one-legged Spacer who had left the FTL merchant trade and opted for onworld shuttle service.

"Depends?"

Captain Ferrarro gave a crinkly smile. "It depends on how much you've got."

His passenger smiled and placed his arm around the fat man. "There must be many ships bound for Jersey today, Captain. Am I right?"

The captain nodded nervously.

"Then I could just…kill you, now, right?" He smiled. "And then I could find someone else, someone more, shall we say, more willing to accommodate me. Am I right?"

A croak.

He leaned closer. "Pardon me?"

"You're right," came the reply.

"Good." He removed his arm. "Then you will accept the standard payment."

The captain smiled an uneasy acknowledgment.

"And please," he said, softly, inserting his index finger in Ferrarro's mouth and squeezing until blood ran down the man's face to meet his thumb, "let us keep to our little arrangement without any, shall we say, deviations."

Captain Ferrarro tried to smile, and swallowed some of his own blood.

"Because I just don't have the time." And he gave out a hollow laugh that was completely devoid of humor, while above the winds, the cries of the dying mingled with the tearful oaths of the newborn…

❧❀❧

Across the ground, the blood of centuries ran, and formed pools, and then scabbed, and then disappeared.

And still the lone body amidst the ghostlike wraiths twisted and turned in a noiseless cry.

The door slid back and the guard walked briskly into the room. Davis-Davis nodded an acknowledgment to the salute and spoke.

"Yes."

"We have an infiltrator, sir." The guard stood rigidly, staring at a piece of wall some four or five feet above the seated man's head.

"Where?"

"Block eight, sir."

"Casualties?"

"Four dead and seven wounded, sir."

Davis-Davis stood up and walked around the desk and behind the guard. "And what exactly is this person doing in block eight, Mr. Bissle?"

The guard winced. When names were used it invariably led to un-pleasantness. "I think he's trying to get to you, sir."

"Then stop him."

"Sir." The guard saluted, pivoted, and left the room.

And the pomp and the circumstance were the seventh day.

Outside the sky grew dark and squalls of rain lashed the windows. "Bloody weather," said Mandrain. He turned back to his cards, chewed his bottom lip for a second, and said, "Okay, three diamonds."

"Where's the boss?" Drewjar asked, peering through a hatch.

Mandrain scratched his head and frowned. "Not really sure. I think he went...went to see Smutbath—" He hesitated. "Yes, to see Smutbath, about something or other. Why?"

Drewjar looked puzzled. "Well, I don't know if it's anything really, but the terminals are acting up."

"No bid," wheezed Flandell, the network controller. He placed his cards on the table and shook a cigarette from a crumpled pack. "Acting up? How?"

Across from Smutbath, Blick pushed his cards together and then fanned them out again. "Are we playing here or what?"

Drewjar studied Blick's cards as he spoke. "Well, they're giving out incorrect information all the time. Work's stopped on data prep until some-one can have a look at it."

"Three spades," Blick said. "Now where the hell's—"

As if on cue, the door opened and DeFatz walked in. He looked un-easy.

Blick said, "It's your bloody bid."

Flandell shuffled around in his chair and coughed loudly. "My dear DeFatz, Mr. Drewjar informs us that the terminals are on the fritz. When did you last check the modem points?"

"Where've you been, anyway?" added Mandrain.

"Let me look at my cards, last Wednesday, and Smutbath's office," DeFatz said to the questioning faces, and he reached for his cards.

Drewjar raised his eyebrows in a what-do-I-do expression.

"What were you doing with Smutbath?" Blick asked.

DeFatz fanned his cards and counted. "Haven't got the faintest idea," he said with a chuckle. "When I got there, I'd forgotten. Must be going senile." He laughed again and stared at the cards.

Mandrain turned to look out the window. Outside, the sky was turning bright ginger in stages.

"You know," DeFatz said, "it's the damnedest thing."

Drewjar leaned back against the wall to wait until the conversation drifted back to the terminals.

"*What* is?" asked Blick in exasperation.

"These cards. I feel I've played this hand a million times."

And he laughed as the winds built up again.

⚜

He listened for footsteps.

All was silent.

He was into block four.

⚜

"Block four!" Davis-Davis screamed, his eyes aflame. "How the holy hell has he got all the way to block four?"

Bissle gulped and stared straight ahead. There wasn't a good answer. The intruder was there, and that was that.

"What are you all doing out there?" Davis-Davis continued. "He's one man, Bissle. One man! Why has he not been stopped?"

Davis-Davis returned to his chair. As he sat down, his composure regained, he said, "I don't care how you do it, but I want him stopped."

⚜

All around, strange colors flashed and lit the heavens while voices boomed across the ever-changing landscape. Voices that screamed and sobbed; voices that laughed and altered tone and pitch, like bad recordings; voices that shook and shuddered, like the sound of a thousand bombs falling together, shaking the firmament.

He lay staring into the resulting voids with eyes of madness.

⚜

Hurried footsteps echoed on the tarmac outside the block four hatch. He slid beneah a large tarpaulin to the right of the hatch and waited, his heart thumping in his head.

The hatch creaked open.

All was silent save for the low hum of the machinery holding the door in place some five feet above the ground. Suddenly a hand appeared inside the hatch, and with a scurry, a guard dropped into the shadows in front of the tarpaulin.

He cursed silently.

He had not been ready.

He listened. The guard inside the block did not move.

He raised his air gun and waited.

A second figure appeared for a split second...and he fired. The air immediately in front of the guard swirled and compressed, and with the start of a shout, the body spun around and crashed into the entry and slid to the floor.

With a scream of defiance, the guard inside the block leapt from his cover in the darkness and fired two shots into the tarpaulin, which jumped into the air, smoking, and then settled again with a *fluump!*

He stood from his hiding place and fired point-blank at the guard's face, then turned and, with a flick of the controls on his air gun, sprayed the entry hatch. Two more guards exploded in a burst of skin and uniform.

He listened for a while and then stepped down.

He switched the hatch door to CLOSE and shouldered the gun.

At his feet was a torso with its left arm and shoulder missing. The legs were nowhere to he seen. The torso breathed in and out quickly, eyes open but unseeing.

The remains of a tag over its breast pocket said BISS.

⋘⊛⋙

And the fear and the horror were the sixth day.

⋘⊛⋙

"I know, I know...but I'm just supposing," said Flandell, mopping the sweat from his face.

Smutbath looked at him disdainfully and shuddered. "Well, don't suppose things like that too often—at least not while I'm around." He dealt the cards into four neat piles on his desk and then picked up one of the piles.

Flandell grunted. "There's just something strange happening and I don't know what it is."

"Must be an epidemic," Smutbath said, sorting the cards into suits.

"Hmmm?"

"Well, yesterday — at least, I think it was yesterday — DeFatz came charging into my office shouting abou — "

The door slammed open and Smutbath looked up.

DeFatz leaned on the desk, panting. "Read this," he gasped, holding out his empty right hand.

⁂

"Then it's the only way?"

"It's the only way. Will you do it?"

She frowned and stared into the empty fire grate.

⁂

"I've been expecting you," the man behind the desk said.

"Huh?" responded Flandell. He coughed and looked around the room he had just entered to ascertain where he was. It was Smutbath's office and Smutbath was dealing cards into four neat piles.

Smutbath finished dealing, picked up one of the piles, and fanned out the cards. Then he placed the fan of cards carefully on his desk and picked up another pile.

He looked up at Flandell, smiled, and then threw the cards onto the table. "Sorry," he said, "that wasn't my line. We'd better try it again." He dragged all the cards together with his hands and started to hum.

DeFatz burst into the office. "Read this," he gasped, holding out an empty right hand.

Outside, the clouds flashed past the mock-up building fronts and all the noise in the world rolled across the stage below.

For a second it all became clear to Flandell. He looked at Smutbath and DeFatz, saw Smutbath rest his head on his desk and begin to sob.

The roar of eternity coming down the corridor outside the door mingled with the strange mauve clouds that had easily conquered the glassless windows and now swirled around the room, removing air.

Then the door disintegrated in a shower of splinters. "Here we go again," Flandell whispered to no one in particular.

⁂

When he awoke, he was sitting across from what appeared to be a statue of Smutbath, frozen in the act of arranging playing cards in his hands.

A table was between them. He looked at his own cards. Seventeen points, seven diamond cards, no spades.

He laid the cards down in a neat fan and reached across to touch Smutbath's arm. It was pliant, cool to the touch, and slightly clammy.

"I know what's happening," he said.

Smutbath did not move.

Flandell rose to his feet and moved from the table to a large desk at the side of the room. On the desk was a tropical-fish tank, only constructed from the sand and soil that lay at the tank's sides. In the water, several small fish swam lazily.

"He's dead," Flandell said. He pushed his hands into his pants pockets and turned to rest against the table. "We sent him back to kill Davis-Davis and he did it. But then years after — of maybe even days after…or minutes — someone or something killed *him*. And that someone or something would not have been there or would not have happened if Davis-Davis had lived." He raised his voice and, looking around the room, said, "Is that about right?"

There was no answer. Smutbath remained deathly still.

"And so now," he continued, his voice lowered, "they're trying everything they can think of to put things right, letting different people know of what's happening and what's happened in the process."

He moved away from the table and walked behind Smutbath. "Good hand," he said, looking at the cards frozen in the process of being sorted into suit order.

A slight movement from the fish tank caught his attention and he walked back to take a closer look. One of the fish had beached onto an island. It wiggled and squirmed, and when he bent closer, Flandell saw that it was sprouting tiny limbs as he watched.

Flandell started to cry.

The door burst open and DeFatz held out an empty hand. "Read this," he gasped. Flandell noticed grimly that DeFatz was holding out his *left* hand.

⁂

"See," said Flandell, "the modems are perfectly in order." He wiped his nose and grunted. "I knew it couldn't be anything to do with them."

"Well it must be something," muttered Drewjar with a scowl. "They shouldn't refuse information from files coded ten and under."

"And what the hell's this message?" Mandrain pointed to the terminal printout and read it aloud. "'Code E005411: Information requested is under construction.'"

"Never heard of it. 'Under construction.' Hmmph." Drewjar snorted disdainfully and straightened up. "Never bloody heard of it."

Flandell remained bent over the machine. "Somebody get me a manual."

"I've got it here," Mandrain called from the rack of books at the other side of the room. "There's no message suite with a code prefix *E*."

"Cock!" said Flandell, and he jumped up and walked briskly over to Mandrain. Snatching the open book, he said, "If there's a message, then it must be explained in the manual."

The others watched as he studied the indices.

He snapped the book shut. "I'm going to see Smutbath," he said, and stormed out of the room.

◆◆◆◆

"Yes?"

"Sir, Bissle's dead," said a voice through the intercom.

Davis-Davis swallowed hard and closed his eyes tightly.

"Sir?"

"Yes, I'm still here."

"What should we do, sir?"

"What's that noise? In the background?"

"That's Block Two, sir. It's on fire."

"He's into Block Two?"

"Yes, sir. What should we do?"

"I have no idea," said Davis-Davis, and he switched off the intercom.

◆◆◆◆

A young paperhanger from Austria lazed on the front lawns of America's White House and the streets were awash with fire and screams, while inside the rambling multicorridored building, a man whose life and principles had in another deal of the celestial cards inspired an entire movement of so-called minarchists stood in an oval wood-paneled room, staring out of the windows.

The man, the third great leader of his great country, absently warmed his hands before a smoldering fire upon which had recently been thrown a revolving chair, the shards of a portable writing desk, a letter-copying device, and a cannonball-weighted clock that told the day of the week. As he watched the event unfolding outside he considered changing his name...a simple matter of making the first the last and vice versa. "Jefferson Thomas," he said, nodding, rolling the words around his tongue to see how they tasted.

On the next lot, Rasputin burned at the stake, his lips flecked with the saliva of the righteous.

Great seams opened and closed continually, spewing out more attempts while mercifully burying those that had no effect.

And the body laughed and clapped to the endless performances, its face dripping with the blood of the millennia.

✦✧✦

And the applause and the shouting were the fifth day.

✦✧✦

The door opened and Flandell walked into Smutbath's office. Smutbath was sitting with his feet on the window ledge, staring into the sky. On the table behind him were four small piles of cards. He turned around and smiled at Flandell. "It's all there," he said. "It's just the way you said — oh, yes...I could hear you."

"Hear me?"

Smutbath stood up and moved to the window. Outside, in the street far below the window, a tall, bearded man was trudging through the mud, jeered on all sides by the gathered crowds. On his back was a roughly made cross constructed of two planks. On one of the planks, the words ACME CONSTRUCTION could be seen clearly.

Smutbath turned from the window, chuckling. "Acme Construction," he said. "Sounds like one of the old cartoons from the twentieth century."

Flandell was frozen in the act of walking across the room, a code manual from the computer building clasped in his hands.

Smutbath walked around the other man, waved a hand in front of his eyes, pushed his shoulder...all to no avail. "You can't hear a word I'm saying, can you?"

There was no answer.

"No, you *can* hear. I heard you, after all. It's just that you can't do anything about it."

Smutbath walked back to the window. "I wonder how long they've been trying...how long this has been going on." He looked out and watched Jesus stagger to the end of the street. As he reached the mound, the figure stopped and the crowds quieted. All faces turned around and looked up to the window. It had no glass in it.

"Forgive them," Smutbath said softly, "for they know not what to do."

The sky turned a violent green and winds blew down the street, scattering both players and props alike.

Smutbath sobbed into his hands. "And *I* don't know what to do, either." When he pulled his face away, he saw that he had cried tears of blood into his hands.

⚜

And the crucifixion and the stigmata were the fourth day.

⚜

"When will you leave?" she asked, stroking his head.

He stared at the spread of playing cards and gently rubbed those still to be turned. "Tomorrow, but you'll hardly know I've gone."

She sighed.

He turned a card.

The fire crackled.

The man looked up at Smutbath and then turned his eyes to Pilking, who had turned around in his seat and now sat staring at him through the sea of faces and backs of heads. He held his cards tightly and said, "Then it's the only way?"

"It's the only way. Will you do it?"

⚜

"I've been expecting you," the man behind the desk said.

He kept the laser trained on the man and searched the smoldering office for opposition.

"This is the end, then," said Davis-Davis.

He nodded and pulled back on the trigger.

But he wasn't listening.

She sighed and sipped her drink, feeling the soft coldness travel down her throat. "When will you leave?" she asked, stroking his head.

"But there is no real danger," Meatle said, rubbing his hand across the bulkhead of the machine. "And he has used it before," he added, turning to smile at the somber gathering.

"But this time we will be altering the entire time flow," Smutbath pointed out in a voice that bore traces of tiredness and something else. "This time, we will be removing a complete piece of history."

DeFatz looked up as the wheel came to a stop and the little white ball slowed. "Finnegan?" he asked.

"That depends," said Captain Ferrarro, "on how much you've got."

"Because I just don't have the time." And he gave out a hollow laugh that was completely devoid of humor, while above the winds, the cries of the dying mingled with the tearful oaths of the newborn....

"We have an infiltrator, sir." The guard stood rigidly, staring at a piece of wall some four or five feet above the seated man's head.

"You know," DeFatz said, "it's the damnedest thing."

Drewjar leaned back against the wall to wait until the conversation drifted back to the terminals.

"*What* is?" asked Blick in exasperation.

"These cards. I feel I've played this hand a million times."

And he laughed as the winds echoed through the room and smashed the rostrum into the air.

<hr>

Already it was the third day, and it was not good.

<hr>

She sighed and stared into the empty grate. He heard the sigh and turned his head on her lap. "Why worry about this one?" he asked. "There have been so many others in the past."

She laughed despite herself. "That's some play on words you've got there."

He smiled at his unintentional pun and sat up. "I've been back before. Please...just don't worry."

"But you'll be altering the entire time flow this time. Think about the things that Davis-Davis must have done in the last twenty years that we don't even know about." She shook her head and moved away from him. "If just one of those things — just one of those millions of things that he did, or would have done — was important, just think of what it could mean to the present. Think how things could change."

He laughed. "Even if something *did* change as a result of his death, then as far as you in the present are concerned, it would always have been that way." He looked into the fireplace. "Ever since whatever it was should have happened or shouldn't have happened...whichever the case may be." He frowned. Something seemed not to be right.

"I don't understand the paradoxes of time," she said with a brave smile. "Don't go."

"I must," he said, wondering why there was no fire in the grate.

<hr>

The sign was directly above his head: BLOCK ONE.

Outside, down the wind, he could hear the voices and cries of the guards. In the last block there had been only the faint hum of machinery and equipment. He now stood against the block one hatch entrance and waited. The smell of burning was spreading everywhere, and his throat and nostrils were stinging.

He laughed to himself. He had made it. He was here.

One more block and he was *here*.

He checked the air gun. It was completely empty.

He bent down carefully, keeping his eyes scanning for any signs of movement, and laid the spent weapon on the ground.

Standing up, he decided it would have to be the laser rifle. He had always enjoyed using the laser rifle.

Unstrapping it from his back, he started across the block.

⚜

"It's kind of like a preemptive defense," Pilking said.

The audience did not respond.

Nobody moved.

One or two were frozen in the act of sleep; one was caught, his eyes half lidded, with a finger up his left nostril; several were looking this way or that; a few were writing.

But all were still.

Pilking walked along the aisles.

"They're playing the odds," he said. "They're trying every trick in the book to make a grand-slam contract."

He reached the front of the hall and, turning to face the immobile gathering again, leaned against the desk. "But how do you make seven of anything when you're missing the ace of trumps?

"They'll even try permutation," he said, his voice almost a whisper. "They'll go back, and they'll go forward. They'll try it over and over again.

"They'll have Germany winning the Second World War...they'll have Gorbachev assassinated...maybe Clinton, Dole, Erikson, Mondayo...all of them, all the ones ever since...and then they'll rerun the whole thing, bringing it up to date, and see if it's worked. Because, let's face it: there's no law anywhere that says gods have to be intelligent."

"And maybe they'll try name-changes, too." He smiled and thrust his hands into his pants pockets, nodding. "Yeah, maybe they'll change your names — all of your names — and my name, too. Hell, maybe they'll even change the Earth's name...change it to —" He stopped and lifted his head, searching for inspiration. "To Valhalla, maybe, or Armageddon." He thought of his beloved president, Jefferson Thomas — ignoring the nagging small voice that seemed to question some important element of that memory—and laughed. "Or maybe they'll even call it Monticello, forgetting the old space station." He placed an arm across his chest and said, in deep sepulchral tones, "'All my wishes end where I hope my days will end, at Monticello.'"

He walked onto the rostrum and sat on the desk. "This is what it's about now: cause and effect, action and reaction.

"And if it doesn't work, then they'll take it all back and try something else...bring it forward again, check it out—no, didn't work—take it back, try something else...and so on."

He smiled and ran a hand through his hair. "Sounds boring, doesn't it? But *they* don't get bored doing things like this. Hell, *they* enjoy it. Death, destruction, pain, confusion...these are the trademarks of a god's work. No sense, no reason, no logic.

"Air crashes, earthquakes, famines...none of it makes any sense.

"So, *why do it?* do I hear you say?" He laughed. "Why indeed." He shrugged. "Because. It. Passes. The. Time.

"That's all. Nothing more."

He rubbed his crotch through his pants and then held up his hand. "See this? What I just did with it?"

Nobody responded.

Nobody moved.

Nobody even breathed, at least not in the usual way.

"I scratched my balls. There. What about that?"

Nothing.

"Important? Nah! But when you get to the stage where you've considered everything else, the seemingly unimportant things suddenly seem like they might be important after all. So.

"I scratched my balls with my right hand. I always do it with my right hand...I'm right handed, for Crissakes.

"What they may do now is go back to every time I scratched my balls—or you..." He pointed to a man in the front row.

"Or you." One in the fifth row.

He pointed to the man with his finger up his nostril. "Maybe they'll go back to every time you picked your nose."

The man, his finger permanently fixed up into the darkness and moist dirt, didn't move.

"And they'll have us do it with our other hand," Pilking continued. "The one we don't usually use. Then they'll run it through again and see if it's worked out."

He sat and watched for a while.

Nobody moved.

"But it *won't* work out. I mean…it's all just a big gamble. And, in the long run, nobody ever wins by gambling."

He stretched out on the table and looked up at the sky. "Hah," he said. "I hadn't ever noticed that the ceiling was gone."

And the second day was a load of balls.

It was/is/soon would be the first/last day.
A time of endings and beginnings.
The possibilities were, at last, exhausted. It would have to be this way.

The hatch was open and all was quiet.
He looked around carefully before he moved inside.
The fires had swept fiercely through the block-ventilation system and the Home Block was already smoking.
He released the catch on the laser rifle and stepped through the hatch to find Davis-Davis, looking very old and very tired, seated behind a large mahogany desk.
"I've been expecting you," the man behind the desk said.
He kept the laser trained on the man and searched the smoldering office for opposition.
"This is the end, then," said Davis-Davis.
He nodded and pulled back on the trigger.
And the winds came crashing through the blocks and whistled across the gashes in the dead man's chest and face; and he felt a tugging in his stomach and tasted the bile in his mouth.
The screams echoed in the tiny office and he dropped the laser rifle and ran. And as he ran back through the blocks, the way he had come, he watched with fascination as the bodies of the dead guards leapt from the ground and ran, first backward and then forward, screaming gibberish in reverse, speeded up and then slowed down. But nobody seemed to notice him as he passed through.
"Then it's the only way?" he panted into the wind. "It's the only way," he replied.
He screamed a frantic refusal and was answered with a sound like mad static.
And now the blocks were gone. All around was bare and deserted.
And in his head, he heard the voices.

※※※※

DeFatz spun the wheel, took the printout, and read.

"We didn't know!" screamed Mandrain, and he watched the little white ball bounce among the slots, waiting for the motion to stop.

The paper carried the legend FILE AMENDMENTS. Under the subheading DELETIONS was the name Davis-Davis, complete with relevant date, time of death, time of birth, personal appraisals, and an estimated MAIN FILE CORRECTION run of 716,421,763 pages containing 8,162,946,344,446 entries. Beneath that was another name. **Finnegan**. It was double-printed, making the word stand out from the rest.

DeFatz looked up as the wheel came to a stop and the little white ball slowed. "Finnegan?" he asked.

Mandrain leaned across the desk, his wet face inches from that of DeFatz. "Look at the date of his death," he sobbed, grabbing the paper and pushing it toward the other man's face. "Look at the date!"

DeFatz looked again at the paper and studied the information carefully. "He was killed sixteen years ago...*after* Davis-Davis was assassinated." His voice trailed off and he looked up at Mandrain. "But if that's true, then how could he go back? What does it all mean?"

Mandrain pulled out a chair and sat down. "It means that Davis-Davis was somehow responsible for the would-be killer of our assassin." He pointed at the paper hanging limply from DeFatz's hand. "Finnegan."

"Oh no," DeFatz said, his eyes wide in understanding.

"Oh *yes*," Mandrain corrected. "And because we had Davis-Davis assassinated, Finnegan lived. Therefore, Finnegan killed our man before he could possibly have set off back to kill Davis-Davis. Thus, Davis-Davis didn't die after all. Therefore, our man *did* go back, and Davis-Davis *did* die, and Finnegan *did* live, and our man *did* die, and so Davis-Davis *did* live, and Finnegan *did* die, and our man *did* live...."

DeFatz was openly weeping.

Mandrain was almost out of breath. "It's beautiful," he said, clapping his hands together in mock glee. "It's beautiful but it's impossible." He looked at the stationary ball in the roulette wheel. "The number is decidedly up and it's a no-win situation. And..." He pointed to the ceiling. "Anytime now, they're going to figure that out for themselves."

⚜

He screamed.

He screamed loud and long as strange forces jostled for control of his body.

Then there came the first and last sound.

The sound was that of a gigantic pack of playing cards being fanned across the sky, echoing around the clouds in time to the distant flares of color that split the horizon into thick, weeping gashes. It reverberated and filled the entire cosmos and bounced off the weakened walls of time, dark winds whipping up the last great fragments of the continuum like street blocks of sidewalk and pavement, bombarding the billowing tattered fabrics of the universe and sending them spinning and pirouetting like enormous gossamer curtains.

The final sound of all amidst the confusion was a rending crash, a clapperboard that signaled the last take.

And the show was abandoned.

As one, all the lights went out.

Everywhere became dark and silent.

And it was good.

> What of liberty and slavery among them, what they
> thought of death and the soul,
> Who were witty and wise, who beautiful and poetic,
> who brutish and underdevelop'd,
> Not a mark, not a record remains—and yet all remains.

> Walt Whitman, from *Unnamed Lands* (1881)

The Invasion

I
t went *what?"*

"Whooooosh!" Jimmy Jorgensson repeated the word in an almost jubilant spray, throwing his arm in a wide arc that nearly removed his can of Sprite from the table and sent it spinning across the floor. "Right over my head," he added, "straight out over the filling station and then down towards the dump."

Adam Showell smiled. "Just like that, huh?"

Jimmy nodded, eyes wide with excitement.

Adam waved his own arm in a clumsy approximation of Jimmy's and said, "Whooooosh?"

Jimmy clicked his jaw. He always clicked his jaw when he got annoyed. "You saying you don't believe me?"

"Aw, come on J.J. — "

"No," Jimmy snapped, getting to his feet and stepping across the spread of comic books scattered across his bedroom floor. "Whenever somebody says they've seen something, you don't believe them. You *never* believe them."

"Did I say — "

"You didn't *need* to say: it's obvious you don't believe me."

"But a flying saucer?"

"I didn't say it was a flying saucer, I said it was an unidentified flying object."

Adam shrugged, drained the last few drops of liquid from his can and crushed it. "Same thing in my book."

"I'm not lying or...or making it up," Jimmy said, a faint note of self-pity creeping into his voice.

"Maybe it was a comet, or a shooting star."

"Maybe." Jimmy sounded unconvinced.

"It's just that if they're always flying around up there, why don't they actually get in touch with us?"

"Because," Jimmy pointed out, leaning forward, "we have wars and we're always killing each other. What have we got to offer them?"

Adam, suddenly feeling disadvantaged by remaining on the floor, got to his feet and slurred towards Jimmy's bed. "Then if we're so lousy, why the hell are they watching us?" He plopped down onto the ruffled covers and folded his arms defiantly. "Maybe if they *are* there, it's them who've screwed up our ozone layer by driving in and out of it."

Before Jimmy could answer, the door creaked open and both boys turned to see who it was. "You guys want any more drinks?" a voice asked. The voice was immediately followed by an old man's head, topped with a creamy white splurge of hair that went in all directions. The head remained disembodied and glared questioningly at the two boys through bifocal glasses, eyebrows raised.

"No, thanks, Gramps," Jimmy said.

Adam shook his head and smiled. "No thanks, Mr. Jorgensson."

The old man's head remained hammered between the partially open door and the wall. "Potato chips?"

"Uh uh."

Adam shook his head again.

"Kick in the ass, maybe?"

The boys laughed out loud, Adam with his eyes and mouth open in astonishment.

"Okay, I'll leave you both to it." The head started to pull back out of the room and then stopped before moving forward again. "This a private argument or can anybody join in?" He waited a second before continuing. "I need to know so's I can tell the folks queueing up outside — looks to me like they been driving quite a while. Noise you fellas're making, must be able to hear you clear over on the Interstate. Folks can't hear their car radios."

Adam chuckled.

"We're fine, Gramps, thanks."

"Well, I'm hitting the sheets so keep it down, okay?"

"Okay." Jimmy scratched his head and looked down at his sneakers. "Mom and Dad in yet?"

"Nope," Ed Jorgensson's voice drifted in as the door closed. "Said they'd be late. 'Bout time you were thinking about bedding down, too."

The two statements seemed entirely unconnected and Jimmy adopted an exaggerated expression of puzzlement. "Okay," he said, managing to contain his amusement. Adam was not nearly so successful and he blurted out a short, braying snigger.

"'Night, Adam," the old man's voice trilled.

"Good night, Mr. Jorgensson," Adam replied, his shoulders shaking like he was fit to burst.

Somewhere down the corridor outside Jimmy's room a door closed softly and, just for a second, its sound seemed suddenly somehow lonely and final. Both of the boys felt it, for that same fleeting instant, and Jimmy was reminded of his friend's recent loss.

Jimmy had hardly mentioned Adam's mother's death, not quite knowing how to start in on the subject. He'd just told him that he was sorry and
let it go at that. But it went deeper. Jimmy couldn't for the life of him figure
out what it must be like to lose one of your parents. It seemed to him like
his own mom and dad would be there forever. He shrugged and looked
across at Adam, all thoughts of their argument forgotten. "You want to call
your dad?"

Adam looked up from his hands, clasped tightly on his lap, and Jimmy
saw the faint shimmer of moisture on his eyes. He shook his head.

"You wanna watch a video?"

"Yeah!" Adam said, suddenly animated. "What you got?"

Jimmy moved across to the small television set and tugged out a bunch
of videos from a shelf festooned with comic books and magazines. "Dad
gave me all his old black-and-whites," he said breathlessly, holding two
videos aloft as confirmation. One was the old Ray Harryhausen epic, *It
Came From Beneath The Sea* and the other was *The Wasp Woman*. "They're
kinda schlocky," he said as he returned them to the shelf and rummaged
about in the others, "but there's some good stuff, too."

"You got any about flying saucers?"

Jimmy turned around and made like he was going to throw an episode
of *The Outer Limits* across the bed and Adam folded up with his hands over
his head, laughing.

The telephone rang, cutting through the sound of laughter and silence
like a knife. The boys looked at each other and Jimmy jumped up. He pulled
open his bedroom door and shouted along the passageway to his grandfather. "You want me to get that, Gramps?"

"You go ahead, I'm taking a — I'm in the bathroom," came the reply.

Jimmy ran down the stairs two at a time and snatched the receiver up
in his left hand before the sixth ring. "Hello?"

"J. J.?"

"Yeah?"

"It's me, Billy."

"Hey, Billy."

"Hey, right back. Listen, you got Adam with you?"

"Yeah. He's staying the night. His dad's going out with some friend of
his and gonna be back late. What's the problem?"

The voice on the other end of the line dropped conspiratorially. "I seen
another one."

"Another UFO?" He pronounced the acronym as a word and not as
three single letters: you-foe.

"Yeah."

"Where?"

Billy Macready paused. "Whadyamean *where?* In the sky, lamebrain, where d'ya think?"

"No, I mean whereabouts?"

"Over the dump. I seen two, truth to tell. Kinda hovering over there and then dropping out of sight."

The news made Jimmy's stomach do cartwheels. But what Billy said next made it do hang-gliding somersaults. He said, "You wanna take a look?"

Ten minutes later, Jimmy and Adam were climbing down the trelliswork beneath Jimmy's bedroom window, with the night standing large and mysterious around them.

⁂

"There goes another one," Jack Turnbull mumbled, pointing his half-empty bottle of cheap wine at the light which passed over the dump. Fred Wessels belched unconcernedly and lifted his own bottle to his lips. He made contact on the third attempt and drank, swallowing noisily.

"That makes seventeen I seen this week alone," Jack said, scratching at the seat of his pants as he watched where the light had gone down behind the auto skeletons.

Fred belched again and shuffled his back against his carpet bag, which he had propped up against an old television set.

Jack Turnbull swayed across to a heap of black bags and leaned on them, spilling wine in the process. "Whe–where d'you think they're from? Hmmm?"

Fred didn't answer.

Jack staggered back from the bags and tilted his head so that he was looking straight up into the nighttime sky. The sky was black now, though the edge to his right contained the reflected glare of the lights of Forest Plains and the cars on the Interstate. "Mars? Venus?" He closed his eyes and breathed in the smells of the dump. "D'you – d'you think maybe Neptune?"

Still no answer.

Jack turned around and looked down at his companion. Fred's bottle had upturned on his jacket and the wine was mingling with the grease and filth and the other stains whose origins were long since forgotten. He had fallen fast asleep.

Jack looked back at the heavens. "Lookit them octobur... octopuses from that movie. You ever see – " He suddenly remembered that Fred was asleep. "Naw, I guess not." He lifted the bottle and took a long drink.

Somewhere behind him, a tin can rattled down one of the piles of trash. Jack turned quickly, arms, legs and head moving without any coordination, like a puppet operated by a complete novice. "You—you hear that, Fred?" he whispered.

Fred smacked his lips and shuffled over onto his side. Suddenly freed from the man's grasp, the bottle rolled onto the ground giving out a soft, liquidy _sploinggg_ sound.

Jack stared into the gloom.

Out across the fields, a dog howled. It sounded frightened.

"Look, tell your mom it's a party, not an orgy."

Dlip, said the radar screen into the headphones lying next to the telephone.

James Farnham moved the receiver into his right hand and turned his chair so that his back was to the equipment. "For God's sake, Carol, you're almost twenty years old."

Dlip

"Well, if you know, why the hell don't you start—I'm not using _any_ kind of language. All I'm saying...Carol, all I'm saying—Look, will you listen to me here? All I'm saying is tell your mom that you're going whether she likes it or not." He closed his eyes and mouthed at her as she started to speak.

The green line went around the screen again, passing the omega letter at the base. _Dlip_, it said.

"There _is_ nobody else I'd rather take, Carol—"

Dlipdlip

"—for Chrissakes."

Dlipdlipdlip...dlipdlipdlipdlipdlipdlip...dlip

"Oh, hell, if that's going to be your attitude—"

Dlipdlipdlipdlipdlipdlipdlipdlipdlipdlip

"I _will_ take someone else."

Dlipdlipdlip

"I don't know who, just somebody."

Dlipdlipdlipdlipdlipdlip

"No, not Mary Clemmons. I do not—No, I do—Carol, for crying out loud, I do not have the hots for Mary Clemmons." He shook his head and looked up at the clock. Eight-thirty: three and a half hours before the change of shifts. "I know I danced with her that one time but, Carol, it was that one time. How man—how many times—Yes, I know. How many times have you danced with somebody else?"

Dlipdlipdlip...dlipdlip

"But I can't go by myself, can I?"

Dlip…dlip

He nodded into the mouthpiece. "Okay. Yeah, okay, Carol. But do the best you can, huh?"

Dlip

"Yeah, me too. Yes I *do* mean it. Yeah, okay. I'll ring you tomorrow. Yeah. Bye. Yeah, bye bye." He rested the receiver on the cradle and turned to face the equipment. "How you doing, radar?" he said, lifting the headphones. As he pulled the earpieces apart, the green line completed its 360-degree sweep.

Dlip, it replied.

⚜

Ted Bannister leaned on his sweeping broom in the glare of the porchlight. "Hey, Marnie?"

A voice answered from inside the house, muffled.

"Come on out here for a minute."

Martha Bannister started talking to him as soon as she left the kitchen, the words getting louder as she walked along the hallway and pushed open the screen door. " — ything done around here if I'm wandering in and out every five minutes at your beck and call, Ted Bannister," she finished as she stepped onto the porch. "What is it, anyways?"

Her husband continued to lean and jerked his head up at the sky. "Meteors," he said confidently.

Martha wiped her hands on her apron and squinted into the night sky. "Where meteors? I don't see anything."

Ted removed one hand from the broom handle and lifted a muscled arm to point. The checkered workshirt hung unfastened around his wrist, blowing in the gentle breeze. "Look," he said, "there goes one now."

High above the hills behind the library, a silver-blue light flashed, leaving a sparkling trail behind in the evening gloom. Whatever it was had gone down over by where Ted knew the filling station was.

"That was a meteor?" Martha queried.

Ted clicked the roof of his mouth with his tongue. "I guess," he said.

His wife shook her head and wiped her already clean hands again on her apron. "What on earth am I doing standing here talking about meteors when I have bread to bake? I declare, Ted Bannister, you've got me near on as crazy as you, you old coot." Ted said nothing and continued to stare at the sky. "And you have a porch to sweep." She turned around and pulled on the screen door. "You do a good job and maybe I'll make you a nice cup of caramel coffee."

"Mmmm…hey!" Ted said as the screen door banged behind him.

Halfway along the hall, Martha heard her husband shout again. "I haven't time," she shouted back, almost choking herself on her own spittle.

"Well, isn't that the darnedest thing…" Ted muttered to himself. Over across town, another silver-blue light had appeared and seemed to be hovering in the sky above the town dump. "If that isn't the strangest meteor I ever—" Suddenly, the light dropped out of sight. Ted Bannister shook his head, took his broom in both hands and looked around the rest of the sky.

❦

The bell above the door to Frank Elmsley's General Store tinkled as his last customer left.

Frank turned around to continue the ritual of closing up for the day. It was almost nine o'clock. He walked back behind the counter, checking things and straightening them up whether they needed it or not. He made sure that the stock and order books were safely on the shelf in their allotted place and pulled open the cover to the switchbox to turn off the interior lights.

Just then, a gust of wind seemed to blow open the door.

Tingalingaling, said the bell, tiredly.

Frank turned around and made to tell whoever it was that he was closed for the day, knowing full well that he had never turned anyone away once they were inside the store in almost thirty-five years. But there was nobody there.

Outside, the wind blew along the darkened street.

Somewhere, far away, a car door slammed.

"We're—we're closed," Frank said to the empty store.

Something moved in his head, softly, gently, rustling and whispering.

Closed? it said.

❦

The door opened slowly and the warmth of the house flooded out onto the path with the spilled light. A small, freckled face appeared around the side of the door, eyes studying the visitor and checking the empty pathway behind him. "Where's Adam?" the face said at last.

Adam jumped out from the side of the house and held his arms wide. "Ta-dah!"

"*Jesus*—Jesus Christ, Adam!" Billy Macready snapped, lowering his voice to little more than a whisper.

Jimmy laughed at Adam's *What'd I do?* expression.

"Don't *do* that," the freckled face of Billy Macready hissed. He waved for them to come inside.

Closing the door gently behind the two guests, Billy said, "Haven't you been listening to the news?"

"The news? Since when do you listen to the news?"

Billy shrugged himself into his plaid jacket. "Well, not the news exactly, but just the talk between records on KWLD."

"Ah." Adam nodded sagely. "*That* news."

"Hey, don't *ah* me, man. I don't like *ah*."

"Hey," Jimmy said, slapping Adam on his arm: "Don't *ah* him, okay? He don' likea da *ah*."

"Jerks!" Billy pulled his zipper tight to his chin.

Jimmy and Adam sniggered. "What did it say, anyway, this 'news'?"

"They seen lights, man. Flashing lights. They seen them all over this county and into the next. And strange noises, too." He shrugged and puckered his mouth. "And, sure, they got some crank calls, too."

"Crank calls? Saying what?" Adam traced an offshoot of the repetitive vine that meandered across the Macreadys' hallway wallpaper, following each curlicue with his finger.

"Oh, you know the stuff: cows being transported by tractor beams, someone seeing the roof of the library being lifted…that kind of thing."

Adam stood back from the wallpaper, straightened up and made like he was a robot, eyes wide, arms held out straight in front of him, "Durn-dur-dut-dut, DAHHH!"

Billy grabbed him and shook hard. "Shhhh! You wanna wake my folks?"

"They in bed already?"

Billy nodded. "Yeah, my old man's hot to trot tonight, hombre. He took my old lady up there 'bout an hour ago, man. They been there ever since. Doin' the old bump 'n' grind, man."

"You hear anything?"

Adam glared at Jimmy and grimaced. "Oh, Captain Gross…pleased ta meetcha, I'm sure."

"Cut it out," Billy said. The sniggering died down. "Okay, let's go." He pulled open the door and removed the key from the inside lock.

"Where we going *to?*" Adam asked quietly.

Billy pulled the door gently and inserted the key. Turning it softly, so that it wouldn't make too much of a noise, he said, "Town dump."

They pulled their collars up against the cold and ran down to the street, making sure they stayed on the grass by the side of the path. But still their feet made noises, thudding through the darkness.

⚜

Jack Turnbull had dropped his bottle and was standing, swaying, above Fred Wessels. "Fred," he whispered.

He felt more sober now than he had in a long time. There had been noises. Strange, slithering noises from the piles of junk which surrounded them. What worried him most was that it might be a bunch of kids come round for a little fun, beat up a couple of bums…maybe even set fire to them, watch them burn.

"Fred!" He bent down and shook the other man's shoulder but there was no response. Jack straightened up and turned around, squinting to make some sense of the gloom. He could see nothing. But still he heard it. *Sensed* it. "C'mon, Fred. Maybe it's the police."

But Jack Turnbull didn't think it was the police.

The faint noises he could make out drifting across the garbage and the old, rusting metal car frames sounded more like the octopuses from that old movie — *War of the Worlds*, he suddenly remembered — clambering across the piles of junk towards him.

He stared through the dark and listened, hardly daring to breathe. Something *was* coming, moving. He could hear it. Hell, he could *feel* it.

The night was cool and a gentle wind blew around his feet.

Jack looked around for the quickest way out.

※◎⁂

"Ted?" The voice cut through the evening stillness and echoed around the wooden porch. "You finished yet?"

No answer.

Her hands encased in bread dough, Mary Bannister paused and held her head on one side, listening. She turned to face the door, mentally cursing her husband for his stubborn refusal to wear his hearing aid, and shouted louder. "Ted, it's after nine o'clock. You come in now before you go get yourself a summer chill, you hear me?"

Still no answer.

She dusted off her hands on her apron and walked sternly through the house. A small frisson of unease uncoiled when she couldn't see her husband through the mesh of the screen door. When she stepped out onto the porch and saw the red-handled sweeping broom lying, apparently cast aside, in Ted's prize rose bushes, the frisson graduated to earthquake proportions.

"Ted?"

The wind took the word and lifted it high into the night. As she followed it in her mind's eye, Mary Bannister saw another meteor whiz through the dark clouds and disappear behind the filling station.

※◎⁂

"Just an old bum," Billy Macready said over his shoulder, in answer to Adam Showell's question. "And the biggest collection of garage sale items you ever saw."

Jimmy Jorgensson tried to pull himself up so he could see but couldn't without dislodging an old washing mangle precariously balanced upon a dirt-encrusted pair of rubber boots, seemingly millions of tin cans, and what looked as though it might once have been a radio. Relaxing his arms, he said, "What's he doing?"

Billy was straddled on the fence, his knees holding him erect and his right foot tucked into the wooden slats. The other foot was over on the other side of the fence, out of sight. "He's out of it, man. Pushing out the big zees. Either that," he added, "or he's dead. Come on. Let's go in."

"What do you mean, *dead?*" Jimmy hissed to Billy's disappearing foot. But it was too late. A dull thud from the other side of the fence told him that Billy was inside the dump. He turned and jumped from the pile of garbage that had been stacked beside the fence and started to clamber up the pile of crates that Billy had used. Once at the top, he looked across to see Billy slowly approaching a figure which lay sprawled against a Mount Everest of black refuse bags. Seconds later he had jumped to the ground.

A few more seconds later, and Adam Showell landed beside him. With a quick glance around the stacks of garbage, the two boys moved off after Billy.

"Naw," Billy was saying as they arrived at his side, "he's just asleep." He sounded almost disappointed. He picked up the discarded bottle of whiskey and sniffed.

"And there's why," Adam said.

Billy took a swig and coughed. "Good stuff," he said between clenched teeth. He offered the bottle to Jimmy who grimaced. "Want some?"

Jimmy shook his head and made the face he used when forced to take bad medicine.

Billy shrugged and turned to his other side. "Adam?"

"Uh uh. *I'll* pass on oblivion, too."

"Suit yourself." Billy hauled back and pitched the bottle high above them. They watched it soar, hover briefly, and then disappear above and old Chrysler shell perched atop a tower of black bags. They waited for the sound of breaking glass but there was only a dull *whump* and the clatter of the bottle rolling down something metallic.

"You shouldn't have done that, Billy," Jimmy Jorgensson said, staring about in the gloom. "Someone might hear."

Billy frowned, accepting the criticism, and followed his friend's gaze.

Adam suddenly grabbed Billy's arm. "Look."

They looked.

"What is it?" Jimmy whispered. "I don't see any —"

"Hey," Billy said. He got up from his crouching position and ran across the passway between the piles of junk and bags. Stooping, he picked up an object from the ground.

"What is it?" Jimmy whisper-shouted.

Adam got to his feet and walked slowly towards Billy. "It's another bottle," he said.

Jimmy glanced behind again and ran over to the others.

"Where d'you suppose he's gone?" Billy asked nobody in particular.

"Where *who's* gone?"

Adam turned to Jimmy and smiled the smile of somebody explaining one and one being two to a preschool infant. "The guy who left this bottle. This *second* bottle," he added.

"Maybe he's taking a pee," Billy suggested.

They thought on that for a while, listening for the telltale sound of splashing water. But only the wind moved around them.

"Maybe he's asleep, too," Adam contributed.

Maybe they've *got him*, Jimmy wanted to say, but it came out as "Maybe we should go back, now."

⁂

"Yes, Mrs. Bannister, I got the description, but—"

A buzz of speech fluttered from the telephone receiver into the stillness of the sheriff's office. Doug Hemmitt placed his pencil carefully on the pad in front of him and rubbed his eyes with his free hand.

"But," he continued, raising his voice slightly, "a person is not considered missing until at least twenty-four hours've gone by. Why don't—Yeah, but why don't you wait a while. Maybe he's just gone off to take a walk." He paused to allow the buzz to make its point. "I don't know why he'd want to take a walk, Mrs. Bannister" — *though maybe I'm getting an idea*, he thought—"but that sounds like the most obvious thing. Maybe he took a walk to see some more of these lights.

Buzzzzzz!

"Sorry, meteors. Yeah, I'm sorry Mrs. Bannister, but that's about all I can suggest."

He looked around at the clock while the receiver buzzed some more. Nine forty-two.

"Yes," he said, "we'll keep our eyes peeled. And you—"

Buzzzz

"Yeah, sure. And you give us a call back if—sorry, *when*—you give us a call back *when* he turns up, okay?"

Buzz

"That's what we're here for, Mrs. Bannister." He leaned back in his chair and swiveled to see if there was still some coffee in the pot. He brightened up when he saw that it was still more than half full. "Yeah, thanks for calling. Yeah, good night, Mrs. Bannister."

The phone went silent.

Doug Hemmitt—"Deputy Doug," as the other guys in the office called him—reached across and picked up the intercom. He would ask Andy Gifford to call by and give the woman a little moral support. After all, it was a quiet night.

※⊙⊛~

"No, no, *no!* For the last time, Carol—for the *very* last time—you are not going. I do not intend to discuss it nor do I have to have a reason. The answer is, no."

Carol Barnes stamped her foot and frowned, staring hatefully at her mother. "It's only a party, Mother, not an orgy," she said, remembering what Jim Farnham had said.

Alice Barnes started clearing the supper dishes. "It may start out that way, Carol, but—anyway, I've said *no*. Now, please. Let it rest at that."

"It's not fair. I'm nearly twenty years old."

"Yes," her mother said, pointing with a plate of gherkins for dramatic emphasis, "and if I have my way, you'll make it to twenty-one."

"What's that supposed to mean?"

"Carol…" Her mother sounded tired now. "I've said *no*. That's it. Let it go."

Carol sat down in the chair with a *thud*, and thrust her face into her hands.

As she left the room en route for the kitchen, her mother called back, "Hadn't you better phone Jim Farnham and tell him?"

Carol got up from the chair and stormed out of the room.

"Who'd be a mother?" Alice Barnes said to the mute milk jug. It didn't have an answer.

Thoughts flooded through Carol's head, mingling with an acute frustration that seemed to color everything with a red tinge and made her want to smash things. She resisted. Instead, she dialed the number of the base at Forest Plains and, when the prerecorded voice asked her to key in the extension of the party she wished to contact, she hit the one and seven keys.

A sinking feeling hit her stomach as, across town, she pictured the telephone ringing on Jim's desk. *Bring! bring!* it went in her mind. *Drurp drurp* said the receiver in her hand.

She pictured Jim hearing the phone — *drurp drurp* — turning around to pick it up — *drurp drurp* — his hand closing around the receiver right now — *drurp drurp* —

Where was he?

Drurp drurp

Why wasn't he picking it up? Did he know it was her?

Drurp drurp

Did he know what she was ringing to tell him?

As the phone continued to ring over in Forest Plains, Carol glance nervously at the clock: nine fifty-three. Over two hours before his relief came. So why didn't he answer?

Drurp drurp

"Oh, go to hell!" Carol snapped into the mouthpiece, and she slammed the receiver down onto the cradle.

Over on the other side of town, in the Forest Plains Air Force Base, a lonely telephone said *bring! bri* — and then fell silent, leaving only an occasional *dlip* from the radar screen and the sighing of the evening wind blowing through the open doors.

⚜

The chair creaked on the old wooden boards of the porch and Martha Bannister looked out onto the world beyond the flickering light; the world that had mercilessly swallowed up her husband. Now she felt strangely at odds with everything, suddenly vulnerable and no longer surrounded by friends. She had managed to resist the urge to cry. Crying was useless, counterproductive — though, "counterproductive" was not a term that figured in Martha Bannister's vocabulary. It was luxury she could not afford because, at its simplest, it signaled the giving up of hope. She could never do that while there was still hope to be had. After all, there was probably a simple explanation. Just like the deputy had said over the telephone. Now, rocking to and fro in her husband's cane chair, she felt a little guilty over giving him a hard time.

Clunk

She stopped rocking and strained to hear.

The noise had come from the side of the house.

Martha leaned forward, her heart skipping through her chest like a young girl. "Ted?"

There was no answer.

She got to her feet, grimacing at the arthritis in her hips, and wiped her perfectly clean hands on her dress. It was her best dress, the red one that Ted liked so much.

"Ted, is that you?"

High up — oh, so very high up! — in the sky, another meteor flew through the night, far above Earth. She walked off the porch into the heady smell of night-scented stocks, with the world standing silent and expectant all around her.

Bu duhh, bu duhh, her heart said, as though warning her.

The side of the house was dark and somehow more inhospitable than usual. It seemed foreign to her. No, more than foreign; it was…She searched for the word. *Alien.* And silent. Nothing moved down there between the fence and the wood panels of her house. Darkness reigned supreme.

"Hello?" She said the word falteringly.

Little voices screamed in her head. *Go into the house. Phone the sheriff's office again. It's an intruder. Ted's going to come home in a couple hours and find you with your head smashed in and your best red dress all* —She stopped herself from going on. It was a strange world that she and her husband were busy waiting to leave, and no denying it. A world where a woman just wasn't safe walking around her own house at night wasn't any kind of world at all, she decided.

Bu duhh, bu duhh, her heart said in percussive agreement.

She took another slow step towards the gloom. "Ted? I hope that's you in there, 'cause I'm coming in."

Then it came.

Soft and gentle, borne on a fragrant wind that was uncharacteristically warm and scented with the most beautiful and intoxicating smells, all fighting for superiority. It wafted out of the darkness before her, like the tinkling of distant bells in some far-off steeple. Or maybe like the sound of bluebonnets rusting against each other as the faery folk ran through them. It made her gasp.

"Marnie?" it said. It was her husband's voice, and not her husband's voice. Or, at least, it was her husband's voice as she remembered it from fifty years earlier, a voice filled to the brim with excitement and hope, determination and resilience, wonder and magic.

She smiled into the darkness and went to meet him. But he was not alone.

✴

Jack Turnbull smiled, too.

Everything was now clear to him. Acutely clear.

All of Jack's friends smiled with him. He felt them.

He felt their happiness and their trust, felt their warm contentment…warmer than any bottle he had drunk from. Warmer than any old newspaper he had pulled around himself.

"Everybody okay?" he asked cheerfully of the myriad chattering voices snuggled in his head.

Okay

Affirmation washed across his senses in a wave, washing the most distant and long-untouched corners of his body and his mind...cleaning him cleaner than any water and soap had ever done.

Noah's Ark. The thought came into his head from nowhere. But it was true. That was what he had become. All of his body, all of his senses. All new responsibilities.

He was a guide. *John Raymond Turnbull,* he thought, *Guide to Earth.* He smiled to himself. It was so long since he had thought of his full name.

A new world to show off. A world he had turned his back on.

He felt completely sober and yet, at the same time, drunker than he had ever felt before. But it was an intoxication that confronted and absorbed rather than one which retreated and repelled. He felt the excitement start in his own mind and then rush through a hundred more, a thousand more, a million more, blazing all before it like a brush fire.

How good it was to be back; to be a part of it all again.

"See you guys tamale," Billy yelled across the street. He made a gunshape with his right hand and pretend-fired two slugs at Adam Showell and Jimmy Jorgensson as they stood watching him, the town dump at their backs. He turned around and started into the alley between Pop Kleat's Soda Shoppe and the realty office. Cutting through the lumberyard at the end of the alley was going to save him precious time, but Billy suddenly felt a slight surge of nerves and his stomach coiled around itself like he needed to go to the bathroom.

"Hey," Adam shouted back, "make sure the saucers don't get you."

"Yeah, watch the skies," Jimmy added. "Keep on watching the skies."

They both laughed.

Billy turned around and gave them the bird, then watched them walking off along Beechwood Avenue, stiff-jointed, a couple of ten-year-old Frankenstein's monsters. He waited until they were obscured by Pop Kleat's window and then turned again to the alley, noting, somewhere deep in his subconscious, that it sure looked awfully dark.

He breathed in deeply, puffed out his chest, and clenched his fists tight. Then he ran down the alley making the sound of a jet plane and slapping each of the trashcans as he passed by.

By the time he reached the rickety gates of the lumberyard, the fear was gone with the impenetrable blackness of the building-shrouded alley. Once again, Billy was beneath the full panoply of the sky. He looked up and watched another meteor flash overhead. It was getting so they were a dime a dozen.

He pulled the gates apart and stepped inside.

⁂

Patrolman Andy Gifford stepped from the black-and-white and walked across the street, towards the old couple dancing around the garden. Trapped in the beam of his flashlight, they stopped running around the flower beds and smiled over at him.

Andy smiled his puzzlement at the old woman, her silver-white hair hanging long around the gathered neckline of her dark red dress. "Mrs. Bannister?" he said. "Mrs. Martha Bannister?"

"Yes?" the woman answered, breathlessly softly.

Andy turned his flashlight fully on the old man. He was walking amongst the flowers, waving his hands wildly, pointing here and then pointing somewhere else, all the time mumbling to himself. "And this is Mr. Bannister?"

Behind him, the car radio squawked in a tide of crackle.

The woman watched him, her head tilted on one side, a smile frozen on her mouth. "Yes, yes it is," she said at last. "Is there a problem, officer?"

Andy returned the smile—it was so infectious, he had to stop himself from giggling—and shook his head. "Well, I don't know. Maybe I have the wrong details or some—"

Mrs. Bannister hit herself on the forehead. "Of course," she said, and the voices in her head mumbled and discussed. "I'm so sorry to have been so much trouble."

Andy started to shake his head, but the woman continued.

"Yes, this *is* my husband," she laughed. The laugh sounded somehow inappropriate. It was the laugh of youth, the laugh of a *young* woman. "And, as you can plainly see, he's quite well."

Andy looked across at the old man. "And this is a garage," Mr. Bannister said to nobody in particular, although, deep in his head, the voices took note: *garage*, they noted. It was all so new, so wonderfully different.

"Yeah," Andy Gifford agreed, "he looks fine to me." *He looks like he just fell out of a tree and cracked his head.* "Okay," he said, "I guess everything's fine here."

"Everything *is* fine," Martha Bannister said.

As he walked away from the house, Andy Gifford heard the old man chattering. It was a frenzied chatter, as though time itself were running out on him. Maybe it was. It couldn't be much fun getting old, he thought. Reaching the car, he turned back and watched them wandering around their house, at one with the darkness. He was glad he had not said all of the things he had thought of saying to them: about not placing missing person reports without due cause; about informing the sheriff's office when that missing person turned up again.

But then it had been one of those nights. As he had driven along Main Street he had seen the lights on in Frank Elmsley's General Store and pulled over. But, just before he had gotten out of the car, he had seen Frank walking around his shelves holding up cans and packets and boxes and then putting them back onto the shelves. Just walking around like he was in a kind of daze. Must be a change in the seasons, he decided.

As Andy slid behind the wheel, Martha Bannister was rifling through some plants and her husband was training a flashlight along the guttering and up and down the water spouting of their house. He could imagine what the old man was saying.

Andy turned the key in the ignition and shifted the transmission into drive. "This is the guttering and the water spouting," he said to the dashboard in as near an imitation of the old man's voice as he could manage.

Back in the Bannisters' nighttime garden, as the black-and-white pulled away from the curb, Mr. Bannister's voices took note. *Guttering...water spouting*, they noted.

⚜

"Hello?"

"Carol?"

"Jim..." She didn't know what to say. Didn't know how to sound. Should she hang up? Should she tell him not to ring her again? It was a battle of wits—protocol: saying the right thing without seeming to be a pushover. "I tried to phone you earlier," she said suddenly, the words slipping out of their own volition while she was busy deciding what to do. "Where were you?"

The voices chattered at the pictures in his mind. They saw a pretty face and long, dark hair. They saw large blue eyes which looked frightened of being hurt. And they saw freckles, lots of freckles, and a short, stubby nose. They inquired.

"Carol," Jim Farnham said, softly.

Carol.

"What?" she asked.

On the other end of the line, Jim Farnham remained silent.

"I said, where were you?"

Jim stammered. "I can't really explain over the telephone. Can you come over to the base?"

"What, now?"

"I'll meet you at the gates in half an hour."

"Jim, I can't come over no—"

Drrrrrrrr, the telephone said, sleepily. Jim Farnham had hung up.

Carol Barnes slammed the receiver down in its cradle for the second time that night and scowled. "Just who the hell does he think he is?" she asked loudly.

There was no answer.

The hall was absolutely quiet.

She looked at the clock. Ten-fifteen.

She listened to the gentle sounds of her parents shuffling around in their bedroom.

She bit her lip, just enough to make it hurt.

⚜

The lumberyard looked almost as dark and inhospitable as the alley he had just run through, and Billy Macready hesitated just inside. He looked back through the gates and along the alley, wondering if maybe Adam and J.J. had turned back and decided to accompany him. But the alley and the small section of Beechwood Avenue he could see at the end were deserted. He was completely alone.

He considered starting back to the street but then he again saw the darkness of the alley that lay between him and it. It had to be the lesser of the two evils, he decided. He was already in the lumberyard, and this *was* the shorter route.

"Okay, boy," he said to the invisible horse between his legs. "Let's go get 'em!"

And he ran into the evening breeze with one hand stretched out before him and the other slapping the outside of his right thigh.

They were waiting for him at the pass.

Billy, they said in unison.

Billy Macready stopped, hand still outstretched, and stared into the darkness of the lumberyard. His heart was pounding, fit to burst. "Hello?" His voice sounded pathetic and small, but that was okay: that was the way he felt, too.

"Adam? J.J.? That you?" Maybe they had doubled back somehow and sneaked into the yard some other way. But he knew that was not possible. The way he had entered—the back way, where the trucks loaded up their deliveries—was the only way in except for the main entrance on his street. And that was...that was miles away.

There was a small glow down among the logs.

Billy stared at it.

We mean you no harm, the glow said, though not exactly in those words. It said it in a strange mixture of pictures and smells and colors and sounds.

And it said it in a thousand tiny voices that both fretted his mind and soothed it at the same time.

Billy wanted to say something—anything—but the words would not form. The glow was growing fainter as he watched it.

We have traveled a long way, said the glow which was many, many voices, snuggled in his head. Its collective voice ebbed and pulsated with the words. *We cannot return home.*

The fear inside him was gone now. He felt rested, peaceful. He felt a great warmth come over him. It was a little bit like pity—like when his father had run over a stray cat and they had knelt beside it and tried to soothe it; but the cat had been beyond help, and Billy's dad had smashed it on the head with a stone. But it was also like extreme happiness—like when school let out for the summer and fall seemed like a vicious rumor, so far in the distance as not having any importance at all. He had so little experience on which to base a comparison. Ten years: what's ten years!?

His brain bypassed the inadequacies of his mouth and spoke to the voices direct.

It spoke in colors and sounds and feelings.

It spoke of the burnished gold of autumn and of the blue-white of the winter snows.

It spoke with the clarity of summer rain and with the fresh breath of spring winds.

And it asked how it, a small boy, could possibly be of help.

You can do nothing, the voices answered. *By your standards, we will die — we are dying now — but death is, after all, only a word used to explain the end of living: it is the connotations of death which are feared, not death itself.*

Billy understood and the voices relished the understanding. They bathed in the young mind's ready acceptance.

We will be gone within two of your days.

Billy saw images of light and darkness, saw them twice. And he smelled the smells of morning and afternoon, of supper and of bed. And he smelled them twice, also.

We only wish to examine and to experience your existence.

The voices were so soothing that Billy failed to notice that the glow by the lumber was gone. But not gone entirely: now it was inside his head.

Many of us are here.

Billy questioned.

Yes, we are all dying.

Billy thought.

He saw the blackness and the immeasurable vastness of space.

He saw the tiny vessels plummeting through the void, like a swarm of starborn seeds, traveling to an unknown future and leaving behind a cold and lifeless planet.

He felt the frustration of time passing without change.

He felt the boredom and hopelessness of tedium and repetition.

And he felt—and marveled at—a determination and perseverance in the face of the certainty of extinction.

He was wasting time. "This, is a lumberyard," he said to the night, so cold and uncaring.

Lumberyard.

"Now, a lumberyard is..."

The voices noted and discussed.

He felt the frustration of time passing without change.

That same night, Carol Barnes slipped quietly out of her house and met Jim Farnham and his newfound friends. She provided a home for the occupants of another craft and, over the following two days, she introduced and explained many facets of her life. She also learned a little herself...and *of* herself.

She came to understand tolerance and with it came a peace that was beyond her almost-twenty years. Although she and Jim would one day drift apart, they would always enjoy a special friendship that could not be explained to the casual onlooker.

Ted and Martha Bannister had children for two days. Like all good parents, they told their children about all the wonders of their world. And, also like all good parents, they grieved at their children's passing.

Jack Turnbull lost his dependency on alcohol but he regained his self-respect. He showed his charges the beauty of the countryside which had become his home and, when they left him, he took his grief back to its leafy consolation rather than taking up a place in society once more. But, for all the rest of his life, Jack enjoyed a special relationship with the other people of Forest Plains, many of whom had been similarly touched on that most special of nights.

One of those was Frank Elmsley.

Frank closed his general store for two whole days, during which he explained many items of produce and their production and why people needed them.

For many nights over the remaining short time of his life, Frank watched the skies hopefully. But, two years later, on a lonely Thanksgiving, he decided he had had enough.

Jimmy Jorgensson and Adam Showell never met up with the invader they had tried so hard to find. But life had so much in store for them that one missed opportunity did not really matter.

And Billy...

Billy Macready played truant for two days.

He drove his parents mad with concern and, when he finally reappeared, they paid him more attention. It's like they say: you don't miss your water until your well runs dry.

The glowing people that, like meteors, had ridden the dark winds above Forest Plains, ceased to exist; at least in the way that we know existence. But, filled with newfound understanding and a wealth of information, they went accepting their fate.

It's all any of us can hope for.

Palindromic

What seest thou else
In the dark backward and abysm of time?

William Shakespeare
The Tempest

It was on the third day after the aliens arrived that we made the fateful discovery which placed the future of the entire planet in our hands. That discovery was that they hadn't arrived yet.

There were three of us went over to the vacant lot alongside Sycamore...that's me, Derby — like the hat — McLeod, plus my good friend and local genius Jimmy-James Bannister and Ed Brewster, Forest Plains' very own bad boy...except there was nothing bad about Ed. Not really.

We went up into that giant tumbleweed cloud thing that served as some kind of interstellar flivver — it had been at the aliens' invitation, or so we thought; our subsequent discovery called that particular fact into some considerable dispute — purely to get a look at whatever this one alien was doing. Jimmy reckoned — and he was right, as it turned out — he was keeping tabs on what was going on and recording everything in some kind of "book."

Not that he — if the alien *was* a "he;" we never did find out — was writing the way you or I would write, because he wasn't. We didn't even know if he was writing at all until later that night, when Jimmy-James had taken a long look in that foam-book of theirs.

Not that this book was like any other book you ever saw. It wasn't. Just like the ship that brought them to Forest Plains wasn't like any other ship you ever saw, not in *Earth vs. the Flying Saucers* or even on *Twilight Zone* — both of which were what you might call "current" back then. And the aliens themselves weren't like any kind of alien you ever saw in the dime comic books or even dreamed about...not even after maybe after eating warmed-over two-day-old pizza last thing at night on top of a gutfull of Michelob and three or four plates of Ma Chetton's cheese surprises, the small pieces of toasted cheese flapjack that Ma used to serve up when we were holding the monthly Forest Plains Pool Knockout Competition.

It was during one of those special nights, with the moon hanging over the desert like a crazy jack-o'-lantern and the heat making your shirt stick to your back and underarms, that the whole thing actually got itself started. That was the night that creatures from outer space arrived in Forest Plains. Then again, it wasn't.

But I'm getting way ahead of myself here...

So maybe that's the best place to start the story, that night.

It was a Monday, the last one in November, at about nine o'clock. The year was 1964.

Ma Chetton was sweeping the few remaining cheese surprises from her last visit to the kitchen down onto a plate of freshly-made cookies, their steam rising up into the smoky atmosphere of her husband Bill's Pool Emporium over on Sycamore, when the place shook like Jello and the strains of the Trashmen's *Surfin' Bird*, which had been playing on Bill's pride-and-joy Wurlitzer, faded into a wave of what sounded like static. Only thing was we'd never heard of a jukebox suffering from static before. Then the lights went out and the machine just ground itself to a stop.

Jerry Bucher was about to take a shot — six-ball off of two cushions into the far corner as I recall...all the other pockets being covered by Ed Brewster's stripes: funny how you remember details like that — and he stood up ramrod tall like someone had just dropped a firecracker or something crawly down the back of his shorts.

"What the hell was that?" Jerry asked nobody in particular, switching the half-chewed matchstalk from one side of his mouth to the other while he glanced around to put the blame on somebody for almost fouling up his shot. Jerry was never what you might call a calm player, and he was an even worse loser.

Ed Brewster was crouched over, his shoulders hunched up, watching the dust drifting down from the rafters and settling on the pool table, his girlfriend Estelle's arms clamped around his waist.

Ma was standing frozen behind the counter, empty plate in her hand, staring at the lights shining through the windows. "Felt like some kind of earthquake," she ventured.

Bill Chetton's head was visible through the hatch into the kitchen, his mouth hanging open and eyes as wide as dinner plates. "Everyone okay?"

I leaned my pool cue against the table and walked across to the windows. By rights, it should have been dark outside but it was bright as a nighttime ballgame, like someone was shining car headlights straight at the windows, and when I took a look along the street I saw sand and stuff blowing across towards us from the vacant lot opposite.

"Some kind of power failure is what it is," Estelle announced, her voice sounding even higher and squeakier than usual and not at all reassuring.

Leaning against the table in front of the window, my face pressed up against the glass, I saw that the cause of that power failure was not something simple and straightforward like power lines being down between Forest Plains and Bellingham, some thirty-five miles away. It was something far more complicated.

Settling down onto the empty lot across the street was something that resembled a cross between a gigantic metal cannister and an equally gigantic vegetable, its sides billowing in and out.

"Is it a helicopter?" Old Fred Wishingham asked from alongside me, his voice soft and nervous. Fred had ambled over from the booth he occupied every night of the year and was standing on the other side of the table staring out into the night. "Can't be a plane," he said, "so it must be some kind of helicopter." There sounded like a good deal of wishful thinking in that last statement.

But wishful thinking or not, the thing descending on the spare ground across the street didn't look like any helicopter I'd ever seen—not that I'd seen many, mind you—and I told Fred as much.

"It's some kind of goddam hot air balloon," Ed Brewster said, crouching down so's he could get a better look at the top of the thing—it was tall, there was no denying that.

"Looks more like some kind of furry cloud," Abel Bodeen muttered to himself. I figured he was speaking so softly because he didn't feel like making that observation widely known because it sounded a mite foolish. And it did, right enough. The truth of the matter was that the thing *did* look like a furry cloud...or maybe a giant lettuce or the head of a cauliflower, with lights flashing on and off deep inside it.

Pretty soon we were all gathered around the window watching, nobody saying anything else as the thing settled down on the ground.

Within a minute or two, the poolroom lights came back on and the shaking stopped. "You going out to see what it is?" Fred asked. Nobody responded. "I guess *some*body should go out there to see what it is," he said.

Right on cue, the screen door squeaked behind us and we saw the familiar figure of Jimmy-James Bannister step out onto the sidewalk. He glanced back at the window at us all and gave a shrug. Then he started across the street.

"Hope that damn fool knows what he's doing." Ed Brewster was a past master at putting everyone's thoughts into words.

The truth of the matter was Jimmy-James knew a whole lot of things that none of the rest of us had any idea at all about. And anything he didn't know about he just kept on at until he did. Jimmy-James—born James

Ronald Garrison Bannister (he'd made his first name into a double to go partways to satisfying his father and partways to keep the mickey-taking down to an acceptable minimum) — was the resident big brain of Forest Plains. Still only twenty-two years old — same age as me, at the time — he was finishing up his master's degree over at Princeton, studying languages and applied math.

Jimmy-James could do long division problems in his head and cuss in fourteen languages which, along with the fact that he could drink anyone else in town — including Ed — under the table, made him a pretty popular member of any group gathering...particularly one where any amount of liquor or even just beer was to be consumed. He was home for Thanksgiving, taking the week off, and there's a lot of folks owes him a debt of gratitude for that fact.

Anyway, there went Jimmy-James, large as life and twice as bold — though some might say "stupid' — walking across the street, his hands thrust deep into his trouser pockets and his head held high, proud and fearless. There were a couple of muted gasps from somewhere behind me and then the sound of shuffling as folks tried to get closer to the window to get a good look. After all, we'd all seen from the *War of the Worlds* movie what happened to people who got a little too close to these objects...and we'd all pretty much decided that the thing across the street was about as likely to have come from anyplace on Earth as it was to have flown up to us from Vince and Molly Waldon's general store down the street. Nobody actually came right out and said it was from another planet but we all knew that it was. But why it was here was another matter, though we weren't in any great rush to find out the answer to that question. None of us except Jimmy-James Bannister, that is.

"Go call the sheriff," Ma Chetton whispered.

I could hear Bill Chetton pressing the receiver and saying *Hello? Hello?* like his life depended on it. It didn't come as any surprise when Bill announced to the hushed room that the line seemed like it was dead. Then the jukebox kicked in again with a loud and raucous *A papapapapapa...*, the needle somehow having returned to the start of the Trashmen's hit record.

The street outside seemed like it was holding its breath in much the same way as the folks looking out of the window were holding their breath...both it and us waiting to see what was going to happen.

What happened was both awesome and kind of an anticlimax.

Just as Jimmy-James reached the sidewalk across the street, the sides of the giant vegetable balloon cannister from another world dropped down and became a kind of shiny skirt reaching all the way to the ground. No sooner had that happened than a whole group of smaller vegetable things — smaller but still twice the size of Jimmy-James...and, at almost six-four, JJ is not a small man—came sliding down the platform onto terra firma…and into the heart of Forest Plains.

We could hear their caterwauling from where we were, even over the drone of the Trashmen telling anyone who would listen that *the Bird was the Word*…and, as we watched, we saw the vegetable-shapes come to a halt on the sidewalk right in front of Jimmy-James where they kind of spun around and then gathered around him in a tight circle. Then all but one of them moved back a few feet and then the last one moved back, too.

At this point, Jimmy-James turned around and waved to us. "Come on out," he yelled.

"You think it's safe?" Ed Brewster asked.

I shrugged. "Doesn't seem to me they mean any harm," Ma Chetton said softly, the wonder in her voice as plain as the streaks of gray coloring the hair around her ears and temples.

"They come all the way from wherever it is they come from, seems to me that if they'd had a mind to do us any harm they'd have done it by now," said Old Fred Wishingham. "That said, mind you," he added, "I'm not about to go charging out there until we see what it is they *have* come for."

"Maybe they haven't come for nothing at all," Estelle suggested.

Somebody murmured that such an unlikely scenario could be the case but they weren't having none of it. That was the way folks were in Forest Plains in those days—the way folks were all over this country, in fact. Nobody (with the possible exception of Ed Brewster, and even he only did it for fun) wanted to make anyone look or feel a damned fool and hurt their feelings if they could get away without doing so. With Estelle it could be difficult. Estelle had turned making herself look a damned fool into something approaching an art form.

"You mean, like they're exploring…something like that?" Abel Bodeen said to help her out a mite.

"Yeah," Estelle agreed dreamily, "exploring."

"Well, I'm going out," Ma said. And without so much as a second glance or a pause to allow someone to talk her out of it, she rested the empty plate on the countertop and strode over to the door. A minute or so later she was walking across the street. It seemed like the things had sensed she was going to come out because they'd moved across the street like to greet her, swiveling around at the last minute—just as Ma came to a stop—and ringing her just the way they had done with Jimmy-James.

They seemed harmless enough but I felt like we should have the law in on the situation. "Phone still out, Bill?" I shouted. Bill Chetton lifted the receiver and tried again. He nodded and returned it to the cradle.

"Okay Ed," I said, "let's me and you scoot out the back and run over to the sheriff's office."

Ed said okay, after thinking about that for a second or two, and then the two of us slipped behind the counter and into Bill's and Ma's kitchen, then out of the back door and into the yard, past the trash cans towards the fence...and then I heard someone calling.

"What was that?" I whispered across to Ed.

Ed had stopped dead in his tracks on the other side of the fence. He was staring ahead of him. When I got to the fence I looked in the direction Ed was looking and there they were. Three of them. Right in front of us, wailing. I'll never forget that sound...like the wind in the desert, lost and aimless.

The door we'd just come out of opened up again behind us and Fred Wishingham's voice shouted, "Hold it right where you..." and then trailed off when Fred saw the things. "I was just going to tell you that some of those things had just turned around and headed over to where you'd be appearing...and, well, you already saw that." Fred had lowered his voice like he'd just been caught shooting craps in church.

Ed nodded and I told Fred to get back inside.

As I heard the lock click on the door, I whispered to Ed. "You think maybe they can read our minds?"

Ed shrugged.

The things were about ten, maybe twelve feet high and seemed to float above the ground on a circular frilled platform. I say "floated" because they didn't leave any marks as they moved along, not even in the soft dirt of the alleyway that ran behind Bill's and Ma's store.

The platform was about a foot deep and, above that, the thing's body kind of tapered up like a glass stem until it reached another frilly over-hang—like a mushroom's head—at the top. Halfway between the two plat-forms a collar of tendrils or thin wings—like the gossamer veils of a jelly-fish—stuck out from the stem a foot or so and then drooped down limply about three feet. These seemed to twitch and twirl of their own accord, no matter whether a wind was blowing or not, and it didn't take me too long to figure out these were what passed for arms and hands on the things' own world.

I looked up at the first creature's top section, trying to see if there were any kind of airholes or eyes but there was nothing, although the texture of the skin-covering was kind of opaque or translucent...see-through, for want of a better phrase, and I could see things moving around in there, shifting and reforming. Where the noise they made came out, I couldn't tell. And we never did find out.

We watched as the creatures moved closer. Suddenly, the one at the front turned around real fast and the hand-arm things fluttered outwards, like a sheet settling on a bed, and, just for a moment, they touched my shoulder. There was something akin to affection there. At the time, I thought

I was maybe imagining it…maybe reading the creature's thought waves or something, but I was later to discover that there was, if not an outright affection, then at least a feeling of familiarity on the creature's part.

This confrontation lasted only a few seconds, a minute at the most, and then the creatures moved back away from us in the direction of the sheriff's office, the wing things outstretched towards us as they went.

"What did you make of that?" Ed Brewster said, his voice a little croaky and hoarse.

"I have absolutely no idea at all," I said.

I kept watching because one of the creatures intrigued me more than the others. This one carried what seemed to be some kind of foam box, thick with piled-up layers of what looked like cotton candy. All the time we'd been "meeting" with the leader—we supposed the thing that had touched me *was* the leader—this other creature was removing small pieces of foam which it seemed to absorb into its tendrils. It was still doing it as the three of them moved down the alleyway. Just as they reached the back of the sheriff's office, the leader put down its wings, turned around and, leaving the other two behind, moved up onto the sidewalk and out of sight.

I turned at the sound of hurried footsteps behind me and saw Jimmy-James running along the alleyway, his face beaming a wide smile. Ma Chetton was following him, her head still turned in the direction of the street to see if any of the creatures were following *her*.

"What about *that!*" JJ said. Then, "What *about* that!"

I nodded and when I turned to look at Ed, he was nodding too. There didn't seem much else to do.

"Did they say anything?" Jimmy-James asked. "Did they say where they've come from?"

"Nope," I said. "Not a word. Just that mournful wailing. Gives me the creeps…sounds like a coyote."

"Or a baby teething," Ma said breathlessly.

"Same here," said JJ. "I tried them with everything I know…English, French, German, Spanish, Russian…quite a few more. And I tried out a couple of hybrids, too."

"Like standing in the United Nations," Ma Chetton muttered testily, her breath rasping. "Or hanging atop the Tower of Babel come Dooms-day."

"What the hell are hybrids?" Ed Brewster asked.

"Mixtures of two or three languages," JJ explained. "In the old days, that was the way most folks communicated…I mean before any one single language or dialect had gained enough of a footing to be commonplace. And I tried them with all kinds of signs and stuff but they didn't seem to know what I was doing. I thought maybe they would have known all about our language by listening to our radio waves out there in outer space. But it was no-go. I can't figure out how they communicate with each other at all," he said. "Unless it's that wailing noise or maybe through that thing that one of them's carrying around."

"You mean the box-thing? The thing that looks like a pile of cotton candy?"

JJ nodded. "He's messing with that thing all the time, changing it even as I'm trying to talk to them."

"Yeah," I agreed, "but did you notice he's taking things *out* instead of adding to what's already in there."

"I'd noticed that," JJ said. "I was wondering if that stuff is absorbed into him and enables him to communicate to the others. Like a translator."

I shrugged. It was all too much for me.

Ed glanced around to make sure none of those creatures had sneaked up on him and said, "We figure they can read our minds."

"Really?" said JJ. "How's that?"

"Well," Ed said, matter-of-factly, "they knew we were coming out here into the alleyway."

JJ frowned and glanced at me before returning his full attention to Ed.

Ed gave a characteristic shrug. "Why else would they come on down here from the street if they didn't know we were coming out?"

While JJ mulled that over, I said, "What do you figure they want, JJ?"

The back door to the poolroom opened and Abel Bodeen peered out. "Is there any of those things out there?"

"Nope, they've gone down to see the sheriff," I said.

Abel pulled a face and gave a wry smile. "That should please Benjamin no end," he said with a chuckle.

The fact was that the creatures *did* please Sheriff Ben Travers, as it turned out. Or they didn't *dis*please him anyway. The truth of the matter was that the aliens didn't do anything to upset or irritate anyone. In fact, they didn't do anything at all.

"Why the hell did they come, Derby?" Abel Bodeen asked me a couple of days after they'd...after we'd first seen them.

"Beats me," I said.

We were sitting out on the old straight-backed chairs Molly Waldon had left out in front of her and Vince's general store, watching the creatures wander around the town, just as they had been doing all the time. But I was watching a little more intently than I had done at first. The folks around town had become used to the aliens after two full days and nobody seemed to care much *what* they were there for. So it's probably fair to say that people hadn't picked up that the attitude of the creatures was changing. It wasn't changing by much, but it *was* changing.

"You've noticed, haven't you?"

I shielded my eyes from the glare of the late afternoon November sunshine and looked across at Jimmy-James. "Noticed what?"

He looked across at two of the creatures gliding along the other side of the street. "They're slowing down."

I followed his gaze and, sure enough, the creatures did seem to be slower than they had been at first. But it was more than that. They seemed to be more cautious. I mentioned this to JJ and Abel, and to Ed and Estelle who were leaning on what remained of an old hitching rail at the edge of the sidewalk.

Ed snorted. "That don't make no sense at all," he said. "Why would they be cautious now, when they've been here two goddam days."

"Ed, watch your mouth," Estelle whined in her high-pitched voice.

"He's right," agreed Jimmy-James.

"Who?" Ed asked. "Me or him?"

"Both of you." JJ got to his feet and strode across to the post behind Ed and leaned. "They *are* getting slower and they do seem to be more…more careful," he said, choosing his words. "And, no, it doesn't make any sense for them to be more careful the longer they're here."

"Nothing for them to be nervous about, that's for sure," Abel said. "They've got us wrapped up neat as a Christmas gift."

The aliens had effectively cut off the town. There were no phone lines and the roads were…well, they were impassable. It was Doc Maynard had seen it first, trying to get his old Ford Fairlane out to check on Sally Iaccoca's father, over towards Bellingham. Frank Iaccoca had taken a bad fall—cracked a couple of ribs, Doc said—and Doc had him trussed up like Boris Karloff in the old *Mummy* movie.

The car had cut out three miles out of Forest Plains and there was nothing Doc could do to get it going again. So he'd come back into town for help, without even taking a look under the hood, and Abel, Johnny Deveraux and me had gone out there to give him some help. Johnny, who works at Phil Masham's garage, had taken some tools and a spare battery in case it was something simple he could fix out on the road. Doc Maynard was not renowned for looking after his automobile.

When we got out there, Johnny tried the ignition and it was dead. But when he made to move around to the front of the car to open the hood he suddenly started floundering and dropped the battery. That's when we found the barrier.

A "force field" is what Jimmy-James called it.

Everything looked completely normal up ahead in front of Doc Maynard's Fairlane but there was no way for us to get to it. It felt like cloth but not porous. JJ said it was an invisible synthetic mebrane—whatever *that* was—and he reckoned the creatures had set it up around the town to protect their spaceship. Sure enough, the same barrier traveled all the way around town…or so we figured. We tried different points on farm tracks and woodland paths and each one came to a complete halt.

Like it or not, we were caught like fish in a bowl. But that didn't seem to matter…at least not until JJ took a look in the creatures' "book."

"There he goes, if it is a 'he,'" said Jimmy-James, pointing to the creature with the box of cotton candy. The funny thing was that the box now looked to have a lot less of the stuff in it than it had done at first. The first time we'd seen it, the thing had looked to be almost full.

"The other thing," said JJ in a soft voice that made you think he was realizing what he was about to say at exactly the same time as he said it, "is they seem not to be touching people with those…those veil-things."

"Yeah," I agreed. "I guess that was what I meant about them being more cautious. Part of it, anyway."

Ed snorted. "Maybe it's a case of the more they see of us the less they like."

Estelle rubbed Ed Brewster's oiled hair and puckered up her mouth. "I'm sure they like what they see of you, honey," she trilled without changing the shape of her mouth. "Anyone would." It sounded as though Estelle was talking to a newborn babe sitting in a stroller. Ed must've thought so, too, because he told her to can it while he readjusted his hair.

"We need to get a look in that box-thing," JJ said.

"How we going to do that?" I asked. "And what good is it going to do us anyway? Just looks like a load of gunk to me."

JJ stepped away from the rail and out onto the street. "That's just it," he shouted over his shoulder as he strode across to the creature with the box. "None of us has seen what's in there, not up close."

We watched the confrontation.

Jimmy-James stopped right in front of the creature and it turned around. Almost immediately, the little veil-arms wafted out as though blown by a breeze and settled on JJ's shoulders, the wailing sound rising a pitch or two in the process. Then it started to back away, its arms still blowing free.

JJ shouted over to me to come on along. Ed Brewster stood up and moved alongside me. "I'm coming, too," he said.

"Now you be careful what you're doing, Ed, honey," Estelle warbled.

"I will, Estelle, I will," Ed said, with maybe just a hint of a sigh. And the two of us walked onto the street to join JJ. Which was how we got into the creatures' spaceship.

The alien with the book kept on backing away from the three of us and we just kept on walking after it. Eventually, we reached the ship where we discovered two more of the creatures standing by the ramp.

The creatures then backed on up into the ship. We kept on following.

A few minutes later the three of us were standing amidst a whole array of what looked to be lumps of foam, all of various sizes, piled up on or stuck against other lumps. Some of the lumps were circular — cylindrical, JJ said — and others looked like tears of modeling clay thumbed into place by a gigantic hand without design or reason.

Up inside the ship, the things' wing-arms were fluttering faster and more frequently than ever…and the alien that we reckoned to be recording the whole visit was mightily busy, removing small pieces of foam with the tendrils and absorbing them. When I glanced inside the box, I saw there was hardly anything in it.

Over to one side of the crowded room a wide lamp-thing stood by itself. Standing beneath the lamp, two aliens were seemingly absorbed in another of the boxes, their wing-arms fluttering like a leaf caught in a draft. This particular box was completely full, a collection of multi-colored shapes and lumps and pieces, all pressed into each other or standing alone.

"We need to get a look at that," JJ whispered to Ed and me.

"Leave it to me," Ed Brewster said. He walked across to the box and lifted it with both hands. "Okay if I borrow this for a while, ol' buddy?" he said, waving the box in front of the two creatures.

The things didn't seem to do anything as Ed stepped back and moved back alongside us, although their arms were fluttering faster than ever. Then, suddenly, the little arm-wings dropped limp and the two creatures turned around. As they did this, the creature standing in front of the other two in the center of the room waved its arms and then it, too, spun around.

"Let's get out of here," Jimmy-James said. "I'm starting to get a bad feeling about this."

As we ran down the platform leading back onto Sycamore Street I asked Jimmy-James what he'd meant by that last remark. But he just shook his head.

"It's too fantastic to even think about," was all he'd say. "Just let me take a look at the box and then maybe I'll be able to get an idea."

We hightailed it back to Jack and Edna Bannister's house down on Beech Avenue and, while me and Ed drank cup after cup of JJ's mom's strong coffee, JJ himself pored over the contents of the alien box. It was almost three in the morning when a wild-eyed Jimmy-James rushed into the Bannisters' lounge and slammed the box onto the table. Ed was asleep, curled up like a baby on the sofa, and I was reading the TV Guide.

"I have to look at the other box," he said. "Now!"

Ed smacked his lips together loudly and shuffled around on the sofa.

I looked up from a feature on *Gilligan's Island* and was immediately surprised to see how much Jimmy-James resembled that hapless shipwreck survivor. "What's up?"

JJ shook his head and ran his hands through his hair. I noticed straightaway that they were shaking. "A lot, maybe…maybe nothing. I don't know."

"You want to —"

"I've been through all of the usual coding techniques," JJ said, ticking off on his outstretched fingers. "I've applied the Patagonian Principle of repeated shapes, color motifs, spacing...I've run the Spectromic Law of shading relationships and the old Inca constructional communication dynamics..."

I held up a hand and waved for him to stop. "Whoa, boy...what the hell are you talking about?"

JJ crouched down in front of me and looked up into my eyes. "It makes sense," he said. "I've made it work...made the patterns fit."

"You *understand* it?" I glanced across at the box of jumbles shapes. "*That?*"

JJ nodded emphatically. "Yes!" he said. Then, "No! Oh, God, I don't know. That's why I need to check. And I need to do it tonight. Tomorrow may be too late."

"I still don't know what you're—"

The resident genius of Forest Plains placed a hand on my knee. "No time," he said. "No time to talk. It has to be *now*."

I studied his face for a few seconds, saw the look in his eyes: there was an urgent need there, sure...but there was something else, too. It was fear. Jimmy-James Bannister looked as scared as any man could be. "Okay, let's go do it."

He stood up and looked at Ed. "What about him?"

"He'll be fine. We expecting any trouble in there?"

"I don't think so."

"Okay. Let's go."

And we went.

The ship was silent and dark. JJ borrowed his old man's flashlight and the two of us crept up that platform and into the depths of the creatures' rocketship. The place was deserted, which was just as well. It didn't take too long before JJ found the second box—the one the creature had been using all the time—and he scooped it into his arms and rushed back out of the ship.

We were back in the house almost as soon as we had left. The whole thing had taken less than ten minutes.

I watched as JJ sat in front of the new box—now containing but a few lumps and dollops of that clay-stuff—wringing his hands and muttering to himself. I couldn't stand it any more and I grabbed a hold of JJ and shook him until I could hear his teeth clattering. "What the hell *is* it, JJ...why don't you tell me for God's sake."

He seemed to come to his senses then and he quietened down. Then he said, softly, "It's the aliens."

"What about them?" I said.

"They're..." He seemed to be trying hard to find the right words. "They're palindromic."

"They're *what?*"

"They run backwards...their time is different to ours."

"Their time is *different* to ours? Like *how* different?"

"It moves in a different direction...backwards instead of forwards — except to them it *is* forwards. But to us it's —" JJ waved his arms around like he was about to take off. "Well, it's bass-ackwards is what it is."

"What the hell is all the goddam noise about?" Ed said, turning over on the sofa. He reached for his pack of Luckies and shook one into the corner of his mouth, lit it with a match.

I didn't know what to say and looked across at Jimmy-James. "Maybe you'd better tell him — *us!*"

JJ sat down at the table next to the two boxes, one full and one almost empty. He smiled and said, calmly, "It's this way.

"I've broken the basics of their language. It wasn't really too difficult once I'd eliminated the obvious no-go areas." He pointed to the almost empty box. "This is the 'book' they're using now...the one that's recording everything that happens *here*...here on Earth."

"Looks like a mound of clay to me," Ed said, blowing smoke across the table and shuffling one edge of the box away from him.

"That's because you're you," JJ said impatiently, "because you're from Earth. To them, it's the equivalent of a diary...a ship's log, if you like."

Ed settled back on the sofa. "Okay. What's it say?"

"It starts at the very moment they opened the doors. It says they found a group of creatures standing outside watching them disembark...get out. These creatures, their record says, held instruments...they thought at first the things might be gifts."

I frowned. "When was that? I never held no instrument."

JJ leaned forward. "That's just it. You didn't. It didn't happen. At least it didn't happen yet." He lifted the box onto his knee and pointed at the shapes inside. "See, it's all arranged in a linear fashion, with each piece linking to others, building across the box in waves and doubling back to the other side. It's like layers of pasta furled over on itself. But see the way that it's arranged...you can pull pieces out of place and the gap stays. It's an intricate constructional form of basic communication. I say "basic" because I've only been able to pick up the very basic fundamentals. There's much much more to it...but I don't have the time to work it out. Not now, anyway."

Ed tapped his cigarette ash onto the carpet and rubbed it in with his free hand. "*Why* don't you have the time? What's the panic?"

"The panic is that the record goes on to say how surprised they all were to find creatures —"

"Not half as surprised as we were to see them!" I said.

JJ carried on without comment. "It goes on to say how they came out and stood in front of us and nobody — none of *us* — moved or did anything. We just stood there. Then we all moved away and went to some structures. They walked around and looked at the outside of these structures and then went back into their ship. They were concerned that they had somehow created the situation by their ship's power."

"Huh?"

JJ waved for Ed to keep quiet and continued.

"Listen. Then it says that, after some early investigations — they say that much more research has to be carried out — after these early investigations, we came on board the ship and borrowed their log."

"Yeah, well, we've got the log," I said. "For what good it's doing us."

"But none of that other stuff happened," JJ said. "This stuff in here..." He pointed at the individual pieces of clay...lifted one end of the carefully interwoven sheet of linked pieces and tiny constructions. "This only amounts to less than one single day. The creatures have been here almost three days now. There's no mention of all the other things that have happened. And bear this in mind...the stuff in here is what's *left*, as far as we're concerned."

I figured someone had to ask so it might as well be me. "How do you mean 'what's left?'"

"I mean, we've been watching the creature remove stuff from this box all the time he's been here, right?" I nodded and saw Ed Brewster do the same. "*And*," JJ continued, emphasizing the word, "what we have here, *now* — and which represents what's left in the box after he's been removing the clay stuff for almost three days — is a record of when they first *arrived*. The creature has been removing the stuff from the *top* — I've watched him...so have you, Derby; you, too, Ed — and leaving the stuff at the bottom completely intact. And that stuff records them *arriving*."

Ed and I sat silently, watching Jimmy-James. I didn't have the first idea of what to say and I was sure Ed didn't either. JJ must have sensed it because he started speaking again without giving us much of a chance to comment.

"Derby, the creatures...have you noticed how they seem always to be turned away from you when you go up to speak to them?"

We'd already figured that the clear part of the mushroom tops more or less worked as the things' faces. And it was true, now that Jimmy-James mentioned it, that the things always had that part of themselves turned away whenever you went up to them.

"That's because at the moment you start trying to communicate with them, they've actually just finished trying to do the same with you."

"That sounds like horseshit," Ed said. "Not even Perry Mason could convict somebody on that evidence."

"And have you noticed how they keep facing you when they move away? That's because, in their time-frame, they're *approaching* you."

Some of it was beginning to make some kind of sense to me and JJ noticed that.

"And we've all commented on how their attitude to us is changing," he said. "You said they seemed to be getting slower...more cautious."

"That I did," I remembered.

"Well, they're getting more cautious because where they are now is they've just *arrived*. Where they were when we first saw them was in their third or fourth day around us. They were *used* to us then...they're not now."

"Okay, okay, I hear what you say, JJ," I said. "Maybe the creatures' time does move in reverse, if that's what you're saying. I don't understand it, but then I don't understand a lot of things. The thing that puzzles me is why you're getting so hot under the collar about this. Everything's going to go okay: we saw them 'arrive'—which you say is when they left—and nothing happened in the meantime. All we have to worry about is our future which is their past...and they've come through that okay haven't—"

I saw JJ's face screw up like he'd just sucked on a lemon. He reached over and pulled the full box across to the edge of the table, held up another of those interlaced jigsaw puzzles of multi-colored clay pieces. "This is the previous diary," he said, "the one before the one they started after they had arrived.

"You remember I said there was an entry in the current ship's log about the creatures being concerned that they had somehow created the situation they found when they arrived?" We both nodded. "Well, that situation is explained in a little more detail in the previous record." At this point, Jimmy-James sat back on his chair and seemed to draw in his breath.

"Okay: the log says that they were following the course taken by an earlier ship—one that had disappeared a long time ago—when they experienced some kind of terrible space storm the like of which had never previously being recorded. For a time, it was touch and go that they would survive, though survive they did. But when the storm subsided, they were nowhere that they recognized. After a few of their time periods—which, based on the limited information in the new book, I would put at quarter days...give or take an hour—there was a sudden blinding flash of light and a huge explosion. When they checked their instruments, they discovered that the ship was about to impact upon a planet which had apparently appeared out of nothingness."

Ed looked confused. "So this explosion went off *before* they hit the planet?"

JJ nodded.

"I don't get it," Ed said.

I said to let Jimmy-James finish.

"There hadn't been any planet there at all until then," JJ said. "Then, there it was. And that planet was Earth.

"They narrowly averted the collision," JJ went on, "and settled onto the planet's surface. After checking atmospheric conditions they prepared to go outside. The log finished with them wondering what they'll find there."

While JJ had been talking I'd been holding my breath without even realizing it. I let it out with a huge sigh. "Are you sure?"

The owner of the best mind in town shook his head sadly.

"But you *think* you're right."

"I think I'm right, yes."

"And they found us, right?"

"Right, Ed," JJ said. "They found us." He waited.

I thought over everything I had heard and knew there was something there that should bother me...but I couldn't for the life of me figure out what it was. Then it hit me. "The blinding flash," I said. "If before that blinding flash there was nothing and after it there was the Earth...then, if the creatures' time *does* move backwards, and their version of their arrival is—or *will* be—our version of their departure, that means the aliens will destroy the planet when they leave."

JJ was nodding. "That's the way I figure it, too," he said.

I looked across at Ed and he looked across at me. "What are we going to do?" I asked JJ.

JJ shrugged. "We have to stop them leaving...in terms of our *own* time progression."

"But, in their terms, that would be to stop them *arriving*...and they're already here."

"Yes, that's true. In just the same way, if we do something to stop them—and I see only one course of action there—then, again in our time, they never actually 'arrive'...though, of course, they've arrived already as far as we're concerned. What we do, is prevent their departure in our terms."

Ed Brewster shook his head and pushed himself off the sofa onto the floor. "Jesus Christ, I'm getting a goddam headache here," he said. "Their arrival is our departure...their departure is our arrival...but if they don't do this, how could they do that...and as for *palindoodad*..." He stood up and rubbed his hands through his hair. "This all sounds like something off *Howdy Doody*. What does it all mean? How can we play about with time like that? How can *any*body play about with time like that?"

"I think it may have been the space storm," JJ said. "I think, maybe, their time normally progresses in exactly the same way as our own…although Albert Einstein said we shouldn't allow ourselves to be railroaded about time being a one-way linear progre—"

"Jesus, Jimmy-James!" Ed shouted, and JJ winced…glancing upwards towards his parents' bedroom while we all waited for sounds of people moving around to see what all the noise was about. "Jesus," Ed continued in a hoarse whisper, "I can't keep up with all of this stuff. Just keep it simple."

"Okay," JJ said. "I figure one of two things: either the aliens always move backwards in time or they don't.

"If we go for the first option, then we have to ask how they found their way into our universe."

"The space storm?" I suggested.

"I think so," said JJ. "If we go for the second option—that they *don't* normally travel backwards in time—then we have to ask what might have caused the change." He looked across at me again and gave a small smile.

I nodded. "The space storm."

"Kee-rect! So either way, the storm did the deed. But whatever the cause, the fact remains that they're here and we have to prevent whatever it was that caused the explosion."

We sat for a minute or so considering that. I didn't like the sound of what I'd heard but I liked the sound of the silence that followed even less. I looked at Ed. He didn't seem too happy either. "So how do we do that, JJ?" I said.

JJ shrugged. "We have to kill them…kill them *all*," he said. He pulled across the almost empty box that we all reckoned was the alien's current ship's log and lifted up the few lace-like constructions of interwoven clay pieces. "And we have to do it *tonight*."

I don't remember the actual rounding up of people that night. And I don't recall listening to JJ telling his story again and again. But tell it he did, and the people got rounded up. There was me, Sheriff Ben, Ed, Abel, Jerry and Jimmy-James Bannister himself. We walked silently out to the spaceship and weren't at all surprised to see faint whisps of steam coming out from the sides or that the platform was up for the first time since…well, the first time since three days ago. As the platform lowered itself slowly to the dusty ground of the vacant lot across from Bill's and Ma's poolroom, I heard JJ call out my name.

"Derby…"

I turned around and he held up his rifle, then nodded to the others standing there on Sycamore Street, all of them carrying the same kind of thing. "Instruments," he said.

By then it was too late. The bets were placed.

As soon as they appeared we started firing. We moved forward as one mass, vigilantes, firing and clearing, firing and clearing. The creatures never knew what hit them. They just folded up and fell to the ground, some inside the ship and others onto Sycamore Street. When they were down, Sheriff Ben went up to each one and put a couple of bullets into its head from his handgun.

We continued into the ship and finished the job.

There were sixteen of them. We combed the ship from top to bottom like men in a fever, a destructive killing frenzy, pulling out pieces of foam and throwing them out into the street…in much the same way as you might rip out the wires in the back of a radio to stop it from playing danceband music. God, but we were scared.

When the sun came up, we put the aliens back on the ship and doused the whole thing in gasoline. Then we put a match to it. It burned quietly, as we might have expected of any vehicle operated by such gentle creatures. It burned for two whole days and nights. When it had finished, we loaded the remains onto Vince Waldon's flatbed truck and took them out to Darien Lake. The barrier — or "force field," as JJ called it — had gone. Things were more or less back to normal. For a time.

It turned out that JJ found more of those ship's logs that night, when the rest of us were tearing and destroying. Turned out that he sneaked them off the ship and kept them safe until he could get back for them. I didn't find that out right away.

He came round to my house about a week later.

"Derby, we have to talk," he said.

"What about?"

"The aliens."

"Oh, for crissakes, I—" I was going to tell him that I couldn't stand to talk about those creatures any more, couldn't stand to think about what we'd done to them. But his face looked so in need of conversation that I stopped short. "What about the aliens?" I said.

That was when Jimmy-James told me he'd taken the old diaries from inside the ship.

Walking along Sycamore, he said, "Have you ever thought about what we did?"

I groaned.

"No, not about us shooting the aliens…about how we changed their past?" Someone had left a soda bottle lying on the sidewalk and JJ kicked it gently into the gutter. The clatter it made somehow set off a dog barking and I tried to place the sound but couldn't. It did sound right, though, that mixture of a lonely dog barking and the night and talking about the aliens…like it all belonged together. "I mean," JJ went on, "we changed our future — which is okay: anyone can do that — but we actually changed things that, as far as they were concerned, had already happened. Did you think about that?"

"Nope." We walked in silence for a minute or so, then I said, "Did you?"

"A little—at first. Then, when I'd read the diaries, I thought about it a lot." He stopped and turned to me. "You know the big diary, the full box? The one that ended with details of the explosion?"

I didn't say anything but I knew what he was talking about.

"I went into more of the details about the missing ship...the one that had disappeared? The last message they received from this other ship was at these same coordinates."

"So?"

He shrugged. "The message said they'd been moving along when they suddenly noticed a planet that was not there before."

"Do I want to hear this?"

"I think the Earth is destined for destruction. The aliens were fulfilling some kind of cosmic plan."

"JJ, you're starting to lose me."

"Yeah, I'm starting to lose *me*," he said with a short laugh. But there was no humor there. "This other ship—the first one, the one that the diary talks about—I've calculated that it's about forty years in their past. Or in our future."

I grabbed a hold of his arm and spun him around. "You mean there's more of those things coming?"

JJ nodded. "In about forty years, give or take. And they're going to be going through this section of the universe and BOOM!..." He clapped his hands loudly. "Hey, Captain," JJ said in an accent that sounded vaguely foreign, "there's a planet over there! And there's no kewpie doll for guessing the name of that planet."

"So, if they're moving backwards, too...then that means they'll destroy us." The dog barked again somewhere over to our right.

"Yep. But if the aliens we just killed were going to do the job, how could the others have done it, too?"

"Another planet?"

JJ shook his head. "The coordinates seemed quite specific...as far as I could make out. That's another problem right there."

"What's that?"

"The diaries are gone. They liquefied...turned into mulch."

"All of it?"

"Every bit. But it *was* Earth they were talking about. I'd bet my life on it...hell, I'd even bet yours."

That was when I fully realized just how much of a friend Jimmy-James Bannister truly was. He placed a greater value on my life than on his own.

"Which means, of course," JJ said, "that we were destined to stop the aliens the way we did."

"We were *meant* to do it?"

"Looks that way to me." He glanced at me and must have seen me relax a little. "That make you feel better?"

"A little."

"Me too."

"What is it? What is it that's causing the destruction?"

"Hey, if I knew *that*...Way I figure it, they're maybe warping across space somehow—kind of like matter transference. The magazines have been talking about that kind of thing for years: they call them black funnels or something.

"But maybe they're also warping across time progressions, too...without even realizing they're doing it. Then, as soon as they appear into our dimension or plane, one that operates on a different time progression...it's like a chemical reaction and..."

I clapped my hands. "I know," I said. "BOOM!"

"Right."

"So what do we do?"

"Right now? Nothing. Right now, the balance has been restored. But the paradox will be repeated...around 2003, 2004." He smiled at me. "Give or take."

We went on walking and talking but that's about all I can remember of that night.

The next day, or maybe the one after, we told Ed Brewster. And we made ourselves a pact.

We couldn't bring ourselves to tell anyone about what had happened. Who would believe us? Where was the proof? A few boxes of slime? Forget it. And if we showed them the blackened stuff at the bottom of Darien Lake...well, it was just a heap of blackened stuff at the bottom of a lake.

But there was another reason we didn't want to tell anyone outside of Forest Plains about what we'd done. Just like nobody else in town wanted to tell anyone. We were ashamed.

So we made a pact. We'd keep our eyes peeled—keep watching the skies, as the newspaperman said in *The Thing from Another World* movie...

And when something happens, we'll know what to do.

What really gets to me—still, after all this time—is not just that there's a bunch of aliens somewhere out there, maybe heading on a disaster course with Earth...but that, back on their own planet or dimension there's another bunch of creatures listening to their messages...a bunch we killed on the streets of Forest Plains almost forty years ago.

Surface Tension

When the rock-thing upped and ate Davenport, he was bringing some of the supplies from the pod, which was sitting in the middle of the "garden," about fifty yards from the dome. The "garden" was a specially cleared rectangle, fringed by small, phosphorous bulbs, that served as the only suitable landing area on Smythe Minor, the smallest of Orgundy's three moons.

Windom had been the first to notice something strange about one of the rocks alongside the pod, and he had called the others over to see. "Hey, come over here and take a look at this rock," he had said. The "rock" had made its move even as they had been making their own.

They had watched from the dome window, frowning in a kind of dumb fascination as one of the rocks behind the first engineer redefined itself, bulged out at the top, had then split itself apart like a big mouth out to catch some starshine. Then it had folded itself over Davenport and eaten him. Just like that. One minute he was bending down and fixing the rear nearside strut on the saucer-pod, rambling into his intercom about how the bearings never seemed to hold up after a couple of landings, with Lace, Orgundy's biggest moon, seeming to lie half-submerged into Smythe Minor's rock-strewn horizon, and then a craggy stand-alone outcropping just seemed to lean forward and envelop him. There had been a single *crump* sound on the intercom, like when you squash an empty soda can, and then a rushing-water noise, and then silence.

Billings was the first to speak, and the words came out kind of like he was laughing at the absurdity of what he had just witnessed. But he wasn't laughing. "Jesus Christ. Did you—"

Then Jayson: "What the hell *was* that?"

"A goddamn Pac-man's what it was," Billings said, unable to keep what sounded like a begrudging admiration out of his voice. "It just ate him up. A goddamn rock Pac-man."

"Pete? Pete…are you there?" Windom flicked the switch on the intercom and waited for a response. There was nothing. He flicked it again and shouted into the microphone, "Pete, come in…respond, please respond." He flicked it again and waited.

Jayson leaned against the Plexiglas and stared out into the darkness. "He's not going to respond." He leaned against the glass and checked the ground to either side in front of the dome.

Billings walked over to stand behind the captain and looked over the man's shoulder at the Chesney Bonestall landscape, so serene and endless looking, both in physical and chronological terms. Behind them, Windom suggested that Pete Davenport just press his "send" button a couple of times if he was unable to speak. "He won't be doing any pressing of 'send' buttons," Billings confided into Jayson's ear. "He won't be doing much of anything anymore, is my guess."

Jayson looked to left and right, seeing only rocks and rocks and more rocks. then he looked straight ahead at the pod, so near and yet so far away. It had only been a few minutes since the rock-thing had eaten Davenport, but already there seemed to be more rocks around the legs of the pod than Jayson seemed to think there had been when they had landed the thing. It seemed that way but then it didn't seem possible. Rocks didn't up and move around. But then they also didn't open their mouths and eat up two-hundred-pound first engineers.

"There's more of them than there were when we landed, isn't there, Captain?"

Jayson nodded in answer to Billing's whispered question.

"What are we going to do?"

That one was more difficult. They had brought additional supplies for the prefabricated meteorological survey dome—including equipment to set up long-distance communication links with Orgundy itself—down from *Tiffany II*, the supply ship that was locked in a holding pattern around Lace, a relatively short distance of some thirty thousand miles. Jayson had told Phil Barittus, the *Tiffany*'s captain, that they would go straight on back to Orgundy.

Simple as that.

He ticked off the points in his mind: the Tiffany was not expecting them back; Orgundy ground control didn't even know they were coming—Jayson had planned to tell then from the pod once he had lifted off again from Smythe Minor; and he couldn't contact either them or the *Tiffany* from the dome because the intercom they had with them was good only for short distances.

Jayson did a quick calculation as to how long it should take them to set up the full communication scanner: if they were lucky, then it might take them only one Earth day. But that wasn't particularly comforting when you took into consideration that they had a very limited supply of air—maybe another twenty hours from the dome's own supply and then two hours maximum in each of the suits' individual tanks. Plus, of course, most of the equipment was still in the pod anyway. Along with the weapons.

Had he missed anything?

Nope. That was it. he had run out of points. They would have to go outside of the dome eventually, whether it was to the pod and the full-blown communications dish-kit it contained or to the small ground shelters containing the dome's tanks: once there, they would be able to hook up the filter pipes to a fresh container...always assuming there was one, of course. Whatever the solution, it involved going outside the dome.

Windom walked across the room and stood beside Jayson. "What do you think they are?"

"Does it matter?"

"Does it mat—"

Jayson cut Billings off in midsentence. "All that matters is that they're there and that they don't seem to like us."

"If I'd only—"

The captain took hold of Windom's shoulder. "Don't even think it, Bob. You saw how fast this thing moved. There was no way you could have warned him."

Windom wasn't convinced. "I could've—"

"What would you have said? 'Hey. Pete, just thought I'd let you know that one of the rocks over there on your left looks like it's turning into some kind of monster thing and we're a little worried it might be gonna eat you?'" He shook his head. "This is the 2051 version of 2051, Bob, not some kind of flaky 1990s interpretation featuring Flash goddamn Gordon. You couldn't have sent that message any more than Pete would've paid it any attention if you had."

Windom frowned but seemed to see the logic of what Steve Jayson was saying.

"Whyn't you go and check on the intercom again. Could be that Pete's just stunned or something and actually still alive inside that thing. His suit could've protected him, maybe...shit, I don't know. If it's possible for rocks to jump up and eat people, then I guess it's possible for—"

"Jesus Christ, will you look at *that!*"

Jayson turned back to the dome window and followed Billings' pointing finger.

The rock that had consumed Pete Davenport had now been joined by two more. The first one somehow reared itself up so that it was about four or five feet taller, then began stretching itself out like taffy. The long, elongated stem rose into the air like a wild rose root filmed over several months with one of those slow-action cameras that the weather boys used back on Earth to film clouds scudding over desert terrain, and that the euthanasia and cryogenics houses then replayed to the accompaniment of ancient Philip Glass soundtracks while they administered the good-bye juice to a bunch of sad old folks who just couldn't stand the progress.

It twisted and turned, dipping and soaring upward, and then traveled back, as though the film were in reverse, all the way back so that the thing was just a rock again. Then it moved its top over toward the ground and rained out pieces of metal and suit fragments.

"Oh, God," Windom said.

"On second thought, Bob, don't bother with the intercom," he said over his shoulder. "Pete's not gonna hear you."

"It's…it's throwing him up," Billings said. "For Christ's sake, the thing's throwing him up."

Jayson raised his hand, shocked to see that it appeared steady and calm, and said, "Take it easy, Billings. Let's all of us take it real easy now."

Windom said, "We're never going to make it past those things. Never going to make it to the pod."

Jayson didn't say anything. He just watched.

It was Billings who broke the temporary silence. "Where'd they come from? I mean, they weren't here when they laid the dome, they can't have been."

Jayson shrugged. "No, they probably came from somewhere out there, or maybe they were somewhere else on the moon when they brought the dome."

"Maybe they were on goddamn vacation," Billings said in mock earnest. "Who the hell cares! They're here now."

"Maybe they just watched us then."

Billings turned to face Windom. "What d'you mean? Why would they do that, just watch us?"

"When they brought the first dome. Maybe they just watched us, kind of waited for the right moment, you know?"

"You mean, they're intelligent?"

Windom shrugged. "Let's say they're responsive to situations. That doesn't always mean intelligence, at least not the way we define it. They respond and they react, sure. Doesn't mean they think, though. Anyways," he added, leaning against the glass and staring across the jumble of rocks and rubble, "maybe there were too many who brought the dome. Maybe they didn't like the idea of trying to take us on in force. Maybe there aren't enough of them."

"You got any more maybes?"

Windom ignored Billings' question and turned to the captain. "How many d'you thing there are?"

"Oh, I—"

Billings suddenly stepped back from the glass. "Look over there, to the right of the pod."

In the shadow of the pod saucer, two rocks had unfolded themselves and were moving around toward the blind side of the dome.

"Well, there are now five that we can see," Jayson said, "and I'm betting there are plenty more."

"What are we going to do?" Billings's voice bore the first signs of panic.

"The only thing we can do is try to outflank them."

Windom frowned. "How?

As he spoke, one of the things grew up right in front of the glass and they stepped away. It seemed to touch the window and then pulled back, like a dog sniffing at a woodchuck's ass. Then it came forward again and rested against the Plexiglas.

"How strong is that stuff?" Billings whispered.

"Strong enough," Jayson said. He pointed to the others to move to either side, away from the thing's direct line of sight. *Could* it see?

As if in response, a thick ridge that ran around the thing's circumference like a necklace suddenly separated and a long row of beady red orbs glistened.

"Oh, great," Billings said from over by the airlock, "the beast with a million — count 'em! — eyes."

Jayson remained in his crouched position a few feet from the thing and lifted his left arm. The eyes — if they *were* eyes — directly in front of it seemed to glow in rotation; first one and then, as that one dimmed, the one next to it, and so on. The thing moved across the glass until it was in front of Jayson's outstretched arm and stopped. The captain held his outstretched arm steady, and the rock creature did its eye trick again. Jayson continued to hold his arm still, the strain beginning to show in his shoulder.

The lights in the thing's eyes dimmed, all of them together, and it moved back across the window.

"Movement," Jayson whispered. "It responds to movement."

Billings grunted. "Great, so all we have to do is stay still until the air runs out."

"No, all we have to do is send out a runner."

"A runner, Captain?" Windom shuffled his back against the table leg and straightened out his legs on the dome floor. The movement caused a sharp ripple of redness around the thing's eye necklace. "You mean, you're gonna send one of us out there, and when they get up close to us we just freeze?"

"If either of you's got any better suggestions, just sing 'em out."

"And then what?" Billings chipped in.

"One of us goes out, makes a run for the crater over to the left of the dome," Jayson said softly. "Then one of the other two goes out and tries to get to the pod and..." He let it go at that and shrugged.

"A decoy."

"That's about the size of it, Bob," Jayson said. "Like I say, if there's a better — "

Billings cleared his throat and said, "Who?"

"Me and a volunteer."

"I'll do it," Windom said, getting to his feet. "I'll get suited up."

Billings watched, partly relieved that he didn't have to go himself and partly horrified at being left behind. "So what...what do *I* do?"

"Nothing you *can* do," Jayson said, reaching across for his own suit. "Keep the home fires burning and a light in the window, I guess." He pulled down the zip on the tunic and started to shuffle into the leggings. Outside the Plexiglas the rock-thing's eyes ran red circles, faster and faster, as if it were about to detonate.

"It's watching us," Billings said.

"It's *reacting*, that's all," Windom corrected. He pulled up the zipper on his own tunic and lifted the fishbowl helmet off the floor by the air lock. "Okay, I'm ready." He pulled the helmet on and secured it, then shrugged into the air-pack harness.

"Whitwonursghosfuss?" Windom's voice sounded like a slow-mo recording played back over wind and sea noise.

"See what he's saying," Jayson said, pointing to the intercom. Billings stood up and walked to the table as slowly as he could, watching the thing at the window all the way. He hit the intercom switch.

Amid a wave of breathing noises, Windom's tinny voice said, "Which one of us goes first?"

Billings turned to the captain and raised his eyebrows.

"Tell him he goes to the crater, I go to the pod. Getting into the pod'll be the tricky part."

Billings flicked the switch into transmit and relayed the message. Windom nodded and gave a circle sign, awkwardly, with thumb and forefinger.

Billings turned back to Jayson. "You ready?"

Jayson nodded and strapped on his air-pack harness. He pointed to Windom and then held up his hands, fingers spread wide, five times.

Billings hit the transmit switch and said, "You go first, Bob, anytime you're ready. The captain'll count to fifty...?" He looked to Jayson for confirmation and received an emphatic nod of the head. "And then he'll follow you out and head for the pod." He turned to Jayson, got another nod. He had heard of more intricate plans, but what the hell...it might work. A thing didn't need to be complex to be successful.

Windom stepped across to the airlock and pressed the release button. The door slid upward with a hiss and he stepped into the airlock and closed the door.

Less than a minute later, they saw him appear at the outside hatch. He stood for a moment, seemingly frozen in midstep, and waited. Jayson and Billings looked across at the rock-thing.

The thing had moved back from the window sufficiently far enough for it to look completely like a large rock. For a second—just one fleeting second—it was as though everything that had happened was entirely in their heads. It was as though they were playing some long-ago game on a far-off planet that none of them had seen for years. Maybe, at any moment, Davenport would wander over to the window and say, *Hey guys, watcha doin'*, the way he always used to do when he was setting somebody up, when he was trying to scare somebody.

But they knew he wouldn't do that. Pete Davenport was just a bad dose of indigestion in some alien's gut.

"He's starting to move." Jayson's voice sounded far away over the intercom. "Start counting."

Billings turned around to look at the rear window. Windom took a single step and then stopped dead. Billings flipped the intercom on transmit and said, "We're counting: one…two…" He heard Jayson echoing the numbers.

Windom had started to move, his strides slow and precise, while, back at the front window, the rock thing moved to the left in the direction Windom was heading at the rear of the dome.

Billings flipped the switch. "Keep counting, but watch out: it's started to move."

"Six," Jayson's voice echoed over the speakers, like he was counting down.

"Oh God, I don't like this," Billings said.

Jayson moved across to the airlock.

"It isn't gonna work. I just know it isn't gonna work."

"Eleven…keep counting and shut up." Jayson opened the hatch door. "Twelve…"

As the hatch door hissed open, Billings saw that Windom had reached the right-hand edge of the rear dome-window. He looked back at the front window. The thing had disappeared.

He spun around in time to see Jayson disappear into the airlock. He flipped the switch as Jayson said "Fourt-" and shouted, "It's gone, the thing…I can't see it anywhere." The hatch door slid upward and locked.

Billings ran to the rear window and pressed his face against the glass. Windom had edged a few feet away from the dome casing. The way ahead looked clear. He ran back to the front window and looked out.

Way ahead, the pod sat serenely on the rocky surface of Smythe Minor. None of the rocks could be seen anywhere. Then he looked down onto a slowly circling line of red lights, just below the lip of the window. He gasped and stepped back.

"Hello? Come in?" His voice was a harsh whisper.

"Seventeen…what is it?"

"It's under the window. It's…"

The respond and they react, sure. Doesn't mean they think, though.

"Shit, it's just sitting there, hunkered down like...like it's waiting for something to happen."

"Nineteen...Bob? You there?"

"Yeah, I'm here. What's up?"

Billings listened to the conversation, trying to make the sound of it drown out the noise of his pounding heart.

"You've got to make a run, Bob. Draw it to you. Start again at one and run on ten, then stop."

"Okay."

"You okay with this, Bob?"

There was no response.

"Bob?"

Windom's response was a soft whisper, like the sound the wind makes—made!—through the grass back in Iowa. "I see it."

Billings flipped the switch. "Where?"

There was no response.

Billings tiptoed across the dome and looked out of the rear window. The rock-thing—or *a* rock-thing—had appeared at the side of the dome casing a few feet from Bob Windom. It was completely motionless. There was no sign of any red eyes but, from this distance, Billings couldn't be sure that that meant anything. He looked down and saw the yellow light flashing on the intercom. "Shit, that's why I can't hear him." He flipped the switch.

Windom was groaning in fear.

"What's happening? Bob, you okay? What's happening back there? Billings? Somebody say something."

Billings flipped it to transmit, said "He's cornered," and switched it back. Then he ran to the front window.

The eyes had disappeared.

He ran back to the rear window. Windom was still there, but now the thing had moved right up next to him.

"Bob? I'm going to try something." Jayson's voice sounded surprisingly calm.

Windom moaned softly.

"I'm going to throw a shovel over behind the thing. I can't see it—I'm out at the front, pressed against the dome—but I can guess. If—*when*—it moves, I want you to make a run for the crater. You got that?"

Another moan.

"Bob, I know you're scared. For crissakes, we're all scared, but you have to do it. We have to do something."

Billings waited silently.

"Oh...okay," Windom whispered. "Okay."

"Right."

A few seconds later, Billings saw a shovel fly past the front window. He turned back to the rear window and looked out. The thing shot away from Windom and out of sight, toward the front of the dome, its eyes flashing like hazard-warning lights on the highway. "Go, Bob…" he said quietly, though the intercom was only receiving.

"Now, Bob, I can see it: go!"

Windom started to move.

In any other circumstances, it might have been funny.

Windom ran in a lumbering slow motion, his feet and legs seeming to stretch endlessly between steps, sending small clouds of rock dust billowing up each time he touched down. Billings closed his eyes but he could still see the pathetic image, could still hear Windom's sobbing.

Billings moved to the front window and looked out to the left. There were two of them over by the shovel, their eyes moving at breakneck speed, staring

reacting…responding…

at the thing between them on the ground.

He looked to the right and could just make out the outline of the captain's body pressed against the side of the dome.

"Bob…how's he doing?"

Billings ran to the rear window. Windom was halfway to the crater, still sobbing—almost hysterically now—but making reasonable progress. He seemed to have found his stride.

He flipped the switch to say Windom was doing well when the yellow light flashed. He flipped it back.

"—stards! They're moving away. *Bastards!* Bob, they're—"

Windom screamed.

Billings looked out.

"I'm going," Jayson said.

Windom had stopped but he was unsteady. The things must have appeared up against him as he was in midstride and Windom was standing on his left leg, his right leg half-crooked to move forward and his arms outstretched, wavering.

Billings turned to the front window and saw the dim figure of Jayson doing a similar slow-motion sprint toward the pod. He looked back.

The things' eyes were glowing fiercely. As if they were angry. As if they had figured it all out. They shuffled up against Windom so that they were touching him, gently pushing, almost, or so it appeared.

"Oh, God…oh, God…"

"Take it easy, Bob," Billings whispered.

"Oh, *God!*"

The thing on Windom's left side was starting to stretch upward.

Jayson's breathing was heavy and forced.

"Ahhgodnah...nooo...*nooooo!*"

The top of the rock had split apart, a huge V-shape facing up to the heavens.

"Captaincaptaincaptaincap—"

Billings flipped the intercom to transmit and stepped back from the window as the top of the rock started down toward Windom.

He leaned back against the wall and banged his head twice, hard. But he could still hear Windom's voice. When he looked out, there were only the two rocks. And their eyes were still revolving.

Billings went to the front window. "He's gone," he said. "They got him." He flipped the switch and watched Jayson, marveled at the fact that he could still run after that news hit him. He looked at the intercom: there was no flashing yellow light. Jayson had nothing to say.

He looked up and saw the rock move out from behind the pod.

Billings opened his mouth but nothing would come out. He moved his hand to flip the switch but found that he couldn't do it. There was still no yellow light, although Jayson had seen the thing. The captain stopped about eight or ten feet from the pod.

Then the things moved in.

They moved like wild animals, smashing Jayson to the ground. He looked at the intercom and saw the flashing light, calmly flicked it.

There was only grunting and groaning.

He continued to watch.

Jayson pulled himself to his feet and moved to the side, towards the edge of the pod, backing all the way.

The things shuffled after him, slowly. It was almost as though they were playing with him...herding him. There seemed to be no hurry. Shit, there *was* no hurry!

As Jayson moved into the pod's shadow, the front rock seemed to lurch on him. The other two moved in.

And now, he couldn't see any of them.

There was a cracking sound and a whoosh, sounds of tearing and grunting, then a shout...a scream. Then silence.

Billings watched.

He flipped the switch. "Hello?"

Silence.

"Hello?" He watched for the yellow light.

Nothing.

"Somebody say something to me...*please!*"

Nothing.

Then he saw movement.

One of the rocks appeared at the front edge of the pod. It seemed to be moving slowly, ponderously...as though it seemed unsure of what it was doing or where it was going. Then, in one perfect movement, the thing toppled forward onto the ground.

Billings watched, his eyes so wide he half thought they were likely to just drop right out of their sockets.

After a few moments, Jayson appeared, staggering, his arms flailing. He stepped around the fallen rock-thing and started walking to the dome, swaying from side to side.

"Jesus Christ!" Billings flipped the switch. "Jesus Christ! Keep goi—"

The other two rock creatures slid out into the open. Even from the dome, Billings could see their eyes revolving. They, too seemed to be staggering. What the hell was happening out there?

Billings drew in air and steadied his voice. "They're behind you," he said. "Just keep moving and don't look back. There's something wrong with them."

Jayson kept moving, tottering slightly but moving all the same. And now he seemed to have greater determination.

Billings looked down at the intercom. There was no yellow light. He spoke softly. "You're nearly there. Go to the hatch. Go straight to the hatch. Do not pass go, do not collect two thousand dollars." He waited.

Jayson was still a few yards away but already close enough for Billings to see that his helmet glass was cracked.

"Oh, Christ."

Jayson staggered once but regained his footing, then moved across toward the side of the dome and the hatch door.

The things were moving more steadily now, gaining ground behind the captain but still moving slow enough to allow him to reach the dome. *Allow?*

Billings watched. The things almost seemed to be dawdling. He moved across to the far edge of the window in time to see Jayson stagger by, his mouth hanging open.

They respond and they react, sure. Doesn't mean they think, though.

He looked back at the things. Now they had stopped.

Billings turned to the airlock and frowned.

The green light came on. Jayson was in the airlock. Just for a second, Billings caught sight of the override switch that sealed the airlock , and then wondered why that was significant.

He turned back to the window. The rock-things were pressed up against the glass. They seemed to be shaking, up and down. Mad? Angry?

He heard the inner door slide up but he didn't turn around. There was something familiar about that movement.

The thud made him turn.

Jayson looked at him but didn't see him. His eyes were blind. Dead blind. The captain's head tilted to the left and then tumbled from the table onto the floor, where it rolled and came to a rest with its nose pressed against the wall.

Billings looked up. The thing bulged from the ripped suit, exploding from it slowly like baking dough, pushing itself through the rips and tears, long strands of the malleable rock extending from the ripped gloves — one of which still held the fractured helmet — until the suit fell in tatters. (Why, he wondered, hadn't he noticed that the captain wasn't wearing his air pack?)

Behind the thing, in sharp contrast to the excited whirling of its revolving red eyes, the green light on the airlock flashed once. As the inner door slid upward, Billings turned away from the brief glimpse of rock, two columns of it, standing on the metallic matting and looked out the window.

The things were still there, even more animated than ever.

Now he recognized it, that movement: they were laughing.

For Bill Gaines, Wally Wood, and Joe Orlando.

Heroes and Villains

(1)

We will never have true civilization until we have learned to recognize the rights of others.

> Will Rogers
> *The New York Times,* 18 November 1923
> ("Imagemaker: Will Rogers and the American Dream,"
> William R. Brown, University of Missouri Press, 1970)

> When all the world is young, lad,
> And all the trees are green;
> And every goose a swan, lad,
> And every lass a queen;
> Then hey for boot and horse, lad,
> And round the world away;
> Young blood must have its course, lad,
> And every dog his day.
>
> > Charles Kingsley (1819-75)
> > "The Water Babies" (1863)

You okay, boss?"

"Yes, Sidney, I'm fine."

Sidney Smolt frowned. His employer neither sounded nor looked fine, or even anything approaching it, but he knew better than to re-ask a question that had already been answered…even when that question was voiced with only the Comedian's best interest at heart. Despite his name and his trademark mischievous and even irreverent smile, the Comedian was neither a patient nor a lighthearted man.

The small fat man shrugged, hitching his pants a little higher at the same time, and checked around the roof. Everything seemed to be in its place and nothing was there that he had not seen before. He keyed the CHECK button on his cellphone, gave a wave to the man standing over by the pool cabins and walked to the south edge of the roof and glanced over the waist-high wall onto Central Park South. It was all clear, just the traffic edging its way up to Columbus Circle or down to the Plaza, mostly Yellow cabs and cyclists braving the early morning rush.

As he walked back to the French windows leading into the penthouse apartment that controlled the Komerdie Building, Smolt glanced at his employer who was standing on the poolside leaning on the railings. The man was dressed only in his shorts, ready for his early morning swim but, at least as far as Smolt could see, he had not yet been into the water.

Was it Smolt's imagination or had the Comedian grown more introspective these past few months?

Pausing before going back inside, Smolt tilted his head and ran his eyes up the Comedian's tanned and muscular legs, over his firm backside and on up the torso. Introspective or not, and no matter how many millions he had stashed away nor how much of the world he controlled, even the Comedian was unable to stop time. With a hint of regret and even sadness, Smolt saw a thickening around his employer's waist—love handles, his mother used to say of his father's girth back during Smolt's long-ago childhood in Cedar Rapids.

But that was before Captain Iowa had caused a building side to tumble onto Jack Smolt's rusting Ford Fairlane, while the so-called "Hero of the Heartland" battled it out with his nemesis, the Gargoyle. It had been an accident, of course, and the Captain was very apologetic — to the tune of an out-of-court settlement of more than $60,000 — but Smolt's father was still dead.

That was twenty-five years ago this year, and the once little Sidney Smolt was now thirty-seven. That made the Comedian...how old? Must be getting on for fifty, Smolt guessed. And in addition to the love handles, the man considered by many to be "the biggest worm in the Big Apple" now had graying hair where once a thick thatch grew so black it was almost blue. It was thin hair now, too, thin around the temples and the crown, and the jowls and the chin on the face beneath it were droopy...looking tired.

Smolt watched the wind blowing the Comedian's hair and then, when the big man—he was still big, at least—shifted over to the little wall looking out over Central Park, Smolt saw the tell-tale whiteness of a piece of paper held in the Comedian's hand which was tucked under the other armpit. It was a piece of mail he had received just this morning: a piece of mail bearing a British postage stamp and a spidery handwriting addressed, simply, to Leonard B. Komerdie, New York, USA. Smolt knew who the letter was from and he knew it wasn't good news. With a deep sigh he went inside.

The Comedian leaned on the small parapet wall of his pool area and looked out over Manhattan. He reached down and picked up his coffee, the mug feeling reassuringly warm in his hand. It seemed chilly suddenly, chilly for June in Manhattan. He looked at the one-page letter and its envelope again, then took a sip of coffee and lifted his face to the sun as he swallowed. Sometimes he felt that only he of the city's denizens was in the sunlight; all others walked only in the shadow of the buildings themselves, scurrying the matrix of streets and avenues like ants, their lives filled with a curious purpose that, no matter how long he considered it, he could not fathom.

In front of him the park loomed green and expansive, its distant thrum of buzzing energy drifting onwards up towards 110th Street where Uptown began, and where the rocky ridge that lifted the Upper West Side continued the gradual incline which began around 59th Street and went all the way to Washington Heights. He scanned the bright blue sky and, amidst the occasional plane moving off from or drifting into JFK or LaGuardia and the ever-present advertising dirigibles that hovered over the park, he noticed a speck coming in fast from the east.

It was too small for a plane or a dirigible.

It was a hero, probably flying in from Queens where The Monitors had their East Coast HQ. The Comedian squinted into the sunlight reflected off the myriad car windshields and windows littering the streets below and tried to see who it was, but he couldn't make him out...if it *was* a "him." There were so many of them these days.

The figure was dressed in green, with a cape which flew behind, stretched out in the air. That meant it was probably Captain Chlorophyll, one of the Monitors — or Grassman, as he was more regularly called. The Comedian smiled at the audacious use of the name, coined by a one-time veteran of the streets who had been caught peddling mind-expanding drugs out of a Hell's Kitchen basement. The boy, hardly out of his teens, had called to the smug Captain Chlorophyll as he was been marched away into the holding cells. "Hey, you all green," the boy had shouted, with that strange clipped delivery and the equally odd reverse-pointing gesture that characterizes and complements the argot of the rappers. "You ain't nothing, man. You just a *grass*man." After that, the green-clad flying wonder had started referring to himself by the new nickname...but that was the heroes for you. To them, nothing was sacred.

The figure swung around Roosevelt Island and lined up with the Queensboro Bridge, heading for Manhattan. Down on the street, people shouted and pointed up at the sky, waving.

Hey, Captain Chlorophyll! they called.

And, *Way to go, Cap!*

And other inanities dreamed up by the small people trying to make something of their small lives. Just like the stars of the celluloid adventures that played the local theaters, the heroes were considered the property of all and sundry. All the gossip magazines were filled with stories of who was dating whom, and the inevitable revelations of infidelity, same-sex relationships and abuse were the order of the day.

Thus Desmond (*Slingshot* to his many adoring fans) Antigones' new and seemingly serious relationship with a balding and bespectacled bank teller in Carmel proved both a new rallying point for the west coast's powerful gay movement and a popular front page feature across the country. And the sudden hospitalization of young Manhattan debutante Cheryl Heggler with "abdominal complications" following an alleged intimacy with off-planet electrical hero *Direct Current* promoted serious doubts for any possible co-habitation between heroes and normals.

Similarly, the lengthy court case promoted by the lawsuit citing mental and physical abuse brought against wealthy socialite Malcolm Benners—*Trapeze* to the world at large—by Benners' young ward, Arnie Leverson (AKA *The Acrobat*) questioned the inevitable effects of power and adulation on the stability of the nation's heroes.

There were more such instances.

The Comedian shielded his eyes and watched as the flying figure slowed down as it came over the park, and then stopped to hover. The Captain was replenishing himself over the green.

The Comedian heard footsteps behind him. Without turning around, he said, "How does he fly? You ever stop to wonder about that?"

"Who, boss?" Smolt said, waiting for an appropriate moment.

"The good Captain Chlorophyll." The Comedian leaned over the wall and watched men and women running through the park's entrances, some of them with kids in hand and others just by themselves. Laughter flooded up over the noise of idling engines—Central Park West had come to a standstill.

The Comedian turned around and leaned against the wall. "I mean," he said, hands thrust deep into the pockets of his shorts, "he has no wings, no jet-boosted rocket pack…how does he do it?"

Smolt shrugged. "Pills?"

The Comedian scowled and jigged his head from side to side. "Maybe. Everyone's on *something*, Sidney." He looked back over his shoulder in time to see the flying figure move off from the park, leaving behind in its wake a muted roar of applause and shouting.

"I wonder what it feels like."

"What's that, boss—flying?"

"No — well, yes, I wonder what *flying* feels like. But I was actually referring to *doing good*. Being wanted…being *loved*." The Comedian fingered the piece of paper in his hand.

Smolt frowned and shifted his weight from foot to foot. "You sure you're okay, boss?"

The Comedian gave a small smile and nodded. "So, you wanted me."

"Yeah." Smolt hitched his trousers and flicked his neck to one side. "The Dummy called. Said he was on his way over."

The Comedian nodded. "That should give the local boys in blue something to occupy them. Anything else?"

The little fat man hitched his pants again, an action that involved his shoulders shooting up a few inches, and clasped his hands. "Well…" he started, glancing back at the French windows where a couple of shadowy figures stood behind the drapes. "We was a little…concerned."

"Mmm? About what?"

Smolt nodded at the paper in his boss's hand.

"This?" The Comedian held it up. "It's a letter from my mother. My having a mother should surely not concern you."

Smolt flexed his fingers while keeping his hands clasped, and looked down at them briefly. "It's not that, boss. It's that we know you ain't spoken with your mom in a long time. And getting letters —" He waved a hand at the paper. " — like that always means bad news."

The Comedian nodded and allowed a small smile.

"Hey, we didn't mean noth —"

"That's okay, Sidney," Leonard Komerdie said in a tired voice. "I didn't mean to be antsy." He turned around and looked down into the street at the sound of a long blast on a car horn. "He's here."

"The Dummy?"

Komerdie folded the note and slipped it into his shorts pocket. "Are we all ready?"

"Yeah, boss."

"Have we heard from the Bomb?"

"He'll be here by nine."

"What time is it now?"

"Twenty before."

Komerdie walked across the roof to the lounger and sat down. "Show them out here when they arrive. Coffee would be good."

Smolt nodded and started to move off.

"And, Sidney —"

The small man stopped and turned back, his eyebrows raised.

"Thanks."

"Hey," he said, waving a hand and — if Komerdie were not mistaken — coloring slightly across his cheeks, "that's okay, boss."

(2)

One murder made a villain,
millions a hero.

Beilby Porteus (1731-1808)
"Death" (1759)

Komerdie was only halfway into the *Times* when Professor Maximillian Skellern's henchmen strolled out onto the roof. The Comedian nodded and continued to read while the men checked the place over in a fuss of un-smiling faces, gray suits and snap-brim fedoras. They looked like central casting walk-ons for Stanley Kubrick's *The Killing*.

After a few minutes, and having apparently satisfied themselves that it was all clear, the men disappeared and returned with a small trunk, which they laid almost reverentially on the mosaic marble area alongside the pool. One of the men flipped the catches on the trunk and opened the lid.

"Jesus Christ," a small voice whined. "I bet it is damned hot in here."

"And how are you this fine morning, Max?" Komerdie called, turning the page of his newspaper.

"Impatient," the voice said, though it didn't sound impatient. The Dummy's voice didn't sound anything: it was just words... always just words.

One of the henchmen leaned into the trunk and lifted the contents out.

The Dummy was "wearing" the body of what appeared to be an eight- or nine-year-old child. The henchman stood the figure down and held it for a few seconds.

"Yes, okay okay," the Dummy said in what would have been, in the voice of anyone else, an emphatic snarl. "I am fine now."

The man let go and the figure, after momentarily staggering slightly, walked across to the nest of chairs and sun loungers by the pool.

The head was slightly bigger than the body—all of which was con-structed from wood and plastic, although skillful painting and the addi-tion of a thick and unkempt thatch of hair had rendered it very believably human, particularly from a few feet's distance.

Inside the head, attached to a complex system of minute pulleys and levers, all operated by electrical impulses generated by the synapses, rested the brain of Professor Skellern, one of the country's foremost authorities on the human mind and, specifically, neural research.

A tragic fire resulting from a laboratory explosion had left Maximillian Skellern with eighty-five percent burns covering his body. In the words of the intern who examined him on arrival at Cabrini Med Center, the professor was a chicken leg that had been left on the barbecue while the cook had gone to answer the telephone. All senses and nerve tissues had been destroyed and only a formidable course of pain-killing drugs had been able to keep him alive.

It was during that time, with his faithful brother Rudie by his bedside, that Skellern reflected on the fire and the fact that the need to cut corners due to a lack of funding had resulted in the loss — effectively — of his life. But perhaps, he had decided, that need not be the case.

Over the following weeks, Skellern had his brother assemble a motley crew of henchman who more than made up for their lack of intelligence with a blind devotion worthy of the most faithful four-legged friend. Then he drafted in Wolfgang Campion from Detroit, a fellow scientist and a vitriolic and somewhat maverick campaigner for state and government funding for his various cryogenic projects. With detailed instructions from Skellern, Campion performed a painstaking operation during which the professor's brain was removed from his ruined body and installed into what amounted to a ventriloquist's dummy.

From there, it was a relatively simple matter of perfecting an effective motor system which allowed basic movements, and only a slightly less simple (for Wolfgang) matter of creating a synapse-controlled mechanical voice box to enable Skellern to speak — after a fashion — plus an Optical Image Translator for him to see and a sensitizer pad developed specially by Warner Bros. Records so that he could hear.

This had taken place in 1996.

The intervening eleven years had seen considerable refinements — not least in the creation of an entire "wardrobe" of artificial bodies of varying shapes and sizes — though such refinements needed money, as did Skellern's band of "helpers."

And so it was that the Dummy was born, masterminding complex burglaries and heists around the country...for Skellern's brain could be housed in bodies that were perfectly capable of getting into seemingly impossible places.

He was here today to make the final preparations to a new scheme devised by his occasional colleague, Leonard Komerdie.

The plan was deceptively simple.

The theft of municipal and currency bonds from The Rock, one of the government's floating fortified warehouses tethered by mile-high tentacle rods to the site of the old Alcatraz Prison. The roll call, such as it was, would be Komerdie, Skellern, and Chester "The Bomb" Urquart, whose impressive exo-skeleton membrane permitted a veritable arsenal of explosives and missiles.

Skellern walked awkwardly and seemingly nervously past the poolside to the special high chair situated well away from the water. One of his henchmen — Komerdie recognized the swarthy pallor of Rudolph Skellern, the Dummy's ever-dependable sibling — moved quickly across and attempted to lift his struggling boss into the chair but Skellern waved him away, his left arm connecting with Rudie's cheek and knocking the man's fedora to the floor. The loud crack echoed over the water.

"I can do it myself, I can do it," the Dummy's squawking voice trilled, with the complete lack of emotion necessitated by the voice-box circuitry.

The Dummy's brother stepped back and replaced his hat, rubbing his cheek with the other hand.

Skellern negotiated himself onto the chair and swiveled around.

"So, where is Urquart?"

Komerdie responded without looking up from his paper. "He'll be along."

"He is late."

"We said nine and it's not yet nine," Komerdie said as he turned the page.

Skellern lifted his left arm and looked at the watch set into his wooden wrist. Komerdie heard the faint whine of gears meshing. "It is almost five before," the Dummy said.

"So he's not late."

"Mmmm."

Komerdie rested the paper on his lap and clasped his hands behind his head. "Why are you doing this, Max?"

"Doing what? What is it that am I doing?"

Even after several years of knowing Skellern, during which time he had engaged in many conversations, Komerdie could still not get used to the complete absence of inflections in the Dummy's speech patterns. It often tended to make communication difficult — the monotone failed to impart emphasis or excitement, displeasure or reflection. Everything was simply delivered on the one level, the vocal equivalent of an EKG flat-line.

The Comedian allowed his trademark smile to broaden and waved his hands in the air. "Everything!"

"I do not understand."

"I mean, why did you want to get involved in the bonds heist? Hell — " He sat forward on his lounger, " — why do I want to get involved?"

"I still do not understand."

Komerdie folded the newspaper and dropped it onto the floor beside his lounger. "It's a simple enough question. Why are you involved? You don't need the money."

The Dummy's head turned slowly to face Komerdie, and the Comedian noticed that something needed a little loosening oil in Skellern's neck joints. "My research," he said. "The money is for my research."

Komerdie leaned forward. "And what research is that, Max? You haven't done any research in years."

The Dummy's gelatin eyes stared unblinking. "It is what I do," the Dummy said at last, and the head turned away with a squeak.

"Have you ever wondered…have you ever thought that maybe you'd like to do something *else*?"

"Such as what? Or perhaps you have in mind to sit me on your lap and have the two of us do a long season ventriloquism act at one of the Vegas gambling hotels, fronting for Connick or Bennett."

The Comedian did not respond.

A tall, good looking young man with heavily gelled hair stepped onto the roof with Smolt. Komerdie's assistant waved him forward and the man nodded with a big smile. He jogged across looking at his watch.

"You are late, Bomb," Skellern droned.

"And a big warm hello to you, too, Max," Chester Urquart said with a broad grin. He nodded to Komerdie. "Comedian."

"Coffee, Chester?"

The Bomb nodded gratefully. "Cool, man. Count me in for the java." He gave a mock salute. "Out last night. Late night," he added with a roll of his eyes. "I didn't have time for no breakfast."

"I didn't have time for any breakfast," Skellern corrected without emphasis.

The young man clapped his hands and nodded to Komerdie. "Looks like we're all ready to chow down," he said.

Komerdie shielded his smile.

As if on cue, Smolt appeared with a tray of coffee and two plates, one containing a variety of Danish and the other bagels, slit carefully in half. A small, covered dish of cream cheese completed the picture. Urquart's mouth watered.

As he poured coffee into the cups—just two, for obvious reasons—Komerdie said, "I'm afraid I have a little bad news."

Urquart lifted his cup and, having first covered it as thickly as was humanly possible with cream cheese, transferred an entire bagel-half straight into his mouth. He grunted questioningly as he chewed.

"Our project will have to be put on hold for a while," Komerdie said, having decided that the best plan was simply to come out with it.

"And why might that be?" Even without inflections, Max Skellern's voice was dripping with annoyance and menace.

The Comedian sat back in his lounger and sipped at his coffee while Urquart ate another danish. "It's a personal matter. I have to leave the country for a few days."

Urquart nodded and made a grimace with his mouth. *Shit happens*, the grimace said. Nothing more sinister than that. Komerdie couldn't help but feel a genuine affection for the young man.

However, Professor Skellern was not going to be so accepting.

"That simply is not good enough, Comedian," he said. This time when he moved his head to stare at Komerdie, the wooden man's neck squealed like nails running down a chalkboard.

"It's my mother," the Comedian said. Somewhere below them, on the Manhattan streets, a siren *wah wah*ed into existence and Dopplered away again. "She's very ill."

"Aw, gee, I'm sorry to hear that," Chester Urquart blurted in a spray of crumbs.

"Is she going to die?"

Urquart winced.

Komerdie refrained from commenting on Skellern's lack of tact and simply nodded. "I'm afraid so, yes."

"She is going to die," Skellern said, "she can do it with you or without you. Either way it will not matter. Our project does mat—"

"I want to see her," Komerdie interrupted. "And I'm going to see her." He drank the remains of his coffee and wiped his mouth on a napkin. Resting the mug on the glass-topped table, he said, "Our project *does* matter, of course, but time is not crucial.

"Next week or even next month would pose no more or, indeed, no less problem than tomorrow or the day after. But—" He turned his head to face the Dummy. "—if you would rather draft in somebody else to handle the arrangements and the organization, then I'll understand."

"Aw, hey, your mom comes first," Urquart said. He looked across at Skellern and affected a big smile. "We can wait, can't we Max?"

The Dummy sat for a few seconds without saying anything. Then he shuffled forward and clumped his wooden feet onto the deck. "I will speak with you, Komerdie. When I have given this some more thought."

Urquart made to say something and then saw Komerdie's single shake of the head.

As Skellern walked stiltedly away, the other two men noticed that even the Dummy's knee joints were squeaking. They looked at each other and hid their smiles. Urquart pushed the bagels away from him on the tray and reached for a Danish. "Great coffee," he said, nodding when Komerdie pointed to the covered pot. He held out his mug gratefully. "And, boy…do I ever need it this morning."

(3)

Ask you what provocation I have had?...
The strong antipathy of good to bad.

Alexander Pope (1688-1744)

Two days later, Leonard Komerdie was walking through the Arrivals gate at London's Heathrow airport, flanked by Sidney Smolt, Archie McIlveen and Janette Skyzcky. Smolt—who looked for all the world a dead ringer for Bud Costello—McIlveen and Skyzcky all carried plastic pistols, each one ready packed with five polished wooden balls fashioned from the darkest mahogany.

Each of them carried shoulder-bags, various magazines and newspapers—including a paperback by Ray Bradbury, its title a line from Shakespeare, which Komerdie had tried to read on the airship but had to give it up because he couldn't stop thinking about his mom—and, in Smolt's case, the travel blanket and set of earphones which passengers were supposed to use during the flight but leave behind on arrival.

Leonard was sporting a ponytail and a goatee beard, an excessively garish shirt and jogging pants outfit, thick-soled sneakers, wraparound Raybans and a Walkman playing *College Standards* by The Lettermen. The strains of "Graduation Day" hovered around the Comedian's head like the smell of cologne. "You know," a dewy-eyed Komerdie confided to Janette Skyzcky as they waited in line at immigration, "these guys were every bit as good as The Freshmen—and not as jazzy. I prefer close harmony without the jazz."

He had made pretty much the same observation just hours earlier on the plane, while Skyzcky had been trying to watch the new George Clooney movie about a man falsely accused of rape ("He could jump on my bones any day," she told Komerdie when she saw the movie advertised in the handout) *and* at a volume several levels higher than was really necessary.

Eventually their turn came and the passports were stamped without any questions. But then, why would there be questions? Archie and Janette acted their parts to the hilt—the wealthy playboy and his consort, plus the inevitable backup in the form of Komerdie and Smolt.

"What now?" Archie McIlveen muttered *sotto voce* as they moved into the main terminal building past rows of people holding up cardboard signs bearing scribbled names.

Komerdie removed his earpieces. "Now we split up," he said.

"Split up? That doesn't seem like—"

Komerdie took hold of McIlveen's arm. "Look, I appreciate your concerns…" He turned to look at Smolt and Janette Skyzcky. "All of you. But I really must be left alone on this trip." He reached into his pocket and produced a letter of reservation for the Piccadilly Hotel which he handed to Sidney Smolt. "This will be all you'll need. I'll see you when I get back."

Smolt opened the letter and studied its contents.

"When will that be?" Archie McIlveen's frown said all that he thought about the arrangement.

Komerdie shrugged. "When I've done what I have to do."

He nodded, almost curtly, hefted his single travel bag over his shoulder and walked away towards the rank of taxi cabs outside the terminal building.

(4)

General good is the plea of the scoundrel,
hypocrite and flatterer.

William Blake
"Jerusalem" (1815)

The cab eventually made its way into London and began threading its way through the labyrinthine network of streets towards King's Cross railway station.

The English capital was changing.

Pollution control had reduced the number of vehicles on the streets to buses and cabs, with occasional delivery vans and, very rarely, private cars bearing permit stickers. And many of the streets themselves were now being fitted with bumps to restrict speed. It gave the whole scenario the air of slow-mo film, with every now and then a bus or a cab or even an occasional bike slowing and bucking, once, and twice, before moving on at a temporarily quickened pace.

"What part o' the States you from then, mate?" the driver inquired over his shoulder as they came to a halt at what looked like being a difficult junction to get out of.

"New York."

"Ah, New *York!*" came the response, as though the very words answered every question about—or corroborated every belief in—America and, indeed, Americans. The driver edged forward, waving at a young man with facial tattoos driving a blue Ford Econoline with the legend

GRAFFITI INK. SAY IT WITH WORDZ

emblazoned on its side panel.

"Never been," he added as they pulled out into a line of cabs heading for Marble Arch.

"No?" Komerdie couldn't think what else to say.

"Never been *any*where in the States, mate," the cabby explained. "Never had no desire. It's your home that's the most important, that's what I always say. I don't mind traveling around England, mind, don't get me wrong. There's a lot of nice places in England. But England is where I'm most comfortable, you know what I mean?"

Without waiting for a response, the driver continued. "Course, you probably feel the same way when you come over 'ere, you know what I mean? You probably think to yourself, 'I can't wait to get back 'ome to them skyscrapers and stuff.' It's what you've been brought up with, that's what important."

Komerdie stared out at the hordes of pedestrians and the gaudy store window displays as they crossed Oxford Circus. "I'm from England originally."

"Go on!" the driver said, locking eyes with Komerdie in his mirror. "When d'you leave, then? You ain't got no English accent, mate. Not one as I can spot anyway."

"I left when I was nineteen. I arrived in New York with a few pounds in my pocket and nowhere to stay."

"You done all right for yourself, though, yeah?"

Komerdie nodded. "Yes, I've done okay. I suppose."

"Course you 'ave. Where'd you live when you was over 'ere, then?"

"Ilkley. Yorkshire."

"Ah, *Yorkshire!*" the cabby intoned. It was like a mantra. "Beautiful part of the world. We love it up in Yorkshire, me and my missus. Went there for our honeymoon, back in '84. Yorkshire Dales. Beautiful! God's country, so they say…and you can believe it when you see it."

Komerdie nodded.

"Why'd you leave, then?"

The Comedian stared at the cabby's face in the rearview mirror and, just for a few seconds, he could see his father's eyes staring back at him, asking him that same question all that time ago. Coming up with an answer now, almost three decades later, was just as difficult as it had been then.

He shrugged. "Why does anyone make a break for the unknown?" He watched the London streets drift by outside the window. "I guess to make something of my life."

"And 'ave you? Made something of your life, I mean…not just making money?"

Komerdie couldn't keep back the smile. "There are some that might say that, yes."

The driver nodded, considering that. Then he said, "'Ave you been back much, since you went over I mean?"

Komerdie turned to the side and kept his eyes focused on the storefronts. "No, I haven't been back at all."

"Blimey! You must be noticing a few changes then."

"A few," Komerdie agreed with a chuckle.

"So why've you come back now, then?"

"To see my mother."

"Mmm." The driver's eyes met Komerdie's in the rearview mirror, studied his face. "So you left…when? Twenty five years ago? Something like that?"

"Thirty-two."

The cabby whistled. "You really *must* be noticing the changes."

Komerdie nodded.

"She sick? Your mum, I mean."

Komerdie nodded again and turned away from the piercing eyes in the mirror. "Dying."

"Sorry to hear that, mate."

"Yeah, well…it happens to us all."

"So they say," the cabby said with a smile.

The car jerked to a halt and Komerdie lurched forward in his seat.

"Jesus Christ, they're worse than bloody kids."

Komerdie leaned forward to find out the cause of the abrupt stop. Ahead of them, a young woman dressed in bright purple leotards, a purple eyemask and yellow boots and gloves was forming out of the wall adjoining a branch of HSBC Bank. A line of people at the ATM alongside were busy either running in one direction or another, or throwing themselves face down onto the sidewalk. Emerging from the bank entrance, and flanked by two burly men wearing bulky earphones and carrying large sacks, a tall man dressed completely in white—even down to the white bowler hat, gloves and what appeared to be a blind man's stick—hefted the cloth bag *he* was carrying over his shoulder, lifted his foot in the air and brought it down with should have been a dull thud. Instead, the resulting noise cut through everything like a pneumatic drill.

The cabby grasped his ears and thrust his head forward against the steering wheel. His mouth was moving, Komerdie saw, though he too was intent on holding his own head to stop the high-pitched whine reverberating through the cab.

And the street.

Store windows burst outwards in cascades of broken glass and the cabby's windshield erupted into a mosaic of vein-like scratches.

Almost as soon as it had started, the sound faded away and, in its place, the sounds of the city were now enhanced by chaos. Sirens shrilly howled, car horns and alarms beeped and whined, and everywhere people's voices called out.

The cabby turned around and pointed to the tall man in white who, followed closely by the two men, was running down the sidewalk to where a white sedan had pulled against the curb. "That's White Noise," the cabby said.

"Who's he?"

The cabby shrugged. "Just another crook, mate...with the usual get-rich-quick schemes." He rubbed his hand over his windshield. "Bastard's buggered my windscreen."

Komerdie watched the man in white slide into the car and bark instructions to the driver. Even as the door was closing, the car lifted effortlessly from the road and moved vertically up the side of the building before maneuvering off to the right and disappearing over the rooftops.

They looked back at the young woman. She seemed dazed and was placating some of the pedestrians.

"Who's she?"

"She, mate," the cabby said, his smile infecting his words, "*was* Malleable Maid." He was leaning forward as they pulled away, staring intently through the pattern of cracks. "But one of them comics companies in the States — don't recall their name: comics ain't one of my things — anyway, they 'ad a bit character in one of their magazines called Malleable Man and they told her she couldn't use that name. Not Malleable *Man*," he added over his shoulder. "Malleable *Maid*."

"So what's she called now?"

As they moved slowly towards Russell Square, with the cabby peering through his shattered windshield, Komerdie saw a bold PP emblazoned on the girl's ample bosom in a yellow circle whose sides fluctuated in and out like an amoeba's.

"Well, her name was Patricia — Patricia Leary — so she changed her surname to "Pending" and now she's —"

"Pat Pending."

"Bang on, mate" the cabby said. "And she says she's going to sue anyone she hears about using her name on a legal document."

"That's going to play hell with intellectual property rights."

The driver frowned and then nodded. He knew diddly about IP. "Bloody people! They're all barmy, you ask me."

"The heroes or the crooks?"

"All of 'em. The heroes aren't much better than the crooks, you ask me. They want to get a proper bloody job 'stead of flying around." He sniffed as he rolled down his window and waved nonchalantly to a bus driver who allowed him to pull around a stationary delivery van. "They want to try driving a bloody cab through London, mate…that'd sort 'em out.

"Yeah, heroes and villains," the driver continued. "They're all the bloody same if you ask me. Not much to choose between any of 'em."

Komerdie smiled as they pulled out onto Kings Cross Road.

"You want dropping at the front, mate…or should I take you round the back?"

"At the front is fine."

They pulled up and Komerdie paid the driver—with a generous tip ("God bless you mate")—and sauntered into the station, buying an *Evening Standard* from a toothless old man at a kiosk festooned with magazines whose covers featured women displaying their anatomy in a variety of poses which must have been extraordinarily uncomfortable.

As luck would have it, his train was at the platform and within minutes he was heading out of London for the North.

He read the *Standard* from front to back page, drinking in the quaintness of the news—such as discovering that the Bank of England financial committee had increased interest rates for the third month running; that the Chelsea football team was threatened with relegation to the second division; and that the Troglodyte and Road Rage had filed a harassment lawsuit against Fastman after the faster-than-light hero had raided their secret (or not-so-secret, Komerdie thought) hideaway. The article was accompanied by a smiling—"smirking" might have been a more appropriate word—Troglodyte and Road Rage, resplendent in their costumes, respectively a dirty brown hooded one-piece and a garish red, orange and yellow tight-fitting outfit topped with what appeared to be a sunburst effect springing from the sides of the man's head. In naming the pair, the caption went on to state that Fastman was unable to attend the preliminary hearing as, in the words of his attorney, he was "unavoidably delayed putting a little light back into a darkening world."

Komerdie looked up as they pulled into Peterborough station and let his eyes play across the faces of the people waiting on the platform in the drizzle. They were as gray as the day itself.

In his sleep, brought on by the soothing motion of the train, Komerdie and many of his contemporaries plus several heroes, all of their uniforms a blaze of color and outrageous righteousness or righteous outrage, stood as though under judgment before a massed throng of miserable-looking people

in a featureless field beneath a persistent rain. One of the watchers—
Komerdie recognized the cab driver immediately…though, in his dream,
he wondered how that could be for he hadn't actually seen the man's face
full on—stepped forward and announced to the throng: *Yeah, heroes and
villains…they're all the bloody same if you ask me. Not much to choose between
any of 'em.*

When he woke up, the train was in Leeds.

Komerdie took a cab to Ilkley and drank in the passing scenery. And
the changes.

When they hit Headingley, just a couple of miles out of Leeds's bus-
tling center, the traffic slowed for no apparent reason. Then, minutes later,
a blonde man wearing silver shorts, silver ankle boots and a matching
sleeveless top appeared over the tops of the cars in front. He was carrying
a petroleum truck, its hood covered by a silver cape fastened somehow to
the wheel arches. Smoke was coming out from beneath the cape in strag-
gling wisps.

"Who's he?" Komerdie asked the driver.

"Silverman," came the response.

"Silverman?" Komerdie turned in his seat as the traffic started to move
again, watching the flying man disappear over the trees and towards Leeds.
"He's a hero, right?"

"Yeah, a hero."

Komerdie turned back and settled in his seat. "So what does he do? I
mean, Silverman? He turn things silver or something?"

The driver shrugged. "I think it's his name—Daniel Silverman. As to
what he does…he flies."

"He flies? And that's it?"

"And he's strong. Those two'll do for starters." He leaned on his horn
and persuaded a Volvo convertible to make the left turn he had been sig-
naling for several minutes. "I lose track."

"He from Earth?"

The driver nodded. "Far as I know. He was a fuel science student here
at the university. The story goes that he was experimenting with some
chemicals and they exploded over him." He shrugged and glanced at
Komerdie in the rearview mirror. "Do I need to say more?"

Komerdie shook his head. "It's a familiar story."

The driver grunted his agreement.

And they passed the rest of the journey in silence.

(5)

What is our task? To make Britain a fit country for heroes to live in.

David Lloyd George (British Prime Minister, 1916-22)
From a speech delivered at Wolverhampton, 1918

As the woman in the blue uniform wheeled the chair towards him, down the delicately paved path of gray stones speckled here and there with tiny shoots like diamonds in the rough, Komerdie's attention was drawn to the tiny figure watching him and he wondered where time truly went.

"She's a little better today, aren't you Mary?" the woman announced as she drew up to Komerdie, seemingly at a sufficiently high volume to interrupt conversations in the neighboring villages of Addingham and Burley-in-Wharfedale. But it was all an act. She had told Komerdie that his mother was unlikely to see out the week. The Comedian had not known what to say then, and he did not know what to say now.

"Hello Leonard," Mary Komerdie said, her voice soft and gentle…the way he had always remembered it.

"I'll leave you two to natter while I put the kettle on," the woman said. Then, to Komerdie's mother, "Now don't go tiring yourself out, Mary."

As the woman walked back up the path to the main hospice building he marveled at her stoicism and her bravery. This was a job he could never contemplate being able to do…chatting animatedly and making people comfortable as they neared their final moments of life. He wondered if she cried at night, when, in the silent solitude of her room, she reflected on her charges.

"Hello Mom."

"*Mom!*" Mary Komerdie chuckled and shook her head, dislodging a wisp of wiry gray hair onto her forehead.

Komerdie knelt beside the chair and rested a hand on his mother's clasped hands. "Why do you laugh?"

"You called me 'Mom' — it's very American isn't it?"

"What, 'Mom?'"

She nodded. "You used to call me 'Mum.'"

He rubbed her hands. "How you doing?"

She looked up into his eyes, and smiled with them. Taking his hand in hers, she let her eyes close slowly. "Oh, it's so good to see you, son."

"And it's good to see you, too. I'm sorry I haven't—"

"You're here now, son, that's all that matters," she said without opening her eyes. "Now is everything."

She let go of his hand and it flopped onto her skirt-covered legs. He felt their thinness and quickly drank in her appearance. There wasn't much of it, save for the ankles and the neck and the face, where the steroids had puffed out the skin.

She opened her eyes and looked at him, her expression a mask of regret, as though she wanted to apologize…to say she was sorry for being old, sorry for being so close to death.

"There's so much to say and to talk about," she began, "but I don't think I have the energy son. You look well, though. Are you?"

"Well?"

She nodded.

"I think I'm okay," he said. "I go for my check-ups every year." He patted his stomach. "Putting on a little too much here…" He took hold of the skin at either side of his chin. "…and here. And my hair's going…" He pulled back his hair at the front to show the expanse of forehead.

"It looks fine to me."

He shrugged. "Well, you can't stop time."

She nodded. "More's the pity."

He wanted to be able to tell her she looked well too, but he couldn't bring himself to lie to her. In the same way, he couldn't bring himself to tell her the truth. He figured she knew how she looked, and it wasn't "well."

"There are some things I want—"

"No, I don't want you to talk, Mom," Komerdie said. "I want you to listen. I've got something to tell you."

She lifted a wattled arm and, with a frail and shuddering hand of skeletal but beautifully tapered fingers, she shielded her eyes from the sun.

"I'm going to make it short and sweet," Komerdie said as he stood up. He lifted one of the chairs from a nearby table of ornate and filigreed white metal and placed it alongside her. "I've—I've made mistakes," he began.

Mary Komerdie's eyes opened wide and she started to speak but the Comedian shook his head.

"No, let me finish." He reached for her hand and held it gently. "I've been wrong. That's the bottom line. I've been wrong and I'm going to change. I just wanted you to know that."

Now an expression of abject horror washed over his mother's face. She pulled her hand free. "No, Leonard. It's me who's been wrong. Been wrong all my life, so it's good to feel that, here at the end—"

"Oh, don't talk like—"

"Now, hush a minute, Leonard," she said sternly. "We both know I don't have long. So does Kathy."

"Kathy?"

"The woman who wheeled me down here. Everyone knows I don't have long — none of us in here has long — so I don't have time to mess about with foolish talk. So listen to me now.

"The garden needs both the sun and the rain," she said.

Komerdie frowned.

"Oh, I knew I wouldn't be able to explain myself," she said. She closed her eyes, lifted a hand to her face and scratched her chin. "It's only the bad days that make the good days seem good." She opened her eyes and looked at her son. "You see, it's me who's been wrong. All these years."

Komerdie started to understand. It was the faintest breath of understanding but it was there, hovering in the back of his mind, getting bigger and growing stronger.

"If there were no *bad* folks," the old woman said, reaching across to lay a hand on Komerdie's shoulder, "then there wouldn't be any need for *good* folks. You *see*," she said emphatically, "what you do is every bit as important as what the heroes of the world do. You provide a balance."

"But what I do is wrong."

She nodded. "Of course it's wrong...but it's necessary.

"Human nature being what it is, we'd get tired if everything was always right. If there was nothing to fight for...nothing to protect against."

"You mean I'm performing some kind of service."

"That's exactly what I mean. The world needs you every bit as much as it needs the heroes."

Komerdie smiled. "The way the garden needs both the sun and the rain."

The old woman nodded.

"You must promise me," she said, squeezing his shoulder. "You must promise me that you'll carry on. Hold your head high and continue what it is that you do...and," she paused to allow a broad smile to wash over her face, "that you do so well, if what I hear about the infamous Comedian of New York City is correct." She removed her hand and squinted at him. "Do you promise?"

Komerdie frowned.

"Can't you just promise me this one thing?"

He thought for a few moments and then he nodded.

"Say it then."

"I promise...*Mum*."

"Good boy," she said.

The nurse *yoo hoo*ed as she came out of the building carrying a tray.

"Tea's here," said Mary Komerdie.

"Great." He reached over and squeezed his mother's hand, not surprised in the least to feel it squeeze back.

(6)

We can be heroes...
Just for one day

Heroes, words and music by
David Bowie and Brian Eno
Copyright © BMG Songs Ltd/EG Music Ltd/
RZO Music Ltd/EMI Music Publishing Ltd.
All rights reserved. Used by permission

Mary Komerdie died in her sleep three days later.

A nurse named Yvonne told Komerdie that his mother had been smiling when the nurse had gone into Mary Komerdie's room to wake her for breakfast. "She looked so happy," she told Komerdie. "And I'm sure it was all because you'd come to see her."

"Yeah, but I came a little late."

The woman shrugged. "But you came. Believe me, not many do."

In the two days that the Comedian stayed at the small guest house in Ilkley, leaving for the hospice before nine o'clock and returning a little before seven PM, he spent the time wisely, feverishly cramming a thirty-year relationship into almost as many hours.

The day on which he was informed that his mother had "passed on," they had planned to go over by the small lake in the hospice grounds and have a picnic. But such was not to be.

There was not much in the way of affairs to put in order.

Mary Komerdie hadn't had any surviving relatives and all her friends were in the hospice, waiting for their own time to be called. As a result, the funeral was a lonely affair attended only by Komerdie, Kathy the nurse, and a sprightly, red-cheeked woman with a voice like a foghorn—and who Komerdie later discovered was suffering from bowel cancer—plus the local vicar, who spoke of the dear departed with practiced regret.

And then, to the lilting refrain of Erik Satie's piano, the simple and surprisingly small coffin slid through the doors and disappeared into the waiting flames beyond.

Komerdie called Sidney Smolt at the Piccadilly and told him he was going to see them back in New York. He was going to hire a car, he told the faithful Smolt, and drive around his old haunts...going to do some thinking.

That thinking continued for four full days and ended only when Komerdie was halfway across the Atlantic, equidistant from his past and his future.

The Comedian arrived in La Guardia a new man...or at least, the old one reaffirmed.

And here he was, on the roof of the Komerdie building, greeting Maximillian Skellern and Chester Urquart who were already waiting for him.

Skellern was wearing one of his android bodies, a tall, hairless olive-skinned man with piercing gelatin eyes that watched Komerdie walk around the pool and flop into the lounge chair beside the table. Urquart was reading a comic book, oblivious to anything or anyone around him.

"Your mother died," Skellern intoned. "My condolences."

Komerdie nodded.

"Yeah," Urquart agreed, shaking his head as he dropped the comic book between his feet. "You okay?"

"I'm fine, thanks Chester." He turned to the Dummy and nodded. "And thanks for your kind words, Max."

Before anyone could say anything more, Komerdie said, "So, we need to get things organized."

He produced a plastic wallet containing plans to The Rock.

"We gonna do it?"

"Of course we are, Max," Komerdie announced with a broad smile. "Whyever should we not?"

The Bomb's smile faded a little. "You're talking...funny," he said, pointing at Komerdie. He turned to Skellern. "He talking funny to you?"

"He is talking good sense," the android said, and, though Komerdie would have put it down to his imagination, the synthetic voice actually seemed to have some feeling in it.

Muted voices from the street below caused Komerdie to turn around, just in time to see a green-clad figure descend onto the roof, its cloak billowing out behind it.

Komerdie dropped the papers onto the table and thrust his hands into his trouser pockets. "Captain Chlorophyll," he said, effecting a small bow. "To what do my friends and I owe the pleasure of seeing you?"

"Cut the crap, Comedian," the hero rasped. "You've been away."

"I've been away."

"And now you're back."

Komerdie clapped his hands once. "Bravo, my dear Kapitan. Your powers of observation are quite impressive."

Chlorophyll jumped down from the small wall as Smolt and two others walked onto the roof. Komerdie waved them back.

"Why does that fact give me cause for concern?"

Komerdie shrugged and held out his hands. "Which particular fact: that I've been away or that I'm back?"

"You're under-dressed, Bomb," the Captain said to Urquart. "And you're as flamboyant as ever, Dummy. A new outfit?"

Skellern nodded. "Just something that I threw on."

Chlorophyll turned to Komerdie. "I know something's going on, Comedian, but, as you know, the Meredith Treaty prevents my using my powers to listen in on conversations or read any materials on your property —" He turned to Skellern and Urquart. "— or those of your accomplices."

"Friends," Komerdie corrected. "They're my friends."

Chlorophyll grunted.

"Why not get a search warrant?"

"I have no grounds save for a hunch…a big hunch."

"It is not noticeable from this angle," Skellern said.

"Most amusing, Dummy." Captain Chlorophyll stepped closer to Komerdie and the Comedian took a step forward. "Just be aware that I'll be watching you," he said. "All of you."

"I'm sure we'll all sleep easier knowing that," Komerdie said dryly. "Now, if you'll excuse us, we have business matters to discuss. Unless, of course, you'd like to stay for coffee — my man Smolt makes a wonderful blend of Samoan cappuccino."

The Captain turned around and thrust his hands into the air, but before he could go, Komerdie called after him. Chlorophyll turned around, frowning suspiciously.

Komerdie walked up to him and extended his hand.

"What's that?"

"My hand," Komerdie said. "What does it look like?"

"What is it for?"

Komerdie shrugged and kept the hand extended. "Let's call it a mark of respect."

"Respect? Since when did you respect anyone or anything, Comedian?"

"I respect that you're doing your job," Komerdie said softly. "I ask only that you respect that I'm doing mine. Yin and yang," he said. "The balance is maintained."

"The balance will only be maintained when you and your cohorts —"

"*Friends!*"

"— when you and they are behind bars. For good."

Komerdie shook his head. "There'll always be others," he said.

"That's true, more's the pity."

"Ah, but have you ever stopped to think what you and *your* friends would do without us?"

Captain Chlorophyll looked away from Komerdie's eyes and down at the outstretched hand. Then he looked up. "Take care, Comedian," he said.

Komerdie dropped his hand. "And you, Captain."

Chlorophyll hopped onto the wall and leapt forward, dropping slightly towards the waiting street before the currents lifted him, and he twisted to the left and headed across the Park.

"Everything okay, boss?" Smolt's voice asked from behind Komerdie.

"Everything is just fine, Sidney," Komerdie said without turning around. "Just fine." He watched the departing figure grow smaller and smaller, until it disappeared completely far out above the trees of Central Park.

**For Kathleen Crowther (1922-2000), James Lovegrove,
Malcolm Poynter and Paul Stephenson...heroes all.
See you in the funny pages, Mum!**

A Worse Place than Hell

If there is a worse place than Hell, then I am in it.

attributed to Abraham Lincoln following
the Fredericksburg collapse, 1862

Prologue

1:30 AM, 15 APRIL 1865, WASHINGTON DC: The tuft of hair is removed almost lovingly by Corporal John Lansing, its thick strands—matted by blood and tissue—carefully removed from the wound by means of a folding-knife that the soldier had bought from a one-eyed trail scout in Abilene the previous year. John Lansing, a church-going Baptist, is not a thief and the "taking" is one borne out of respect, admiration and profound loss.

At this time the patient is still alive, lying diagonally across a walnut bed in a room measuring fifteen by nine feet, but he is unconscious, lower extremities cold to the touch, pulse feeble. As Corporal Lansing steps back from the table, he places the swatch of hair in the fold of a theater handbill and, his hands now clasped across his stomach, he stealthily refolds the handbill before dropping it into his tunic pocket.

One of the two medical men present—name of Leale—proceeds to cover the body with mustard plasters. Lansing looks away, his eyes traveling the topmost circumference of the room, and he immediately feels a tell-tale tear roll down his left cheek. After almost thirty minutes, the other doctor—Barnes—straightens up and drops the shiny instruments onto the small folding table by his side. He cannot locate the bullet, a small lead ball less than one half-inch in diameter, which is embedded amidst shards of pulverized bone fragments in the anterior lobe of the left hemisphere of the brain.

When Doctor Barnes speaks to the people in the room, his voice is tired and without hope: further explorations will be of no use, he tells them.

Soon, he will be free, the doctor says. *We must simply wait.*

THE PRESENT: A bizarre mixture of smells floated across the dark, early morning street, the gentle wind blowing the disparate elements into one single aroma: a cloying, olfactory amalgam of smoke, sweat and rotting flesh.

The sixteenth President of the United States of America had been alternating running with brisk walking for several hours now, feeding off a heady adrenaline cocktail of wonder and fear. He stepped out of the shadows onto the pock-marked sidewalk and once again breathed deeply the myriad aromas of New York City.

It was almost five hours since his escape and with each passing minute the smells floating on the wind had strengthened, grown bolder. He had made good speed, at first moving without clear knowledge of where he was going save to put distance between himself and the doctors but then weaving his way across the city and then heading down towards Greenwich Village.

For the past few hours he had been lying on a bench in Washington Square, reputed — according to his map — to be a park but which in truth amounted to the barest scattering of trees, several concrete pillars (the function of which he could not fathom) and what appeared to be a huge fountain though it contained no water.

The entire area had been littered with homeless people who drank boldly from brown-bagged bottles an elixir which, while it did not provide any answers, at least fogged some of the questions. He had picked a piece of wall against which he sat and watched. And though he tried with all his might, he could not get out of his head another image — Devil's Run, when the Union forces had been overrun by a Confederate charge on the second day at Gettysburg — of men equally bereft of hope and stamina, propped against mounds of soil piled up into gullies by a constant barrage of cannon-fire.

But now he was back on the street, a little replenished.

A plaque set into the concrete wall across from him reflected the orange glare from the intermittent sodium lamps:

THE BOWERY

it said.

Half-crouched, so as to avoid or at least delay discovery of his current position, he looked back along the way he had come. Could this dark and dismal street truly be the same Bowery that he had passed along, albeit briefly, on his last visit to New York City? Of course, it must be: after all, could there be *two* such famed thoroughfares? Presumably not. But the broken and occasionally boarded-up windows and the graffiti-festooned building fronts were indeed a far cry from the gay and picturesque entertainment center he remembered…for his memory did not accord with the actual passage of time which had taken place.

This street stretched far away to his right, a generous pathway more than wide enough for four sets of coach-and-horses to ride abreast. A distant humming noise sounded and lights bathed the street. Lincoln stepped back into the shadows and watched in fascination as another of the infernal mechanical carriages bounced out of the street across from him and disappeared up the street to his right.

Could it be looking for him? It seemed unlikely. Not that people would *not* be looking for him, but rather the apparent lack of any urgency on the part of the vehicle suggested an altogether different and more leisurely motive behind its appearance. Though what could bring any respectable person out into the streets at this time of night — or rather *morning* — was quite beyond him.

He looked again at the sign and then removed the folded paper from his coat pocket, scanning down its key of landmarks until he reached the one he wanted. He then referred to the map and noted the position of his destination. He had been right: The Bowery led into it. He refolded the paper and returned it to his pocket, checking the gloomy buildings opposite for any sign of someone watching him, but everything seemed deserted.

Along the other way, towards the city's heart, it was the same, though there the pathway seemed to curve gently to the left. As he stared into the shimmering, orange-hued gloom, something moved from the protection of the left-hand wall. It moved slowly, apparently cautious at first, and then it stopped and seemed to settle in the middle of the road. He knew it was watching him.

He squinted and rubbed his eyes. Was it a cat? A dog, perhaps? *It's a rat*, a secret inner voice whispered to him, though such a suggestion was surely ridiculous. The thing was ten — nay, *twenty* – times bigger than a simple vermin, even bigger than the battle-bloated carnivores that inhabited the areas outside the circles of protective light on the fields at Fredericksburg and Antietam Creek, where the dead and dying lay on the bare ground and the blasted and torn limbs were stacked as high as piles of pumpkins in the fall. He shook his head, breaking up the quickly-forming mental picture into a series of half-remembered shards.

But the smell remained: the smell was here, now.

He straightened up and stood his ground, removing the white gloves — now somewhat stained, he noted disapprovingly — and slowly inserting them into his coat pocket. The fact that there were other gloves in there seemed somehow reassuring. Lincoln lifted his head, jutted out his chin, and, rubbing his hands down the sides of his legs, stared, concentrating all of his attention on the creature on the path as though it were the only thing in this Godless place.

The thing's eyes seemed to wink and it shrank lower upon itself…either trying to hide or preparing to attack. Lincoln straightened his hat and stepped forward.

Quick as a flash, the creature turned and darted along the street a little way and then off at a right-angle into the shadows surrounding a series of metal containers, leaving behind it an insidious echoing patter of tiny clawed feet.

Interlude 1

8:10 PM, 26 JUNE 1892, BY THE COLORADO RIVER, NORTHERN ARIZONA: Prentiss Ingraham, noted dime novelist, holds the young man tight, the roar of the river blustering over to the right. The man's collarbone protrudes from his shoulder, a thin slice of bluish-white bone, while the jumble of intestines that has partially spilled from the gash in his belly now lies quivering on the folds of his ripped shirt. His partially severed left foot sits limply on the rocky slab beside his hip, the leg above it twisted and broken like a piece of driftwood. The man's lips are the deepest blue that Prentiss has ever seen. He will use that fact in a story the following year.

Yore not gonna make it, boy, Prentiss tells the man — whose name is Jedediah Lansing, only surviving son of Captain James Lansing, late of the Union Army — over the sound of the water.

In the background, sounding like excited children at play, muffled calls ring out as Cody and the others wade into the shallows as far as they dare in order to retrieve the waterlogged provisions from the smashed raft. Jedediah shifts awkwardly and cries out in pain, momentarily losing consciousness, but he manages to remove the leather pouch from his pants pocket and presses it into the writer's hand. Responding to Lansing's nods, Ingraham leans forward so that the dying man might speak into his ear.

As he listens, his eyes open wider and he glances down at the pouch.

THE PRESENT: Lincoln relaxed and lifted his head, listening.

It was not silence that he heard, he suddenly realized, but rather a faint humming, like some kind of electrical generator. He looked around at the darkened street and saw only dereliction and waste. This was not a hospitable place. In that respect, it was not dissimilar to other places of confrontation. For that was what this was, a battlefield of sorts though the combatants were not visible. Rather, this war was one waged from a distance. And the hum he heard was the hum of the city itself, breathing with a life of its own.

Suddenly it seemed as if there were three possible sides to this conflict: the forces of law, the forces of chaos and some intermediary power, a sentient being imbued in the bricks and mortar and coldly glowing streetlights.

Staying within the comforting shadows, the President edged his way along the sidewalk. Somewhere in the distance, a howl rang out, rising and falling in pitch. He stopped and waited. To his other side, again far away, a second cry sounded, its mournful wail echoing the first and seeming to build in intensity until, quite suddenly, both faded away.

And only the hum of the city remained.

Interlude 2

4:30 PM, 11 MAY 1895, A FUNERAL PARLOR IN GUTHRIE, OKLAHOMA: Having removed all of the clothing from the bullet-riddled bodies of the two men — whose names, his sheet of paper tells him, are Charlie Pierce and Bitter Creek Newcomb — Doc Hinkel, a medical man of some questionable repute as well as philanderer and unsuccessful gambler, proceeds to remove their boots. In the lobby outside the room, two Deputy US Marshals go through the details of the ambush again for the benefit of a newspaper man up from Oklahoma City.

The newspaperman — whose name is Dan Remington — plans to headline the piece:

DESPERADOES EARN THEIR FREEDOM!

In Pierce's left boot the doctor discovers a wad of papers. He unfolds them as he listens to the re-enactment in the hallway. The first paper is a likeness of a man and a woman. The creases make any formal identification impossible. The second paper, a folded fifty-dollar bill, the doctor slips into his waistcoat pocket. After careful examination of the third and final paper — a crumpled theater handbill advertising a play entitled *Our American Cousin*, containing a lock of hair which still bears traces of skin and dried blood — and the scribbled writing on its reverse, Doctor Hinkel places this also in his pocket. Then he washes the excess blood from the bodies and clasps the two pairs of hands neatly on their respective stomachs.

As he calls for the newspaperman to come and take the photograph, the doctor thinks excitedly of the potential betting power of his new prize. Tonight, he will be lucky, he tells himself: tonight, he has himself a fine stake with which to play.

THE PRESENT: Crossing 4th Street, Abraham Lincoln went over the events of the past few hours.

The last thing he remembered was sitting in a private box at Ford's Theater watching a play of some kind. He could not remember the name of the presentation itself, although the name Tom Taylor seemed familiar. Could that be the title of the play? He did not think so. Perhaps it was the name of the writer.

He remembered that it revolved around a Yankee lighting his cigar with an old Will and Testament, thereby sending up in smoke his chances of inheriting some $400,000. It was not a bad play, but then it was not a good one, either.

A sound to his right caused him to pause.

A stooped man carrying a small paper bag of some kind stumbled out from beneath the awning of a store, the nature of whose merchandise — boldly displayed in the two large windows — the President could not discern. The man, clearly the worse for the effects of alcohol, held his ground, body tilted to an extreme side-angle while his feet remained stationary...as though they were in fact attached in some way to the sidewalk. With his free hand, the man was attempting to pull up his fly. The front of his trousers was wet and, behind him, in the doorway, a widening pool could be seen snaking its way towards the sidewalk.

Lincoln considered trotting off the street and into the shadows but, even as he weighed up the likelihood that he could do it without being seen, the man looked up, gave a loud rasping belch and saw the President. Almost immediately, he started laughing.

Interlude 3

1:30 PM, 16 MAY 1920, DISTRICT SCHOOL #94, NEAR PECATONICA, ILLINOIS: It is the first year of teaching for Miss Erna Meyer. She is in the middle of conducting a crayoning project for the first grade. Charles Buntjier, privileged earlier that morning by being assigned the task of holding the flag to which the rest of the class pledged their allegiance, is talking to his friend, Leland Meiers. Unaware that the teacher is watching him, Charles hands over the fieldmouse to Leland and accepts in return a small leather pouch and a large beetle through which a string has been pulled and knotted.

Charles, Miss Meyer calls out, *Leland.* The class, as one, stops what they are doing and all eyes turn to the two boys.

Yes, Miss? their eyes say, though their voices remain silent.

Please come to the front of the class, Miss Meyer says. *And bring with you whatever it is that you are playing with.*

While the other children wait and watch, Miss Erna Meyer studies the objects set before her on her desk. Leland and Charles stand at the other side of the desk, their hands clasped behind their backs.

The teacher drops the unfortunate beetle into the waste basket by her side.

She calls for Keith Fisher to take the fieldmouse outside and set it free.

Opening the small leather pouch, Miss Meyer asks, *And what is this?*

Part of President Lincoln's head, miss, says Leland Meiers.

THE PRESENT: Still laughing, the man staggered forward and then back again. He lifted his free arm and pointed at the President...or, more accurately, at his hat. "Shum kinda fancy dress, huh?" the man said.

"My attire may not be entirely to your liking, sir," Lincoln responded, "but neither is your attitude acceptable to me. I suspect it would be equally distasteful to any right-minded folk. I suggest you be on your way." And, with that, he turned on his heel, removed his white gloves from his pocket and strode onto the sidewalk. His destination was just another two or three blocks ahead, he remembered. Time was wasting.

Interlude 4

8:45 AM, 6 JANUARY 1946, A RESIDENTIAL HOUSE ON HOUSTON'S GOLD COAST, RIVER OAKS: Ex-Governor William P. Elkins hands the contents of a small metal box to his wife, Oveta. He says, *You must guard this with your life,* though the cancer has affected his vocal chords and his voice is too soft for her to hear above the sound of her own grief.

He settles back onto his bed, the pillow momentarily engulfing the sides of his head, and he breathes out a final breath slowly. It is a deep breath, a luxurious and well-earned last breath, and it carries with it the inseparable dual scent of jasmine and goodness. He can die happy now, he thinks, content in the knowledge that his wife will preserve his treasure for prosperity.

Oveta Culp Elkins recognizes her husband's release from life, sees the unseen veil lift from his pain-stricken face, and she cries out in desperate sadness. As she stands from the bedside chair to throw her arms around her dead husband, the small metal box drops from her lap and rolls under the bed.

THE PRESENT: He recalled the upholstered rocking chair in which he had been sitting. There had been two other people in the room: his wife and a guard. The guard was fully armed and had, for the most part, remained at the rear of the box. However, now that he thought about it, the President clearly recalled the man moving down closer to the stage and taking a seat to his right.

Had that been a part of some elaborate plan to take his life?

Then there had been a slight chink of light, as the door behind him opened. He remembered paying no heed to it, suspecting that it was merely John Parker checking that all was indeed well inside the box. Then...

Lincoln shook his head and staggered as though momentarily faint, stretching out his left hand to the wall for support.

Then there had been the noise and a flash as bright as that produced by Mathew Brady's exploding gunpowder contraption, and a searing, profound pain in his head.

The next thing he remembered was coming to in a brightly-lit room. He was lying on a table, surrounded by people—each wearing a white half-face mask—and a profusion of gleaming equipment which appeared to be of a surgical nature but the like of which he had never before encountered.

Where am I? he had asked, in a sleepy voice. *Has the play finished? Did I pass out?*

The two people leaning over him had smiled then—he had recognized their smiles even through the masks—and had looked at each other triumphantly.

Where is my wife? he had asked. *Where is Mary?*

That is when they had told him a story more fantastic than the most far-fetched dime novel, stranger even than the strangest dream.

One of the men—there were six men and two women present—explained that he was in New York City but, in addition to his having to endure a physical displacement of several hundred miles, he was no longer even in his own time.

Abraham Lincoln looked up at the towering buildings that lined the street, gray-bricked and mirror-windowed monoliths that stretched way, way up into the early morning sky, and he marveled at the advancements that had made such constructions possible.

New York City but a handful of years short of the turn of the millennium...and a New York that was more than a century older than the one he had visited so recently. This was indeed some rare kind of magic.

As though to emphasize the sense of wonder, a Yellow Cab turned out of 6th Street and headed up to Cooper Square.

Interlude 5

10:10 PM, 23 OCTOBER 1989, WELLS, MAINE: Having changed hands sixteen times in nine states over 125 years, the lock of hair once belonging to Abraham Lincoln is discovered in a collection of virtually mint comicbooks, *Big Little Books*, *Classics Illustrated*, animation cells and cinema lobby posters cautiously valued in the upper single millions.

The collection belongs to the widow of the recently deceased Jonathan Morrill, whose lifetime of collecting has amassed some 14,000 items and has caused the couple to spend almost $100,000 on customizing their home to accommodate the vast bulk.

In addition to the "Tuft of Lincoln," as it has become known, the collection also includes a small selection of similar personal effects removed from equally auspicious bygone notables, primarily those involved in the art of writing. A twine-headed hammer, for example, allegedly used by Henry David Thoreau to construct his one-room hut by Walden Pond; the quill pen and notebook used by Laura Ingalls Wilder; and assorted other items of interest.

The comic books and cinematic collectibles have been sold at auction over a three-day period at a special convention in Atlanta's Hilton Towers Hotel.

Generally considered to be of little financial value, the non-comic book-related ephemera has been sold as a single lot to William H. Goddard, a wealthy New York-based garment manufacturer whose grandmother was one of the survivors of the tragic conflagration at the Triangle Shirtwaist Company in 1911.

On the train returning home to New York, the new owner now considers his purchase and discovers Lincoln's hair. As it turns out, it is one of two almost identical artifacts…but the unquestionable connection between them goes beyond mere physical similarities.

THE PRESENT: They had talked to him of a special process known as cloning, the art of extrapolating the DNA of a living creature from part of its skin…or, as in his own case, from the follicles attached to hair-roots which were still alive when removed.

Could you bring back my Willie? the President had asked, in something of a daze, not quite catching the snigger from one of the men at the rear of the room. *He died only —*

He had been going to say that his eleven-year-old son, William Wallace Lincoln, had died only three years ago but, of course, it was much, much longer now.

And...and Mary, my wife?

The man had shaken his head.

A woman had stepped forward and said, *She died in 1882, Mister President.*

"Oh, Mary, Mary," he said now to the cold buildings and the unblinking lights.

There was no response, only more grief.

Interlude 6

10:10 PM, 12 DECEMBER 1993, THE BEECKMAN TOWER RESTAURANT, NEW YORK CITY: William H. Goddard hands over a case to a man he knows only as Dolman. Quite how the man came to know that he had the artifacts he does not know. He will never know. He knows only that the man — and presumably the woman with him — are in the employ of the government.

More than this does not seem to matter. Even *this* does not seem to matter.

Goddard is in need of the funds this transaction will bring him. It has not been a good year in the garments business and a pending divorce settlement looks set to take most of his remaining capital.

The case is handed across a plate-festooned table overlooking the lights of First Avenue. Dolman, a fat man who perspires a lot, accepts the case. A few minutes later, he hands a small envelope to Goddard who smiles and places the item carefully in his waiting billfold. The billfold is then returned to Goddard's inside jacket pocket.

The woman with Dolman — Goddard does not know her name — considers the contents of the leather pouches passed to her by her colleague. She matches Goddard's smile: she knows they would have paid twice as much if they had been pushed. Goddard's smile grows even broader as their eyes meet: he knows he would have accepted half the amount he has now pocketed.

Below them, the sirens continue their litany of amusement.

THE PRESENT: He rubbed his hands down his legs. Everything felt and seemed the way it had always done and yet this was not his body...as the people had explained. They had explained but he had not understood...artificial, they had called it: a mixture of plastic, rubber and silicone, only one element of which he was familiar with.

But what did it matter what he was constructed from. Without Mary, it did not seem important.

All that was important was that he was here. And, even more important, that he did not want to be. Now, all he wanted to do was rest.

They had left him alone in the room at his request, telling him that there was someone they wanted him to meet, but while they were gone he had slipped out of another door, walked along the brightly lit corridor and down a seemingly interminable series of stairs until he reached the street. Then it was simply a matter of running straight ahead, away from the river, and occasionally turning left when a street appeared suitably deserted. Then it was right again for a way, then left again and so on until he reached the park which was not a park…and all the veterans of the war of life. It was there, checking his bearings after his rest, that he stopped a young man and asked where he was.

The young man seemed reluctant to speak to him at first but then, with an expansive sweep of his arm, announced *Enn Why You*. It was an enigmatic response which the President decided not to pursue further. Instead, he inquired how he might reach the Cooper Union Building and the man had given him a small handbill and a map of the city…some of the street names on which he recognized and remembered. He had decided to walk the route.

The President had passed by several small restaurants and what seemed to be drinking establishments, from which loud and raucous music bellowed, despite the lateness of the hour. Clearly, the Prohibition movement which started in Maine in 1851 and spread to New York State in 1855, had been repealed.

He had passed by grocers' stores, whose wares were stacked resplendent on large trestle tables which extended way out onto the sidewalk.

And he had passed by a series of young ladies clad in the most minuscule of clothing who offered amusement, wry smiles and even an occasional expression of sympathy. He had, however, been unable to contain his amazement when two of these "women" had turned out, on closer investigation, to be men. Lincoln immediately recalled Jefferson Davis's capture near Irwinville, Georgia, dressed as a woman so as to evade atonement for his crimes against humanity. The President wondered what it was that these individuals sought to escape.

All the way along his route, Abraham Lincoln had watched the jumble of people and faces, noting the mixture of color and realizing that the state of "insurrection" he had declared on April 15 just four short years ago had not been in vain. For here, all had a place and, or so it seemed, all were equal.

When at last he reached the Cooper Union Building, he felt more at ease though he was tired, his energy sapped by the need for stealth and an almost overwhelming grief and profound loneliness.

Interlude 7

12:45 AM, THE PRESENT, NEW YORK UNIVERSITY MEDICAL CENTER, 1ST AND 30TH:
The latest search party returns...again unsuccessful. Meredith P. Sansome,
Head of Bio-engineering and the doctor in charge of the cloning project,
slumps into a chair and closes his eyes.

Dwight Jablonski, right-hand man to the Joint Chiefs of Staff and now
specially appointed temporary Director of the Center's security, steps out
of the washroom and runs his hands through his hair. He looks tired. When
he opens his eyes he looks around the room, studying each face in turn.
Great, he says, *just great. From the team that brought you Nagasaki, Agent Orange and AIDS...a resurrected former President left to wander around modern-
day New York.* He shakes his head. He has no idea as to how the elaborate
security arrangements were so easily breached, though his mind has reflected on similar embarrassments over the years, Kennedy, Oswald,
Kennedy and Reagan to name only four. He knows that questions will be
asked and answers will need to be found. *If anyone here has any balls to
spare, just leave them on the table,* he announces to the hushed room. *We'll
need a hell of a lot of them to satisfy the media. Any that we have left will make up
a nice pie for the President.*

It's not the end of the world, Sansome says. He doesn't sound totally
convinced.

No, but I'm sure we'll get around to that next week.

On the table is a large file of other "possibles" — including a rock and
roll singer from Memphis, a draughtsman-turned-dictator from Austria
and a much-loved architect from Wisconsin — all of whom were considered either inappropriate ("no Spielberg factor," was how Jablonski put it)
or, by virtue of the source materials available for their respective "re-awak-
enings" (the alleged piece of John Kennedy's brain being an obvious example), deemed unlikely to succeed. Because of the enormous costs involved in the complex process, the first one not only had to be right...it
also had to be popular.

In the cloning of one of the country's most revered statesmen and one
of its favorite literary figures — each of whom, being contemporaries, had
spoken highly of the other (though they had never actually met) and both
of whose reputations had survived the intervening years entirely intact —
had seemed to provide all the necessary elements to win the nation's support. But now, all bets were off. When — *if!* — they managed to track down
the President, the entire project would have to be shelved. Jablonski had
already explained this situation — and its implications — to Sansome.

Where the hell has he gone? Jablonski asks nobody in particular.

Maybe the muggers have got him, somebody says.

Don't even joke *about it,* Sansome says. *How about the poet?*

One of the men says, *Marilyn is down there with him now. Seems they've been having a few difficulties.*

Difficulties? Sansome leans forward in his chair.

The door bursts open and a woman rushes into the room. *He's on,* she says. *We had a few problems with the fact that the hair was clipped and so there were no complete follicles present.* She walks across the room, lifts the Mister Coffee pot and pours it into a cup.

Sansome stands up. *But he's up and running?*

The woman nods as she takes a drink. *Mmm, that is so good,* she says. *He's a little groggy but he is up and running. We had to sedate him, though.*

Sedate him! Jablonski slaps his forehead dramatically. *Jesus Chri—*

Keep calm, the woman interjects, *keep calm. We had to give him a little something to keep him loose while we explained the situation.*

Sansome says, *And how did you do that?*

The woman smiles awkwardly. *We told him he was in Heaven,* she says. *We told him that we had created a magical futuristic version of New York City and that Abraham Lincoln had gone missing. "Where would he go, Mr. Whitman?" we asked him.*

Did he know? Jablonski says, hardly daring to wait for the answer.

The woman nods, smiling. *The Cooper Union Building,* she says. *He saw him there in 1861.*

THE PRESENT: Walt Whitman sat in the car between two unsmiling angels in gray suits and marveled at the scenery they passed by.

"I am so delighted at this opportunity, gentlemen," he said. "It is here—where we are now going—that I first saw the President."

Meredith Sansome, turned around in the front passenger seat, nodded and smiled beatifically. This was how he thought an angel would smile.

"He was—and, I presume, still is—a man of unusual and almost un-couth height and, on this occasion, he was dressed entirely in black with a similarly dark complexion and an insolent composure." Whitman smiled and stuck his neck forward, running his hands through his hair. "A bushy head of hair—equally black—and a disproportionately long neck." He laughed and shuffled excitedly in his seat. "What a man!"

Huge buildings scraped the night sky of this dream-world, its dark-ness now softening on the horizon, and everywhere was lit by bright lights and colorful displays. Perhaps this was indeed Heaven, he mused silently, watching his own thoughtful expression reflected in the window of the car.

The last thing he could recall was lying in his room, a gentle rain falling outside, and saying to Horace Traubel — dear Horace! — that he should take something with which to remember him. He had reached out then and, with a pair of nail clippers, had removed a sizable chunk from his beard. This thatch he had presented to Horace with a sad gleam in his eye.

Whitman saw that gleam again now, reflected in the glass before him.

The vehicle in which they traveled pulled out to overtake a colossal vehicle which sprayed water over the gutter and sidewalk, following with a mechanical brush that swept it clean. Whitman stared at it as they went by and turned to watch it through the back window. It seemed for all the world like some gigantic creature, lumbering through this wondrous kingdom of Heaven doomed to a single purpose: to clean. He presumed that everything here would be similarly employed.

The man in the driving seat periodically checked the rearview mirror, shaking his head each time he saw the shaggy-bearded man whose eyes blazed with each new revelation.

They had tried the Lincoln Center.

They had tried City Hall, where the President's body had lain in state while 120,000 grief-stricken New Yorkers had filed past to pay their last respects.

They had even tried the Lincoln statue in the park, combing the grassland and paths surrounding it for hundreds of yards.

But it had all been to no avail.

Then the poet, when he came round and could respond to questions, told them the Cooper Union Foundation Building was where the President would go. It was the only place that would be familiar to him, Whitman had explained. The only place where he would feel even a little comfortable.

Minutes later, they were there.

The car screeched around the corner into Astor Place and pulled up in front of the red-bricked building on the left. As the driver turned off the engine, Sansome pointed towards the shadows by the reception entrance.

There, his stovepipe hat in his hand and his head bowed, President Abraham Lincoln stood looking up at the early morning sky.

"Let's go," Sansome snapped.

They got out.

"Mr. President," Sansome called as soon as he was out of the car. "That was quite a chase you led us on."

The President turned to face the small group that walked across the road towards him. If he was surprised or fearful, Sansome thought, then he certainly didn't show it.

"We have brought someone to see you, Mister President," he called, and he flicked the protective seal off the hypodermic nestled in his jacket pocket.

Lincoln frowned at the portly man with the bushy mane of beard hanging from his chin.

"Mr. President," Walt Whitman said softly, "I am indeed honored to meet you."

His face a mask of smiles, Sansome walked calmly by the poet and around behind the President.

Whitman, his attention momentarily attracted to the angel who had brought him here, watched as Sansome plunged a weapon of some kind into Abraham Lincoln's back.

The President gasped and, dropping his hat, reached out for support. But the chemical now coursing through his artificial veins was swift and powerful. The darkness rushed up to greet him, to soothe him and to take away the pain of remembering and loss…to restore the freedom he had earned, the freedom he had fought for all of his life.

"Mister…Whitman?" he said.

Then he crumpled to the ground.

Sansome knelt by the body and felt the President's neck. He looked up and smiled sadly. "He's gone," he said. "Again."

Walt Whitman stared in disbelief. He looked at the other angels he had traveled with, saw one of them remove a shiny object from his jacket pocket. Shaking his head, he watched as the man—a normal man, not an angel at all—stepped forward and jabbed the hypodermic into his arm.

Somewhere, way in the distance, a siren wailed its shame.

Epilogue

THE FUTURE, THE FOGGY BOTTOM CAFE, 25TH STREET, WASHINGTON DC, CLOSE TO THE KENNEDY CENTER: The man called Jablonski walks across to pay the bill.

The man called Dolman makes a final entry in his notepad. Both men are relieved at the way the entire "Tuft of Lincoln" matter has been resolved, particularly in that they have retained their positions and that the project has been given a second chance so soon.

While his colleague pays the bill, Dolman glances at his pad. There are two lists of names. The first is a column of pairs, couples, all of whom have been thoroughly checked and rechecked for their suitability. All are "good" people, people whose deaths would be felt by the entire nation…people whose subsequent rebirths in the event of their deaths would be greeted with unanimous acclaim. Two of these pairs of names — one married couple noted for their philanthropic work and a two-man song-writing partnership — have been ringed in red ink.

The second list, a column of six names only one of which has been ringed, comprises operatives who would, if asked, be prepared to effect the sanction even knowing that to do so would result in their own deaths. These people would be told that they would themselves be brought back at a later date and with a new identity. Although his colleague has not said as much, Dolman knows that such a potentially disastrous loose end could not be permitted.

He closes the pad and smiles up at Jablonski, happy in his work.

In blowing airs from the fields back again give me my darlings,
give me my immortal heroes,
Exhale me them centuries hence, breathe me their breath,
let not an atom be lost,
O years and graves! O air and soil! O my dead, an aroma sweet!
Exhale them perennial sweet death, years, centuries hence.

Pensive on Her Dead Gazing
by Walt Whitman (1865)

For Dr. Keith D. Sorsby

Halfway House

As silent as a mirror is believed
Realities plunge in silence by...

Hart Crane (1899-1932)
Legend

Space.

He thought it would have been different, more than just an empty void with a few dots scattered around the blackness. It should have been the ultimate adult playground, where the long-suppressed swashbuckling spirit of Man could re-emerge and run free, dabbling in countless adventures and weird landscapes.

But it was only black.

He looked around and strained his eyes for something — anything — in the blackness; but there was nothing, nothing save the occasional star twinkling its silent laughter at him.

"I can think of worse things to do for a living," dad says, rustling his newspaper.

His mother slides the plate in front of his father and gives her husband an icy stare before returning to the kitchen.

"What do you think, Mum?"

Impatient noises of pans clattering drift through the open door.

"You know what I think, Karl," comes the reply. "There are plenty of good jobs down here without you tramping about where you've no right to be."

His father glances myopically over the top of his newspaper and smiles, his head gently shaking from side to side.

"You know what you want to be and what you want to do, son," the man says softly, the words soothing and encouraging. "I can think of worse things."

He watches his father turn a page, hearing his words replaying, hanging on the still air. He realises that, for all that his parents have adopted different stances, one thing is common between them: fear.

It's a new sensation.

Before now, his chosen route had never given him cause for fear: not at school, or at university; not in his early days with the Royal Air Force nor even when his transfer to NASA came through. But now…

What was that?

He tried to turn, to see…and there it was…something…

It was gone now. But he had seen something, briefly, just out of vision, out of the corner of his eye.

He strained, attempting to swivel around in his clumsy suit. But it was too difficult.

His mouth locked in a tight grimace, muscles tensing, he tried to rock around, twisting his body. Eventually, after much effort, he managed to turn. He breathed a sigh of relief and accomplishment and opened his eyes.

Blackness. Nothing everywhere but plain blackness.

Had he managed to turn around? How would he be able to tell?

He shouted into his helmet, "Blackblackblack…" and sobbed. A tear edged its way out of his left eye and trickled onto his cheek. He felt it. And he felt the stickiness in his throat. "Just fucking blackne —"

"Who said that?"

The rest of the boys turn in their seats to stare at him. He feels conspicuous, feels the blood burning in his cheeks and in the lobes of his ears. He knows he is caught, knows that everyone knows it was him. He stands up.

The teacher places his book almost lovingly on his desk, a desk littered with carved initials of pupils dating back through two world wars, walks across the rostrum, clumping as he goes, and steps onto the wooden-tiled floor.

"Ah, Mister Glogauer," he says, sarcasm and venom dripping from each word like treacle from a spoon. He walks along the aisle, hands clasped behind his back, black gown flapping at his sides, and stops beside the boy's desk. "What a surprise."

Sniggers from all around the room disturb the stillness and stroke the tension.

The teacher turns and barks, "Quiet!"

The room hushes and small faces turn back to open books so as to avoid the stony stare which confronts them.

He feels his heart pounding and his hands go cold and clammy.

The teacher turns back to face him, his eyes burning with cold contempt.

"Do you want to make something of yourself, Glogauer, hmm?" he says. "Do you want to be something when you grow up?"

"Yes, sir," he answers softly.

"Hmm? I can't hear you, Glogauer. Speak up boy."

"Yes...sir," he answers again, emphasising each word carefully, unable to keep the indignation and the annoyance out of his voice.

Another snigger from somewhere in the classroom.

The teacher spins around to find the source but it has disappeared as quickly as it formed. He turns back.

"Get out," the teacher says. "Get out of here."

※※

If only he *could*, he thought. But there was no chance of that, no chance at all. He was going to die. He knew that.

Out here, death was a fact. Not like back on Earth, where death was hidden and ignored; swept under the carpet...out of sight, out of mind. And now he was going to die. Slowly. Painfully. All alone and yet surrounded by an infinite number of worlds...worlds with people walking and talking, killing and loving...while, high above them all, he acted out his little drama. A drama without appreciation, a performance without an audience.

"A man is measured by the tears cried at his funeral," his grandfather once told him in a deathbed-moment of rare lucidity.

Nobody would cry at his funeral, he thought. Would he even have a funeral? The people back at the depot, back on Earth, would know that he was dead. Perhaps they would arrange a funeral and bury a load of bricks or something. That would count, surely. Wouldn't it?

"Please let that count," he shouted to the void. He started to cry again, shaking in his suit, each sob jarring his bruised and scorched body.

His parents: he hadn't thought of them before.

It would kill them, the shock. Especially his mother. She would simply go to pieces.

He thought of her face and smiled, thought of her concern at his well-being. His eyes started to sting again.

"Mummy..." His voice was no more than a whisper.

※※

"He's what?"

"Mrs. Glogauer..."

"Oh, no...dear God, no...please Arthur, don't let it – "

"Mrs, Glogauer, please...sit down."

She will sob and the sad man by her side will hold onto her hand: the hand will be more frail but it will be her hand. Both of them will look old. Old in loss-terms and in experience-terms, not just as a measure of time.

"Now, Mary..." her husband will say. He will try to comfort her, but it will be no use. "Karl knew it could happen," he will say. But she will not hear these words. Not really.

Her face will be drawn and her eyes open wide, staring. Her head will move very slowly side to side, stifling the anguish which craves an outlet.

The man in the uniform, looking very official, will be half-standing behind his desk unable to decide whether to stand completely upright or to sit down. He will regurgitate memorised words, in a soft Midwestern accent redolent of the plains and the cornfields surrounding his hometown. "He would feel nothing," he will say. "It would all be over very quickly."

The old man will ask how.

"Meteor shower," will be the answer. "There was nothing they could do about it."

⚜

The memory came flooding back...

⚜

"Jesus Christ!"

"What is it?"

"Meteors...hundreds of them."

"Captain..." A voice from behind.

"Not now." The captain turns, terror in his eyes, skin drained white. "We've had – "

The crash, the earsplitting noise of metal cracking and buckling inwards; of instrument panels and complex circuitry erupting in showers of glass and sparks; of people screaming and crying; of people running nowhere.

He watches, helpless in his suit, preparing to take density readings on one of the struts outside. He watches but he cannot move.

He sees the captain, clothes and hair billowing flames, screaming until one of the rocks takes him away. He watches the navigator, with a large hole where his chest was, still standing...his face showing no sign of concern or of pain.

Through the hole, he watches the lights flicker on the CPU's myriad panels.

Vomit bubbles into his mouth. He cannot swallow it, it makes him gag. So he opens his mouth and allows it to froth down his chin until it forms a pool above the elastic neck of his suit. His mask steams up and he closes his eyes; the noise and the chaos continue in his brain.

An explosion rocks the ship. He feels the heat, great searing heat, envelop him and he feels himself whisked away. He tries to open his eyes but his brain will not allow it. He crashes into something and the breath is knocked from him momentarily. Then he hears another explosion and a deep sucking noise. Then silence.

When he opens his eyes at last, there is only blackness.

The ship is nowhere to be seen.

⚜

The memory made his heart beat faster…or was it the fact that his air was going? He sniffed and breathed in, almost choking on the smell of vomit, but the air seemed to be okay. But what would it be like if the air were running out?

He breathed in again and thought back to the times when he used to hide under the bedclothes from his mother. Maybe it would be like that.

How much air was there in these tanks anyway? Was it four or six hours?

Six, he hoped.

Four, he thought.

He could not remember.

How long had he been floating like this? He had no way of knowing. Perhaps it was hours, but he forced himself to believe it was only a matter of minutes: perhaps thirty or forty, no more.

"Think about it logically," he said to himself and the universe around him. "The depot knew exactly where we were when it happened so they'll probably have sent another ship by now."

He smiled to himself and stared at the blackness, searching for tell-tale dots of light that would signify a rescue ship.

"I bet it's on its way right now," he said, though the blackness was absolute and totally uncommunicative. "I'm just going to have to stay put and wait."

He stared into the gloom, still searching for that pinprick that would grow into the ship that was going to save him.

"Now," he said to himself, "how long would it take them to reach me?"

How far had they been from the depot? He tried to remember. They had been taking density readings along the Harding Four belt, which was only about two hours from the substation. When should they have reported in?

If the personnel checked the wide range scanning equipment for the ship's blip they would see it wasn't there. But would they check? And, anyway, the ship may still be in one piece — when the hull cracked, pulling him outside, any fires would have been extinguished immediately.

So, if they weren't due to report in for hours yet, and the station could still see the blip, they wouldn't attempt to get in touch until the routine call was overdue.

Suddenly he felt something brush against his back.

He jerked to the side and tried to paddle his way around, but it was no good. And he was using up valuable air in the attempt. Instead he tried to move forward, head over heels.

It still took some considerable effort but, at last, he watched the distant shimmering stars change and he tumbled forward on himself, slowly…until he came face to face with Vincente Carioneri.

He screamed out into his helmet and thrashed his arms and legs wildly.

The universe was staring through the hole in Carioneri's chest while the navigator's eyes stared wide and calm. The man's face looked black, as though it were shadowed, and little black sores, like tiny rosebuds, ran along both of his lips. His outstretched arms floated limply by his side, as though he were trying to fly, and one of his feet was missing.

He whimpered now, trying to back away but knowing that he could not.

The realisation of his own fate suddenly dawned on him. He would never be saved. There would be no rescue ship.

"Please…" he said, pushing the corpse away from him. "Please…"

But it was no use. Finally he decided to pull Carioneri towards him so that he could gain more force. He closed his eyes and grabbed the corpse's shoulders, pulling it near. Then, his eyes still closed tight, almost locked in an embrace with the dead man, he pushed with all of his might. When he moved his arms in front of him he could feel nothing. It seemed to have worked but still he did not open his eyes. Instead, he thought.

He tried to remember when he had first heard of death and what it had meant to him.

It wasn't the sort of thing a father would explain to his child without a request or at least an expressed interest. He couldn't remember.

Perhaps he had always known it. Perhaps the knowledge was passed on in chromosomes, generation to generation. And when the brain worked under parental guidance in a person's early years, the stored data was simply released. Then you knew.

But maybe there was a halfway house, a kind of limbo…a gap between the firmaments of life and death.

Maybe that was where he was now, lost in that halfway house, existing but not existing, alive but yet not alive...

⁂

"Ashes to ashes, dust to dust..."

He looks up into his mother's sorrow. "Don't cry, Mum, please don't cry."

His father looks down and pats the small worried head that stares with concern at his wife as they all stand in an incessant drizzling rain beside the lonely newly-dug grave.

"She'll be alright, son; don't you worry. Nana's gone to Heaven, so we won't be seeing her down here anymore. But she'll be watching over us all – you especially – so don't you worry. Your mum'll be alright."

He looks down at the wooden box and feels the tears well up behind his eyes; his throat feels dry and he has to cough, but he is not exactly sure why he feels this way. Everyone looks so serious, standing in the cemetery in their somber colours and their new hats and their drawer-creased ties.

All around him, the graveyard seems cold and heartless through the December mist. He is frightened and confused, seven years old. "Are we going to leave Nana here, Dad?" he asks.

His father ruffles his son's hair without looking at him. He has his other arm around his wife, who is shaking uncontrollably. His father says, "Shhh..." but he is not sure to whom he is saying it.

"From the earth ye have come," the sad voice drones, "and so shall ye return to the earth."

⁂

But *he* had come from the Earth, too. Did that mean...?

He opened his eyes and, with great relief, he discovered that the dead navigator had drifted away apparently out of sight. He looked around and then saw him, over to the left, still floating. As he kept looking, he saw that the figure was actually still moving, dwindling in size. And then he looked at the diamond-encrusted blackness to either side of the figure—and to either side of himself—and saw that *that* was moving also.

"Oh my God," he said. "It's *me* that's moving!"

He opened his arms wide and tried to flip himself backwards, in the direction he was traveling. At first it didn't seem to do any good but then, on the fourth attempt, he felt himself moving over.

As he turned, watching the distant star clusters change shape, he realised that he would always be up here, floating forever in some nameless part of the galaxy. There was no conceivable reason, he now accepted, for the search party—assuming one had even been sent—to ride around indefinitely looking for crew members who had just *happened* to have their suits on when the meteors struck...and had just *happened* to escape with the air when the hull was breached.

He smacked his lips, smiled calmly and folded his arms. "Face it, Karl old man," he said. "You've had it."

He started to laugh and then jumped at the noise, so strange amidst the blackness.

Was he going mad? Was he finally losing it? Was the oxygen running out after all? He doubted it. Facing up to what appeared to be a certainty had brought a wave of relief.

He was going to die and it was going to be a new experience. He must retain his faculties until the end. He must study it.

Somewhere down there, he suddenly realised — or was it *up* there? — were his parents. He jerked his head up and down: which was it?

"Where the hell *am* I?" he shouted to the memory of Vincente Carioneri.

⚜

"I just don't know where the hell you're at any more," she shouts in desperation, waving her arms in the air as she paces the floor. "You tell me this...you tell me that..."

She stops pacing and kneels beside him. "I tell you, Karl Glogauer, you are one dumb bunny. Dumb!"

She stands again, re-adopting her earlier pose.

"You're dumb because you won't say what you want; you're dumb because you think you owe me something...that you're 'not good enough' for me..." She shakes her head.

In a softer voice, she says, "I love you, Karl."

He stares at her, feels a hurt inside himself.

"I love you and I want to be with you — I want to be with you any way you want...but I do want to be with you." She pauses and looks away from him before adding, in a still softer voice, "always."

He shakes his head, not knowing what to say.

"Please don't hurt me," she says.

⚜

"I won't hurt you, Monica," he shouts to the hard, cold blackness all around him. Just for a second, he thinks he can see her face, etched on a white and shimmering cloud maybe a billion miles away, but it's just the stars laughing at him.

⁂

He sits in his car waiting for her.

She comes out and waves to him, slamming the door behind her.

He starts the engine, hears it purr all around him, mingling with the comforting sounds of London's busy streets.

She jumps in and leans over to give him a kiss. He leans his cheek towards her and accepts the affection with a smile.

As he pulls away from the house in Ladbroke Grove, he feels at one with the universe...at one with it and, somehow, even in control of it.

They both laugh at nothing in particular...and move into the next seconds of their brief time together.

⁂

"Please...please, dear God," he sobbed, his breathing now becoming more and more difficult, gulping down his air as the tears rolled down his cheeks.

"Help me..." he shouted to the stars.

"Kill me," he whispered, "but please don't keep me here waiting."

"There's no use begging, son."

The voice startled him.

"You're in a fix and no amount of pleading will do you any good. No good at all."

"Dad?" He stared at the figure, shaking his head, not really believing.

"You got yourself into this and it's you that's going to have to get yourself out of it."

At first, he wondered what his father was doing without a suit on, and then he realised. Monica appeared by the old man's side and smiled, though it was a smile filled with sadness and regret.

"Why, Karl? Why did you do it?"

Do what? Finish with her? Join the Academy? *Meet* her?

He shook his head but it only made him feel dizzy. The air *was* going after all.

He thought of reasoning with her, asking for her help...for her understanding. But why waste the effort. She didn't exist. And neither did his father...at least not out here. Nothing existed out here.

He watched as the thing that looked like Monica seemed to sit down — though there was no sign of a chair — and then buried her face in her hands.

He tried to turn away but, when he did, Monica and his father had also moved over to his side.

How long left? It must only be a matter of minutes now. He breathed deep the thin air now hissing into the helmet as he scanned the blackness for some small sign of hope. There was none.

Dad shakes his head in the same kind of mock disgust he used to use when he was trying to encourage him. "Come on, son," he says. "That's like looking for a needle in a galaxy-sized haystack. It's time to bite the bullet."

He closed his eyes and tried to calm himself, chest heaving, starting to wheeze at the effort of breathing.

"Yes, come on now, Karl," Mum says bravely. "You know I never wanted you to have any part of this but what's done is done."

He kept his eyes closed and thought back to the cries of the media, the cries of mankind: "…life on other planets!" "…life on Mars!" "…life beyond the solar system!"

"There's no life anywhere," he said to his friend the helmet.
"Oh—"

" —God, Karl: do you believe in God?"
The vicar smiles across the table at the small boy as he stirs his cup of tea.
"Yes I do," the boy replies emphatically.

"But why does he always take the good ones?" his mother says between sobs as she stands beside her mother's grave.

The boy looks on, listening, taking everything in.

"Now, Mary," his father says, comfortingly. "Try not to be bitter. He takes all of us eventually." He holds his wife's hand to his chest, his face a mask of pain.

The boy remembers that face from another time.

He had been showing off his hamster to a visiting cousin when he had accidentally allowed the wooden playrun his father had constructed to fall on its neck. The hamster had been strangely still and unresponsive, its neck all bendy and its eyes vacant and slightly bulging.

He had carried the unmoving creature out into the garden where his father and his uncle were talking. "Daddy," he had said earnestly, "Blinky's hurt. Make him well…please make him well."

It was the first time that he had seen his father cry.

The memory of that time still fresh in his mind, he watches his father cry again, holding onto his mother as a lifetime of bravery seems to peel away. Almost as though she is unaware of anyone else present, she shudders, unashamed, uncaring, as the tears come.

But she is not unaware, he realises. He watches as she grips his father's hand.

He opened his eyes and smiled at his mother. She nodded to him, returning the smile.

"Do you need any help?" she says.

He shook his head.

His father put his arm around his mother and they both shimmered and faded into the blackness, leaving a colour darker for short moments.

Monica stands and moves slowly towards him.

"Let me do it," she says. "It's my —

— privilege."

They are sitting in a restaurant called Break For The Border, *just up from Cambridge Circus. They have been buying books at the shops in Charing Cross Road.*

Monica is keen to demonstrate that they are a partnership. She is opening her purse to get money for another round of Tecate beers.

He puts his hand on top of hers and says, "You don't need to do that."

She frowns at him, puzzled, and says, "Who needs to do anything. I want to do it, that's all. Please don't — "

— stop me," she says.

He smiled and watched her hands reach to either side of his helmet...then lifted his own hands to help her.

"That's better," she says.

"Yes," he agreed. "Better."

It was difficult to speak now. The sound of hissing air had stopped. Everywhere was silent.

He felt rather than heard the sound of the clasps lifting on his helmet.

For a second, he was frightened. But Monica smiled again. He had forgotten how beautiful she was when she smiled. He had forgotten so many things...

He kisses her face as she reaches down between her thighs and guides him.

"Oh...oh God," he says, sinking deep within her, a moist warmth enveloping him.

Monica's head moves back on the pillow and, her eyes closed, she smiles. "Easy baby..." she says. She moves so slowly, so gently...

⚜

"Easy, baby," she says again.

He watched with mild interest—he was suddenly so tired...tired of holding his breath—as she started to lift the helmet. He waited for the jolt as it pulled free from the neck-brace. But no jolt came.

The silence flooded in like a river, silence on silence, infinite peace.

The last thing he saw before he closed his eyes was his helmet, floating by his side...and then—

⚜

She takes his hand and holds it in her own hands. "I want to talk to you," she says.

"Talk to me?" he says. "What about?"

She lifts a curl of blonde hair that has tumbled across her eyes and straightens it back onto her head.

"Well," she answers, thinking. "About what happens next?"

He smiles back at her and brings his free hand to grasp both of hers. "You mean, what happens to us, right?"

She lets out a small chuckle and drops her eyes to watch his hands kneading hers. "Yes," she says. "What happens to us."

Suddenly, he sees her for what she really is and he sees, at the very same instant, what she really means to him.

He has been holding onto the letter from the Academy for over a week now, not knowing what to do. But now it seems obvious. After all, does the world really need another astronaut that badly?

"What about us getting..." He stops deliberately and watches her face lift up, watches the smile spread like sunshine chasing clouds across a summer field.

She raises her eyebrows, urging him to finish.

He smiles and pulls her towards him, laughing.

And then he finishes the sentence.

They stand at the stretch in the face of death,
Delighting in surface change, the glitter of light on waves,
And I roam elsewhere, my body thinking,
Turning toward the other side of light,
In a tower of wind, a tree idling in air,
Beyond my own echo,
Neither forward nor backward,
Unperplexed, in a place leading nowhere.

Theodore Roethke (1908-1963)
Journey to the Interior

There is no death. Only a change of worlds.

Seatlh, Suquamish chief (1786-1866)

Elmer

Less than an hour after he concealed his father's body, Oswald Masylik stared into the early-morning sky and thought of the past.

Thinking of the past was something Oswald had been doing more and more since he had hit fifty-nine, and now, with the big six-oh straddling the horizon of his future like a stormcloud, what had already gone seemed a sight more appealing than what lay ahead.

There are some places where the past seems to sit on the air like a ribbon tangled up around an overhead wire, blowing and fluttering in the wind like it's about to spin off somewhere...but always staying right where it is.

Oswald had heard other folks talk of these special places: sometimes they were triggered off by the wafted scent of a familiar old perfume, sometimes by the shape or coloring of a once-familiar building, and sometimes by a long-ago familiar sound...like a floorboard settling down for the night that sounds just like a throat being cleared by someone you don't see any more.

Oswald Masylik's "place" was a mixture of *all* of these.

For Oswald, the past would always be two things: the first being a sensory amalgam comprising the acrid smell of diesel fumes, the sight of the old aluminum sidings of a thirty-four-ton freight rig, and the unmistakable sound of shifting gears and air brakes; and the second being the memory of the old schoolhouse from his childhood days.

And maybe there was a third thing: the old ravine where he made The Great Discovery.

Out of all the weeks that stacked like building blocks to form the many-roomed mansion of Oswald's early life, one stood out as being special. And that was the week of The Great Discovery.

Looking now out over the one-time barren rockface of the ravine, the events of that week came tumbling back to him.

It was April 1946.

In those days, Oswald was simply "Ozzie." His father was a long-haul driver for the Pacific Intermountain Express Company — or PIE for short — handling the Illinois leg of the ten-man tag-team needed to get freight from Oakland to Chicago.

Ben and Eleanor Masylik and their son lived in a little town called Pecatonica, about twenty miles west along US20 from Rockford.

To say Pecatonica was "little" in those days was kind of underplaying the truth. The fact was that it was tiny. The best example of this was the school.

District School No. 94 was one of the best one-room schools in the country (or so everybody kept on telling the students), with one teacher — Miss Meyer — teaching all of its fifteen-strong, six-grade "Class" of '46 at the same time.

A typical day in that bygone era might have seen Miss Meyer assign a study problem to the seventh grade and then get the first graders busy crayoning. Second graders were then put to work at the blackboard doing arithmetic and the fifth grade were sent into a corner to compose a letter. She might then assign some reading in geography to the sixth grade while she went through homework with the third. There was no fourth grade in 1946, which maybe made things a little easier that year.

The simple fact of the matter, however, was Miss Meyer never seemed flustered by anything she had to do. She would stand there in front of the blackboard as calm as you please, a book open in her hands while she read to one of her grades, one foot standing toe-down behind the other like she was one of those big birds that sleep standing on one leg.

In 1946, Will Jenner and Ozzie were the entire third grade. They were seven years old, reaching impatiently and anxiously towards double figures like kids on a carousel reaching for the brass ring that meant a free ride.

The days leading up to Ozzie's Great Discovery were exceptionally dull ones — that's "dull" in meteorological terms.

The weather was stormy, even for early April, and most recesses saw the students of District School No. 94 confined to the classroom staring out of the long windows as rain lashed down on grass they should be out playing on. The privy was out there, too, so they were all having to work at holding bowels and bladders.

The immediate postwar years were another world as far as kids of the late 1990s were concerned. Most of the kids at District School No. 94 walked to their studies each day — sometimes two or three miles each way — although one or two got lifts from their fathers in beat-up pick-ups and rusting Pontiacs, Mercuries and all manner of other autos with mufflers that sounded like low-flying aircraft.

Pecatonica was not a wealthy town. Not by any means.

Ozzie's mother never learned to drive and his father was away most every weekday so Ozzie's feet were his transport. Will Jenner was the same.

Will had a younger sister, Irene — who was in 1946's first grade — and an older brother, Homer, who worked for a delivery company in Belvidere. Homer was twenty-two years old and the family didn't see much of him since he'd moved away from home.

Irene was a cute kid, with wavy blonde hair and a smile that Shirley Temple would have died for but she drove Will batty, always running up to him when he was talking to Ozzie about comic books or radio shows, asking him things. But, while Ozzie could see how frustrating she was — with her lisp and that wild shriek she had when she was happy — he also kind of envied Will having someone he could talk to if he really needed to.

Ben and Eleanor Masylik had just the one child.

Ozzie's mom used to delight in telling him, while she was ironing her husband's uniform or Ozzie's school shirts, that it meant they could give all of their love to him. But, over in the corner of the room on these occasions, reading the newspaper or listening to the radio, Ben Masylik would add that a good motto was "never make the same mistake twice." Eleanor would glare across at him, and he would just raise his eyebrows and shuffle the newspaper or shake a cigarette out the creased pack in his shirt pocket: a *what did I say?* kind of look that he would always postscript with a wink and a smile to his son when Eleanor, hiding a knowing smile, wasn't looking any more.

This little ritual always made Ozzie laugh, even though he had seen it a hundred or more times.

But the truth was, Ozzie was lonely.

Some of the other kids had pets. Dogs and cats, mostly, though one or two who lived on farms and other smallholdings kind of adopted things like chickens and sheep.

Billy Morrison had a pet pig that went by the name of Lamont (after the guy in *The Shadow* radio show) and Martha Toffel told everyone she had befriended a woodchuck that she called Millie but nobody ever saw it. But that didn't bother Martha because she had a twin sister and the two of them seemed to be together all the time. Ozzie didn't have anybody: no brothers or sisters, and no pets.

Ellie Masylik had an allergy to fur, which made her wheeze like a stalled train, so the idea of keeping cats and dogs was out. And they didn't have a farm or any land to speak of — even though the house was surrounded by woodland — so keeping some other kind of animal was also a nonstarter. Ozzie's mom, who felt mightily guilty about her affliction, said Ozzie could have a bird if he wanted but, somehow, keeping a bird in a cage didn't seem as attractive as having something to take out for a walk.

Then, right at the end of that dismal, overcast week, Northern Illinois got the mother and father (plus a few aunts, uncles and cousins!) of all storms. None of the kids had ever seen anything like it and even the usually placid Miss Meyer seemed a little rattled by all the banging and crashing of the wind against the old schoolhouse and the sight of the privy door pinwheeling across the field before taking off like something out of *The Wizard of Oz*.

And so it was that school let out early that day and all the kids got taken home by Billy's father in Mr. Morrison's old backboard truck, all of them sitting huddled up in a mess of interlinked arms and legs against the back window of the cab, being lashed by the wind and rain and laughing fit to burst.

There were fourteen of them that day — Martha Toffel had stayed home with a temperature — and Will, Irene and Ozzie were the last ones dropped off at the end of the road that split into two and led down one way to the Jenners' house and down to the Masyliks' the other. Right in front of them, an uprooted tree lay across the road.

Mr. Morrison leaned across Billy and rolled down the window. "Can't take you any further. You kids gonna be okay here?"

Ozzie and Will nodded enthusiastically, the wind blowing rain-soaked hair down over their eyes and then whipping it back again. "Sure thing, Mr. Morrison," Will shouted, holding up his sister's tightly clasped hand as evidence.

"Okay," Mr. Morrison said, a note of reluctance in his voice. "You run right on home now and stay indoors," he shouted over the whine of the old truck's engine and the steadily increasing wail of the wind. "It'll blow itself out before too long, but it's my guess we haven't seen the worst of it yet."

Will and Ozzie followed Mr. Morrison's gaze across the flat grassland leading down to the highway. Every now and then they could see pieces of tree whipped up into the sky and just whisked out of sight, and what was left of the trees themselves was bowed right over towards the ground as though they, too, were trying to get out of the storm. It was only a little after one o'clock, but black enough to be near nine at night.

The three kids nodded and Will pulled little Irene close to him, clasping her hand still tighter.

"I'm fwitened," Irene said, her face so screwed up she looked like she was going to start bawling. Will waved to Mr. Morrison's truck as it trundled back up the road and then hunched down by his sister. "There's but a few minutes walk and we'll be home," he said, pulling the collar of her jacket up around her neck and managing to give her a reassuring hug in the process. He turned to Ozzie and nodded with all the gravity that a seven year-old can muster — and that's a mighty lot of gravity — and patted his friend's shoulder.

"You take care, Ozzie," he said.

"You too, Will." Ozzie glanced over at little Irene and couldn't help but smile. "You too," he said. "Look after your brother now, hear?"

Hanging onto Will's left hand, her face suddenly lightened. She had a responsibility, she now realized. Someone other than herself to worry about.

"I will," she said somberly, suddenly grabbing hold of her brother's arm with her free hand. But her words were lost in the wind.

A couple of minutes later, over the tree and running through every puddle he could see, Ozzie turned around to wave but Will and Irene were gone. For a few seconds, he just stood there looking at the distant horizon. Clouds were roiling in clumps, tumbling over each other like playful puppies. About midway, on the flats, uprooted bushes were rushing across the grassland like tumbleweed, bouncing occasionally when they hit uneven ground. Now and again one of them would flash high into the air, pirouetting madly before falling back.

Ozzie turned back to the track that led home and started to run again, tucking his chin deep into his chest to preserve the ability to breathe. He could hear the high-pitched whine of the wind now, like the siren attached to the old schoolhouse to warn of a possible nuclear strike.

He was suddenly scared. Maybe that's what this was. Maybe it wasn't a storm at all. In a strange way, the sound of his own whimper comforted him.

The first leg of the dusty track that eventually lead to the wood-frame house he shared with his parents wound flat for a couple hundred yards beyond the fallen tree before curving to the right, overlooking a steep ravine, a place of barren rock and scrawny bush skeletons, and up to a tree-lined crest. Looking up briefly, his legs pistoning forward, feet occasionally catching lumps of rock and clumps of grass, Ozzie could see that some of those trees had gone.

Ozzie knew, staring into the wind through watering eyes, that the track dipped sharply and without protection in an ambling curve around the mouth of the valley and several square miles of flat and exposed scrubland. That single thought gave him additional cause for concern when the wind bent a tree alongside him all the way to the ground before uprooting it entirely and sending it cartwheeling across the track, where it suddenly disappeared out of sight down into the ravine.

The surge of wind stopped him almost dead in his tracks and he bent even further forward, noting as he did so that his body was virtually horizontal to the ground. He could have stretched out a hand and touched the grass beneath him.

With renewed effort, Ozzie reached the crest and fell down beside a stump of tree. Pushing his body in against the bark, he turned his face into his chest and gasped for air, glancing back the way he had come.

That's when he saw it.

Coming out of the clouds in the distance, lightning flashing all around it, seeming even to be originating from it, came what looked like a cross between one of the planets illustrated in Miss Meyer's science books and a giant mudball, like the ones Ozzie used to make with Will Jenner when they were both little kids out in the Jenners' backyard.

Without even realizing he was doing it, Ozzie raised his right arm like he was going to salute the thing, lifted it so that the forearm was almost over his eyes, lifted it so that it might protect him when that thing hit him square on, pounding him into a million zillion bits of bone and gristle. All serious thought vanished: he did not think of escape or of hiding or of the pain the thing was going to cause him. All he thought of was…where did this thing come from? It wasn't a bomb and it wasn't an aircraft: it came from *out there*.

Out there!

Just the words filled Ozzie with awe. The thing was some kind of comet or meteor, hell-bent on hitting the Earth after spending — what? After spending how long out in space? Maybe this thing was older than the Earth itself. Maybe it had been flying around out there when Jesus had trudged up the hill with His cross…maybe it had been zipping around when the dinosaurs had idly looked up, wondering at the high-pitched whine as they munched the treetops.

He watched as the planet/comet/meteor spiraled and glimmered, shimmered and twirled, huge forks of light glancing across its gnarled surface.

He didn't have time to consider moving, to think about shielding himself or flattening out against the ground. All he could do was stare at it, leaning over at the very last second as it came hurtling by, feeling its heat, smelling its surface — a mix of old vegetables, the inside of aluminum cans and clothes fresh from a windy day on the washing line out back.

At the very last second, as the thing hurtled down towards him, Ozzie covered his face and shouted, although he could hear only the sound of the high-pitched whine, making sure he kept a small gap to see through.

The thing filled his vision then, a seething mass of ridges and knolls, of troughs and valleys, promontories and clumps of what looked like thick, stringy hair, whorls of gray and blue and black, eyeless sockets formed of silt and dirt and mud, made hard by time and the airless cold of outer space.

No sooner was it in front of him than it was past, missing him by what seemed like only a few yards, its whine like a police siren passing him by and moving off. Out of the corner of his eye, Ozzie saw the gigantic mudball strike the ground to his right, just above the ravine. For a few seconds nothing seemed to happen and then, still twirling around and spinning, grass and dust and dirt billowing into the sky like a curtain, the thing just rose up again, still spinning, already growing smaller.

It was only then that the ground beneath him shook and Ozzie jumped up to his knees fearing that it was going to open up and swallow him.

He jumped up and down, jumped sideways, first one way and then the other, swapping feet, holding the one foot in the air, arms stretched out, watching the ground, waiting for the first splits to appear. But nothing happened. He landed from one of the jumps and stayed put, both feet on the ground, spread wide, half crouched like a mountain cat waiting to spring away.

He looked to his right, up after the mudball, and squinted into the settling dust. He could just make out the shape of the meteor through the haze, growing steadily smaller, still spinning and twirling, up into the sky and back into the depths of space.

Ozzie staggered a little, feeling like a freshman sailor on the deck of his first ship. He plopped to the ground against the tree stump and waited, though he had no idea what exactly he was waiting for.

The wind had dropped. Now there was only a pleasant breeze.

Ozzie looked up and saw a slight break in the clouds, a tear in all that gray and darkness through which gold rays shone. Okay, it was only a slim break but it *was* a break.

Dust was settling all around him, settling on his outstretched arms like bathroom powder. He looked down at himself, checking to make sure there were no tears in his jeans or sweater. Everything seemed intact. Then he looked down at the ground to his right, where the meteor thing had hit before bouncing out to Alpha Centauri and all points north, and he gasped.

There was a thick gouge out of the earth that looked like the heaviest airplane in the history of aviation had just taken off carrying the entire contents of Fort Knox in its belly. There was a deep runnel starting just a few yards from where Ozzie was sitting and carrying on to just a few feet shy of where the land dropped away into the ravine.

Plants — most of them weeds — had been either crushed or uprooted; a bush seemed to have been torn in two, one half sitting same as ever and the other half gone out of sight; and the whole area of ground seemed indented, as though a boulder had been rolled to the ravine and just let go over the edge. But most of all, the ground was torn, soil and dirt chavelled into deep gouges and tears, the grass and brush razed away like skin peeled off, exposing the glistening surface of blood and muscle that lay beneath. Ozzie stared.

Something was happening to that ground.

He blinked and rolled to one side, thinking maybe it was the light from that gap in the clouds or maybe his close brush with death and destruction had left him a little light-headed. But no, what he'd thought was happening was still happening, no matter which angle he looked from or how many times he rubbed his eyes.

Keeping his body as close to the ground as he could manage, Ozzie crawled forward on his stomach, pulling the rest of him along behind like he was some kind of human snake. When he got to just a few inches away from where the comet must have made its glancing blow, he stopped and watched.

On the ground in front of him, covering the grooves and runnels and smashed earth, lying up alongside and across the bruised ground, were what looked like the amoeba things Miss Meyer had talked about one time in her introduction to biology, all flattened out and frilly around the edges. They looked like a cross between a frying egg, a wad of gum and the bald head of Elmer Fudd, the little guy who was always the butt of Bugs Bunny's antics in the cartoons they showed on Saturday mornings at the movie theater over in Rockford. The things were a kind of dull, light brown, like a Band-Aid strip, and they seemed to undulate when they moved along, their sides rippling.

Creeping nearer, Ozzie stared.

The things seemed to be merging themselves onto the chavelled soil. They would shuffle along, their sides rolling up and down, and then they would stop and…and they would just kind of disappear. There was no other way to describe it.

There seemed to be hundreds of the things, each one just a few inches in diameter. As he looked around the ruined path left by the comet, Ozzie saw that the things seemed to be congregating at the edges of the swath, then they would stop and disappear. Seconds later, more would reach the edge of *that* spot and then they would disappear. And the piece of ground that they had covered, momentarily smooth, would change.

Ozzie gasped in astonishment. "Wow!" he said to the gently soughing wind and the upturned earth. The pieces of earth recently covered by the things had started sprouting grass stalks, each shoot slowly nuzzling its way free and standing proud.

He got to his feet and moved still closer, bending over where the things were working—he supposed "working" was a reasonable description of what they were doing. The grass coat destroyed by the comet was being replaced.

He looked up away from where he was standing and allowed his eyes to travel along the comet's graze to the edge of the ravine. The width of the path between the untouched grass was narrowing. Soon there would be no sign of the comet having been there at all, save for a gently rolling indent of the grassland.

Already, the section directly beneath him had met in the middle. And as the graze was healed over, the process seemed to speed up, with the amoeba things having less of a distance to travel in order to carry out what could only be termed a healing or restoration process. Now, Ozzie saw, the ground was recovering some of its earlier greenness, albeit with a distinctly hollowed-out appearance. It looked for all the world as Ozzie imagined a piece of ground might look after something huge had been removed from beneath it.

With the whole process having taken only what seemed to have been a minute or two, there were few of the things left. Those that remained settled on small areas of exposed soil, some of these areas no bigger than a dime or a nickel, and simply faded from view. Then Ozzie saw one of the things shuffling across some recently "re-seeded" grass heading for a thin welt of exposed soil.

His heart pounding in his chest, Ozzie tentatively reached out his hand and, grimacing, tenderly took hold of the thing between thumb and forefinger. He was prepared for pain, maybe a stinging sensation or some kind of shock, but there was nothing. What did happen was that his finger and thumb suddenly felt quite numb.

He placed the thing on the palm of his other hand and watched it closely. For a few seconds, Ozzie thought that it was dead, that the sudden pressure of his fingers had somehow traumatized it, but then, with a flick-and-swirl of its tiny skirts, it shuffled slowly across his palm towards his fingers.

"Whatcha doin' fella?" he said softly, moving his free hand beneath the fingers of the other so that the thing would plop to safety when it reached the tips of his outstretched fingers. There was no answer, of course.

Once on its new surface, the thing simply trundled its way towards Ozzie's wrist, apparently exploring.

Ozzie looked up at the sky and saw that the sun was definitely now out. The ground in front of him was now completely healed. There was no sign of any of the amoeba-things.

He looked down at the thing on his hand and smiled as it continued to swish its sides as it moved slowly over his wrist. Then he placed the other hand beneath his arm and allowed the thing to crawl back onto his palm.

"You sure are a wittle wascal," Ozzie chuckled, trying to mimic Fuddsy's voice. "I'm gonna call you Elmer," he whispered, cupping both hands, ensuring that the thing had no way to escape. Then he set off for home.

⁂

Ozzie had expected his mother to be full of excitement about the comet—after all, she must have seen it—but she said nothing, although she was pleased to see him home safely.

"That was quite a storm," she said, looking out of the window. "But it looks like it's clearing up just fine now."

Ozzie nodded. He had trapped the amoeba-thing in his right hand and that hand was now thrust deep into his pocket.

"You go get washed up now," his mother said. As Ozzie turned and ran out of the kitchen, she called after him: "Supper will be ready in a few minutes."

In the sanctity of his room, Ozzie carefully placed Elmer into a glass bowl he had been using to store marbles. Across the top of the bowl, he placed a thin sheet of cardboard. As an afterthought, he used his penknife to cut three small holes in the cardboard in case he suffocated his new friend. Then he placed a carton of toy soldiers on top of the cardboard for added security, making sure that the carton didn't obliterate the life-preserving holes. When he was satisfied that the thing was both safe and secure, he went downstairs.

That night, it being a Friday, Ozzie's father was home. But there had been a problem at the depot. One of the drivers scheduled to take a rig out on Saturday had called in sick so Ben had to do the drive from Moline across to Chicago. It had all been arranged, he explained to a disappointed Eleanor while Ozzie lay on the floor reading comic books. Tom Nelson was due to take a rig from Iowa City across to the West Coast and so he was going to take Ben down to Moline, drop him off and continue on to Iowa City where he would pick up at the PIE depot there. Ben reckoned he would be back late on Saturday night and that they would at least have the Sunday together as a family. Unaware of the fine points of this conversation — or of the silent glances and nods between his parents — it was a surprise when Ben Masylik suddenly announced that he could use a little company.

"You feel up to that, Ozzie?" Ben inquired, his face looking serious.

"Huh?!" Ozzie was amazed. He loved to sit in the big rigs and he had never been out in one when it was actually moving. "You bet!" he said, getting to his knees.

"Your father has to be up and away early, now," Eleanor announced as she stacked clean dishes by the sink. "Means there'll be no time for dawdling around."

"Yes, ma'am!" Ozzie said. "I mean, no ma'am," he corrected himself. He thought about reminding his father about company policy stating that drivers' kids couldn't travel with them on the rigs but decided against it. Nevertheless, he was reassured that his father wouldn't be getting into trouble when Ben Masylik explained that he had had a word with the crew foreman and, seeing as how Ben was helping them out of a tight spot, it was going to be okay for Ozzie to make the trip.

Even better, Ozzie thought. It's official.

Up to bed earlier than usual that evening to make sure he was rested for the 3 AM. get-up the next morning, Ozzie was surprised to see that the holes in the piece of cardboard over the bowl containing the amoeba-thing had disappeared. The cardboard was as good as new. For a second, fearing that his friend from the comet had suffocated, panic set in. Ozzie lifted cardboard off the bowl and reached inside. He breathed a long sigh of relief when Elmer responded to his prodding finger.

"So, you don't need no air, then," Ozzie whispered to the thing as it trundled around his palm. "That makes things a little easier anyways," he said. He had been wondering how he was going to carry Elmer around with him when he and his father went on their adventure the next morning. The fact that the thing didn't seem to need oxygen the way humans did meant that he would be able to carry it in one of the jars his mom used to store her homemade jam.

Feeling that life sure had a way of making things turn out okay sometimes, Ozzie returned Elmer to the bowl, ensuring that the cardboard and the carton of soldiers were firmly in place, and got ready for bed.

The following morning, Ozzie felt like he hadn't been to bed at all. It was only the prospect of the forthcoming adventure with his father that finally woke him up sufficiently to have some breakfast. And even then, he almost forgot to take Elmer. He finally remembered only when Tom Nelson's car's headlights washed across the still-drawn kitchen curtains, when he made a big thing out of going to the bathroom before they set off. Amidst the confusion of Ben and Eleanor shaking their heads in frustration while they greeted Tom that Ozzie snuck out of the kitchen with one of his mother's carefully-washed screw-cap jars from the cupboard beneath the sink. Minutes later, the jar safely tucked into his jacket pocket with its passenger intact and apparently healthy and happy, Ozzie climbed into the back of Tom Nelson's Pontiac and they set off for Moline.

The trip down was fine.

Ozzie sat quietly, hunched up on the back seat, watching the landscape drift by and listening to his father trade stories with Tom Nelson about guys at the depot and workloads and how summer couldn't come soon enough. They'd had their fill of the winter, which in 1945/46 had seemed to go on forever. Hauling the big rigs around on roads slick with rain and sometimes sleet took an awful lot of concentration, Tom explained over his shoulder to Ozzie. Ozzie's father seemed to agree wholeheartedly but Ozzie saw him give some kind of shake of the head to Tom, after which Tom went to great lengths to say just how great a job this was and how he wouldn't be caught dead doing anything else. Ozzie's father said it was amen to that, whatever that meant.

Having left the house at a little after 4:30, the trio hit the outskirts of Moline just after eight o'clock, after stopping for coffees and donuts at Bohlman's Cafe, one of the PIE drivers' favorite stopovers, in Sterling. The place was little more than a shack at the side of the road but the parking area was filled with eighteen and twenty-four wheelers, sitting ticking and clicking in the early-morning gloom. Ozzie sniffed in the smell of hot metal and diesel fumes and the scent made him feel like he could fly.

Inside the cafe all you could see was peaked caps, smiling faces and steam from the back room. The place smelled of cigarette smoke, frying bacon and hot coffee. Ozzie couldn't decide whether he liked this smell better than the parking lot or the other way around.

Waving bye to Tom Nelson made Ozzie feel a little wistful suddenly and his father must have sensed it. "Okay, trusty navigator," he said to Ozzie in a loud voice, wrapping his arm around the boy's shoulders. "Let's go get ourselves a rig."

And that's exactly what they did. Eventually.

Delays crossing the Rockies through bad weather had put hours onto the schedule and the rig that Ozzie's father was due to drive to Chicago didn't arrive until almost one o'clock. It was another hour after that that they finally set out from the depot, Ozzie loaded up with candy bars and comic books bought for him by different men in the depot, all of whom had treated him like he was the President or something. But when they pulled out onto US6, Ozzie's father muttered darkly.

When Ozzie asked what the matter was, Ben Masylik pointed to the sky. One side was almost pitch-black and the other was sunny. Ozzie guessed straightaway that they weren't heading for the sunshine and, sure enough, the road wound round to the right and all that was ahead of them was dark.

The rain started almost immediately, a drizzle at first but soon building up to a full-scale downpour.

With the windshield wipers going, making a squeaky sound like chalk on a blackboard (which Ozzie didn't much care for), reading his *Action* comic was pretty much out of the question concentration-wise, even though the story about Superman and two magicians called Hocus and Pocus looked like being a doozy. So he chewed on a *Tootie Frootie* bar and took out the jar containing Elmer.

"What you got there?" Ozzie's father asked.

At that point, they were about six miles from a place called Atkinson, which Ozzie thought was a strange name for a town...until he thought about Pecatonica. Ozzie had seen the signpost.

There were to be lots of occasions down the years when he would wonder whether what happened next was a direct result of his pulling the jar out into the open, momentarily distracting his father's attention from the road ahead. But each time he was to think that, he would discount it.

The road wound sharply to the right, almost a hairpin bend, and the rain was hitting the rig's windshield like someone had a hose trained on it.

Before Ozzie could think of how to answer that question without having to tell his father about the meteor and the way the little amoeba-things had repaired all the grassland, the road was going off one way and they were heading on another.

Rocks added to the situation, or detracted from it, rocks freshly loosened by the rain and fallen down onto the road..

Ozzie watched his father holding onto the steering wheel and shifting down the gears; he felt a sudden lurch and then another, and his father said, as calm as could be, "Blowouts."

He looked across at exactly the same instant as Ben Masylik looked down at him, just a brief look — couldn't have been more than a second or two — but it contained a lifetime of sadness, regret and guilt. Then he looked back at the road and gritted his teeth.

As Ozzie's father slammed a foot down hard on the brake pedal, he reached out with his right hand and pulled the boy close to him, folding his face into his jacket. Ozzie could smell the sweet aroma of perspiration and soap, of cigarette smoke and body-warmed material. The last thing that Ozzie saw before he nuzzled into his father's jacket was the edge of the road, approaching fast, and a steep drop behind a two-rail fence. Right in the middle of that fence — and right in the middle of the windshield — Ozzie also saw a tall pole with some kind of sign on it.

His face in the jacket, Ozzie felt the rig jerk once, heard the sound of breaking glass, heard — and felt — his father grunt, felt the back of the rig jackknifing around behind them, turning the cab over to the right, and then there was a sudden weightlessness, just for a few seconds, and then he was pulled by some unseen and unimaginable force from his father's arm against something solid, just for another second, and then he fell back against the seat and down onto what had to be the floor — he had his eyes closed but, jerking out his hand, he felt his father's foot pressed down on a pedal.

There were a lot of crashing sounds all around, and Ozzie was buffeted up beneath the front dash, and then everything went quiet. Just the sound of rain hitting the cab and the distant hiss of water on hot metal.

Then just one more sound.

Ozzie listened, hardly daring to open his eyes in case they were still falling through space and were about to hit some valley bottom a hundred miles down at the other side of the fence. He could feel the coldness of outside.

The sound he could hear was coming from his father.

Now Ozzie opened his eyes.

He was still lying on the floor, the bench seat behind his back and his face pressed against the rubber mat. All he could see were his father's feet, still pressed down on the pedals and trapped beneath a thin sheet of flooring that had peeled back.

The feet were not moving.

Ozzie wanted to say, *Hey, it's okay Dad, you can take your feet off the pedals now: we've stopped,* but something deep down inside told him that it wouldn't do any good.

He struggled to his knees. Parts of his body groaned at the movement and he felt a couple of sharp jabs in his back but it didn't feel much different from when he crashed his soapbox into a tree over by the creek last year. And he was still around to tell the tale of *that* one.

Ben Masylik was lying back on the seat, his head slumped forward onto his chest. Ozzie saw straight away that there was blood. In fact, there was a lot of blood, and it seemed to be increasing as he watched.

His father must have sensed him reaching forward because his father's head moved. It was a slow and precise movement, and, when Ben Masylik's head was in a position where he could actually see his son, he let his eyes do the rest. They looked sleepy.

"Dad, you okay?"

Ozzie shuffled forward and took hold of his father's hand.

The eyes closed, slowly, and then opened again just as slowly. "Go get help," he said. The voice sounded like a cross between a whisper and the hoarse croak you got after a bad head cold. Ozzie noticed that the flow of blood seemed to increase with the words.

"You're hurt, Dad." Ozzie realized how ridiculous that must sound. His father had probably worked that fact out all by himself.

The eyes closed and opened again, this time more slowly...like they didn't really want to open at all: they just wanted to close up for good and take Ozzie's father off into a nice deep sleep where the pain wasn't there any more.

Ozzie reached across and lifted his father's head.

The piece of windshield fell out of Ben Masylik's throat and slid down his chest. As it moved, a thin spout of blood sprayed up into the air. It was only then that Ozzie realized the windshield had gone and they were covered in pieces of glass, some of them large but most of them tiny shards that crunched under his knees.

"Dad!"

Ben looked at his son with a profound sadness. His mouth started to move. *Get out,* the mouth said without any sound, the eyes drooping closed again. He lifted a shaking hand and moved it to his neck. Just before the hand covered the wound, Ozzie saw just how bad things really were.

Ben Masylik's neck looked like someone had taken a saw to it. There was blood everywhere, some of it spurting — even now, around his hand — and some of it just seeping out, in tiny waves.

Ozzie clenched his eyes tight and then opened them again.

He's dying, a tiny voice said in the back of his mind. *He's dying like they die in the western movies and in the* Mr. District Attorney *comic books, only this time it's your dad who's doing the dying…and my, isn't there a lot of blood.*

Ozzie took hold of his father's free hand and almost gasped at the coldness of it. It felt clammy and frozen, already dead. Even at seven years old, and without so much as a First Aid certificate to his name, he knew that his father would not last until Ozzie could get out and bring help. He patted the hand and said, "You'll be okay, Dad." His father's slow and gentle smile made him turn away.

Then he saw the jar.

It had rolled up against his father's door. He must have dropped it in the crash. Ozzie leaned across his father's knees and picked it up.

Ozzie let go of his father's hand and ignored the way it simply flopped down onto the seat. He quickly unscrewed the cap and tipped the amoeba thing into the palm of his hand.

"Got a job for you, Elmer," Ozzie whispered. Was it his imagination or did the thing actually seem to be listening? Certainly, it wasn't moving, which it usually did when it was given a brief moment of freedom.

"You got to fix up my dad," he said.

Then, being careful not to drop the creature, he leaned over his father. As he pressed on his father's legs, reaching around to the neck wound, Ben Masylik whispered, "Eleanor."

Very carefully, holding the amoeba thing tightly in his right hand, Ozzie lifted his father's hand from the wound. It was no consolation that the spray of blood seemed weaker now.

Ozzie placed Elmer on the gaping gash and moved his hand away.

For a few seconds nothing seemed to be happening at all—in fact, Elmer seemed not to know what to do, but just sat there or stood there…or whatever it was it did. But then the creature seemed to ebb and flow, to contract and expand. Ozzie leaned down closer so he could see what was happening.

It seemed that Elmer's underbelly was being pushed into the wound like clay into a mold. The process lasted only a few seconds, and then the amoeba thing stretched itself out thinly across the neck like a membrane, its edges continuing that same fluid rippling movement. Soon even that stopped and there was no movement at all. In fact, as he looked so closely that his nose was almost touching his father's neck, Ozzie could see no trace of the creature at all. But best of all, there was no sign of the wound.

Ozzie moved back on his haunches and took hold of his father's hand again. It didn't seem to feel as cold.

Ben Masylik raised his other hand and lifted it to his neck where he rested it on the spot that, just a few seconds ago, Elmer had worked its wonders. He opened his eyes.

"Ozzie?"

"I'm here, Dad."

"Are you...are you okay?" Ben moved his head around and looked straight at his son. The eyes seemed brighter now, seemed to contain life.

"I'm fine," Ozzie said. "A little bruised is all."

Ben smiled and closed his eyes. "Good," he said. Then he slept.

Ozzie considered lighting one of the emergency flares he found in the compartment beneath the dashboard but decided it wasn't necessary — after all, it wasn't completely dark yet and the road up above the ravine was well traveled. And anyway, he didn't know how to light them.

He got out of the cab and crawled back up the ravine to the road, the rain still lashing down on him, waving his arms when he got to the top like he was trying to take off. The first car he saw also saw him, swerved a little and pulled in at the side of the road a few yards ahead.

⁂

The events which filled rest of that afternoon kind of got watered down over the years.

Ozzie's father said that he was traumatized, which was probably right.

The truth of the matter was that the man — a Mr. Ward Henshaw from Princeton — drove Ozzie into Atkinson where the sheriff called an ambulance and everyone went back out to the scene of the wreck. By five in the afternoon, Ben Masylik was sitting up in bed in Geneseo District Hospital looking for all the world like he could climb a mountain, although two thick plaster dressings on his forehead and newly-shaved scalp suggested that wouldn't be a great idea.

Eleanor arrived at a little after eight o'clock, given a lift by one of the men from PIE who seemed almost as concerned for Ozzie's father's condition as anyone else. Turned out that the rig wasn't too badly damaged. PIE had an empty rig out at the site before midnight and the load was on its way again by six AM. Nothing damaged and all present and correct.

In the hustle and bustle, the people at the hospital had removed Ben's clothing and it had been thrown into the trash. While it had caused a few raised eyebrows on the part of the doctor and nurse attending Ben's wounds, the sheer amount of blood on the shirt had been ignored. And why not? There were just two gashes on Ben's head and both of them had been sutured. There didn't seem to be any other injuries to speak of...although, while he was drifting under the anesthetic, Ben had rambled on about his neck being sawn almost completely through. This did cause a couple of smiles. But not from Ben's son who was quickly shooed out into a large waiting area containing a big table littered with copies of *Life* magazine and *The Saturday Evening Post*.

Flicking through the bright pages of a *Post* and keeping one eye on the door behind which his father slept, Ozzie decided to keep quiet about the amoeba-thing. Telling everyone seemed like it would cause more problems than it would solve.

And he maintained that silence all through his father's life.

Ben Masylik had a good life and a long one. In fact, there were times when Ozzie for one thought it was maybe just a little too good and too long. Nothing ever seemed to ail Ben...although, inexplicably, he took to sitting outside a lot after the accident, simply staring into the night sky, watching the occasional comet or shooting star hurtle through the gloom.

Eleanor died quietly in her sleep in 1996, by which time Ozzie was long gone from Pecatonica, having moved away to Forest Plains in 1959 where he was now happily living the life he had made for himself. Ozzie's mom had fought the cancer that ravaged her body but in the end it simply overpowered her. Ozzie's father said to him, quietly, that maybe if cancers could think, this one might just recognize that Eleanor Masylik had been a worthy opponent. Ozzie thought that was a nice thought.

Ben had seemed to be okay. Ozzie stayed for a few days after the funeral, quiet days during which — overlooked by the ornate urn containing Eleanor's cremated remains — Ben spent long hours going through drawers and wardrobes, marveling at each new or just forgotten discovery of his wife, sniffing (when he thought his son couldn't see him) at notes she had left or clothes she had neatly folded...all in an effort to recapture, albeit briefly, the scent of her fingertips or the lingering perfume of her warmth. But the time came that Ozzie had to go back to his own home, though he asked his father to come back with him...even if it were only for a visit.

But, no, Ben wouldn't think of leaving Pecatonica.

Then, less than a week later, Ozzie answered the doorbell to discover his father standing on the other side of the screen door, looking more frail than he had ever looked in his life.

Beside him on the floor stood a small valise.

In the crook of his left arm he held the urn containing Eleanor's ashes.

Ben nodded and, seeming to draw breath in from every corner of his body, announced, "I'm going now, Ozzie. I just came to say good-bye."

"Going?" Ozzie said, pushing open the screen door. "Going where?"

Ben drew breath in, head shaking slightly, and for a second Ozzie thought the old man was just going to fall down right where he stood.

Ozzie helped his father into the house, hoisting the old battered valise carefully only to discover it was so light it might well have been blown inside by a stray gust of wind.

Minutes later, lying on the sofa in his son's lounge, Ben Masylik was fading fast. "Take it easy, Dad," Ozzie told him. "Just get your breath."

"No time," Ben Masylik said. "I know what you did, son."

"What I did? What I did when?"

"The thing"—he patted the side of his neck—"it told me."

Ozzie felt a shudder build up around the back of his shoulders.

"Sit down, son."

Ozzie sat.

"Everything makes sense now," Ben Masylik said, his voice little more than a whisper. He gave out a little chuckle. "All those evenings I'd sit out there on the porch, staring up into space." Ben shook his head. "I was looking for some sign…some sign from out there."

"Out there?" Ozzie leaned forward and rested his hand on his father's knee. "What are you talking about, Dad?"

Ben put a finger to his mouth. "No time for questions," he said softly. "Just let me speak."

Ozzie nodded and settled back in the chair.

And so Ben Masylik explained about the endless blackness and the swirling planets, whispered of the cold journey on the meteor. Then he told of how the meteor grazed a large colorful planet, and how the thing that his son had placed on his neck all those years ago had been tumbled off onto the ruined ground. There had been many of them, Ben explained, but only one of them had been unable to find something to repair… something to put right.

"Thanks to you," Ben said, interrupting his own story, "and thanks to a couple of blown tires on a hairpin bend and a careless driver too intent on looking after his passenger, it didn't have too long to wait.

"And so it's been repairing ever since," Ben continued, "putting right anything that happened to go wrong or even looked like it might go wrong. Kind of like shoring up weak beams in an old mineshaft.

"It fixed cells and blood flows, straightened and strengthened brittle bones, massaged strained muscles." He rubbed his head briefly and let his arm flop down to his side. "Even looked after my follicles," he added, with just a trace of a smile. "My father was bald as a coot, and his father before him." Ben pointed at Ozzie. "And if you didn't see fit to grow the half-dozen hairs you still got near on down to your waist before swirling them around your ears, folks'd see that you too was pretty much shiny up top."

Ben shook his head and chuckled, and then his face took on an expression altogether more serious. "But there are some things that get broke that *nobody* can fix. Not even the little doodad you put on my neck."

"Elmer," Ozzie said.

His father frowned.

"I called it 'Elmer.'"

Ben licked his lips tiredly. "Well, the time came when your mother died that…that I just didn't want to carry on. It wasn't so much a case of breaking a leg or pulling a muscle or cells splitting every which way…it was a case of me simply wanting to close up the shop and go home."

"But you *are* home," Ozzie said, pointing down at the floor. "This is your home, or it could be."

"No, your mom is my home," Ben said, though Ozzie had to lean a little further forward to catch the words. "She was my easy chair; my cool breeze in the summer and my fireside in the winter. Fact is," he added, a single tear brimming from each eye, "I can't go on. Don't want to go on.

"And that's something your doodad *can't* fix: a busted heart."

Ozzie knelt down beside the sofa and took hold of his father's hand between his own.

"I guess that was when it spoke to me…in here." Ben tapped his head with his free hand. "Asked what was happening…though it didn't do it in those words, of course. It did it…" He paused and frowned. "Heh, I don't know how in tarnation it did do it, but it did. Pictures, sounds…" He shook his head.

"And then it told me all about what happened. And how it, too, wanted to go home."

Ozzie started in amazement. "Back into space?"

"No, home is where the heart is, son, and the heart is where your loved ones are and where your friends are. Applies to every living thing. Now, we don't have a lot of time left to us," he said, struggling into a sitting position. "Here's what you have to do."

Ozzie listened.

At first he was astonished.

At first he refused.

Then refusal became reluctance; and reluctance became "maybe." And that's when he knew he was going to do it. No matter how strange the request might seem, he was going to go through with it. He was going to go through with it because he had just said "maybe" to his father…the way his father and his mother used to say "maybe" to him, back when, all those years ago, he had asked if he could stay up to listen to a show on the radio or have an extra dime's allowance to buy a new comic book. He knew—and he remembered—"maybe" was just a delayed-action version of "yes."

Ben Masylik died sometime between 10:45 that same day and 5 AM the next.

He died someplace between Bloomington—where Ozzie had pulled in at an all-night diner because his father had seen the trucks parked out in the lot—and Rockford, where they stopped for gas with the first rays of autumn sunlight bathing the pumps in the filling station. The way Ozzie had it figured, his father had died soon after the truckstop, just upped and drifted away—the urn containing the last remains of his beloved Eleanor nestled beneath his arm—with the familiar smells of the old rigs calling him home stronger than ever.

Although the final few miles out on Highway 20 to Pecatonica were driven in silence, it seemed to Ozzie that the inside of the car was awash with the sounds and smells of his youth.

The old turnoff down to his parents' house looked the same as ever, but somehow, on this morning, it looked extra-special. Standing there on the early-morning roadside beside his car, Ozzie couldn't help but feel that if he ran down that left-hand fork, he'd see his father and mother standing waiting for him. Couldn't help but feel that, if he turned around real quick, he'd see a seven-year-old Will Jenner creeping up behind him, breath held, arms and clawed hands at the ready to squeeze his sides. But Ozzie knew that Will wouldn't be there if he looked...but maybe he would be if he didn't. So he didn't look. He left him be, creeping forever in his memory.

Ben Masylik's neck looked like a mountain cat had got a hold of him and been interrupted. The only good thing was that there was no blood. The amoeba-thing had waited until Ben was gone before it detached itself. Ozzie pulled the old man clear of the door and laid him gently on the ground. He stood the urn right next to his father's arm, actually considering wrapping it around the urn before deciding that was maybe just a little ghoulish. Then he took the rock-hammer out of the trunk.

Elmer was sitting—or standing: Ozzie still couldn't figure out which—on his father's checked shirt pocket, looking just as sprightly and fit as it did all those years ago. He placed the creature gently into a small plastic bag and placed that in his jacket pocket. Then he lifted his father onto his shoulder, placed the urn beneath his arm, grabbed hold of the rock hammer and set off for the edge of the ravine.

The way down was a little difficult and Ozzie half expected to hear a car pull up and someone shout down to him

Hey, you need a hand with that dead body, mister?

but no cars appeared and no voices called. Only the wind and the insects and the birds made a chorus of sound that seemed somehow wholly appropriate.

The whole job took around about an hour.

Scattering his mother's ashes over the body took less than a minute.

The hardest part was breaking up the rock; pulling enough stones out of place to expose a suitable area to conceal the old man; putting them back seemed a whole lot easier. He watched his father's body grow smaller as the rocks were carefully replaced to ensure maximum coverage.

Then he removed the plastic bag from his pocket.

He took Elmer out of the bag and nestled it in his hand. "Hey, wittle wascal," he said, "how you doing?" He hadn't expected an answer.

But there had been an open blister on the palm of his hand, caused by wielding the hammer, and the amoeba-thing immediately folded itself across it.

Then the world opened up wide inside Ozzie Masylik's head.

He saw/felt/heard/smelled the vastness of space.

He understood — as if he'd ever doubted it — the power of friendship and the security of belonging.

And he learned the power and wonder of watching the future unfold before him in a swirl of color and sound and texture and aroma and taste.

He looked down at his hand and saw Elmer detach itself from the blister. Reaching out, he placed the creature on the freshly split rocks and watched it scurry along a seam amidst the dust.

Then it disappeared.

Then, out of the crack between that rock and the one alongside it, thin shoots of mossy grass appeared, tentatively testing the wind and the air, folding in on themselves and curling out again, spreading each way until they had reached the end.

Then the moss spread to the other cracks between all the other rocks.

As he watched, Ozzie saw the construction of haphazardly-placed rocks heal over and knit together with a lush green, forming a kind of rock garden of tiny swaying fronds and smooth granite.

All the way up to the top of the ravine the rocks were being welded together with the moss.

Ozzie got to his feet, hefted the hammer and started scrambling back up to the top of the ravine.

By the time he had reached the car the first flowers were already appearing, a myriad of colored tiny petals sprouting out of thin stalks, spreading all the way along the bowed path of that long-ago visitor from outer space.

As he started the car he realized what it seemed like: it seemed like jubilation. It seemed like coming home.

Setting Free the
Daughters of Earth

Oaths are but words, and words but wind.

Samuel Butler

The addict hunkered down beneath the bridge, leaned into the support and blew warm air into his cupped hands. His breath came out like steam, pooled around his hands and then drifted slowly up against the blackened stonework of the bridge, weaving its way through the filigreed metalwork of the railings to mingle with the exhaust fumes of the occasional overhead traffic.

Somewhere off in the distance, beyond the towering Residential Blocks that littered the Edge, sirens sounded—maybe a traffic accident, another Midtown thruway littered with fallen debris. The addict knew it had to be Midtown because the Prowlcars didn't come out here often—hadn't come out here regularly for a long time, long before the addict had become hooked.

He looked over his shoulders, surveying the litter-strewn dry canal-bottom whose bank he now crouched upon, and stared out into the night, watching the pirouetting light beams scratch the sky around the Business Blocks, where the surrounding blackness was already lightened by the glow of life, a glow that never went out. Not like the old days, the days he had heard folks talk about around the occasional fires here on the Edge, days when work stopped on an evening, slowed down on a weekend, that mythical pause in commercial motion when all but the most essential services ceased for a day.

Sunday, it had been called.

The seventh day. A day of rest.

But Sunday had long gone.

Now time was marked strictly by the Julian calendar, a five-digit identification that did not recognize individual days or their characteristics.

His mother, before she died, had told him all about Sunday, and about the other days, information passed down to her by *her* mother who had had it passed down to her by *her* mother!

About how his mother's great-grandfather, in that long-ago mythical time before the addict was born, would go out for A Drink on Friday, the fifth day, with his friends.

And about how, on a Thursday — which had been the day before Friday — the two of them, his mother's great-grandparents, would sometimes go out to see a moving picture show…in the days before TAP came in. And about how some folks had gone to church on Sunday.

That was long gone, too.

And she had told him about how the different months used to have different characteristics.

Months? he had asked.

His mother had smiled and ruffled his hair. Months had been groups of four weeks, sometimes four and a half, which occurred at different times of the year. The seasons, his mother had called them, speaking their names reverently…though she had never known them herself.

The addict could remember their names — summer, winter, autumn, spring — but not their order. It didn't matter.

The seasons, his mother had explained, had been differentiated by the weather. Sometimes it was hot. Sometimes it was cold. And sometimes it was getting close to being one or the other, but not quite there yet.

One season, his mother had been told, the sun shone and people got out of doors, walking around or lying on the grass, drinking in the sunshine, feeling it recharge their bodies.

Then, in another season, folks started to wrap up more, had started to wear more clothes, and the trees had started losing their leaves.

And still another one, the one after that one, snow would fall out of the sky. Snow…even the word had a magical resonance to it. In reality it was rain, frozen into tiny white cereal flakes of coldness, that fluttered down and lay on the ground, blown by the wind into banks and drifts of white against buildings and fences. The addict did not know snow. But he hoped that, one day, he would see it…watch it falling from the sky.

And then, last of all, she had told him about how, after all the coldness and the snow, the temperature would ease off and plants would start to sprout new shoots, the trees would grow new leaves, and people would rummage through closets and wardrobes and old chests in the hallway, sifting through piles of clothing until they found the light stuff, the stuff with hardly any sleeves or hardly any pants-legs…getting ready for the heat.

But that had gone, too. All gone.

Everything was gone.

The snow, the wind, the heat.

No days. No seasons. No weather. No beliefs.

People worked. And people TAPped.

And that was it.

For those who did not work, those lost souls who had drifted out into the dead areas of the Edge, on the periphery of the dome-covered Cities that now covered the inhospitable world, a brief nomadic existence was on offer…brief because they invariably drifted out of the domes, pulled by the lure of the open land glimpsed through the murky Plexiglas. Then there was only lingering death. But there was a sense of the way things used to be…if you were interested and if you could be bothered to look for it.

On this night, as it was with every night, the addict looked.

Still crouched down, the addict carefully stepped out from beneath the bridge and breathed in, fighting off the urge to cough.

Once free of the overhang, he looked up and saw a skybus negotiating the tight corner of Vicar Lane and The Headrow, a handful of empty emotionless faces staring out of the fluorescent-lit interior and down into the gloom of the streets and the darkened buildings. The bus stopped against a loading platform and a stooped figure carefully stepped down. The addict imagined he could hear the sibilant rush of the pneumatic doors — *ssssshhhh!* — opening and closing, and then the bus moved off into the stream of intermittent traffic, steam jets pumping from its rear and its underside.

The stooped figure watched the bus for a minute and then turned away, lugging what looked like two huge mailbags, limping onto the railed walkway that traversed the residential block.

The addict watched the figure go and then allowed his eyes to drift down the building, floor by floor, until he was staring straight at a man sitting on the stone armguard of the bridge. The addict was about to duck out of sight, but it was clear that the man was not interested in him. The man wasn't interested in anything at all, save the current running from the box in his lap — the addict assumed that was where the box was although he couldn't actually see it — and up the wires to the terminal bolts grafted into his temples.

The man was a TAPper or a Frankie, oblivious of everyone and everything while his bolts were being fed, thrusting whatever particular images and sensations made up his own particular pleasure.

A cab passed overhead, its underside light sweeping the bridge and then the ground before returning to the bridge and fixing momentarily on the man. An airhorn sounded — *horrrk!* — as the cab wheeled left and passed over the addict, moving towards the dense forest of residential blocks closer to the dome edge.

The addict turned to watch it go, watched its taillights blinking, and, just for a second, before the cab turned again to move along Boar Lane, he saw the distant reflection of its headlights in the Plexiglas between two blocks on the corner of Boar Lane and Commercial Street. Then the glass was dull again, unseen, just a wall of darkness at the end of Commercial Street.

He looked back at the bridge and saw the man shaking, watched him near the end of his hit. The man would be in Heaven for a few hours now, swirling down the blissful aftermath of the hit until reality crowded in again and he would have to seek out another supply.

The addict shrugged his coat up on his shoulders and scrambled up the side of the embankment onto the walkway. Everyone had his or her way of dealing with life in the domes, particularly those who lived on the Edge…his or her way of escaping the way things really were.

But some methods of cerebral escape were considered to be even more heinous than the artificial stimuli that could be scored for a few credits from any street corner or the shadowed recesses of the second-cellar bars in Downtown. Of these — of all the recreational drugs openly tolerated (and even encouraged) by an increasingly dependent society — one and only one was completely forbidden. And this was the substance favored by the addict.

The penalty for being caught with his particular tipple was termination.

No questions, no excuses, no trial. Just lights out, and good-bye.

He shrugged his shoulders and stared along the walkway.

The sound of the city was stronger up here, so strong that the addict could barely hear the man on the bridge coming to the end of his hit. But he could still hear it just a little, and he hurried his step to get out of range.

The air smelled of smoke, cold and fuel.

The puddles on the walkway and the rain-slicked ledges of the buildings were all rainbow-hued, the constant drizzle of fuel particles having eaten into the surface to come out with the water and swirl in eddies of various shapes and colors. The addict looked up into the darkness. He couldn't see the dome's ceiling, let alone the sky beyond, but he could feel the gentle drizzle from the sprinkler system, drifting down over the town.

Now and again, when the system broke down, the authorities would send rainships circling the building-tops. He had seen one once, coming down onto the dock at the filling station across town, its bulbous tanks gleaming in the fluorescent lights, its contents spread across the streets.

With crops grown outside the dome in separate covered areas and all water for domestic use fed into the City, rain was something the population didn't actually need any longer. The official line was that the daily spraying was a token gesture to simpler times: the consensus, however, was that the nightly downpours were used to quell disenchantment and insurrection.

Sometimes, when he was feeling particularly low and particularly bold, the addict thought about leaving the city.

Sometimes, at night, lying in his cot, wrapped up in his coats, he dreamed of the deadly open spaces beyond the Plexiglas.

He dreamed of dusty roads winding between grassy hills, and of clouds silently drifting across an endless blue sky.

He dreamed of wooden shacks and picket-fenced garden areas, of clear lakes and a vast ocean lapping a sandy shoreline. He even dreamed of gleaming, brightly-colored automobiles humming along rolling highways, attached to the roads themselves instead of flying around the building-sides, and he dreamed of panting trains hammering along a ribbon of track that snaked between frozen-rain topped mountains…and grass…and forests.

He dreamed these dreams because of his addiction. And his addiction was a direct result of those dreams.

A voice spoke from the darkness.

The addict stopped and squinted into the gloom beneath the canopy of a block entrance, his hands out of his pockets and ready for confrontation.

"I said, you *need* anything?" the voice said, the words accompanied by a thick waft of smoke pouring out into the street.

"Uh-uh," the addict lied. He did not want to detail his problem without first seeing the identity of the person asking the question. There were too many dummy-dealers out in the darkened streets, Prowlers looking to pull you in for a few hours…to spend some time in the Prowlhouses. In there, amidst the old tried and tested methods of persuasion, the Prowlers could find out all they wanted to know.

A man stepped out of the entrance, the darkness peeling away from him like a cellophane covering. The man took a deep draw on his pipette and, throwing his head back, blew out more smoke, making a circle of his mouth at the end to cause smoke rings which shimmered and then dissipated.

"What you need?" the man asked.

The addict took a step back. "I said, I don't need anything."

The man nodded. He removed the pipette from his mouth, wound it up until the bowl was fixed into the center and then placed a shiny clip around the stem. He dropped the apparatus into an already bulging pocket in his ankle-length coat and said, "Everybody need *some*thing."

"Not me."

The man nodded but carried on. "You want uppers or downers? You want head games?"

He leaned forward and the addict shuffled back some more.

"I not hurt you," the man said, "just looking see you been fitted…see if you a TAPper."

The addict subconsciously lifted a hand to the skin of his left temple and then dropped the arm to his side. "Well, I haven't," he said. "There's no such thing as Total Audience Participation. It's a con."

The man nodded, not wanting to get into a conversation. Maybe not even knowing what this guy was talking about. "Just looking, too, see you Prowler," he added, although he had clearly decided that such was not the case.

The addict raised his arms in supplication. "Do I look like a Prowler?" he asked.

The man considered this and then said, "*Every*body look like Prowler."

The addict relaxed. "Well, I'm not," he said.

"I can see." The man leaned back against the wall. "So, maybe you need smoke, little weed maybe."

"No," said the addict.

"Glue capsules? DNA droppers, wood-burners, sharkfins?"

"Never use 'em," said the addict.

"How's 'bout some dreamboats—got new supply in this week, help you sleep for month, sleep so long you wake up starving. Got some LDs, too—keep you going for 'nother month, never need to sleep, laugh all time."

"Don't need to go Long Distance," the addict said. "And I get all the sleep I need. Every night. Like a baby."

The man gave out a raucous laugh. "Ain't nobody sleep like baby, man," he said.

"Well, I do."

"Okay," the man said with a carefree shrug. "You don't need nothing, I might 'swell go."

"Wait." The addict looked back along the path. A limo-car was passing overhead, a couple of levels up, its headlight beams splaying the embankment where he had just been. The TAPper from the bridge had gone. Maybe he had fallen or even jumped, his head filled with ejaculation thoughts, his mind convinced that he would survive the drop…or maybe hoping that he wouldn't.

"Hey, listen," the man was saying, "I got places—"

"Okay," the addict said, "show me."

"Show you? Show you *what*?"

He shrugged. "Everything. I want to see it all."

Now it was the man's turn to be suspicious. "You *sure* you not Prowler?" He drew the word out, emphasizing the two syllables, "prow" and "lurr."

The addict shook his head and stepped closer to the man. He could smell the man's dirt now, could smell his sweat and the smoke on his clothes, the piss stains on his plastic coverall pants, the oil and grime in his matted hair…which the addict now saw was gathered into two small pigtails resting on the upturned collar of his coat, each one tethered with a tiny length of tubing. He had stepped so close that he was touching the man, could feel the man's body up against his own, could feel the man's hand trapped against his own stomach.

"I just want to be sure before I make a decision."

"Yeah?"

The addict nodded. "Call it window-shopping. I don't know what I want until I see it." He looked into the man's face, stared into the hooded squinting eyes. "You can understand that," he said.

The man waited for a few seconds, watching the addict, and then straightened up. He lifted his right arm, pulling it up between them, and showed a long bladed stiletto tube-knife, a capsule already loaded into the see-through trigger guard. He smiled and flipped the safety. A sheath unfurled along the blade and the guard slid into the handle. The addict's eyes were wide open.

"Had be sure," the man said. "You coming on strong."

The addict nodded and gave a shrug, watching the man drop the tube-knife into his coat pocket, heard it clunk against the pipette.

"Okay," the man said, unfastening the toggle-catches down the front of his coat, "take look." He pulled the two flaps open. "Take *good* look."

Somewhere behind him in the night, the addict heard air horns. They sounded like he imagined hump-backed whales might sound, or dolphins, swimming lazily beneath a dark sky, not fully knowing where they were going or even where they had been…only that they *were*.

It was a sound of exhilaration and of simply being.

But it was also something else. It was a fanfare for the contents of the man's coat, each item held into place against the lining by carefully sewn straps and inlaid pockets. It was true, the addict thought, his eyes jumping from one attachment to the next. You really could get anything here, here in this shadowed entrance to a seedy residential block, with the rain still falling in a thin spray. He allowed his eyes to wander, drinking in the sights inside the man's coat in the passing overhead glare of a limocab.

There were gaudily-colored packets, shining phials and glow-in-the-dark tubes, and alongside them, against the man's right armpit — the smell! — were electrical bolt-leads with cushioned clamps; and long, winding pipettes and smoking bulbs; long-nosed syringes and dum-dum needle-heads; speed-dipped nipple-pins, testosterone pustules and a whole array of penile and labia adornments and sex embellishments.

Against the other armpit were sublimated chest-pads, toe-capsules for a guaranteed slow climb and heavy-duty army surplus amphetamine suppositories for the instant peak.

Down around the man's upper thighs an array of bottles hung suspended from his plastic coveralls by the slimmest of threads, their contents like the sweets of old, varying colors and shapes and sizes…SUNSHINE YELLOWS, one label proclaimed; MEADOW GREENS boasted another; BLUE DOWNS said a third, all in the same shaky writing.

Some were cylindrical capsules, mostly for anal or vaginal insertion, and of the oral varieties some were flat and circular while others were square or cuboid to delay movement into the stomach.

A sewer-cover rattled over to the right of them and steam bellowed from the depths beneath. At the same time, a distant siren wailed and someone howled to the night, the aggression of the single drawn-out cry quickly dissipating into a deep-throated sob of anguish. The cry was abruptly cut off.

"You see something?" the man asked.

The addict turned back from looking along the deserted walkway and shook his head. "Just a little jumpy," he said.

The man shook his head in exasperation. "No, I mean you *see* something?" He let go of one side of his opened coat and pointed to the rows of bottles and packets and artificial stimulants. "You see something *here!*"

"No," the addict said sadly. "You have nothing I need."

The man grunted and fastened his coat. "What you need then? I get it for you. What you need?"

The addict stared at the shadowed outline of the man's head, wondering if it were safe to tell him. He looked back along the walkway, saw a news broadcast and share information feeding its way silently around one of the Residential Blocks, and breathed in deeply. Looking back, he said, "Pages."

The man took a step back against the doorway.

"You said," the addict reminded the man. "You said you could get me what I needed. Well, I need pages."

The man moved quickly out of the doorway and stood in front of the addict on the walkway, his face now exposed to the dim light, his eyes wide open. "You mad," the man said. "No pages." He waved his hands to underline the statement. "No pages," he said again, to underline the underline.

"You said." The addict reached into his back pocket with one hand and pulled out a thick wad of credit notes. With the other, he reached down between his legs, flipped open the Velcro prosthetic flap on his left upper thigh and produced an old Prowler gun, its greased-up snub-nose coated in talcum powder.

The man raised his hands. "*Prowler!*" he whispered.

"No, I'm not a Prowler," the addict said.

The man pointed. "Prowler *gun.*"

"Yes, it is a Prowler *gun* but I'm not a *Prowler*." He waved the credits, wafting them in front of the man's face. "I will pay you," he said, spreading the words out so that the man would be able to understand.

"Pages bad."

"Yes, pages are dangerous," the addict agreed. "If you get *caught*. We will not get caught." He pushed the wad of notes back into his coat pocket and pulled out three forties. He reached out and stuffed these inside the lapel of the man's coat. Then he slipped the gun into his other pocket, raised both hands to show that they were completely empty. "I pay you well."

The man was clearly considering his chances...wondering whether to break for it, to run a zig-zag path along the walkway, risking being shot in the back for—how much? he pulled the notes from his lapel and looked...120 credits—when maybe he could get more. Maybe much more.

"You come," he said at last, pocketing the credits as he turned and started to walk.

The addict followed.

⚶

In all his days and nights of wandering the City, the addict had never been this way. It was as though the way was a special secret way, one which could only be traversed at a certain time on a certain day.

There was a strange sentience to the darkened walkways and the pair moved carefully and slowly, feeling the dank silent doorways and the hooded windows sightlessly following their passage. The addict listened for signs of movement amidst the shadows but heard only the sound of his feet and those of his guide, occasionally echoing on girders and occasionally thudding on stone flagging or rotting boardwalks.

The man led the addict into parts of Downtown that he had not realized existed, and it was not until they had been walking for several minutes that the addict noticed that the sounds of the City had disappeared.

He halted for a moment and the man in front stopped also, turning to look at him through the gloom. "Okay?" he whispered.

"Listen," said the addict.

The man cocked his head to one side and then to the other. "Don't hear nothing," he said.

"That's right," said the addict. "No sounds."

"Good," came the response.

"No," the addict said. "There are no sounds of *anything*."

The man appeared to consider this. "Good," he said again and, turning sharply, he resumed the trek.

Along they went, then down twisting narrow steps that led to a thin walkway along a culvert, its sides curving steeply to meet below a silent stretch of still water.

They walked along the side, trailing their left hands across the wall as they passed, leaning slightly to avoid the feeling of falling...or of wanting to jump. Beneath a curved stone bridge, they came to more steps, this time going up. The man ran up the steps two at a time, his coattails wafting behind him, and the addict followed, pleased to be leaving the culvert behind.

At the top of the steps they turned sharp right along a narrow street between what appeared to be warehouses. The road here was cobbled and uneven, its surface shiny with water and slick with something else. Now there was a smell.

The addict breathed in deeply.

The scent of decay and oldness was at once repellent and attractive. He thought it might be like the smell of the sea.

At the end of the street they turned left, the man glancing over his shoulder to make sure the addict was still there. The addict suspected that the man could not care less either way and, as they continued, he half-expected the man to make a break for it. He wondered what he would do if that happened. He had absolutely no idea where they were.

A little way along another street that sloped gently downhill, the man stopped and moved to the side where he stopped and pressed his back against the wall.

"Are we there yet?" the addict asked, pausing for breath.

"Where?" the man asked.

The addict shrugged. "Wherever it is that we're going."

The man did not respond. Instead, he backed along the wall until he reached a section of boarding. He backed onto the boarding and began to tap with his knuckles, beating out a discordant rhythm that seemed to go on and on. After a few seconds, the addict thought that the man was simply playing for time...that the rapping was a nervous tic...but then he stopped.

The addict sensed that they were now waiting for something.

He listened.

Then, there it was...a distant and faint rapping, a faraway syncopated melody of hand on wood. It came from behind the boarding.

The man rapped again. And waited.

A sudden litany of noise sounded, and stopped.

The man stepped aside and waved for the addict to join him against the wall. As he stepped forward, the addict heard a faint scratching rasp, metal on metal, from behind the door. He leaned back against the wall and waited, hardly daring to breathe.

At the far end of the alley a figure appeared, seeming to step straight out of the wall itself. Without moving his back from the wall, the addict craned forward to see if he could discern some kind of door but the wall seemed to go on right to the end of the street.

The figure jogged noiselessly across the street, where it disappeared momentarily, folding itself into the shadows. Then it re-emerged and jogged to the end of the street, its bulbous head darting first one way and then the other, checking the street that crossed the end of the alley for any signs of movement. The figure came back and stood for a few seconds looking down at the addict and the dealer. Then, with a short wave of an arm, it backed up into the shadows.

"Is he waving at us?" the addict whispered.

The dealer shook his head and pointed down the alley, away from the waving figure.

The addict looked around and saw a second figure, its head as huge and unwieldy as the first, stepping back into the shadows. The wave had clearly been some kind of signal, perhaps confirming that the streets were clear of Prowlers, and the addict waited quietly for further developments. He did not have long to wait.

The rasping noise came again, louder this time as though whoever or whatever was making it no longer felt such a need for stealth. The noise grew louder still until it stopped with a dull thud. Then came a metallic jingle and the sound of keys being inserted and turned to give a solid thunk.

The dealer stepped away from the wall and held out his hand to the addict. "Credits," he said. "Give to me."

Momentarily wrong-footed by the sudden use of the preposition, the addict pulled out his wad of notes without thinking and peeled off five.

The dealer took them, gave them a quick flick and shook his head. "More."

"How much more?" the addict asked. "I haven't even seen anything yet."

The wood paneled boarding began to rise.

"Many pages in there," the dealer hissed, nodding to the rising boarding. "Give ten like others."

"Which others? You brought other people here?"

"No," the dealer snapped. "Like other *notes*." He patted his coat pocket.

"Forties!" The addict made a quick mental calculation. "That's more than five hundred credits," he said.

The other man thrust the notes he already had into his pocket and then jabbed his empty hand out again. "Yeah, right. Give."

The addict counted off the forties and placed them in the dealer's hand. The man thrust his payment into his coat pocket and ran off down the street, his steps echoing through the gloom.

Turning around, the addict watched as the boarding reached the top of the surrounding brick and stonework and stopped. The addict frowned. There had only been a wall behind the boarding. He was about to turn and shout to one of the shadowy figures at either end of the street when the wall shimmered and another figure stepped through it and out onto the pavement.

Before he stepped out of the shadows, the addict transferred the old Prowler gun from his pocket to the prosthetic flap on his upper thigh.

The new figure wore plastic coveralls and a large bulbous helmet. Holding the gun steady, its muzzle pointing straight at him, the figure lifted its free arm and flicked a button on the helmet. Amidst a blur of crackling static, a deep male voice said, "Who was he?"

"Who?"

"Your friend. The guy ran off?"

The addict shrugged. "Dealer. He brought me here. I asked him."

"Why'd you do that?"

"I wanted something he didn't have."

"What was that?"

"Pages," the addict said. "I need some pages."

"You carrying?"

The addict shook his head.

"Lemme check."

The addict lifted his hands and fell forward against the wall while the man frisked him.

"Okay," the man said. He turned slightly and looked up the street. "Hill…see anything? That other guy gone?" he said. The addict looked up at the figure at the top end of the street and saw it walking down towards them. Clearly, they were communicating by some sort of short-wave system.

The figure with the weapon turned to the other end of the street. The deep voice said, "How 'bout you Brooks? Things look okay?"

The addict turned and saw the third figure walking towards them from the lower end. It waved an arm.

"Seems you okay," the deep voice said.

The addict nodded, fighting back his excitement. "I am. I just need some pages."

The man hefted the weapon onto his shoulder and said, "Okay. Walk through the wall." He raised an arm and pointed. "Merry…switch it on. Our guest is coming through."

The addict stepped up to the wall, hesitated and then stepped forward. There was a brief blurring and the addict was inside…

…in another world.

He looked ahead and he looked upwards.

He looked to the left and he looked to the right.

He even looked down.

And he breathed in the smell.

Around him and above him and below him were metal gantries, walkways similar to the one on which he now stood, stretching forward and crisscrossing each other, layer upon layer, tier upon tier, with each one traversed by silent people, men and women, each dressed in a similar garb of green and white, sweater and pants. To either side of them, be they up or down or to left or right, set back behind protective rails, were huge piles of paper sheets, littered with colored marking cards jutting out sometimes at angles and sometimes straight ahead or at 90 degrees to one side. Each pile was held in place by what appeared to be plastic sidings, their sides a graffiti mosaic of scribbled writing and accompanying numbers, the numbers occasionally crossed through and new numbers scribbled alongside.

"Anything in particular you have in mind?"

The first man had followed the addict through the wall and was standing just behind him to the left. He had removed his helmet and was standing with his weapon propped against his right shoulder.

The addict shook his head, unable to speak.

He breathed in again, closed his eyes, and analyzed the smell.

It was simply paper, aging paper, and maybe the sweet underlying waft of metal and oil and wood and plaster.

But it was more than that to the addict, much more.

The smell was an olfactory amalgam of words and phrases, knowledge and ideas, dialogue and thoughts. It was the largest collection of history the addict had ever seen, larger even than he had ever dreamed about, dreamed about in the quietest moments of the loneliest days and nights huddled tightly in his cot.

Here were snippets of stories and articles, sections of treatises and criticisms, chapters of opinion and belief. Vowels and consonants, prefixes and suffixes, prepositions and adverbs, nouns and adjectives...

The accumulated smell of the words came at him in a tumult, soared up his nostrils into his brain in a flood of imagined images.

The vast emptiness of space...the swirling cold depths of the oceans...the ancient monuments long forgotten to today's diluted version of humankind.

Though he had not yet stepped forward to glance at even one of the millions—perhaps billions—of pages torn from the old books, the addict knew it was all here: Dickens, Homer, Tolstoy, Shakespeare...Melville, Bradbury, Updike, King. The great literary minds of every century in the planet's history gathered together under the one roof—he looked up again and saw that it was a composite of roofs, a cavernous covering that had, at one time, protected perhaps a whole range of warehouses.

"Wow!" he said, unable to think of anything else.

"Quite a collection," the man ventured.

"Quite a collection," the addict agreed. He pushed his tongue against the back bicuspid on the right and swallowed the fractured enamel. Then he bit down on the tiny microchip button, felt the brief tingle of vibration of the homing signal.

The man stepped forward and looked at him, frowning. "You okay?"

The addict swallowed and smiled, thumped his chest as though he had indigestion, eyebrows raised in apology.

"It always gets people, the first look," said the man, nodding that he understood.

"Hey, I'm fine. Absolutely fine."

"So, what's your poison?" The man smiled and nodded to the walkway straight ahead of them. "That way is mostly twentieth century literature. Same for the next two tiers down. Most come at twenty credits a page, six for one hundred. You buy more, we can do a deal."

"Right," the addict said. "A deal. We'll definitely have to do a deal."

"The next three tiers up are nonfiction, philosophy, science, religion. The two after that have classical works, including poetry, and sheet music."

"Sheet music?"

The man shrugged. "The words and notes to the old songs? I dunno. Not my bag. Not any of it."

The addict looked puzzled. "You don't...you don't use any of this stuff?"

"Nah." The man shook his head vehemently to emphasize the point. "Don't see the attraction. Just words and stuff. Doesn't mean anything."

The addict nodded and smiled. "The daughters of earth."

"Say again?"

"'I am not so lost in lexicography, as to forget that words are the daughters of earth, and that things are the sons of heaven.' Doctor Johnson said that, almost three hundred years ago."

"Yeah, right." The man frowned momentarily and then his face lightened. "You like all this stuff, huh?"

He turned back and walked to the rail, leaned on it and looked down. "Yes, I like all this stuff." He scanned the myriad pages before him. "Must've taken a long time," he said, "stripping all these pages out of the original books."

"Sure did. Not many books left after the wars, and a lot of folks who, like you, feel they need to drink it all in." The man moved up alongside the addict and leaned over the rail. "When you have one book and maybe a thousand customers, you gotta think of ways to satisfy the demand."

"Sure," the addict agreed.

"Could have sold the whole book for maybe 50 credits, which is pretty much all anyone can afford. Maybe 100 for the more popular ones — the ones folks remembered reading — but the supply isn't infinite. The demand is infinite, but not the supply. You know what I mean?"

"I surely do," the addict said.

"So we strip 'em out."

The addict tried not to let the man see him wince.

"That way, six hundred page book gives three hundred sheets; three hundred sheets at twenty credits apiece gives —"

"Six thou."

"Right. Six thousand credits. Against, what? Against 50 or 100."

"It's a case of simple economics," the addict said. "Commerce."

"You got it in one."

"It's not a new concept."

"Say again?"

"They used to do it in the old days, the dealers, guys like you." He turned around and leaned back against the rail. "They see the demand and feed it. Used to be that way with comic books."

The man frowned. "They the ones with pictures?"

"They're the ones," the addict said, smiling, jabbing a finger at the man. "Superhero stuff, stuff like Superman, Batman, all that stuff. So few of them survived the Second World War, they became collectors' items — we're talking, what? Two hundred years ago? Two fifty?"

The man shrugged. "No idea."

"No, well, folks bought them for crazy prices, squirreled them away in protective bags. Each time one was sold at such and such a price, the dealer whacked it up the next time he got a copy of that mag."

"You know a lot about this stuff."

He shrugged. "It's a hobby."

"Everyone needs a hobby," the man said, pointing to the two bolts fixed into the skin of his temples. He gave a big grin.

The addict returned the grin, and said, "Then it was books. First editions, limited signed editions…all that stuff. At first, it was just the signature that made the limiteds special. Then they came with extra chapters, special introductions, special afterwords.

"Then folks got tired of that and turned their attention to the old paperbacks." The addict whistled and waved his hand as though he'd burned his fingers. "Those were crazy days."

"Hey…you weren't there? You couldn't have been."

"No, I wasn't there. But I've spoken with people who have spoken with people who knew people who knew people…you know what I mean? Time marches on."

The man shuffled side to side impatiently. "Ain't *that* the truth."

The addict ignored him and carried on. "Condition was always a big thing, but then, when all the great condition books and magazines had been bought or had simply deteriorated into a lesser condition, the prices for those went through the roof." He paused, nodding. "Course, you have to remember that people had different levels of spending power then, it wasn't governed by the State the way it is now."

"Right," the man said, his voice indicating that he didn't really follow what this guy was going on about.

"Yeah, and then the shit really hit the fan after the wars. Every country—and I mean *every* country—decimated. Billions wiped out over the space of the first eight, nine years, and billions more over the next fifty or so. The new global State didn't want folks looking to the old books and the old ways, didn't want them making themselves dissatisfied…questioning the status quo. So they took steps to remedy the situation. They got rid of whatever books they could find."

"That the Blanking?"

"Yes, that was the Blanking." He turned and looked at the piles of pages towering the aisles, a cityscape of white monoliths, and he dreamed of a life which could be long enough to read them all. "Have you ever wondered," the addict said, his voice low, "if it hurts them?"

"What?"

He looked over his shoulder and nodded at the piles. "If tearing out the pages hurts the books."

There was a silence. Then the man said, "Look, I don't know what you're talking about mister. What say you just tell me which part you're—"

"I'm interested in all of it," the addict said.

"Well, okay, just tell me what you want."

The microchip in his mouth buzzed once and then again.

It was time.

Turning around from the rail, the addict smiled and said, "I want it *all*."

The man frowned, gave a half-smile, not understanding. "You want it—"

The addict kicked out once and sent the man's helmet skittering along the gantry, where it spun and swirled a few times, taking it closer and closer to the edge until it disappeared over the side. The next kick took the man in the crotch, like the next kick and the one after it, each one delivered by the addict in quick succession with alternate feet.

The addict pulled his hand back, flexed the fingers into a right angle, and plunged the hand forward into the man's chest, a single jab. There was a dull crunch and the man coughed. He coughed again, dropped his weapon, and fell to his knees. The next cough brought up what looked like food and some pieces of splintered bone.

Lifting the weapon from the floor, the addict brought the butt down on the top of the man's head. The man was dead even before he fell face forward.

He wiped the blood in a long smear along the man's plastic coveralls and, after a quick inspection, flicked off the safety guard. The barrel hummed quietly.

He turned to the rail and quickly scanned the gantries in front of him. Nobody seemed to have noticed the scuffle. But he was still going to have to move quickly. He backed along the gantry until his back was against the wall. He was a little more sheltered here, safe from a casual glance by one of the people tending the stacks of paper. He crouched down to make his presence still harder to detect and turned to face the wall through which he had stepped just minutes earlier.

It was a simple destabilized molecular sheet. Although the outside had been treated to give the appearance of brickwork, the inside bore no such illusion—just a flat expanse grafted onto the real brickwork at either side. Fixed to the wall at the right was a small panel with four buttons. There was no writing on the panel.

The addict duck-walked to the panel and studied it.

Four buttons. Two red, one green, one black.

He shook his head. What was he thinking about? The color coding could mean anything and time was already against him.

As if on cue, he head a metallic voice talking through static.

The addict moved to the side of the rail and cautiously looked over. Just a few feet below, on a protruding stanchion, was the helmet. The voice was coming from inside. The addict knew it was asking about him.

He shuffled back to the panel, took a deep breath and pressed the green button.

Nothing happened.

He pressed one of the red buttons.

He almost dropped the weapon when the siren started. It whooped and wailed, so loud he could feel its vibrations in the metallic gantry beneath his feet. Somewhere behind him he could hear the sound of shouting voices, almost lost beneath the siren.

He pressed the black button.

The wall shimmered and became translucent. He could see shapes standing beyond it, outside on the street.

Then he pressed the other red button.

The siren stopped.

But the voices continued. And now he could feel other vibrations...running feet.

He spun around as the first shape came through the wall, crouched down, gun at the ready. The shape looked down at him, just a glance, the black visored helmet nodding once, and then it moved forward, further along the gantry.

A second shape appeared, then a third and a fourth, each of them moving quickly to the side, computerized laser rifles primed and already sweeping the tiered gantry system for signs of movement.

A fifth shape handed the addict a telephonic headset.

A sixth dropped a rope and grapple at his feet and then moved forward.

The addict slipped the headset on. Immediately there were voices, voices shouting instructions...to get the ones on the ground first; the others had a long way to go. To watch out for anyone moving towards wall panels which could mean self-destruct instructions.

Then one voice said, "You okay, Reader One?"

He nodded, looking up at the shapes. He couldn't tell which one was asking the question.

"Then get down to ground level," the voice said. "Main office must be down there. They'll be aiming to get rid of it all. And when they do that, they'll do it from the ground."

The addict looked at the rail.

"We must preserve the pages," the voice added. "Jesus Christ, I have *never* seen so many as this." There was a pause and, turning back, the addict caught sight of a black shape standing just inside the wall, staring up and down, shaking its head. The figure fitted the grapple onto the rail and tossed the rope over the side; then it turned to face him and waved a hand.

"Go," the voice said.

The addict shouldered the strapped weapon and rolled over the edge, allowing his hands to slide down the rope as it swirled beneath his interlocked legs and feet.

Already the sound of the lasers was deafening, drowning out the voices from the headset. But it wasn't deafening enough to drown out the screams. Or maybe it was just that he knew they were there...could imagine what they sounded like.

He allowed himself to slide down.

As he passed each gantry tier, he slowed and stared at the piles.

So many sheets of paper. So many pages. So many millions and billions and trillions of words.

A shot hit the metal alongside him and he braced himself, expecting the man to get a better aim, trying to spin himself around and jam one foot onto the gantry to steady himself enough to be able to train his own weapon.

Halfway around, already swinging the rifle up to let off a few hopeful shots, the addict saw an overalled man burst apart as one of the lasers hit him from behind. The arm that bounced against the gantry to his side still held its weapon.

Through the smoke, covering his face against the smell of burned flesh, the addict saw the black shapes swinging across the gantries up above, ropes attached to the roof by suction pads. It was almost balletic. If it were a TAPped presentation there would probably be music piped over the top of all the noise...the sounds of people shouting, people screaming.

People dying.

He let go of the rifle and felt it swing by his side as he let himself slide down to the floor.

He landed awkwardly, a few feet in front of a man in an overall punching the ammunition clip on his rifle. The man's head raised to look at him and the addict could see the eyes...just for a second.

They were filled with fear and with anger.

Then the head dropped down again as he declipped and then pressed it home again.

The addict lifted his weapon and fired. Twice.

The shots sent the man flying back along the corridor, bouncing against the gantry supports before skidding to a halt alongside the rear wall.

The addict crouched and followed.

The place was a maze of metal and smoke.

"How you doing, Reader One?" a tinny voice asked in his headset. It was not the voice he had heard earlier.

"On the ground," the addict shouted into the mouthmic.

"See anything?"

Something touched the top of his head and he fell forward, spinning, bringing his weapon around. On the floor, his knees bent up against the gantry, he saw a sheet of paper flutter, side to side, until it landed, slithering beneath one of the supports.

When he looked up, he saw the rest of them.

The air was filled with sheets of paper, their surfaces covered in the spidery blackness of type. Some of them were burning, leaving tiny trails of smoke as they descended.

He grabbed at a sheet and shook out the flames, glancing at the words between the blackened edges of the page. It wasn't something he recognized but the simple commitment of thoughts to paper, of the recording of opinions or beliefs or even complete fiction filled him with awe. The way it always did.

They had always hoped that one day they would find a stash like this one. They had hoped but had never dared believe.

He looked around and saw the black figures swinging down onto the ground level now. As he looked up the tiers he saw other black figures on the edges of the gantry, their weapons readied but nobody to fire at. Several of these figures were already giving the all-clear.

It took them sixteen days to move all of the pages, filling the cavernous interior holds of the stripped-down water carriers, delivery modules and old skybuses before lifting off shakily into the sky to carry the pages to a hundred safe-houses scattered around the City.

Watchers were placed at street corners, upper-story windows and on rooftops for two square miles of the warehouse, each fitted with a mouthmic and a "lights out" implant in a rear tooth to be used in the event of capture. The operation went smoothly thanks to the fact that the warehouse was in a sector that nobody ever visited any more. During the repeated pickups, the addict realized just how much of the City had fallen into disuse. It was this fact that most depressed him...perhaps even more than the criminalization of reading, the fact that the city was somehow being run down beneath their very eyes...turned into something else.

This was why the organization had been necessary. The People's Literation Society, a middle ground between the authorities which sought to suppress literature and the entrepreneurial pushers who sought to benefit from the suppression. If asked, the addict would have found it difficult to say whom he despised the most.

The first drop took place during a busy lunch period, from an old delivery module that skirted the monolithic towers of the business district three times before its load was dispatched. Then the module slipped into and amidst the tiered traffic flows until it was gone. Two Prowlcars arrived minutes later, by which time the module was safely "home" and already being dismantled, its tell-tale livery being replaced or restructured or redesigned. The addict estimated they "set free" more than half a million pages of around three hundred to four hundred words a page.

The sheets released on that first drop fell from the air onto the dirty streets and walkways of the City like confetti.

A TAPper propped against a building side outside a recreation brothel stooped to pick up a sheet that had brushed his bare legs. As he lifted it for a closer look, another sheet landed to take its place. The sheet contained pages 69 and 70 of *The House at Pooh Corner*. The TAPper frowned and studied the words, wondering just what, exactly, a "tigger" might be. When he got to the end, he wanted to know more about Piglet and about the blue braces of Christopher Robin (whoever *he* was). The boy scratched at the rash around his cheek-studs and watched another sheet flutter down towards him. Maybe that one would provide some answers...or maybe he would have to search around—even ask around—until he found other sheets...

A man wearing a banker's sarong picked up a sheet containing pages 175 and 176 of John Steinbeck's *The Acts of King Arthur*, glanced around nervously and then scrumpled the paper into his waist-pouch. Seconds later he was lost in the crowds watching the pages rain down upon the city, heading home where he could read in safety. He felt gloriously excited. A few steps further along he stopped and grabbed a fistful of sheets which he thrust after the first one…

An old woman, bald and bearded, watched a sheet flutter through the gloom of the lower levels, watched it waft to and fro, easing itself finally onto a ledge just a few feet away from her. Maintaining her muttered conversation with herself, she abandoned the metal shopping cart containing her entire life's belongings and retrieved the sheet—pages 85 and 86 of Jostein Gaarder's *Sophie's World*—and, returning quickly to her possessions, slipped it beneath a makeshift pillow whose stink of urine and sour breath she no longer noticed. The world had come back to her, suddenly, contained on a simple sheet of paper. The streets had been opened.

"What came first?" she asked a passing Hostess, reading from the paper and wagging her finger to the heavens. "The chicken or the 'idea' chicken?" The Hostess pushed her to one side and moved quickly to an elevator platform: she obviously didn't know the answer any more than the old bearded hobo woman. But as she stepped onto the platform and pulled the gate across, the Hostess went over what the old woman had said…

High above the streets, two men leaned on the protective rails outside a middle-level nicotine store, watching.

"Snow," the addict said. "It's snowing."

"It's snowing seeds," the man beside him answered, nodding. "The seeds will find accommodating soil and they will be nurtured. They will find warmth and care and they will form roots and grow…grow into knowledge and curiosity and emotion." He pointed to a young man walking determinedly through the fluttering sheets without stopping. "Some, like him, will ignore what's happening. They will turn a blind eye—but only at first. Eventually even they will want—*need*—to know more. Those with a two-page sheet from *Moby Dick* will want other sheets, more story…the same with those who have read—*lived*—brief moments from *Dracula* or *Oliver Twist* or *The Wind in the Willows*. They will want to read and to live other moments."

"And what if they can't find them?" the addict asked.

The other man shrugged. "Then they will construct their own stories inspired by the tasters they have received today. Thus has it ever been, thus will it ever be." He stared out across the City, turning his face to the gently wafting pages. "There can be no turning back. Not now."

"God, but I hope you're right," the addict said.

The man beside him smiled and said, in a loud, proud voice:

"'Scatter, as from an unextinguished hearth

Ashes and sparks, my words among mankind.
Be through my lips to unwakened earth
The trumpet of a prophecy! O, Wind,
If Winter comes, can Spring be far behind?'"

"Ah, Shelley," the addict said, nodding as he suddenly remembered the old order of the seasons. "Famous last words?"

His friend shook his head. "Prophetic *first* ones."

The sirens, when they began, did not sound frightening. They sounded afraid.

Late Night Pickup

I couldn't see the sun because it was very dark in space.

From Ozark Mountain farmer Buck Nelson's testimonial
following his alleged 1955 ride in a flying saucer

(1)

B en opens his eyes and shakes his head. He must have nodded off.

Seeing he's awake, the fattest of the two cops (it's a close-run thing) slides his ample backside onto the tall seat behind the front desk and gives a big smile. "It'll be okay, just tell us the whole thing from the top," he says with a slight lisp, folding his hands calmly and carefully on the desk in front of him..

"How'd you like your coffee?" The cop over by the *Vendarama* machine beams a toothy grin as he adjusts his peaked cap. He hikes his belt up over his belly and rests his hands on his hips like he's just run over from the next-but-one county. The belt returns to its more comfortable position, looking like a smile in a face mostly obscured by an eyeless mask of shirt.

"Like tea," Ben says. He's concerned to see that his hands are shaking but he puts that down to the accident—he's not completely sure of the nature of the accident but he knows he's been in one. Something to do with the car. "White, no sugar," he says. "I don't see why I can't just go," he adds, turning to the cop on the seat beside him. The truth is, he can't completely understand why he's here…wherever "here" is.

The cop at the machine either doesn't hear Ben or he's simply ignoring him. He turns away, frowning as he pushes his peaked cap back off his forehead. Scratching at the newly-exposed graying thatch of hair, he reads up and down the small menu inset into an illustration of steam billowing from a wide-brimmed cup, his extended pudgy finger stopping at each selection. Around and behind the cup a trio of smiling faces hover, their noses extended over the steam, their eyes closed in either orgasmic delight at what they're supposed to be drinking or extreme frustration at the cop's seeming inability to find the correct button.

Ben reaches into the inside pocket of his jacket and, lifting out a pack of Marlboro Lights, he looks around the one-room office...first over to the double-doors—a thick beam crossing them, resting in two curled metal cradles, one at either side fastened to the wall—then at the windows, feeling a strange sense of alienation from the massed cloud of stars up in the night sky. Then he glances at the tall counter, festooned with yellow legal pads, piles of papers, and all manner of cardboard cups. After shaking out a cigarette, and looking across at the coffee machine, he begins checking his side pockets. "Damn," he says.

The cop behind the counter opens his eyes wide.

"You got a light?" Ben asks. "Must've left mine in the car."

"A light?" The cop frowns and glances around the room as though he's looking for something. "You think it's—"

"His cigarette, Frank," the second cop says as he sets a cardboard cup of swirling brown liquid in front of Ben. He nods to the ashtray and the matchbook over by a pile of papers. "He wants a light for his cigarette."

Frank rolls his eyes and shakes his head. "Oh, sure," he says as he reaches across for the matchbook. He pulls out a match and attempts to strike it on the front of the matchbook but not on the brown stripe.

"Just forget it," says the other cop. He looks across at Ben, sees the puzzled expression on Ben's face, and pulls his gun from his holster. "Sorry," he says to Ben.

(2)

Ben opens his eyes and shakes his head. He must have nodded off.

Two policemen—sheriff's men by the look of them, two fat boys...late forties, early fifties—are leaning over him, beaming big shit-kicking grins. The fatter of the two stands back and sidles onto the tall seat behind the front desk and keeps that smile trained on him like a hunter's rifle. "Feel better?" he says.

Ben nods and watches the other cop back over to a *Vendarama* machine by the side wall.

"It'll be okay," the cop on the tall seat says in a gentle voice. "Whyn't you just tell us the whole thing from the top." The cop has trouble saying words with esses in them and, against his better judgment, Ben wants to smirk at the hissing noise he makes.

"How'd you like your coffee?" the cop over by the *Vendarama* machine asks, adjusting his peaked cap. He hikes his belt up over his belly and rests his hands on his hips like he's just run over from the next-but-one county. The belt returns to its more comfortable position, looking like a smile in a face mostly obscured by an eyeless mask of shirt.

"Huh?" Ben says, staring at the belt. "Oh, like tea," he says, feeling a familiarity in the words…not just because that's what he always says when anyone asks him how he takes his coffee but because the whole thing seems a mite familiar. Like the belt. *Deja vu*, he figures.

He looks down at his hands and is concerned to see that they're shaking, but he puts that down to the accident—he's not completely sure of the nature of the accident but he knows he's been in one. Something to do with the car. "White, no sugar," he says. "I don't see why I can't just go," he adds, turning to the cop on the seat beside him.

The truth is, he can't completely understand why he's here…wherever "here" is. He looks across at the cop by the machine, trying to get away from those piercing eyes and straining to think what might have happened to the car. His *mother's* car.

He looks from one cop to the other, watching those dumb yokel grins.

The cop at the machine either doesn't hear Ben or he's simply ignoring him. He turns away, frowning as he pushes his peaked cap back off his forehead. After reading up and down the menu of selections, the cop hits a button.

Ben reaches into the inside pocket of his jacket and, lifting out a pack of Marlboro Lights, he looks around the one-room office…first over to the double-doors—a thick beam crossing them, resting in two curled metal cradles, one at either side fastened to the wall—then at the windows, feeling a strange sense of alienation from the massed cloud of stars up in the night sky, then at the tall counter, festooned with yellow legal pads, piles of papers, and all manner of cardboard cups. He slides a cigarette into his mouth and pats his jacket pocket. Maybe he's hurt somebody. Maybe he's even killed somebody. Jesus Christ. Now he pats his shirt pocket, pants pockets. "Damn," he says.

The cop behind the counter smiles like a cat that just got the cream. "You need a light?" he says, shooting a quick smile across to his partner.

Ben nods and shrugs. "Must've left mine in the car."

The second cop strolls over and sets a cardboard cup of swirling brown liquid in front of Ben. He nods to the ashtray and the matchbook over by a pile of papers.

Frank reaches across for the matchbook and strikes it, holding it out. Ben leans forward and lights his cigarette, pulling the smoke in and then breathing it out with a sigh. "Mmm," he says as he leans back, "that's better."

He lifts the cardboard cup and takes a sniff. It doesn't look like tea—doesn't look like coffee, either—but he takes a sip anyway, carefully, so he doesn't burn his lips. It doesn't taste of anything at all, but it's warm.

The cop whose name is not Frank moves around and leans on the counter. "Okay?"

Ben nods. "It's warm." When the cop glances across at Frank, Ben says, "It's fine…really," and takes another sip to prove it.

"Okay," Frank says. "So, you want to tell Ed and me the full story?"

"The full story?" Ben shrugs.

The full story. Ben frowns, trying to think, watching the two faces in front of him. He was driving…driving somewhere;that much he can remember. In a car. Yes, a car. His mother's car. He was driving…where? Where was he driving to?

"You okay?" Frank asks.

Ben folds his hands around the cardboard cup, grateful for the heat. It's cold here in the cops' office. He looks around to see if he can see a heater but there doesn't seem to be one. "I already told you all I can remember," he says. "Didn't I?"

"You told us you were driving."

"That's about it," Ben says. "And that isn't much. I'd just as soon get off and out of your hair."

Frank looks across at his partner.

Ed pulls another stool across to the counter and hitches himself onto it. He removes his cap and sets it on the counter, moving the ashtray away. "You're not in our hair," he says. "Not at all."

"You want to pass that over here?" Ben says through a cloud of exhaled smoke. "The ashtray?" He smacks his lips. The smoke has left a bitter taste in his mouth, like the cigarette is stale.

Ed nods and slides it across, watching as Ben taps ash into it.

Ben leans back in his chair, takes another draw on the Marlboro and looks up at the ceiling, squinting at the glare from the overhead light.

That was it!

There was…there was a light. A light outside the car.

"There was a light," he says dreamily.

"A light?" one of the cops says—Ben doesn't see which one because he's still looking at the light on the ceiling.

"Go on," the other cop says, "in your own time."

Ben looks at them. "I guess that's about it. I was driving along, minding my own business, and then there's this humming noise—" he hums and wiggles his hand by way of demonstration "—and then a light—a blinding light—and then, voila, next thing I know, I wake up here in the station with you guys."

"Voila?" says Frank.

"You taking any drugs?" Ed asks.

"Do I *look* like I take drugs?"

Ed looks at Ben's clothes, his eyes traveling down the tweed jacket, shirt and necktie, off-white Chinos, tasseled moccasin loafers. "I don't know. How should you look if you take drugs?"

"What's your full name?" Frank interrupts.

"Ben," Ben says. "Benedict Dussenberg, but everyone calls me Ben."

Frank scribbles something on the paper in front of him. He scribbles for what seems like a long time…a long time to write 'Benedict Dussenberg.' Ben pulls on his cigarette and glances at the other man, the cop named Ed.

Ed smiles and nods an "it'll be okay" smile-and-nod combo.

"And where were you born?" Ed asks without looking up from his notes.

"Where was I *born*? Does that *matter*?" Ben lets out a nervous laugh and looks from one cop to the other. There is no response.

"Just for our records," Ed says, nodding and smiling again.

Ben sighs. "Kissimmee, Florida." He stubs out the Marlboro. "I'm that rarity amongst men: someone who was actually born in Kissimmee."

"A rarity?" Frank looks up, his eyes wide.

Ben chuckles but the chuckle fades away as the two cops watch him. "It was a joke? You know? A funny?"

"Funny," Ed says, rolling the word around like a candy someone has given him and he isn't too sure about the flavor.

"Yes, funny." He shrugs and crosses his legs. "I'm sure there are lots of people who were born in Kissimmee. I was being ironic."

"That's like funny, 'ironic'?"

"Well, not funny *exactly*. I mean—Say, can we just get on with this so I can go? It's been a long night." Ben lifts his left arm and looks at his watch. "Four o'clock! Jesus Christ," he says, jumping to his feet, "I need to make a call."

"Sorry, you can't do that," Ed says, the smile still in place but the nod now replaced by a slow side-to-side shake of the head.

"But I need to call my brother." *That's* where he was going. His brother's house. Out in…in…in Daytona. Daytona Beach. "Daytona Beach!" Ben says excitedly. "That's where I was going—to see my brother in Daytona."

"Good," says Frank.

Ben waits a few seconds, sitting as still as he can. "Look, if I'm being accused of—"

"The phones are down," Frank says.

"Lines," Ed says, a slight hiss of impatience in his voice.

Frank bites on his lower lip. "Lines?"

Ed smiles and nods some more. "The lines are down."

Frank turns back to Ben and shrugs. "Lines and phones," he says, "they're all down."

They sit in silence for a few seconds, each one of them looking at the others in turn until, at last, Ed slaps the counter with his hand. He turns to his partner and says something. Frank pulls back, as though physically hit by the words...if words they are. It sounds more like twigs breaking and water rushing over rocks...sounding something like...something like "sherwantimum."

Ed visibly cringes and clamps his mouth shut, turning to face Ben.

"*Sherwantimum?*" Ben says, looking at the two men.

They don't say anything.

"What was that?"

"What was what?" Frank asks.

"That...what he said." He points at Ed. "Sher-something. That some kind of official term? Some kind of acronym?" How could it be an acronym? Ben thinks. It was a word, not individual letters. He suddenly wishes he hadn't mentioned it. The cop called Ed looks pissed. "I just didn't catch it," Ben says. "But then I probably wasn't meant—"

Ed reaches down to his side and produces a gun, points it at Ben. He's starting to say something—it could be "sorry;" his eyes look like they're apologizing—but Ben can't hear the words above the roar and the blinding flash of jagged light that stutters from the gun's barrel.

(3)

Ben opens his eyes and shakes his head. He must have nodded off.

Two policemen—sheriff's men by the look of them, two fat boys...late forties, early fifties—are leaning over him, beaming big shit-kicking grins. The fatter of the two—though there isn't much in it—stands back and sidles onto the tall seat behind the front desk and keeps that smile trained on him like a hunter's rifle. "Feel better?" he says.

Ben half nods. The truth is he feels pretty sick. His face stings, his gut feel like it's been kicked by a mule and his arms hurt. But the cop asked if he's feeling better; maybe he felt worse before...though he can't remember any before. He makes to look at his watch but it isn't there.

"It'll be okay, you just wait and see," the cop on the tall seat says in a gentle voice. "Whyn't you just tell us the whole thing from the top." The cop has trouble saying words with esses in them. Even though he feels so bad and it's against his better judgment, Ben wants to smirk at the hissing *thuh* noise the cop makes—*juthuh-t...thuh-ee...uh-thuh.*

"How'd you say you liked your coffee?" The other cop is over by the *Vendarama* machine, adjusting his peaked cap. Ben smiles — this guy has a lisp, too. "I didn't," he says.

The cop hikes his belt up over his belly and rests his hands on his hips like he's just run over from the next-but-one county. The belt returns to its more comfortable position, looking like a smile in a face mostly obscured by an eyeless mask of shirt.

"Like tea," he says, loving the line as he always did. "I never drink coffee."

The cop turns around and crouches down so his face is inches away from the menu on the front of the machine.

Ben can't understand why he's here…wherever "here" is. He looks across at the cop by the machine, trying to get away from those piercing eyes and straining to think what might have happened to the car. His *mother's* car. He tries to move in his chair but his back sends a stabbing pain to his brain and he slams out his right hand to hold onto to something…anything. He hears a clunk. When he looks at his right wrist, he sees his wristwatch.

Ben reaches into the inside pocket of his jacket and, lifting out a pack of Marlboro Lights, he slides a cigarette into his mouth and pats his jacket pocket. Maybe he's hurt somebody. Maybe he's even killed somebody. Jesus Christ. Now he pats his shirt pocket, pants pockets. "Damn," he says.

The cop behind the counter smiles like a cat that just got the cream. "You need a light?" he says, shooting a quick smile across to his partner.

Ben nods and shrugs. "Must've left mine in the car."

The second cop strolls over and sets a cardboard cup of swirling brown liquid in front of Ben. He nods to the ashtray and the matchbook over by a pile of papers.

Frank reaches across for the matchbook and strikes it, holding it out. Ben leans forward and lights his cigarette, pulling the smoke in and then breathing it out with a sigh. "Mmm," he says as he leans back."

"Feel better?" Frank asks.

Ben folds his hands around the cardboard cup, grateful for the heat. It's cold here in the cops' office. He looks around to see if he can see a heater but there doesn't seem to be one. "I already told you all I can remember," he says. "Didn't I?"

"You told us you were driving."

"That's about it," Ben says. "And that isn't much. I'd just as soon get off and out of your hair."

Frank looks across at his partner.

Ed pulls another stool across to the counter and hitches himself onto it. He removes his cap and sets it on the counter, moving the ashtray away. "You're not in our hair," he says. "Not at all."

"You want to pass that over here?" Ben says through a cloud of exhaled smoke. "The ashtray?" He smacks his lips. The smoke tastes like bad medicine, leaves his mouth feeling furry.

"So you were born in—" Ed looks down at a pad "—in...Kiss me?"

"Kissimmee. It's in Florida." Ben frowned. Of course it was in Florida. *He* was in Florida, for crissakes. "How'd you know that?"

Frank says, "You already told us?"

"I *did*?" Ben tries to think back to telling these guys anything at all...tries to think back to...The Accident, wondering when they're going to get around to telling him about that but not really in any rush. *It's going to be bad*, a small voice whispers in the back of his head. No, not rushing to hear that news at all. "I'm that rarity amongst men," he says, picking up the thread and letting rip with another favorite line. "Someone who was actually born in Kissimee."

"A rarity?" Frank looks up, his eyes wide.

Ben chuckles but the chuckle fades away as the two cops watch him. *Here it comes*, the small back-of-the-head-voice confides, *Nope, a rarity is someone who turns a little old granny into roadkill.* The voice does a pretty good impersonation of the two cops...and just as Ben thinks that, isn't it strange that both cops sound exactly the same? even down to the lisp? the voice says, *You've done it now, hotshot.*

"It was a joke?" he says, weakly. "You know? A funny?"

"Funny," Ed says, rolling the word around like a candy someone has given him and he isn't too sure about the flavor.

"Yes, funny." He shrugs and crosses his legs, fighting off the urge to tell them he was being ironic—*These suckers wouldn't know anything at all about ironic*, the voice whispers.

"I'm sure there are lots of people who were born in Kissimee." Ben smiles, raises his hands palm up. "Hey, and why not?"

"Why not what?" Ed asks.

Ben shakes his head and watches as the cop scribbles some more.

"I think I should make a call." He looks for his watch and then remembers it's on the other wrist. He looks anyway. "Shit," he says. "It's stopped." He shakes his wrist, listens to the watch and doesn't hear anything. "Batteries," he says.

Frank nods and makes another note.

"You guys got the time?" He looks at them, allows his eyes to move to their wrists. He cannot see any watch, not on either of them.

As Ben looks around the office for one of those big old schoolhouse clocks, Ed says, "We got all the time in the world."

Now *here it com*— the head-voice begins but Ben shakes it silent.

"Sorry, you can't make a call," Ed says, the smile still in place but the nod now replaced by a slow side-to-side shake of the head.

"But I need to call my brother." That's where he was going. His brother's house. Out in…in…in Sherwantimum! Ben lets out a short guffaw. Where the hell was *Sherwantimum?* His brother lived in Daytona. Daytona Beach. "He lives in Daytona Beach!" Ben says excitedly. "That's where I was going—to see my brother in Daytona."

"Good," says Frank.

Ben waits a few seconds, sitting as still as he can. "Look, if I'm being accused of—"

"The lines are down."

Frank turns back to Ben and shrugs. "That's why you can't make the call."

Ben watches as Frank writes more notes. He looks across at Ed and squints. "There something you not telling me?"

"Not telling you?" Frank says.

"Like what?" Ed asks.

"Like…"

Ben thinks carefully about what he's going to say.

Here he is in some hick town…some yellow-headed boil on the backside of Americana, a Norman Rockwell flipside not found in the pages of old issues of *The Post*, where he's dealing with a couple of local yokel Sidney Greenstreet-lookalike cops for whom the only Miranda in their cerebral databank is probably the girl with the overbite and the big tits who serves Sears Tower-sized stacks of pancakes down at the obligatory 24-hour Diner, where the ashtrays never get cleared, the jukebox still plays 78s and the indigenous youth population are able to look left and right at the same time while they play banjo at the speed of light. They could just lock him up and throw away the key forever…sweep out his bones next spring with a big brush made out of hawthorn twigs and bound in twine…muttering Latin prayers as they scatter his ashes on the fields to promote crop-growth. *Hell,* the head-voice adds, *looking at those bellies, maybe they're gonna* eat *you.*

Ben doesn't like the sound of that idea.

"I don't believe you about the phones," he says, filling the suddenly uneasy silence, "that's like what."

Frank looks genuinely puzzled. "Why should we tell you that? You don't believe us?" He turns to his friend. "Can we do that? I mean—"

"Go try them," Ed says. He points to the telephone alongside Frank on the counter. "Go ahead," he says, nodding again. And smiling.

Ben walks across and lifts the receiver, listening. The line is dead. He looks across at Frank and at the paper in front of him. The lardbucket isn't taking notes at all: he's doodling. A series of small shapes and squiggles already cover half of the sheet.

Replacing the receiver, Ben says, "You want to tell me what all this is about?"

"Storm," Ed says. "Took all the lines down. That's what you saw. Lightning."

"I didn't say anything about seeing anything," Ben says. *Did I?* he thinks. Then he remembers that he did see something…some kind of light…a light over the car, following him along the road…no other cars around —

"That's what he saw," Frank agrees in a Howdy Doody voice, interrupting Ben's train of thought.

"You said you saw a light," Ed says, sounding for all the world like Sylvester the cat. *Thufferin' thuccatash!* the head-voice whispers. "It was lightning."

"Lightning?" Ben sniggers. "That was not lightning. I have seen lightning, let me tell you that. Back home, I've seen electrical storms that lit up the world for miles around. And this thing tonight — this light — that was not lightning."

Ed unfastens some of the buttons on his jacket and shakes his head. "Well, that's what it was. A storm. Took all the lines down —"

"Yeah, so you said. And *I* said —"

"And you crashed your vehicle."

"I *crashed* it?" Now they were getting down to it. The routine…good cop, bad cop. Only thing was, Ben couldn't figure out which one was which. "That's my mother's —" Ben lifts his hands and feels his chest and his legs. "I crashed the car? So how come I'm not hurt?"

"You were unconscious. Car went off the side of the road."

"And I was in it?"

Ed nods. No smile.

"I don't remember it. I don't remember any of it."

"That's not unusual," Ed says.

Ben looks at him and then glances across at the man's partner. Then he looks at his watch again. "How long have I been here?"

"A while," Ed says. "You been here a while."

"Yeah, but how long's a while?"

He pats his body exaggeratedly, feels his head. "And, whaddya know…no injuries. I've been out cold and I don't even have a lump on the head. Something's going on here —"

"Who said you'd —"

Ed reaches across to Frank and takes a hold of his jacket sleeve, but Frank isn't having any of it. He shakes his arm free and continues.

"Who said you'd been out in the cold?" The smile beams across his face.

Ben leans across the counter. "You did, that's who."

"Me?"

"It was me," Ed says. "It was me said you'd been unconscious."

Ben straightens up. "Well, it was one of —"

"Unconscious? That's 'out in the cold?'" Frank whispers.

Ed pulls a gun from his holster, places it on his fat lap, shaking his head, smoothing the side of his face with his free hand. "Out cold," he says tiredly, "not out in *the* cold." He looks across at Ben.

Just for a second or two, Ben thinks he can see regret in those piggy eyes.

"Okay, okay…that's it. I'm out of here, cold or not." Ben walks across to the doors and takes hold of the beam: it doesn't move. He makes to turn the handle, figuring that maybe that'll dislodge the beam. That doesn't move, either. He kicks at the doors—not even a shudder of wood in the frame.

Then the office seems to go brilliantly white…as white as the massed stars outside the window, glimmering at him in his hour of need.

(4)

Ben opens his eyes and shakes his head. He must have nodded off.

Two policemen—two fat sheriff's men…late forties, early fifties—are leaning over him, beaming big shit-kicking grins. The fatter of the two sets a cardboard cup of swirling brown liquid in front of Ben. He nods to the ashtray and the matchbook over by a pile of papers. "Smoke?" he says, pronouncing it *thu-moke*.

Ben nods, closes his eyes and tries to straighten himself up in his chair. "Sorry about that," he says. "Tired." No, not just tired, he realizes: he's sick. His body feels like it's on fire, his breath is rasping and he can hear wheezing from his chest. And his head feels tight. If he could only move his hands…

One of the cops reaches across for the matchbook and strikes it, holding it out. Ben says, "Can't move my han—"

"That's okay," the other cop says. He reaches over and shakes a sorry-looking cigarette out of the pack, spilling tobacco on Ben's pants. *My but those pants look in a sorry state*, a small voice in Ben's head whispers as the cop jams the cigarette into Ben's mouth.

As the first cop holds out the lighted match, the cigarette drops from Ben's mouth. He tries to say "sorry," but can't. Instead he watches as the match flame suddenly finds new life, first licking at the skin on the cop's fingers and then taking hold, growing bigger. His eyes wide, Ben looks up at the cop's face, watching the big man watching the flames, seemingly ignorant of any pain.

"Jesus Christ!" Ben says, trying to shuffle himself back, feeling the pressure on his head...trying to get away from the flames...which have now reached the cop's shirt cuff. And, hey...the other cop has pulled a gun from somewhere. Big barrel, Ben thinks. Doesn't look like any —

(5)

Ben opens his eyes and shakes his head. He must have nodded off.

Two pairs of legs are standing at either side of him. One pair steps back as Ben struggles to move and sidles over to what must be a seat behind the desk in front of him. "Feel better?" the legs' voice says.

Ben sends out sensory feelers before he attempts to answer that. It doesn't take long: he feels like shit. Every single part of his body feels like it has been kicked for hours. He's bent over in a chair, his head almost between his knees. He looks down and sees that his off-white Chinos are now very off-white indeed. At first glance, they look like they've been splattered with mud...and then Ben recognizes the marks as dried blood. The sides of the trousers have been ripped up the seams, only one of his tasseled moccasin loafers — the left one — is still there; the other foot is bare, bare and swollen.

"My God," Ben says. "Have I been in an accident?" His voice sounds like that guy in the wheelchair...the one who wrote about the history of time.

Hands pull him upright and he sees he's in an office. It's night outside the window...lots of stars. There are two cops in here with him...cops who never heard of the word 'diet.'

"That's what *we* want to know," one of the cops says.

The other cop sets a cardboard cup of swirling brown liquid in front of Ben. He nods to the ashtray and the matchbook over by a pile of papers.

"Smoke?" he asks.

Ben struggles forward, feeling sharp pains shoot down each arm. "You bet," he says. The cop reaches into Ben's jacket pocket, pulls out a pack of Marlboro Lights. Ben stares at the ragged sleeves of his own jacket. "Good God," Ben says. He looks up at the cops and sees them both watching him. For a second, he wants to cry...wants to tell them enough...no more — but...enough? Enough *what*? No more *what*?

The cop shakes a cigarette out of the pack. It's the last one. *Boy, you got through those fast*, a small voice in Ben's head says. *Wasn't it full when you set out?*

Set out? Ben says to himself silently. Set out where?

Sherwantimum, the head-voice whispers with a chuckle. *Where else?*

The cop places the pack on the counter and Ben frowns at the faded packaging. Must be the light in here...or maybe he's damaged his eyes in...in what? In the accident, that's what. There's no way he's going to look like this — his pant-legs looking like he's been through a swamp, his jacket in tatters — unless he's been in an accident. He looks at the two cops. The thing is, has he hurt anyone?

Placing the cigarette in Ben's mouth, the cop strikes a match and holds it under the end. It tastes bad...stale and old. Maybe he's had some kind of medicine...some kind of pain-killer...making the cigarette taste so —

Without realizing, he's managed to raise his right hand, reaching with it for his cigarette to remove it from his mouth so that he can breathe. The hand comes into view, his jacket, his shirt-cuff...and something else...something faintly-white and plastic-looking...like a membrane glove covering the hand...and the hand looks...looks lumpy underneath that glove. As he reaches for the cigarette, the glove splits open at the wrist and something gelatinous

that's you, amigo, the head-voice chuckles, *that's you leaking all over the damned floor*

pouring out in thick rivulets, hanging down like cuckoo-spit.

Then there's a muttering sound...like twigs breaking and water rushing...and then there's a flash from somewhere in the office.

(6)

Ben opens his eyes and shakes his head. He must have nodded off.

Two fat faces are leaning over him. Cops. Their eyes are steely cold, their mouths unsmiling.

"How'd you feel?" one of them asks.

Ben tries to speak but the words won't come. His body feels like it's in a vice and his ass feels like it's got something inside it — something long and cold: he tries to clench his buttock muscles but it hurts.

He closes his eyes and tries to gather his thoughts.

Where am I? What has happened? He can smell shit. Smells bad, like some kind of crop nutrient...fish manure.

He opens his eyes again, slowly this time.

It's an office...a police station, Sheriff's office...something like that. Outside the window it's dark. Ben can see stars...lots of stars...clusters of them looking so close they could be scratching the window.

"I got you a Like Tea," a voice says.

Ben grunts acknowledgment and tries to lift his right arm, give a wave of thanks, but it won't move. He tries the left one—same thing.

He closes his eyes again, retreating once more into the safe darkness. "Can't...can't move my arms," he says.

"Yes you can," the voice says.

Ben feels hands on his head, hears a soft scraping noise. The pressure on his head eases a little and he feels a wave of pins and needles start in his upper arms, moving slowly—slowly but surely—down to his forearms and his wrists, then his fingers. His fingers feel like they're about to explode out of the ends and, for a few seconds, he wants to cry out...and then the sensation goes.

"Try now," the voice says.

"I got you a Like—"

"He knows about the Like Tea," the voice snaps.

Ben lifts his right arm slowly, lifts it to his head and feels around gently. His fingers scratch at his head like crab-claws...like they don't have any skin on them. But the crab-claws feel something...he's wearing some kind of metallic head brace. He drops the hand to his side without trying to look at it

Sherwantimum—maybe that's what the thing on his head is called... and he starts to sob.

"You want to try sit up?" the voice asks.

Ben lifts his head and looks at the voice's owner. It's one of the fat cops—poor guy, got some kind of skin complaint: flesh all bunched up on either side of his head.

The face nods, the flaps moving around. "You're going to be—"

"Hey," the other voice interrupts, "your face."

Ben watches two hands come up into view...watches the hands take hold of the two skin-flaps and pull them tight, back to the ears. As this takes place, a thin tear appears down the man's forehead, snaking to the bridge of his stubby nose.

The man closes his eyes for an instant and then seems to fall on top of Ben.

Ben grunts, the air knocked from his lungs. When he opens his eyes he sees the man's face right in front of his own...the forehead ripped right down past the nose now. There's something glistening behind there...something greenish and yellowish, moving side to side, a thin, translucent film flicking up over it and then disappearing. When the man speaks, fumbling with his hand—Ben can't see what he's doing—Ben smells something old and rancid.

"Sorry," the man says, pushing something hard into Ben's stomach.

Ben frowns. *Sorry?* he thinks. *What fo—*

(7)

Ben opens his eyes. He must have nodded off.

Wherever he is, it is silent. Not so much as the sound of a breath.

He instinctively tries to shake his head but nothing seems to happen…no sense of movement. He can't even turn his head. Can't seem to move anything…can't even feel anything.

He's in an office. A sheriff's office, looks like…or some kind of police station. Two cops are sitting in front of him, lounging back on a couple of low-backed summer-chairs, their heads only a foot or so above the ground…and yet, directly in front of Ben. Ben thinks that's a little strange perspective-wise but he lets it go. Behind the cops, behind the counter, is a high window: outside it's night…lots of stars…whole bunches of them, like clouds. He can't see the moon. Right in front of him is the edge of a table—he's *on* the table, he suddenly realizes…actually on the damned table.

One of the cops—both of them are really fat…huge…and they've got some kind of skin problem—one of them stands up, moving with difficulty, and comes over to Ben. The cop is holding something in his hand, something shiny looks like…something catching the glare of the stars outside in the night, making their light dance across the office.

The cop bends down in front of Ben.

He looks sad, this cop. And tired.

The cop holds up his hand and Ben sees a glass jar.

On top of the jar are two eyes, secured in gauze-like material attached to a wooden board. There are tiny lights on the board, recessed back from the eyes themselves, twinkling like the stars outside the window.

Running from the board into the jar—which is attached to a whole clutter of wires and springs and pipettes and which appears to contain a dull-looking gray fibrous lump—are two spindly, glistening wires. These two wires lead, like umbilical cords, back behind the jar to a glass tank surrounded by a lot of flashing lights.

In the tank—submerged in the water or whatever it is—somebody has dumped a whole carcass'-worth of entrails and organs…Ben can see a heart pumping silently. And outside the tank, attached to another wooden board is a pair of ears held in place by an elaborate system of wires and clamps which, in turn, connect up with the apparatus attached to the side of the tank and to a tall speaker standing by itself.

Ben tries to frown. But can't.

He tries to blink. But can't.

He tries to speak. But can't.

The thing in the man's hand is a mirror—Ben sees that now. But if it's a mirror, why can't he see *himself* when he's looking at it?

The cop puts the mirror down out of sight and lifts a small box with a switch on it. He places this on the table in front of Ben and flicks the switch.

Sound fills the silence…the sound of distant engines humming, the sound of muted voices…strange voices babbling from somewhere in a metallic tone…sounding for all the world like twigs breaking and water rushing.

Into this comes a voice. The voice of the cop, Ben realizes as he sees the man's lips moving.

"It'll be okay, just tell us the whole thing from the top," the cop is saying with a slight lisp. He folds his hands calmly and carefully on the desk in front of him.

Ben hears a loud screaming noise, building and building and building…it seems to be coming from somewhere behind him…just behind him, where the tall speaker sat on the tabletop.

And then the cop shakes his head and flicks off the switch, stopping the screaming. Stopping everything…returning the office to silence.

The cop reaches down to his holster, starts to draw his gun and then stops. He lifts his hands to his head and begins to pull his face open. His lips are moving again—briefly, until they come off in the cop's hands amidst folds of wrinkled skin—but Ben can't hear anything…except maybe the memory of a scream. Hoarse now. Tired.

If only he didn't have to look…

Songs of Leaving

The final ships go up reaching for the stars in the closing days of what is to be the last winter of the world.

They ride interlocking plumes of power and steam like anxious fingers of smoky fire, colored sunset orange and cornfield yellow in the still afternoon. And each of them belches out a tumultuous roar, a hymn of steam and gasoline, a cadence of harmony and discordance, a syncopated symphony of regret and anticipation.

A song of leaving.

They have already left from Islamabad and Jerusalem, these ships—or ships like them...like them in intent if not in appearance—and from the arid wastes outside of Beijing and the heat-shimmering flats of Florida; from the snow-covered plains surrounding Moscow and the scorched tundra of Kenya. From a thousand thousand places, the ships have lifted into the sky in these tired days, with the distant horizon darkened not only by their sheer number but also by the approaching asteroid.

The towering silver points of the final ships rise to hit the clouds and then puncture them, pulling them down and around their midriffs, bellies bulging with the almost-last people of Earth, their pinpoint faces turned to the grimy windows, acceleration pulling at muscle, sinew and flesh as they watch the cities and the meadows fall behind, and the endless gray ribbons of highway and the veiny drifts of water drop down and down until they are at first partially obscured by the clouds and then completely obliterated by swirling whiteness.

On the ground, silent faces—some alone, some huddled in groups— also watch as the last ships dwindle in the azure blue, growing smaller until they are no longer ships but merely glittering shadows, and then distant needles and then, at last, merely the tiniest specks in an otherwise clear sky.

And then they are gone.

Ahead of the ships lie the domed cities of the Moon and Mars. Beyond those, a series of space-borne stations littering the heavens, some finished and some still under preparation. A colossal paper chase of metal and plastic, stepping stones of rivet and cable, leading humanity's survivors across the airless void and on towards untold adventures and undreamed-of destinies. The ships will touch down and their passengers and crews will consolidate and plan their next steps, always looking with one eye to the darkness before them and the other to the ghost of the doomed planet they have left behind. Only some of them will survive the journey. But that's something they do not think about.

Back on the Earth the silence rushes in to remove the memory of the ships' engines, runs along the worn-down pathways of a million forests and the dusty streets of a million towns, replacing their throaty roar with the sound of the wind through the trees and the creak of swinging store signs.

⚜

The asteroid was first noticed by amateur astronomer Julio Shennanen, through the $199.95 telescope bought as a thirtieth birthday present by his brother Manuel from the *Keep Watching the Skies* store on Bleecker Street and erected in Julio's backyard in the Brooklyn suburb of Park Slope.

Julio, who was a native of New Orleans, had moved north when his wife Carmen had gotten herself a job as a child-minder to a wealthy couple in a penthouse apartment overlooking Central Park. Initially referred to as "Shennanen's Folly" by a skeptical sky-gazing fraternity, the object reported as a shadow over Alpha Centauri turned out to be a whole lot more substantial and a whole lot nearer when it could be viewed by something costing a little more than a week's grocery bill. It turned out to be a whole lot more menacing, too.

At the request of its discoverer the object was renamed "Fat Tuesday," ostensibly because that was the day on which it was first spotted (and because, at roughly the size of the entire Eastern seaboard, it was big). But the underlying reason was an acknowledgment of Julio's hometown—inasmuch as "Fat Tuesday" was a literal translation of "Mardi Gras," the name now regarded as the entire celebration but originally intended as referring only to the final day…a day of feasting. It was also—and perhaps more significantly—a recognition on Shennanen's part, even in those early days of the object's arrival in our planetary skies, that the Carnival's days were numbered…the Carnival being Earth and all who lived upon it. A kind of "lucky" cosmic coming-together of events for would-be wordsmiths with nothing better to do with their long New York evenings than star-gaze.

But there was nothing "lucky" about the appearance of Fat Tuesday, particularly where Julio Shennanen was concerned. By that time, the writing was on the wall for the world, and there were some in the world who held Shennanen responsible—sad and bitter folks who had spent a lifetime blaming others for anything that happened to them. And so it was that, on the evening of the anniversary of his discovery, the computer programming sky watcher was shot and killed outside his home, with Carmen looking on from the bedroom window. When Julio's screaming wife ran out to help him, she got a bullet in her back for her trouble.

In a letter of pasted newspaper copy sent to the *New York Times*, the assassin said that he (or she—nobody ever found out) was committed to ridding the world of this blight on humanity (Shennanen) and, in so doing, remove the threat of Fat Tuesday. (Though quite how those two items could be connected was beyond all but those who sent fifty-dollar bills to PO Box addresses posted up on TV screens at the end of an afternoon session of down-home "back to basics" sermonizing on cable.)

The assassin was never caught—at least, not by the authorities—and the threat to others in the scientific community remained. Despite the fact that the media and pretty much everyone she spoke to or heard from condemned the action with vigor, a now wheelchair-bound Carmen Shennanen left the excesses of New York State and returned to the Big Easy where she disappeared into an anonymity worthy of the FBI informant protection program and one that even Julio's brother Manuel could not pierce.

⁂

Meanwhile, Fat Tuesday blunders on.

According to one pundit, the asteroid is on course to "kiss" the Earth in the early afternoon of February 8, 2007, just seventeen months after its first sighting. "The particularly bad news is that this is going to be no platonic peck on the cheek," NASA's resident expert in "heavenly affairs"

Professor Jerry Mizzalier goes on to tell Oprah Winfrey in a show interview whose transmission is debated for a full week before eventual release to a waiting and increasingly despondent world. "It'll be the full enchilada," Mizzalier continues, "a big smackeroo on the lips and the tongue right down the throat."

"And then?" Oprah asks in an uncharacteristically trembling voice.

Mizzalier's shrugged response says it all: the kiss is just the foreplay. After that, mankind gets fucked. Big Time.

⚜

When you put your mind to it, you can do a lot in nine months.

Throughout 2006 and into the January of Earth's final year, all potential solutions were considered while, at the same time, work continued feverishly on the construction of spaceships that would, if all else failed, carry the seed of humanity — and as many of its fellow planetary inhabitants as could be realistically mustered in so short a time — to the stars.

The alternatives were running out fast. Nuclear missiles failed to have any effect. "It's kind of like trying to blow up an elephant with a .45," Jerry Mizzalier explained colorfully to Dan Rather. "You may get lucky and dislodge a nickel-sized chunk of meat but that's about all." That was Mizzalier's last TV appearance. Two days later, he told the *Washington Post* he was going down to the Keys to make his peace with God — "And maybe do a little fishing on the side."

Four attempts at landing a hand-picked crew of demolition experts *a la* the *Armageddon* and *Deep Impact* movies of the late 1990s got no nearer to Fat Tuesday than a few hundred miles. It seemed that either real-life Bruce Willises and Robert Duvalls were somewhat thinner on the ground than their celluloid counterparts...or movie-makers and screenwriters had simply got it wrong (hard as that was for many to accept).

Perhaps not quite so colorful as Jerry Mizzalier but no less succinct was the nonagenarian British astronomer Patrick Moore's verdict on BBC television's *Newsnight*. "One should liken it to a game of snooker," the monocled scientist explained to Jeremy Paxman, with a characteristic pinwheeling flourish of his arms, "with Earth sitting defenseless in the middle of the table, right in the path of the white ball."

On the other side of the Atlantic a couple of days later, Colorado physicist W. Martin Parmenter picked up the analogy on a special edition of *The Jerry Springer Show* when, along with other luminaries of the scientific es-

tablishment, he was invited to hypothesize the outcome of the "Big Kiss."
"I don't know diddly about snooker," Parmenter said laconically, "but if
we switch to the game *I* play, then we're the eight ball on a table in a pool
hall in Denver…and we're about to get hit full on with enough force to
drop us — or what's left of us — in the corner pocket on a table in a cellar
barroom in Mexico City."

The disappearance of Springer from the airwaves following the show
was openly considered by many to be the single silver lining in the approaching dark cloud that was Fat Tuesday…that and the appearance of
an advertising board carried by a barefoot man down the full length of
Broadway, his handiwork proclaiming, in hand-scrawled letters that were
a mix of caps and lower case, "It's official — Fat Tuesday is a load of balls."

By the time of Earth's last fall, with the browning leaves bidding a
fond and final farewell, all continuing attempts to avert the inevitable catastrophe were cosmetic at best. The real energy was now being channeled
worldwide into the construction of spaceships, huge gleaming monoliths
that grew quickly on hastily-prepared launch-pads around the globe. That
not all of these vehicles would survive the trip was accepted, as was the
inescapable fact that, statistically speaking — particularly considering the
haste and the resulting corner-cutting of their translation from blueprint to
steel and wire and circuit board — many of the ships would not even make
it off the ground. But it was a risk that an escape-mad humanity receiving
its quota of "lottery" tickets ("Life's a lottery," ran the impassioned ad cam-
paign, "so make sure of your tickets today") was more than prepared to
take.

⚜

When the last ship to successfully depart the green hills of Earth lifts to
relative safety above the planet's atmosphere on February 4 2007 — a Tuesday, appropriately enough — the tally of successes against failures (for anyone remaining on Earth who might be interested) is an impressive 3.718 to
one.

And then they are gone.

Small ships, sleek pointy-nosed sliver-shaped missiles bearing ten- or
twelve-strong crews snuggled amongst carefully-secured boxes of artifacts
and flags and religious ornamentation, and huge-bellied blunderbusses
carrying cryogenically frozen embryos of the Earth's animal and insect
populations and thin trays of seeds containing all manner of florae and

faunae...all have disappeared over the months and weeks and days, up into the sky and far away. Now all that is left are the unlucky ones, the ones whose lottery tickets haven't paid off.

There are billions of them in mountains and valleys and towns and cities, all the distant off-the-beaten-track communities from China to Scotland, from the wine-growing regions of France to the sidewalk cafes of Vienna, all of them paradoxically breathing a sigh of relief as the last gleaming means of escape passes behind the clouds — in much the same way as the terminally-ill patient relaxes when all the fit-and-well visitors depart the hospital and leave the slowly dying to get on with the job in peace and quiet. "Misery loves company," is the way it's often described.

But the truth of the matter is that, in these final hours, there is little sign of misery.

Movies and literature which, in the last half of the previous century, foretold of anarchy and chaos in the face of humanity's end, couldn't have got it more wrong. With the last spaceship now a memory of chances missed and debts now to be paid, a strange calm falls across the cities and towns and villages of Earth.

What little looting there has been has been dealt with swiftly and without mercy. A do-it-yourself system of law and order has grown throughout the winter months, bringing with it an acceptable face of vigilantism in which people are openly but unemotionally intolerant of any among their number who fail to live up to the dignity now expected of the last remnants of the species.

Because, after all, what use is a new video recorder? Or precious jewelry? And anyway, most storekeepers simply leave their stores open and go home. So stuff is there for the taking but most people leave it be: gleaming Chevys and Cadillacs sitting in unmanned showrooms; the very latest fashions from Gucci and Versace adorning silent mannequins in the windows of stores whose doors lie carelessly and casually ajar; and rare first issues — in mint condition, no less — of silver- and golden-age DC comic books, their costumed impossibly-super heroes staring off the covers regretting that there's nothing even Krypton's first son can do to avert the disaster spiraling closer with every passing minute.

Everywhere is quiet.

People stay home, make love gently and talk feverishly, trying to pack all the thoughts and hopes and love they thought they had left into the few hours that remain. Sons and daughters return home like it's Thanksgiving or Christmas. In between their conversations, minds idly drift to thoughts of what it will be like when the end finally comes, wondering what it will be like, sitting in a fifteen-story apartment building and seeing a wave of water thundering towards the window blotting out the blood-red sky…wondering what it will feel like to have your Midwest home blown up from around you while you crouch with your family behind the sofa or, if you have one, in the cellar listening to the sound of Earth breaking up. Consequently, most folks don't leave potential talk- or love-making-time empty.

The last ship has gone.

Fat Tuesday's kiss is now accurately scheduled for 2:17 PM on Saturday.

On Wednesday, the Earth gives up its dead.

✦✦✦

"Hey."

The boy turns around and looks at the man standing out on the street by the white picket-fence gate. "Hey yourself," he says, shielding his eyes against the sun's glare. It's almost midday and the California heat is stifling but, even so, the street is busy with people.

The boy's name is William Freeman—his friends call him Billy; his parents, Will—he is twelve years old and suddenly acutely aware that, as far as he had been concerned, the street had been pretty much deserted the last time he looked. And that was only a few minutes earlier.

"You must be Will," the man says, beaming a big smile and resting a liver-spotted hand on the gatepost as he looks William up and down.

William nods. The man must be a friend of his mom and dad, someone who's maybe been out of town for a while and has come back to more familiar surroundings for when the asteroid hits. Right now, though, William is more concerned with a tall thin man standing across the street with his back to them. This new man's hands are resting on his hips and he's shaking his head staring up at Mr. and Mrs. Manders' place, seeming to take a lot of interest in the new glass conservatory Mr. Manders tacked on a couple of summers back.

"Don't you want to know who *I* am?" the old man at William's gate asks in a voice bearing more than a hint of amusement.

When William turns back to the man he can see the distant shape of Fat Tuesday over to the east, hanging on the horizon like a party lantern.

"Who are you?" he asks, wondering if it was his imagination or if the man suddenly seems a mite familiar.

The screen door squeaks open behind him, whines shut and clatters twice. William turns and sees his mother walking across the lawn, picking her steps real careful, like she was walking on thin ice. Her left hand is up to her mouth, her right holding a hank of hair at the side of her head. She's staring—with a mixture of frown and wide-eyed amazement—not at William but over his shoulder. William looks back at the old man.

"Hello, Pooch," the man says.

"Daddy?"

George Chinnery was the first to make contact. It had to be *some*body and, as luck would have it, it was George.

George slipped away to new adventures in the spring of 1998, leaving behind him a breathless cardiac arrest team, a callous flat green line on a bedside monitor and a weeping daughter. William had been almost four years old but still young enough to forget quickly. Forget and accept…or maybe the two were the same thing.

But while George was the first, over in the quiet suburb of Hawthorne, an area in the sprawling Californian conurbation that was famous for producing one of the last century's most enduring musical acts, the others quickly followed.

Hillary and Sam Arnold sit on the bed in their son's room.

Around them are strewn the collected ephemera that is all that remains of little Joseph Arnold: comic books, a Millennium Falcon toy spaceship— that looks nothing like the huge ships that have so recently left Hillary and Sam and the rest of the Earth far behind them—and a few favorite pieces of clothing that Hillary just hadn't had the heart to throw out when the tumor took their little boy away.

There are no tears. The tears dried up years ago. Now there is only a grim and quiet resignation that sometimes fades right into the background…only to return when they least expect it, usually in the mornings when, on waking, the imminence of Fat Tuesday—or even its very existence — seems for just a fraction of a second to be the remnants of a very bad dream. Only it isn't a dream at all.

"You want me to get some pills or something?" Sam Arnold asks his wife in a voice that is just above a whisper. He runs his hand down her back.

She shakes her head and folds the sleeves of little Joseph's sweater, laying the garment gently on her son's pillow.

"Jack Mason says old man Phillips — you know? down on Times Square? — he's giving them away to any that wants them. Wouldn't take me — "

"I couldn't bring myself to do that," Hillary tells her husband, turning to look at his face, seeing the darkness beneath his eyes. She recognizes that darkness: it isn't fear, it's the helplessness he feels at being unable to do anything for those he cares about. Since the death of Joseph and their decision not to try replace him, that "those" is just her.

He runs his hand up to her neck and gently kneads the skin between her hairline and the collar of her housedress. "It wouldn't hurt," he says. "Jack says old man Phillips said — "

"How do they know?" Hillary says in a tired voice. "And, anyway, it's not the hurt I'm bothered about."

"Then what is it?"

She shrugs and looks up at the window, imagining the cold skeletal trees of Central Park just a couple of blocks away. "No idea." She moves closer to him on the bed and wraps her arms around him, smelling his musk of fading cologne and skin mingled with cigarette smoke. "I had the dream again last night," she whispers.

"Little Joe?"

Hillary nods. "He said he was coming for us."

Sam pushes her back gently, holding her at arm's length. "Is *that* why you don't want me to get the pills?"

Hillary's eyes search her husband's face for some indication of an answer to his question. "I don't know," she says at last. "Maybe."

"Oh, honey," he says, "I wish it could — "

The knock on the apartment door sounds like a rifle crack in the stillness of the New York afternoon. And yet, for all that, it is a small knock…a delicate knock. And outside the window there seems to be some kind of commotion and lots of shouting…like a parade, maybe.

The news traveled fast, spreading like wildfire fueled by the wind of the approaching asteroid. Dead people were coming back to life…kind of.

It sounded comic book-crazy but it was true.

Telephones the world over buzzed and hummed with the news: sons and fathers, daughters and mothers, uncles and aunts and sisters and brothers…they were all coming back, sauntering down paths and knocking on doors, drifting into backyards and onto porches, peering through once-familiar kitchen windows and smiling never-forgotten smiles.

At first, the people who heard the news thought it might be some byproduct of the asteroid…like something dreamed up by George Romero and Stephen King, a plague of flesh-eating cadavers shambling the highways and byways of the doomed world in a final devastating flourish of death and destruction. But then their own doorbells and buzzers sounded or their own windows rattled with a distantly familiar tapping or mailboxes clattered open to allow long-ago special calls in long-ago special voices that had lived on only in dreams and wishful memories. Sure, it just had to be something to do with Fat Tuesday, but the animated corpses seemed to possess not only no malice, evil intentions or appetite for human skin and cartilage but also no idea of how they had gotten there.

They came in droves, huge processions of men, women and children, some young and some old, some no more than babes in arms carried by another of their number, and all of them marveling at the things they passed by, each of them making their way to a familiar place and to familiar faces.

They came into towns and cities, along arterial blacktops empty of cars and trucks, and along the narrow roads that are the blue veins connecting communities. And a few came by other means…

❧⊙❧

The Mississippi River is almost 2,500 miles long, drifting and winding from a stream you could step across in northern Minnesota and washing miles wide through the country's heartland and down into the Gulf of Mexico.

If you counted the Missouri—which feeds into the Mississippi from the Rockies just north of St. Louis—and the Ohio, which gets in on the act around Cairo, IL, and the Red, the Arkansas, the Tensas and the Yazoo…you'd be talking about getting on for 4,000 miles of river system. Only the Nile and the Amazon are longer.

The Mississippi and its tributaries drain almost one and a quarter million miles, including all or part of thirty-one states and some 13,000 square miles of Canada. Through Prairie du Chien in Wisconsin it drifts, where French fur traders exchanged goods and services with the Winnebago; down through Cave-in-Rock, Illinois and into Vicksburg, with its vast Civil War battlefield where, on a still night you might just hear the cries of Southerners still withstanding General's Grant's forty-seven-day siege; and on down to Hannibal, boyhood home of Sam Clemens, who took the *nom de plume* of the riverboat captains' calls for measuring the water's depth—"Mark Twain!"

So many places along that drift of water, so many swirls and eddies, you could imagine many things getting out into that watery flow to sail along.

So maybe you could imagine this: a huge, gaudily-painted floating palace pulled from the secret depths of the river somewhere where nobody has ever been, a pair of enormous paddle wheels rucking up the frothy water, its saloons decked out in gilt and scarlet and velvet, bright white paneling and the sound of banjo-picking…sailing slowly, drifting between the West Bank and Algiers, drifting under the Huey P. Long bridge upriver near Harahan, and then settling, just a stone's throw from the Moonwalk promenade of the French Quarter where, on an evening in the dog days of the world, a saxophone's lilting refrain merges into the sound of accordions and the smell of tobacco and the whoops and cries of people making the most of their unearned death sentence.

And as the riverboat nears the side, it sounds its horn, a mournful but somehow strangely exultant wail that breaks through the sounds of sometimes reluctant and sometimes forced revelry, causing it to stop, not all at once but itself like a wave, a wave of silence washing through the port of New Orleans where Mardi Gras is in full swing, a true "farewell to the flesh." And there they are, hanging from the sides of the riverboat in all manner of clothing, old and young alike, hanging onto railings and wainscoting, leaning against funnel and gate, waving for all their worth to folks in the crowds that soon gather around the moorings.

At the front of the throng of hand-holding beer-drinking revelers sits a woman in a wheelchair, frowning in a mixture of disbelief and an excitement she thought she would never feel again. For now, in this magical short final era of the history of Earthbound humanity, a new ability holds sway…an ability known only to children, the mythical race that knows the power of the darkness and the light alike, that knows the real power of acceptance without reason.

"The dead are here!"

The cry moves through the crowds like the wind itself, touching every one of them as they recognize faces on the riverboat, return smiles and waves, anxiously waiting for the boat to dock so that they may all be reunited.

Then, "There's another one!" someone calls.

And there, up the river, is another boat just like the first one, paddle wheels thrashing the surf of the old Mississippi, churning it up like watery thunder. And behind that one, itself bedecked with a hundred or a thousand waving bodies, comes another, letting out its steamboat whistle cry…only this one doesn't sound mournful at all; this one sounds like the biggest cheer that ever was…until the boat behind it, just coming around the bend now, pulls fully into view and lets rip. Now *that's* the *biggest* cheer that ever was…at least for a minute or two, a deep-throated calliope wheeze that sets folks to holding their ears and laughing and crying all at the same time.

They hear the clarion call out in the plantations surrounding New Orleans, plantations with names such as Rosedown and Destrehan, where the *garconnieres* are already filling with old familiar faces…work-clothed men in overalls wading through the cotton plants or the rice, indigo, hemp, tobacco, sorghum, corn, peanuts, potatoes and sugar, beaming grins big enough to crack the whole face wide open, or appearing from around majestic live oaks bedecked in Spanish moss and from behind centuries-old camellias and azaleas, the watery sunshine dappling them like fireflies.

As the ships reach the dock one by one the people jump and drop and sometimes just walk right off. Their clothes are sometimes yesterday's fashions and sometimes straight out of the turn of the century, a mix of zoot suits and linen jackets, lettered sweaters and gingham dresses, and all kinds of uniform—army, navy, air force…and many of them stylistically different, too. But all of them touch down on the riverside walkway beaming big smiles, their eyes scanning the crowds trying to pick out the faces they've come to see. And every time one of the waiters greets one of the visitors— be the newcomer old or young—their first word is often their name followed by a query.

"Poppa?"

"Sandy, is it really you?"

"Son? Welcome home…we're real proud of you."

And then come the questions…lots of questions. But the answer is always the same: "I don't know…I just don't know."

In the massing thrusting pushing throng of people, some searching and some who have already found each other, a wheelchair threads its way to the water's edge where the big paddleboat sits, its deckboards creaking and its funnel hissing softly. The woman in the chair searches the faces and the bodies, ignoring the good-natured jostling as she watches the arms outstretch, thinking each time that the arms are for her but then realizing that the clothes are wrong or the color of the skin is wrong or—

"Carmen. Over here!"

She feels emotion well up in her stomach, feels a tingle down her legs that she hasn't felt for what seems like a lifetime, and she feels the tell-tale tickle of a tear on her cheek. "Julio?"

Her eyes scan the knees and legs that surround her as she struggles to lift herself from the chair that has become her home, and amidst the mustaches and the sideburns, the long-tail coats and the swirling crinoline, she sees him.

And he sees her.

❦

It's Saturday morning.

Just another Saturday morning, to look at the folks strolling the streets of New Orleans. But if you sneaked and looked into the French Quarter—not that you'd need to sneak: you can hear the hullabaloo clear across town—you'd think that maybe the Saturday night partying has started just a little sooner than usual. Either that, or the Friday night session is going on past its usual cut-off time.

But then it isn't just another Saturday morning. In fact, it isn't just any morning at all: it's the last day of the world, and the songs of leaving it all behind fill the air like the scent of summer jasmine, thick and wistful.

The light is soft, like a late fall afternoon, with Fat Tuesday now sitting squarely between the sun and the ground, plummeting on to keep its scheduled appointment at 2:17 EST. Just a little over four hours from now.

All of the farewells have been said—most of them many times during the past three days. But there's been a lot of greetings, too.

Now the dead walk and sit alongside the living, chewing the fat, tapping a foot to the music that seems to wash around everything like the early-morning mist that sometimes spills over from the river.

Over on Bourbon Street, Fats Domino and Mac Rebbenack are duetting on a couple of Steinway Grands rolled out into the street from Jeff Dickerson's instrument store, while Alvin "Shine" Robinson powers up and down the fretboard on the Earl King favorite, "Let The Good Times Roll," while Robert Parker's sax wails and whines. The crowd cheers at every bum note that spills out—they've been cheering since well before dawn—as long as the constantly changing band has been playing (and drinking...so you can forgive the musicians a lot). Truth to tell, you can forgive anyone pretty much anything this morning.

In the audience, watching Fats and the good Doctor hammer the ivories, are Professor Longhair and Lloyd Price, Huey "Piano" Smith and Joe Tex, Ernie K. Doe and Lee Dorsey. They'll all get a turn on the instruments and many of them already have. And if and when folks fancy a little oration between the music, former governor Huey Long is all set to bend their ears for one last time...though right now, just like everyone else, he seems content to whoop and laugh and slap his leg, spurred on by Democratic congressman John Breaux, the pair of them having given up trying to talk over the music.

The truth is, it's impossible to figure out who's dead and who's alive. Some of these folks you recognize straight off, and you wonder to yourself...wonder as you grab another bottle of beer from a passing waiter...you wonder just which is which. Not that it matters.

Sitting at one of the tables outside Cafe du Monde, at the corner of Decatur and St. Ann, working their way through a plate of beignets and their third cup of cafe au lait while listening to Allen Toussaint play a little boogie-woogie on an old stand-up wooden piano, are Anne Rice, William Faulkner, Ellen Gilchrist and British publisher John Jarrold (who, in all his years in the business, has never missed a convention in the Big Easy). Meanwhile, leaning against the front wall chatting to the driver of a horse-drawn cab, Jack Kerouac and Allen Ginsburg seem to be sharing a joke with Truman Capote and John Kennedy Toole...with Kerouac holding up a copy of Toole's Pulitzer Prize-winning A Confederacy of Dunces and shaking his head. Toole just shrugs and allows a slow trickle of water into his glass of absinthe, watching with satisfaction as the liquid turns a pale green.

On the riverfront round back of Cafe du Monde, hookers provide final—and occasionally first—sensuous experiences to men and boys on the steps and amidst the foliage, the sound of their anxious enjoyment permeating the already filled air.

A shoe-shine boy stops Julio Shennanen—"A high five for the shine and just your thanks for the time," he says, holding his right hand in the air, fingers stretched out like twigs. "Gotta have clean shoes to meet your maker."

"I'm fine, but thanks," Julio says.

"How 'bout you, missie?" the man asks, a grin from ear to ear exposing bridgework gaps you could suck pickles through. "Polish up them wheels so fine you could make the sun put on *his* glasses."

Carmen laughs and claps her hands. "No, really," she tells him, reaching out to touch his arm. "We're both fine. Thanks."

The man shrugs and tells them to have a good day, and then he shakes his head and chuckles as he walks off. Alongside him, in the bushes next to a telescope overlooking the river, a tall, red-headed woman is sitting astride a young barefoot man. Carmen and Julio can see only the woman's back and the man's feet poking out from beneath her long skirts, and, just for a couple of seconds, they watch the woman moving slowly up and down and they listen to her voice, soothing and encouraging.

Carmen looks up at Julio and feels new strength from his smile.

"Wheel me over to the steps," she says, nodding to the gap in the railings overlooking the river. "Then you can get me out of this damned chair so's I can sit on land again."

Julio does as she asks.

The two of them sitting on the steps, Carmen looks up at the black hole that is Fat Tuesday. "You know," she says, closing one eye and squinting, "if you look at it just right, you can almost believe you could reach out your hand and feel it." She reaches up with her left arm to demonstrate, feeling around with her hand.

Without turning around to look at him, Carmen asks her husband, "How close do you think it is?"

"Close," comes the reply.

For a few seconds, Carmen doesn't say anything. Then, "You know," she says, "I think I'd like to go swimming."

There are already folks in the water, swimming slowly out in the middle of the river but she thinks that maybe Julio will say she shouldn't do that. Instead, he stands up and takes off his shirt and pants, dropping them into a neat pile beside her. Then he takes off his shorts.

Firecrackers light up the now dark sky and a chorus of cheers and trumpets sound above the already cacophonous din.

"You want me to help you?" he asks.

Carmen's mouth is wide open in a mixture of shock and excitement…the kind of excitement that comes only when you think you're doing something naughty. "Maybe with my pants and hose," she says, giggling as she unbuttons her blouse. "And then you can take me down to the water."

"Take you down to the water?" Julio says. "Heck, you can just fall in." And he gives her a push before diving in after her.

Carmen hits the Mississippi in momentary panic, sinking immediately beneath the surface, staring up through the swirling water at the dark shape that looms overhead. Then she sees another shape, the thin brown outline of her husband, cut into the water alongside her and she feels his arms wrap themselves around her and lift her gently to the surface.

She emerges spluttering and shakes her head. "You damned fool," she says, "I could have drowned."

For a second, neither of them does or says anything, they just float there, Julio paddling with his feet and keeping them straight with his left arm treading the water. Then they both burst into hysterics.

"I wonder…I wonder what time it is," Carmen says as she allows her husband to turn her over onto her back and swim, pulling her with him.

There's a wind in the air now, a strong wind.

More fireworks light up the sky, turning the darkness into a daylight of sorts. The glow of the fireworks momentarily illuminates the surface of Fat Tuesday and she sees, suddenly, that it looks just like the ground out back of their house in Brooklyn. No more mysterious than that.

Somewhere over in the town, they can hear Dr. John playing "Such a Night."

"Who cares," Julio says, "we've got eternity…and we've got the river."

Carmen nods and squeezes Julio's hand. "Amen to that," she says.

> The great Mississippi, the majestic, the magnificent Mississippi, rolling its mile-wide tide along, shining in the sun.
>
> Mark Twain
> *Life on the Mississippi*

Story Notes

"Some Burial Place, Vast And Dry"
(*The UFO Files*, 1998)

All writers have favorites in their own stories and this is one of mine.

The theme is a familiar one—a lonely man in the twilight of his life reflects on his past. The differences here are (a) the man is actually the last survivor of an expedition that landed some years earlier on a faraway planet and (b) the nostalgic reflections coincide primarily with the annual visit of a decidedly strange airborne monolith that takes the form of a collection of architectural structures.

I spent absolutely ages putting this tale together, reading up in volumes of architecture and visiting different areas to get the correct feel of not only the various forms of construction but also the eras that they were from. And all for a short story—little wonder that my agent tears her hair out!

The theme for the book—one of those wonderful little DAW anthologies put together by Marty Greenberg and Tekno Books—was a simple one: unidentified flying objects.

I had two ideas—one of them was a rather hard-edged tale of abduction and alien investigation (which would eventually see the light of day as "Late Night Pick-up") and the other was a treatise on loneliness disguised as an SF yarn and delivered in a Bradbury-esque style. Ever a lover of Bradbury's work (and always keen to work in that "voice"), I opted for the latter...and even turned up a couple of extracts from Walt Whitman (of whom Bradbury himself is a big fan) that seemed appropriate.

For a time, the story was going to be called "All the Haunts and Homes of Me" (from Whitman's *Salut Au Monde*) but, for some reason that escapes me now, I opted for a line from the same poet's *Debris*. I think, with the benefit of hindsight, I made the wrong choice...but that's just a matter of taste.

When the tale appeared it received some very favorable reviews, one of which came from David Truesdale, who at the time was producing the remarkable (and much-missed) *Tangent* magazine. Dave and I were fellow judges for that year's World Fantasy Awards and his kind and generous comments proved to be a pleasant distraction from the seemingly endless practice of swapping emails several times each day on the merits (and demerits) of the towering piles of books and stories we were charged with evaluating. Thanks, Dave. But by far the best thumbs-up I received was a nice note from Bradbury himself saying how much he had enjoyed the story. Almost better than being paid. *Almost.*

"The Killing Of Davis-Davis"
(*Free Space,* 1997)

The first version of this story appeared in a very small-press British magazine in the late 1970s. It was one of the stories that, as soon as I had returned to writing fiction in the late 1980s following a long rest, I always wanted to rework...but I didn't really know how. So it went into the reference files to wait for an appropriate time.

Ed Kramer, with whom I had edited a couple of anthologies, gave me a call and asked if I would like to try him with something for a book he was working on with Brad Linaweaver. "What's the take?" I asked, ever a sucker for writing stories for themed anthologies. "Libertarian SF," came the reply. *That's more damn research,* whispered the little voice in the back of my head. "Sure," I told Ed, ignoring the voice. "I'll try you with something."

Brad and Ed's original idea had been inspired by the Prometheus Award, given annually by the Libertarian Futurist Society, which honors science fiction that takes politics and economics seriously. And in "The Killing of Davis-Davis," I had the makings of just the tale, albeit one that needed some extensive tinkering.

In his introduction, Brad called the story "a sophisticated meditation about the game of power politics." Maybe that's so...but it's also a consideration of godhood and time travel paradoxes. *You* decide which is closest to the truth.

"The Invasion"
(*The Ultimate Alien,* 1995)

Once again, a very different version of this tale appeared in the 1970s, serialised in a short-lived (mercifully so, as it turned out) magazine delivered free of charge to homes in the west-Yorkshire town of Leeds. Even free of charge, the magazine was overpriced. But I was thankful to them for accepting the story (and for paying me money!) and it was nice to see it unfold — complete with illustrations — over a few issues.

When John Betancourt called from Byron Preiss's office to see if I had anything suitable for an anthology of alien stories (cunningly titled *The Ultimate Alien*) I decided the time was right to update "The Invasion" and re-set it in my fictional small US town, Forest Plains. It was one of those wonderful jobs — reworking some particularly clunky dialogue, making the whole thing tighter and, best of all, spending a little time in the company of some old friends — and I confess to feeling mighty pleased when I sent it off for consideration. Of course, I felt even more pleased when John accepted it.

As a footnote, I must say that I'm happiest when I'm writing gentle stories filled with wonder than plain-and-simple scary tales. That's not to say, of course, that I can't or won't occasionally take a break — "Late Night Pick-up" (about which, more later) is one such vacation from sweetness and light while "Bedfordshire," my story for the Campbell, Dann and Etchison anthology *Gathering the Bones,* is as dark and bleak as I've ever been. I mention this just in case you make the mistake of taking me for granted!

"Palindromic"
(*First Contact,* 1997)

I had the outline of this story in my file for several years before I finally got around to tackling it. The reason was pretty understandable: it's a very difficult idea to pull off...as I think you'll see. I only hope you feel that I did manage to pull it off.

For a brief — very brief — period, there was a chance that it might end up as a collaboration with Ian McDonald, with whom I spent several very pleasant summer evenings going through it over a few beers...but we both got busy on other things and, anyway, it was — as I say — a very difficult idea to pull off even with the two of us going at it.

Once started, the story required repeated reworking and back-filling in order to make the whole thing hang together (you'll see why when you read it) and make sense. Rereading it now, it occurs to me that I should try to go back to that town and those characters and tackle the aftermath of (or events leading up to!) their actions...and it'll be a fairly cosmic tale. One of these days, I'll do it

"Surface Tension"
(*Monster Brigade 3000,* 1996)

I've loved comic books for as long as I can remember, particularly the SF fare put out by Bill Gaines's EC company and the two Julius Schwartz-edited DC titles, *Mystery in Space* and *Strange Adventures.*

There's a big difference between the two approaches, with DC going at it fairly straight (if, on reflection, a little ridiculous — one tale I recall had an alien stealing the entire continent of North America simply because one part of its outline was a perfect replica of his own profile and he needed it to enter an interplanetary competition) while the EC tales were invariably constructed around a twist-in-the-tale: one which springs readily to mind had an unpleasant astronaut goading his fellow botanist crew member by pulling petals off a flower to see if his girl back home still loved him; the man's comeuppance arrived when the ship landed on a planet populated by sentient trees and bushes "who" performed a similar ritual.

It's the EC twists, later developed by Roald Dahl and Fredric Brown, that most interested me, so when another of those wonderful calls came in for an anthology — this time with a theme of "monsters" — I thought I'd have a go.

"Heroes and Villains"
(*Villains Victorious*, 2001)

Another favorite. This manages to mix in my love of, once again, comic books — but this time the costumed superhero type — with my feelings for my mother.

When I was writing it, my mum was very close to death and we were coming to the end of a short (*mercifully* short, when I hear of what some other folks have to go through) but horrific month which itself came at the end of a six month battle with breast cancer. That final month began with my mother being told that the mastectomy (and all the follow-up radiotherapy) had failed: the doctor gave her three to six months. As it turned out, she moved on to new adventures halfway through the fourth week.

But, terrible though it was (and it *was*), one can learn things from just about any situation and, in those agonizing days, I learned a lot more than I thought I knew: not only about loss and love and the magical bond that exists between parents and their children…but also about the fear we all have not simply of going but of leaving others behind to grieve. Indeed, my mother's opening gambit (when she told me the news…and she was sitting holding hands with a wonderful district nurse) was to tell me she was sorry — and it was clearly *me* she was sorry for, not herself.

She was stoic to the end, and there were some black moments — which, thanks to the morphine, she laughed at even while they were happening — and they'll all find their way into stories eventually. But, when I was deliberating takes I could use on the old chestnut of Villains (that was the book's theme), I got to thinking about how we all have parents…even the bad guys. And, assuming that not every bad guy is the result of a broken home or parental abuse, how does a bad guy react to the news that his mother is on her last legs? And for that matter, how could one ever define goodness or badness if we didn't have both? And therefore, isn't each of those traits equally important?

Well, that was all I needed: thus, amidst a daily routine of pill and potion administration (my mother lived with us until fifteen hours before she died) and bathroom duties, I took the title of a much-loved Beach Boys song from my youth and set out to write an obituary for my mother that she could maybe read before she clocked off from her shift. Sadly, impatient as ever to get on with something new and exciting, she left me before I got it finished. Thus it remains one of several stories I've written — and to whose number I will undoubtedly add more — purely for her.

"A Worse Place than Hell"
(*White House Horrors*, 1996)

This was a strange one.

I've long wondered — and increasingly so, as time goes by — just how someone from the past would react and cope with being suddenly brought back to life in the modern world. I usually drift into this reflective trance when I try to imagine my dad — who died in 1972 — being brought back to life in 2004…computers, cellphones, internet, terrorists, cable TV, keyhole surgery…And I had had a note to that effect in my ideas folder for several years, with nothing coming of it.

Then came another of those magical themed anthology invitations…this time for a horror story set in or around the White House. Just a few days later, I had the seed of an idea…but I didn't start the story right away: I wanted a new slant in the telling of the tale, not simply the concept of it. (You can only do this writing lark if you learn to listen to the muse: it'll tell you when the elements are all in place — you should never, *ever* try to rush it or sidestep the process.)

If you're like me, you could well be reading these notes before you've read the actual stories…so I'm not about to spoil the fun by blabbing what it's all about. But I enjoyed immensely the cutting backwards and forwards in time and it's something I think I would like to do again.

"Halfway House"
(*Pawn of Chaos*, 1996)

One of the stories that impressed me most about Ray Bradbury's *The Illustrated Man* when I first read it was a little tale entitled "Kaleidoscope." I was twelve years old at the time, and I think it was the first time that the fact that I was going to die one day truly hit home. I often wonder — now…I didn't do it at the time — when my two sons first "embraced" that idea. I wrote the original version of the story many years ago but I considered it far too downbeat even to try selling it. Then along came the opportunity to write a story featuring one of Mike Moorcock's Eternal Champion incarnations and it just seemed to suggest itself right away…along with the idea of using the protagonist from *Behold the Man* and *Breakfast in the Ruins*.

"Elmer"
(*Alien Pets*, 1998)

Yet another anthology invitation called this one into being — *Alien Pets*…I ask you! But it didn't take too long for an idea to present itself, and as usual with my stuff, the real point of the tale is the back-story…with more considerations of the human condition, and love and loss clearly on display. When the story kicked off, it was pretty much straightforward — though I wanted the pet to be as unusual as I could make it (in other words, a far cry from Space Ranger's shape-changing sidekick, Cryll from DC Comics' old *Tales of the Unexpected* title) but as the effects of the scenario unfolded, it called to mind consequences…and prices to be paid.

"Setting Free the Daughters of Earth"
(*Future Crime*, 1999)

This one has antecedents (in *my* head, anyways) in Bradbury's *Fahrenheit 451* and Anthony Burgess's *The Wanting Seed*, but I wanted to delve more into a future society that could well evolve from the drugs-dependent and hedonistic areas that most of our big cities are becoming.

"Late Night Pickup"
(*Alien Abductions*, 1999)

I was very excited when the invite came to write an alien abduction story, and I decided to write a tale where *all* the people on Earth (except for a "lucky" few) were abducted...just for a little while, like maybe overnight, and then returned. Except when they came back, they were different. So I set off, frantically typing, enjoying myself (as I always do when writing short stories) and then I discovered that not only was the first section (around four pages) a single sentence (Jack Kerouac, eat your heart out!) but this was shaping up to be a long tale.

I called Marty Greenberg's office and spoke with the indefatigable Larry Segriff and explained my dilemma—"Don't worry, Pete," Larry said, laid back as ever, "just go ahead and see how it turns out and we'll take a look."

I should say here that I regularly overshoot on stories: give me a max of 5,000 and I'll turn in 6,000 or maybe even 7,000. Give me a max of 10,000 and I'll turn in 12,000. I don't do it on purpose, it just seems to happen that way. The absolute worst example of this shortcoming was a story I did for an anthology edited by Schafer and Sheehan (two Bills I'm always happy to encounter) containing stories based on J. K. Potter's artwork—that hit the wire at 23,000 words, despite having an eight-to-ten-thou max. (Thanks chaps, by the way.)

Anyway, Larry and the other guys at Tekno Books know me of old and so they were prepared to give me my head. So I carried on. Pretty soon, I had hit the ten-thou marker and there was absolutely no sign of bringing the tale in. Another call. This time, Larry agreed that I should maybe think about a different idea—the tale I stopped at that point, incidentally, turned into the 35,000-word novella *Darkness, Darkness*, the first in a four- or five-book cycle of SF/horror novellas entitled *Forever Twilight*...and it wouldn't have existed if it hadn't been for Larry and the Tekno Crew, so big thanks are due to them.

Anyways, I turned immediately—that very same day—to a story-beginning I'd had on one side since the *UFO Files* project (see first story) about a man who's had a traffic accident on a nighttime road and he's being questioned by the cops. The problem is that he can barely recall anything about the accident...and, of course, it all goes downhill from there.

At first, there seemed to be a lot of humor in the story but as it progressed, the chuckles I'd been having kind of dried up.

"Songs of Leaving"
(*Mardi Gras Madness*, 2000)

A few years back — 1994? 1995? — The World Fantasy Convention hit New Orleans.

I had been there with Nicky and the boys a few years earlier but for some reason the place hadn't really made much of an impression. Yes, I know...it sounds ridiculous to me too, now.

Anyway, I attended and I took every opportunity to go out walking around...sometimes with other con-goers and sometimes by myself...and I fell absolutely in love with the place and the people. Highlights?

First off, being confronted by this shoeshine boy whose street patois just blew me away — I could have sat and listened to him all day (and he'd have let me so long as I was paying for his time — and why not?).

Secondly, walking along the side of the Mississippi and hearing a steamboat's mournful wail — I actually called Nicky up on one of the public telephones right there beside the water and held up the receiver so she could hear all the way across in England, where it was late evening and she was baking a cake. I wept, right there on the jetty...at the sound of the boat, the slowness and mystery of the river, and the simple fact that, at least in those halcyon pre-9/11 days, the world seemed like a pretty fine place..

And lastly, at the fantastic street parties they had every night. I spent hours down there often watching from a balcony cafe or bar and, on one night — one particularly boisterous night — I went down and mingled. Fantastic — fabulous place, fabulous people.

So, of course, being asked by Russell Davis to try him with a story about the Mardi Gras was a joy. But, as ever, I wanted to do something special.

I actually recall finishing this story, printing it off and rushing out into the garden where Nicky was sunbathing and I read the whole thing to her (not exactly what she was looking for on a hot summer's day when she was trying to get some shut-eye in the sunshine)...and when I got to the end, I choked up. And that's when I knew it was a pretty good tale. I think. I *hope...*

So there you have it...another collection of tales to amuse, to cause discomfort and to strum on the heart-strings. I'm particularly pleased with this one simply because it's pretty much all what you might call SF...as opposed to the dark fantasy material that I'm perhaps better known for.

But SF, dark fantasy and even crime/suspense…I think they're all fairly recognizable as my stories. Okay, some of them are a little darker than others but I think there's a humanity present in them all. I hope you enjoy them and, as ever, I'll be interested to hear from you either way.

Look after each other…and happy reading!